The Road Not Taken

Emily Tudor

A Hart Sisters Novel

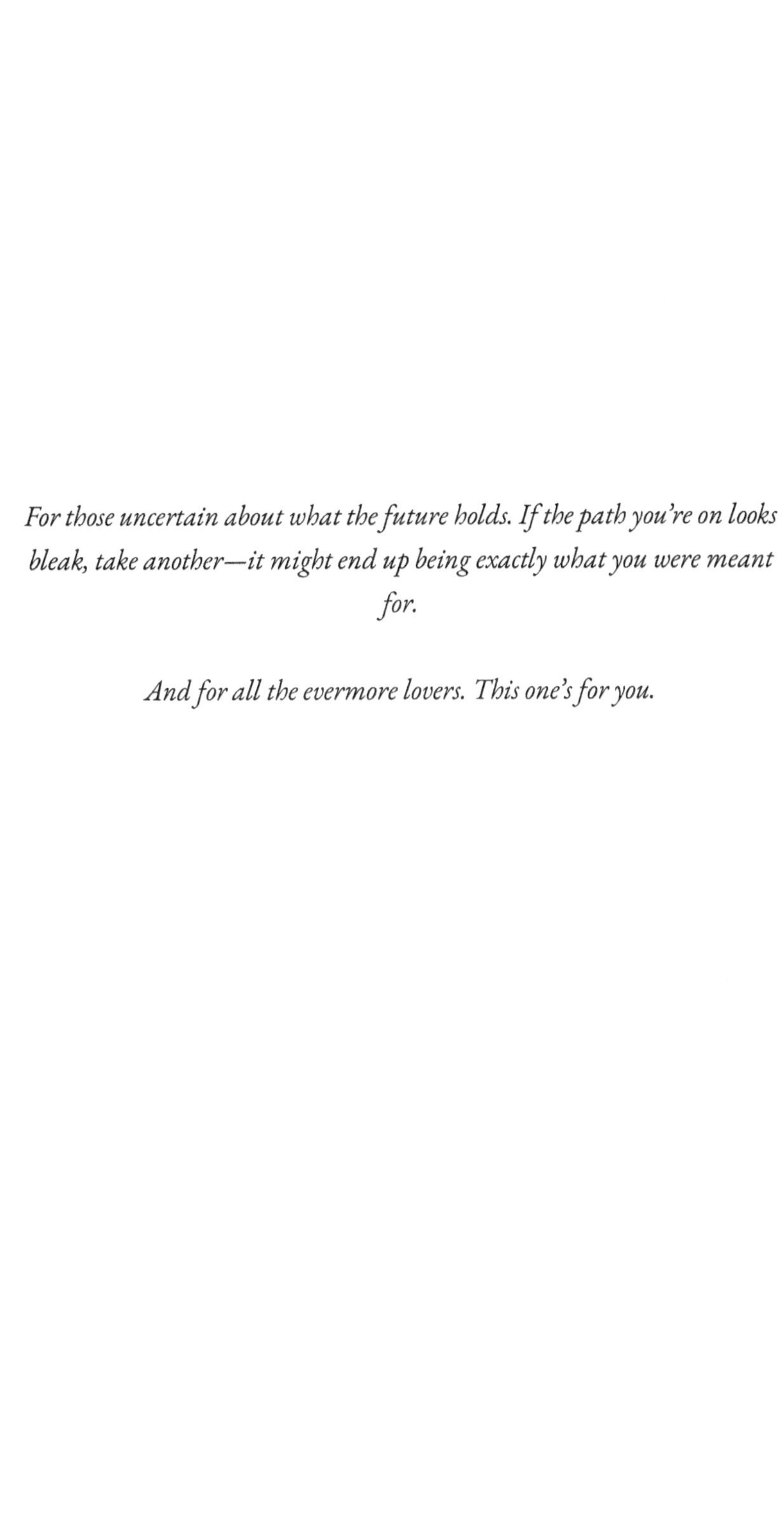

For those uncertain about what the future holds. If the path you're on looks bleak, take another—it might end up being exactly what you were meant for.

And for all the evermore lovers. This one's for you.

Content Warnings

This book deals with suicide (not on the page), talks of suicide, death of a family member, grief, neglectful parents, mentions of stalking, and sexually explicit content. Your mental health matters. Please proceed cautiously.

If you or anyone you know struggles with dark thoughts, call, text, or chat 988.

Playlist

The Fall — Gregory Alan Isakov
Something More — Chelsea Cutler
4runner — Brenn!
Closure — Taylor Swift
20 Something — SZA
Sunday Best — Surfaces
Butterflies — Kacey Musgraves
It Will Come Back — Hozier
Northern Attitude — Noah Kahan Ft. Hozier
Ivy — Taylor Swift
I Think I Like You — The Band CAMINO
Don't — Ed Sheeran
When Emma Falls in Love (Taylor's Version) — Taylor Swift
Falling — Chase Atlantic
Glue Song — Beabadoobee Ft. Clairo
Heaven — Niall Horan
Nothing New (Taylor's Version) — Taylor Swift Ft. Phoebe Bridgers

Coney Island — Taylor Swift Ft. The National

Holocene — Bon Iver

You, Love (Interlude) — Lizzy McAlpine

Body Talks — The Struts

Sink — Noah Kahan

Gold Rush — Taylor Swift

Margaret — Lana Del Ray Ft. Bleachers

Dorothea — Taylor Swift

Robbers — The 1975

It's Time To Go — Taylor Swift

Skinny Love — Bon Iver

Evermore — Taylor Swift Ft. Bon Iver

Unknown / Nth — Hozier

Good Grief (Reorchestrated) — Bastille

Right Where You Left Me — Taylor Swift

Anchor — Novo Amor

Supermarket Flowers — Ed Sheeran

Meet Me in the Hallway — Harry Styles

Olivia — One Direction

Thinking Bout You — Ariana Grande

Scott Street — Phoebe Bridgers

Renegade — Big Red Machine Ft. Taylor Swift

About You — The 1975

Lover, You Should've Come Over — Jeff Buckley

Boys of Faith — Zach Bryan Ft. Bon Iver

This Is What The Drugs Are For — Gracie Abrams

Happiness — Taylor Swift

Tolerate It — Taylor Swift

Run Away — Chase Atlantic

This Love (Taylor's Version) — Taylor Swift

To the Mountains — Lizzy McAlpine

Forever Winter (Taylor's Version) — Taylor Swift
Someone to Stay — Vancouver Sleep Clinic
'Tis The Damn Season — Taylor Swift
Home — Phillip Phillips
Marjorie — Taylor Swift
Sweet Nothing — Taylor Swift
Fine Line — Harry Styles
Long Story Short — Taylor Swift

I shall be telling this with a sigh
Somewhere ages and ages hence:
Two roads diverged in a wood, and I—
I took the one less traveled by,
And that has made all the difference.

—ROBERT FROST, *The Road Not Taken*

Prologue

— THE FALL BY GREGORY ALAN ISAKOV

WHEN I WAS LITTLE, I loved going to the grocery store with my parents. It always felt like such a magical place, with so many people bustling around. Of course, as a kid, you find ways to make everything around you magical. The expressway feels as mystical as a carpet ride. The sticks you find in your yard become magic wands that you can cast spells with.

When you're a kid, you can't wait to grow up. You can't wait to be able to drive your own car somewhere, and to have a credit card. You can't wait until you can do all the adult things that look so fun when you're young. As a kid, I was always hurrying to get my life started, so much so that it felt like a race. I was in such a rush that I forgot to stop and look around and savor all the good parts. A time that I, like most people, take for granted. Because you can only get older, you can't rewind time and go backward. You can try, but one day you'll look back and wish you were twelve again and nothing bad had ever happened to you.

Because when you get older, you experience so many things that will make you yearn to be young and carefree again. Nobody tells you that as you grow up, the world gets less magical. Those rose-colored glasses slip off your face, and you see the harsh reality of everything around you.

Everyone around you is just doing their best to make it through today. Because tomorrow will come, and you have to repeat the same day over and over again.

As a kid, you go into the grocery store, and it feels like a never-ending castle filled with different rooms. You feel like every time you enter, there's always something new to discover. But as an adult, you'll start to get mad when they change the aisles around because now you can't find the damn oranges!

I never imagined that I would one day be employed in the magical grocery store my family and I went to every Saturday. I never imagined that the place I swore I'd never end up, would soon become the place where I was stuck.

Emotionally and physically.

As I watch customers trickle in and out, I create stories for each of them. The guy holding flowers and staring at his watch is probably late for a date. The young woman reading the get well soon greeting cards might have had someone close to her get hurt—or maybe they're sick.

All the stories I create for these people make me happy. They're out in the world. They're *living* whereas I'm only existing. I have nobody to share my oranges with. I have nobody to blow out candles in front of. I'm directionless and alone.

This big magical place I once thought of is now holding me hostage. I had love once. I had people around me once. I had someone to grocery shop with on the weekends and laugh with when our groceries dropped through the bag. I once had someone to argue with over who was allowed to push the cart. I once had someone who would peel my oranges for me when we got home.

Now, my oranges sit and rot in the bowl on my small kitchen table. I have to throw them away most of the time. Yet, I still buy them because it reminds me of something I once had.

Is that all life is? Yearning for things that you once had, but not chasing after them?

Inside a grocery store, life can be whatever you want it to be. But outside? Outside in the real world is where reality smacks you in the face, and you're still a twenty-six-year-old girl who has no idea what she's doing with her life.

Not much has changed in my six years in this store. Except once, I had a friend here. A person. *My person.* At least, that's what I thought.

But he left four years ago, and I haven't talked to him since he stopped communication four months after he left. He's out living his life somewhere far away from me, and I'm still here at home wishing something could've worked out in my favor for once.

But that's not how life works.

Part 1
—Now—
August 2026

Chapter One

— SOMETHING MORE BY CHELSEA CUTLER

"Is it possible to reach over the counter and slice some of their fingers off?" One of my coworkers asks me as I wipe down the counter.

"I think that goes against a few health code violations." I smile at her while she laughs.

"I know, but honey, some of these people are—how do I say this nicely—fucking annoying." Jackie, one of my coworkers, laughs as she takes another order from the counter. Fridays usually aren't too busy, but today has been since all the college students are coming back after the summer break. All of them are shopping with their parents and buying all sorts of things to fill their dorm rooms with.

I remember doing that.

Stop it, Livvy.

I shove those memories down and continue to clean up the department. The same department I've worked in since I was a college student and had no idea what I was going to do with my life. It's been four years since I graduated, and I'm *still* waiting for someone to tell me that everything will just fall into place as I thought it would. "That's customer service for you."

"I never knew working with the public could be like this. Why didn't anyone warn me?" My coworker Cal says, clearly joking, as he comes back from his break.

"Cal, please. Everyone loves you. You're like a giant teddy bear come to life." He smiles when I tell him that because he knows it's true. He's around 6 feet tall and has light brown hair that curls at the end like fusilli pasta. Cal is one of my favorite coworkers, and sometimes we hang out outside of work, so we've slowly become friends.

It's been nice having someone to talk to who understands my mind. Cal is one of those people. He dropped out of school because it wasn't his thing, and now he works here while selling some of his art on the side. He's *really* good at painting and even has a couple of pieces hung around the store we work at. He understood me when I would tell him for years that I had no clue what I was doing and how I felt so burnt out trying to figure out what to do. Now, here we are, years later, and still stuck where we were.

Cal also helped a lot when *he* left me here and went off to live his life, but everyone at work knows not to mention his name. *You're a coward, Livvy.*

No, I was just really, *really* fucking sad. But life has moved on. *I* have moved on.

As much as I can, at least. It's hard when everything you do and everywhere you go reminds you of someone you tried to forget but couldn't.

It's the three of us working this morning, along with Joe, but he's putting a bunch of boxes away in the cooler. Joe is like my work Grandpa. He and I have a bunch of inside jokes—one having to do with caramelized onions—and I always like working with him because he keeps things interesting.

"Do you need a break, Liv, or can I go to lunch?" Jackie asks me as she takes off her apron.

"You're good. I'll go after you get back." I tell her as she grabs her purse and walks toward the break room. I turn to Cal. "She only talked shit about three customers while you were gone."

"That's got to be a record low. How interesting." He looks at me for a second before speaking again. "Are you feeling okay? I know things have been tough recently."

"Recently?"

"Okay, excuse me for checking in on you," he chuckles.

"I know. I'm sorry. Things are the same as usual. I'm twenty-six, still have no direction in life, and will probably die while shaving deli meat for someone's children." I laugh, even though no part of what I said was funny. "I have a degree in English Literature from a college fifteen minutes from here. Yet, I'm still stuck in my hometown in the same routine I've had for years because I can't figure out what I want to do with my life."

"Oh! Don't forget the breakup from six months ago. Your string of failed relationships makes my life look like a cakewalk." He laughs, and I can't help but join him.

"Sometimes, I regret confiding in you about every aspect of my life."

"What else is there to do while we're stuck here?" He makes a good point. "Plus, we're friends. I'm supposed to give you shit for this, but I'm also allowed to bring wine to your apartment when you're sad."

"True, and even though that boxed wine was *terrible,* it still makes for a funny story." After my last breakup—if you can even call it that—six months ago, I texted Cal that I was moping in my apartment with a carton of ice cream. He then came over after his shift with wine, more ice cream, and tissues. We watched a bunch of movies so he could distract me from how sad I was. Funny enough, I wasn't even sad about the breakup. I was sad that, yet again, I had another failed relationship.

Every time this happens, I feel more stuck than before. The first boy I loved broke my heart, and now it's just been one after the other. One endless string of failures and heartbreak because my heart still hasn't properly healed from the first one.

But yeah, I've moved on.

Cal got so drunk that night that he fell off my second floor balcony, and I was too drunk to help him. It took an hour for me to call someone to make sure he was okay, because the two of us were laughing so hard. He didn't break anything, just a few bruises and a sprained ankle. He's as good as new now.

"What the hell are you two chatting about out here?" Joe asks us as he wheels the cart out of the freezer.

"We're reminiscing about the time I sprained my ankle trying to cheer Livvy up." Cal smiles at him, knowing that it didn't work, and to this day, I profusely apologize for what happened.

"Ah, yes. That story never gets old. You two becoming friends reminds me of a tornado making landfall—it's chaos." He smiles at us.

"So, what are you going to do tonight while I'm stuck here? One of us should do something fun, and you need to get out of your apartment more." Cal asks me.

"First of all, I could have plans already. Second of all, I *do* get out of my apartment." I scoff at him as a customer comes up to the counter, and I take their order. When I turn back around to grab what they wanted, Cal is almost keeled over from laughing so hard. "Seriously? What was that for?"

"Oh, I'm sorry. I thought you were telling a joke. I know for a fact you don't have plans tonight unless Parker is dragging you out kicking and screaming." He stops to laugh a little bit more. "And coming here to work doesn't count as getting out of your apartment, Livs."

I swallow down a *fuck you* toward him because swearing in front of customers is not something I want to get fired for today. I hand the customer her stuff, and she walks away, not before I flash my best customer service smile at her. Whenever I'm in front of customers, I always try to be the sweetest I can be. I even have a few regulars I enjoy talking to, but sometimes it's hard.

Because people are idiots, but I read somewhere once that even if people are idiots, you should always be nice to them, so I am. I've received a few comments about my sunny disposition and cheerful attitude, but anyone who knows me knows I put up that kind of front at work. Because the truth is that sometimes it's hard for me to get up in the mornings. Most days, I would rather stay in bed until my covers consume me because putting on that face every day feels so hard, especially when I'm as unmotivated as I was four years ago.

Nobody tells you how fucking hard adult life is when you have no clue what you're doing. The worst thing is that there's no instruction manual. I wish there was because it would be much easier to blame that than myself for feeling like this.

"Parker has as much of a life as I do. I think she has some work to do tonight, so she'll be at the office late."

"So it's going to be another night of you being alone and wallowing in your self-loathing? How fun," Cal teases me, and I know he means well by trying to get me out of my shell more, but I don't want to.

"Leave the girl alone, Cal. After working here all day, Livvy probably needs to recharge that social battery. God knows you use all of it up." Joe smiles at me.

"Yeah, yeah. Fine. But one of these days, Liv, I'll get you to be a going-out type of person. Even if it takes me years, so help me, I will do it."

"Good luck with that," I say as I take my apron off. As Jackie returns, I grab my bag and head off for my first fifteen-minute break. The store gives you two small breaks and one that lasts half an hour when you work an eight-hour shift or longer. I'm not too hungry yet, so a short break will suffice. As I sit down, I pull out my phone and water bottle, taking a few sips as I swipe to my messages.

Liv: You're working late tonight, right?

Parker: Yeah, I have a proposal due at the end of the week and no help.

Liv: Gross. Is that one girl still making things difficult?

Parker: Yes. She's a pain in my ass. Why are you asking? Are you going out? Or is Livvy Hart possibly bringing a date home?

Liv: Haha. Calm down, no dating for me, remember? I'm focusing on myself for the time being. I'm out at three today, which is earlier than normal, so I'm not quite sure what to do with myself.

Parker: Right. How could I forget the no dating rule? I guarantee that will be broken as soon as you see a cute guy walk into the store.

Parker: Bonus points if he has brown hair and is taller than you.

Liv: I'm going to ignore that text because I don't have a type. But I'll see you later? I'll grab some ice cream before I leave, and we can watch a movie when you get home.

Parker: Sounds good. Try not to fall in love with anyone in the next five hours!

I switch to scrolling through Instagram for the remainder of my break. I swipe past a bunch of publishing house posts about all the new books releasing soon, and my heart lurches.

I wish that could be me.

When I settled on my major in college—English literature—I felt like my life finally had some direction. I always loved writing short stories and random things in my journal, and the idea of being able to do that as a career felt thrilling. Until my brain decided that it was not a good way to make a sustainable living, and my imposter syndrome snuck up on me and told me I'd never be good enough. Then, after everything happened, I felt stuck again, and I didn't bother digging myself out of that hole this time. I let it bury me and haven't been able to get myself out of it since.

I'm just scared. Scared that everything I do will fall flat and nothing will be good enough. There's no way I could be like some of my favorite authors and writers. No fucking way. They have *actual* talent. I'm a girl who grew up writing her feelings in a journal and thought she could do anything if she wanted it badly enough.

The real world is terrifying, and it would chew up and swallow people like me. There's no way I can make a living off of something I like doing for fun. God knows my parents remind me of that all the time.

"Olivia, you need a real job. A daydream cannot sustain you in life."

I heard that every time I tried to bring the conversation up when I was in college. Always the same thing, and eventually, I stopped asking altogether. I've written and published one book all on my own. It was a great learning experience, but writer's block has officially started to kick my ass. Maybe I'm only meant to write one book. Maybe that's all my dream career will ever be.

Dreams cannot become reality, no matter how much you want it or will it. They're just dreams, after all. Fantasies that we wish could become reality. Kind of like love. Love is something that everyone searches for their entire life, and when it finally breaks them, they wish for something that will last through every bad thing that could happen.

But love doesn't work that way. Because you can love someone more than yourself, and in the end, they'll still leave. Love and dreams will *never* be enough when the real world is there to slap you in the face anytime you dare to think it could work out.

I sigh heavily as my alarm goes off, signaling the end of my break. I rub my eyes before cleaning off the table I was sitting at and heading back to my department. Joe is still filling things at the case furthest from our department, Cal and Jackie are laughing about something as I enter the department and start washing my hands. When I finally get my cut gloves on—we have to have them on at all times for safety purposes—I swing over to the case where we have our daily packages available. I make a note of all the things I need to replenish as I open the freezer and shove things into my arms.

As I'm putting stuff in the case, careful not to drop anything, I hear Joe talking to someone in my peripheral. It's probably one of his fan club members—which is what I call the older ladies that come in here to see him. They flirt with him even though he's happily married, and sometimes, he can't remember their names, even though it looks like he's known them forever. It's hilarious, and we all laugh about it in the department.

A tap on my shoulder interrupts my thoughts, and when I turn around expecting a customer to need help, I'm met with a gut punch instead. My toes start to go numb, and my heart starts to beat erratically as I look at the man in front of me.

Is he really here? Is he really standing in front of me right now after four years? Or is it just the ghost of everything I thought he was?

"Livvy," he says to me as he looks deep into my eyes. I think I've forgotten how to breathe, and I feel some packages slip from my arms and onto the floor, but I don't move to pick them up. I'm frozen where

I stand, and suddenly I'm young again, watching him get on the plane without me. *How can he still affect me this much after all this time?*

"Tristan."

Chapter Two

— 4RUNNER BY BRENN!

"How long has it been since you've been back?"

A car horn blasts from behind me as I notice the light has turned green. *Fuck. I need to pull it together.* "Uh, four years, give or take."

"Shit, man. I thought you'd visited between then and now. Are you sure you don't want the boys and me to hop on a flight? We don't mind coming early. I mean, obviously, we'll be there for the funer—"

I cut him off. "It's fine. I have some stuff to take care of beforehand. If I need you guys, I'll let you know."

One of my best friends in the world, and one of the nicest guys I know, sighs heavily on the other end of the line. "Tris, you can't take all this on by yourself. The guys and I are here for you, you know."

"Ethan, I know that. Trust me, I do. I don't want to burden you guys with all the nothingness that surrounds this fucking town. There's no need to drag out your misery." I'm making excuses. I know that, Ethan knows that, but he doesn't say a thing about it.

"Okay, fine. Where are you headed now? To your mom's house?"

"Yeah, but she asked me to make a stop at the grocery store before I came home. She needs a few things." He laughs directly into the phone, which practically blows the speakers out in my car. "Is something funny? I didn't hear a joke."

"Isn't it weird as fuck to walk back into a place you once worked at to go shopping? I'd fucking hate that, dude."

I pause, having never thought of it like that. I guess this store does have some memories attached to it. *Memories of her.* I shake that thought away because she's obviously not going to be there anymore. I assume she's off doing bigger and better things, like I always knew she would.

Good for both of us that we've made something of ourselves.

Really fucking good. Even though she hasn't answered any of my correspondence in years, I assume she's moved on and is living the life she always wanted. A life that doesn't involve me for some reason.

"It'll be fine, I think." I hear him stifle a laugh again. "I'm about five minutes away, so I'll text you and the guys when I'm home."

"Okay, dude. Best of luck. Give your mom a hug for me."

"I will." As I hang up the phone, another wave of guilt washes through me. Or maybe it's panic. Or maybe it's both.

Or maybe it's the fact that I'm back in a place that holds memories that make my body ache.

I'm silently cursing my mom for making me stop at the old store I used to work at, but I'd never tell her no. Especially now, with everything that's happened.

I pull into the parking lot that's barely full and park my car in one of the front spots, but I don't get out immediately.

Four years. Four whole years since I've seen this area, seen this tiny corner of my world. I remember how I always dreamed about getting out of this small Pennsylvania town and how I was never going to look back.

Well, here I am. Looking back. And I wish I had never left. I wish I stayed because maybe the things that happened wouldn't have. And maybe *he* would still be here. Maybe I would still have *her*. And maybe I would be happy rather than wanting to run my car off the highway.

But I can't. I have a family—my family—to take care of.

I take a deep breath before exiting my car, and then I find my body walking through the double doors, and into this old space. *It looks exactly the same*, I think to myself. Nothing has changed except what fruits and cases are in the front as soon as you walk in.

Maybe I haven't changed either. How do you tell? Is there a formula of sorts that I can use? Because four years ago, I left here feeling confident, self-assured, and excited.

Now, as I come back, I can't help but think that every decision I've made since then has been wrong.

I grab a basket from where they sit at the entrance and pull up the list my mom sent me on the phone. It's a bunch of supplies for a casserole. *That's weird.* I whip out my phone to text my younger sister, Teagen.

> **Tristan: Why is Mom making me buy shit for a casserole?**

> **Teags: I don't know. There's a shit ton of food here.**

> **Tristan: Should I still get it then?**

> **Teags: Mom will be upset if you don't. I think she's trying to distract herself as much as she can.**

> **Tristan: Has she cleaned the whole house yet?**

Teags: Yeah, she's also redone your room about fifteen times. I told her I could help, but she told me to sit back and relax.

Tristan: Fuck. I'll be home soon, okay?

Teags: Sounds good. See you soon.

Tristan: How's Theo doing?

Teags: He's not here yet.

Fuck. His plane should've landed a while ago. He's coming from South Carolina, so judging by that, he should be home now. Great. Now I'm going to have to track him down, too. Another thing to add to my list of shit I don't want to do today.

But I guess I'm used to it since I'm the oldest and have to clean up everyone else's messes. I never *asked* for this to be my role, but when my dad died, someone had to step up.

That someone was me at the ripe age of eleven years old. Now, as a twenty-seven-year-old guy, I had hoped I didn't need to keep doing that. But yet again, I've proved myself wrong.

"Fuck, okay. In and out, here we go," I say as I grab the first few things on my mom's list. As I turn the corner, it feels like a thousand memories are punching me in the gut. I find myself unable to move before I feel a hand slap me on my shoulder.

"As I live and breathe, Tristan West. I never thought I'd see you again. I figured I'd be six feet in the ground when you finally came back."

I know that voice well. I turn to see my former colleague, Joe. Christ, he looks the exact same. "Joe, my man. How's life treating you? And has your fan club grown exponentially since I last saw you or what?"

"Ah, yeah, it has." The two of us laugh before he holds out his hand.

"What's this?" I ask as I take his hand and shake it.

"I was sorry to hear about what happened. I saw the obituary in the paper. I assume that's why you're back?"

"Yeah, it is," I say, feeling my mouth suddenly get drier.

"I'm sorry for your loss. I can't even imagine what your family is going through. If you need anything while you're in town, let me know. My wife and I will help in any way that we can."

I feel myself softly smile. "Thank you. That means a lot." I pause, willing my legs to stay upright before I change the subject. "So, how's the department been? Any new hires, or are things mostly the same?"

"A few have come and gone in the years since you've been here, but your girl is still here."

What? "My girl?"

Joe points over toward one of the cases, and I swear my heart stops beating—no, it beats faster because I thought she would've been gone by now.

She's still here. Why is she still here?

Did I walk into some parallel universe or something? Is she actually in front of me right now? She's not facing me, but there's this magnetic pull toward where she stands. I don't exactly feel my legs moving, but they are, and before I can explain what I'm doing, I tap her on the shoulder.

As I see her turning around, that surprised and sorrowful look on her face, it takes everything in me not to ask her what happened all those years ago.

To ask her what happened to us.

She's still fucking here.

I can't believe she's still here when she practically disappeared on me that day.

"Livvy." I can barely get the word out of my mouth, but I remember how much I used to love saying her name like it belonged to the both of us, not just her.

She turns around, and when those blue eyes lock on mine, a few packages slip from her hands and she doesn't move to pick them up. She stares at me as if she's not sure I'm really here. "Tristan."

The two of us are quiet for a few seconds as we stare into each other's eyes, but the trance is easily broken when she realizes that she's dropped a few things. She looks down, and before she can do it, I reach and grab them for her. Only we both do it simultaneously, and end up bonking our heads together. "Fuck, sorry."

"Can you just...let me do my job, please?"

Ouch. I guess I deserved that. "I'm sorry."

And then she looks up at me with those eyes I used to love looking at so much, and I know that those two words can mean a bunch of different things.

I'm sorry I knocked heads with you.

I'm sorry I left you four years ago.

Why didn't you answer my calls? Why did you stop sending letters? Why did you cut me off with one note? Why, Livvy? I thought we were real, and I'm sorry if I was too much, if the distance was too hard.

I should've come back. I should've stayed.

I'm sorry. I'm so sorry. For all of it.

"I—"

"Tristan! You're a sight for sore eyes! Come here, and give me a hug!" My old coworker, Jackie, runs up to me and doesn't give me time to say no before she wraps her arms around me. She was always a bit colorful before, but now she seems even worse. *Yikes.*

"Don't worry, I'll handle the counter," Cal says, another familiar face.

"Hey, Cal. How's it going?" I ask him, and he shrugs, gives me a weird look, and walks away. *Okay then.*

"Everyone acting like this is some sort of meet and greet is ridiculous. Let's get back to work and let Tristan leave again. It's what he's best at, after all."

"Oh gosh, I bet you two have lots of catching up to do," Joe pats my back again as he says that. "Feel free to go on your lunch break now, Livs."

She looks clearly uncomfortable as she tries to answer. "But I just got back from break."

"It's dead in here! We'll handle the counter." Jackie shoves her a little bit, and she trips, but before she can fully fall, I catch her.

She then scrambles out of my arms, brushes her clothes off as if I've lit her on fire, and sighs. "Fine." She turns around and heads back into the department, takes off her apron and disappears into the back cooler. I know for a fact she's grabbing her lunch, though I'm sure Joe would give her another one since she might not even eat during this one.

But they were right; we *did* have a lot to talk about. But she might not even want to talk about it since it's been so long. It's worth a shot, though, right?

She stops in front of me before she speaks. "I have to go punch out, but I'll meet you in the cafe breakroom."

"Are you still one of the few people that uses it?" I smile, kicking myself at the memories that are hitting me the longer I'm in here. *I need to get out of here. I can't fucking do this.*

"Yeah. I'll see you over there."

I nod before she takes off toward the time clock and wave to my old coworkers as I walk over to the table in the corner of the breakroom. *Her favorite.* Or it was, maybe that changed too, but when we used to work together, she always sat at this table.

This could either go really good or really bad.

I silently hope for the former as she sits down across from me and doesn't say a word.

Chapter Three

— CLOSURE BY TAYLOR SWIFT

I'VE ALWAYS HEARD THAT if you talk first in an argument, you'll lose. So as I sit across from a man I used to love, I say nothing. What is there to say, anyway? *He* left, not me. *He* ruined everything and was the one who halted communication between us. Now, he's the one who has to explain himself. After all, he's the one who waltzed in here like he's the fucking man of the hour.

God, why does it still hurt? Why does just being in his presence still make my body ache the same way it did when he left?

His face looks older too—not in a bad way—but he looks different. These past four years have aged him nicely. He's still got all those muscles, but he seems...tired. Then again, he's probably saying the same about me in his mind right now. I called my younger sister the other day, just to check in, and she told me that I need to be sleeping more. When I asked her why, she told me that my voice sounded tired. I didn't have the heart to tell her that I'm always like this. Exhausted from the weight of being here and existing.

I guess being unmotivated and frozen in life will do that to a person. It's not only your body that's tired. It's your mind, your soul, your voice, your posture, your everything. It all aches to *feel* something again, but I don't know how to turn that part of me back on. I don't know how to fix it. I can't ever remember feeling like I had a path laid out for me, like everyone else. I never had that one big goal in front of me that I spent my entire college career chasing. It never came, and here I am four years later, still feeling the same.

And here he is. He shows up here after four fucking years and finally wants to talk. I don't think that's why he came originally, because based on the basket he's carrying, he's shopping for himself. *Or someone. A special someone.* I don't care. I don't even care! Why am I thinking about this right now? And why hasn't he said anything? We just keep staring at each other, but I'm not the one who has to explain something.

He came here. I didn't go to him, so he should be the one—

"You're still here." I feel like it's a figment of my imagination that he whispered that, but I know I heard it. "Livvy, why are you still here?"

"You've missed a lot these past four years." His face twinges as if I've hit him, but it goes away in seconds.

"I know." And now we're back to silence again. I don't feel like I owe him an explanation for why he can still find me at the same job I've had since college, but I offer it anyway.

"After graduation and everything else that happened, I felt like I didn't have a path forward. You know that. I had no clue what I was doing, and even though my heart wanted to chase my dream, my mind—and every goddamn person around me—told me that I'd never make it. That I was never going to be good enough."

"I remember you feeling the same way before I left. I thought staying was the right choice for you. I thought leaving would—"

"Don't." I can't bear to hear him say that he thought by *leaving me* it would help me figure out my life. *I was supposed to go with him.* I don't regret staying—Tristan told me to stay—but I do regret everything that unfolded after he left. I don't even really know what happened. I try not to think about it often, or ever.

"I'm sorry. I—I don't know what to say, or what will help in this situation." He runs a hand through his already messy hair. "I'm back indefinitely."

"Why? Why are you here, Tristan? What could've caused you to leave your cushy place in Silicon Valley to come back here? I thought you had burned every bridge when you left this place." That was a bit mean, but I can't help it. All of these buried feelings are coming up, and I can't stop them.

"I'm back for a funeral."

"Oh." *Now I feel like a bitch.* "I'm sorry for your loss."

He swallows hard before answering a few seconds later. "Thanks."

"Was it an immediate family member, or...?" I trail off, mentally kicking myself for even asking that question because he clearly doesn't want to talk about it.

"Yeah, but—"

"You don't have to say anything. I'm sorry I even asked, just forget it." I pause, wondering if I should offer any comfort toward him, or if I should stay where I am. Would he lean into it? Would he pull away? Would he let it linger because he missed it? I choose the former, reach across the table, and grab his hand. "If there's anything I can do—"

He lets go of my hand and places his arms underneath the table. *Ouch.* "It's fine, Olivia. I didn't expect you to know."

Olivia. Why does him saying my full name make my chest ache so much? "Right."

His gaze pierces mine. "I'm okay. Really, I am." He's saying the words but I don't believe him. His mouth is saying one thing, but his tense shoulders, dark circles, and disheveled hair are saying otherwise. He hasn't been sleeping, and he clearly hasn't started grieving yet.

Typical Tristan. He was always one to put the rest of his family before himself, and I know he's in full man-of-the-family mode like he's always been. Which is why it was such a shock to me when he told me he always dreamed of getting out of here. I thought for sure that he would want to stay close to his family, but he did the opposite. He left, and they let him because his family wanted him to stop worrying about them for once. They wanted *him* to chase his life, not squander it to keep taking care of them.

At least that's what he told me in one of the letters he sent me before they stopped coming altogether. "How long do you have left?" he asks me.

"About ten minutes."

"You should eat then. I'm sorry that I barged in like this. I never thought I'd see you here. I never meant to interrupt."

"It's okay," I say as I start to grab my lunch bag from where I set it on the floor.

"Can I guess what's in there?" My heart lurches when he asks me that question. It used to be our little tradition that we would try and guess what the other brought for breaks at work. It's good to know all those little moments meant the same to him as they did to me, or maybe they didn't and he just feels bad. Either way, it fucking hurts. Talking about the past and bringing up all this buried shit is not something I want to do right now—or ever, if I'm being honest.

"Go ahead," I say to him.

"Hmmm. Okay. My Livvy is a creature of habit, so I'll guess that there's a turkey and provolone sandwich with mayo and lettuce in there, a bag of carrots and ranch dressing, and some wavy chips." *My Livvy.* There's that nickname I used to love so much. I hate how easily it slipped out. Our old patterns are emerging, and it's killing me.

I pull out all of those things and I see a smile turn up on his face. *God, it's just like old times.* "I'm not your anything anymore. Remember?"

His smile falls as soon as I say that. "Right. Of course." The two of us are quiet for a few moments before he speaks again. "Look, about what happened—"

"Please don't. I—I can't do this here, and you shouldn't be focused on the story of us right now."

"I know, but Liv if we could talk at some point. About all of it. I really feel like we should."

"What's there to say, Tristan? You left, and that was fine. I'm still here and that's fine too. We weren't meant to be, or anything like that. I've had closure about us for a while. You don't need to explain anything to me."

"Livvy, you know that's not true." His eyes lock with mine, and it takes everything in me to hold his gaze and not tear my eyes from his out of pure guilt. I know what I'm saying is false, and so does he, but I can't stop myself.

"It was only a year." *You're hurting him, Livvy. Stop.*

His gaze bores into mine. "And it was the best fucking year of my entire life."

It was the best time of my life, too. It's the only time I remember feeling as much as I did. The only time I remember feeling true happiness, and feeling like I deserved it. I remember how he used to look at me, all that longing in his gaze before we got together, trying to convince myself that it wasn't real—that he would never want me. I remember kissing him for the first time and feeling like my body had woken up from a coma. I remember watching him leave, and how he took a piece of me with him on that plane. I remember getting his first letter and hearing him read it to me in my mind—a tradition that we started in class all those years ago, that we tried to make stick but couldn't. I remember all of it, and those memories linger in my mind like smoke that will never clear.

Tristan may have physically left, but throughout the past four years, he's never left my head. He's always been in the back of my mind, floating there as if he was standing right next to me while I ghosted my way through life. Looking in his gaze now brings me back to all the times when I thought I could drown in those eyes of his. Now, I only see traces of who he once was—who we both were.

Everything is different now. We're older than we were, we're different, smarter, wiser, and I've had so many moments without him that he doesn't know about, and vice versa. Now he's going through something, and I want to reach across the table and comfort him, but I don't think I know how to. At least not this version of Tristan. He practically pulled away earlier as if he hated how I grabbed his hand to try to comfort him. "Oliv—"

My alarm cuts him off. "I have to get back to work."

"Okay." Both of us stand up and as I walk by him, trying to get out of this situation as soon as possible, he catches my wrist in his hand and turns me around to face him.

I don't pull away at first. I know I'll regret that later, but I can't pull away because it's all so familiar. The way my head reaches his neck and how he always used to rest his chin over the top of my head, his cinnamon cologne permeating my senses.

I guess some things never change, but maybe too much of *us* have changed for anything to be like it was. So yes, this is all familiar, he's familiar, but the two of us are fundamentally different from when we were meeting each other for the first time in college.

Before I pull away, I wrap my arms around his waist, wanting to comfort him and take any part of the pain he's feeling away at this moment. *He lost someone,* I say to myself. *That's all this hug is for. Comfort.* "I'm sorry," I whisper into his shirt.

"I'm sorry, too," he says as he brushes a hand on my back. *Familiar.* It's all too fucking familiar. I pull away and take a few steps back before he reaches into his pocket and holds something out to me. "My new number. Use it, please."

"How do I know you'll answer?"

"I'll always answer for you, Livvy. As long as you call, I'll always answer." I want to tell him that he didn't answer all those years ago and that he's a liar, but I don't. He presses a quick kiss to my cheek before I can move away from him, and then he leaves.

He leaves and doesn't look back at me. Not once.

Just like last time, I'm stuck where he left me. Watching him walk away with part of my heart in his hands for the taking.

I know that this time, I'll survive it. I've done it before, therefore I can do it again.

Part 2
— Then —
Four Years Ago

Chapter Four

September 2022

— 20 SOMETHING BY SZA

As I SIT AND stare at my laptop, willing my homework to do itself, my best friend, Cassie Flemming, sits across from me in the student center.

"You look like shit," she tells me, and I roll my eyes.

"That's because I feel like shit."

"Your parents still?"

"Yup." I tolerate my parents, but the constant pressure from them to get a good job after college sucks when you have no idea what you want to do with your future.

"I'm sorry, Livs. But don't carry that weight around with you. You'll figure it out. I don't know why society wants everyone on earth to have their entire lives figured out at such a young age. You have time. One more year to figure out a path, and even if you don't, you'll be okay."

"Damn, you're definitely going into the right field. Anyone would be lucky to call you their therapist."

She winks at me. "Damn right. *Future* therapist."

I feign a smile while returning to my computer screen. Our senior year of college may have started two weeks ago, but I'm already feeling the burnout. *Just get through this week, Liv.* I repeat that mantra about eighty times a day. I repeat it every single week, and though it helps to have those small things to look forward to, I find myself hating this repetition. I hate that I'm just existing right now and that all the days start to blur together so much. I'm not getting *through* anything. I'm ghosting. I'm floating through school, homework, and classes because I'm so fucking tired.

All of this is a waste, anyway. I'll never chase my dream of becoming an author, so what's the point? My parents will force me into some nine-to-five job that pays my bills, and I'll be unhappy for the rest of my life. I can practically see my future now, and I'm not looking forward to it. I miss the little girl who used to see the world with bright-colored glasses on. I don't think she'd be proud of us for not going after what we want, but sad that we've succumbed to the expectations of our parents.

Summit University, the school I've been destined for since I was a kid, continues to stomp on me every chance it gets. My parents always wanted me to go here since we live so close to it, so I didn't have a choice when I was applying to schools. I got accepted, and before I knew it, I was moving into the dorms and out of my childhood home. It's a nice school, but I've never felt at home here. Don't get me wrong, I love all the old-fashioned architecture and stone buildings with ivy running up them, but I always assumed that when I went to college, it would feel like I was starting a new life.

Something about being here feels like I'm in someone else's body. It just doesn't feel *right.* But if I told my parents that, they would tell me I'm being ridiculous, just like every time I try to talk about my feelings. They shut me down and move on.

"Have you figured out an internship yet?" I ask Cassie, and she goes on this long spiel of how she's doing one at this nearby psychiatrist's office. I love seeing the look on her face when she talks about it. She's so passionate, but part of my soul starts to ache because I can't remember when my eyes lit up at something I was doing like hers do. I nod with a smile, not wanting to bring my friend down when she's clearly so excited about this.

"Woah, Cass, breathe. You're talking so fast that you're going to run out of oxygen." My other friend and roommate, Parker Owens, came and sat with us.

"I know, I know, I'm just excited!"

"We can tell." Parker flashes me a smile before slumping back in her chair. Parker is a lot like me—introverted and prefers books and fictional characters over people—so she understands how it feels when Cassie, our very outgoing and extroverted friend, is around in full swing.

Cassie is as fiery as the red hair falling from her head. It's long and wavy, constantly all over the place, but always seems to look cute. Her hazel eyes and high cheekbones remind me of Jessica Chastain, and freckles pepper her skin beautifully.

Parker's dirty blonde hair falls right to her shoulders, having cut most of it off of her head before school started. Her blue eyes pierce your soul—especially when light shines on them. Her brown-framed glasses fit her face, making her eyes appear even bigger—when she wears them. Parker often neglects her glasses, opting not to see. Which is understandable. Some days, I've seen enough.

Cassie was good for getting Parker and me out of our shells during freshman year, and we often go out together, but sometimes it gets exhausting.

Or maybe that's just the weight of all my expectations that I'm feeling. *Probably!*

"How have the first few weeks been treating you, Parker?" Cassie asks her.

"They've been fine. I have to say, though, having my dad as a professor is the weirdest thing ever. I don't think I'll ever get used to it."

"Yeah, I don't think I could deal with that. You're stronger than me." Parker's dad teaches statistics here at Summit. Parker is majoring in astronomy and has been pushing this class off with her dad for three years. Now that she's finally in it, I bet it's a weird adjustment.

"So, Liv, how's your day been? Any progress on figuring out your life?" Parker asks, like she does every single day. It's not to be mean or to put more pressure on me. She thinks that one of these times, I'll magically know what to do.

"Nope. But I did sign up for two new elective classes." I smile, excited about my choices. Even though the semester has been going for two weeks, I had a few gaps in my schedule to fix, so I added two right before the cutoff date.

"Which ones?" Cassie asks me.

"Some sort of coding class or something, and creative writing—though technically, I need that one for my major requirements." I smile at the thought of writing stories again. I've always loved writing; I've done it ever since I was little, whether it was writing short stories in my journal or writing down all of my feelings. Writing helped me sort through all of my feelings when they felt too jumbled to sift through in my mind. The same goes for books. There are some characters that make you feel like you're looking in a mirror when you read about them, and it always made me feel less alone when I found one that understood me.

"Creative writing? Does that mean you've been writing again? Can I read something? I loved that one short story you read to us that night freshman year." Cassie practically sifts through my bag, trying to find my notebook, but she won't find it.

"Cass, chill out. Also, you basically forced Liv to read you her story when she told you a thousand times it wasn't done."

I giggle at the memory. One of the first times we got drunk together, Cassie found my writing journal and forced me to read her something from it after she found something that I started but never finished. All I had written was a smut scene, which Cassie found *very* entertaining, and I blushed the entire time while reading it aloud. Parker just cringed, but the next week I walked into our dorm and she was reading one of my favorite romance novels, and when she finished, she told me not to speak of it ever again. Parker loves reading like me, but it's mostly thrillers, fiction, memoirs, and biographies. It's not that she *hates* the romance genre, but she doesn't prefer it, and that's okay.

The three of us talk for a few more minutes until they both realize that they have class soon and rush out of the student center. "I'll see you at home, Liv!" Parker practically shouts at me while almost running into someone on her way out the door. Cassie heads in the other direction, walking with her boyfriend to class. I throw a wave at Bryce, her baseball-playing boyfriend, before he threads their hands together. *Adorable.*

I have a class in an hour, so I keep staring at the notes that I took for my public speaking class. My professor assigned us all a two-minute short introductory speech, and being the worst public speaker ever, I've been on edge all day. I also barely slept last night, so I'm practically running on pure anxiety. I keep reminding myself that it's only two minutes, but nothing seems to calm me down.

Half an hour later, after about a thousand leg shakes, I get up and head for the snack area. I grab a bag of my favorite sour candy and a bottle of water. I hand my ID to the cashier and she swipes it before handing it back to me.

I grab my food, wanting to get back to the things that I left on my table, but when I turn the corner to go back, I run straight into someone and almost fall over. The stranger catches me by my waist and even saves my snack and water bottle from falling as well. *Impressive.*

"Shit, I'm sorry! I should've looked where I was going," a deep, gravelly voice says as he sets his now empty coffee cup on a nearby table, along with my stuff that he caught. Only then does it hit me that his coffee is now on my shirt, and I'm all wet. *Fuck.* I look at the guy who caught me, and he doesn't look familiar at all, but he must go here because his hoodie says *Summit Baseball.* He's probably around a head taller than me, maybe 6'2", with brown curly hair that falls just the right way. His eyes are a warm brown, and his jawline could probably cut glass. *God, he's beautiful, and I've been staring at him for far too long.*

"It's fine," I say as he grabs some napkins and hands them to me. "Thank you."

"Are you in a rush or something?" he asks, and I remember that I have my presentation soon.

"Fuck," I whisper to myself, knowing that I don't have time to run back to my place across campus before my next class. "Fuck, fuck, fuck."

"You didn't hit your head, did you? Do you want me to take you to the health center?"

"No, it's fine." I don't turn around as I grab my stuff and head back to my table, but I feel him following me. When we reach my table, I dig through my bag, hoping another shirt magically appears, but I find nothing. *Shit.* I left my jacket in my apartment because it was pretty warm out today. I look over and see this guy staring at me as he sits at my table. "Why are you following me?"

"I feel bad for spilling coffee on you, and you look stressed out. What can I do to help?" He smiles at me, and I suddenly feel very awkward because I don't know this guy.

"Nothing. Just go back to whatever you were doing."

"I wasn't doing anything before this. Let me help since I was the one who spilled coffee all over you."

"Technically, I ran into you," I say, and he shakes his head at me. "What?"

"I'm taking the blame. I was on my phone texting my brother and not paying attention. Plus, my mom always used to tell me to be nice to pretty girls. So, why are you freaking out, and how can I help?"

I scoff at him, not wanting to dive deeper into what he said. *Did he just call me pretty?* "Considering I don't even know your name, it's fine. I have a class to get to."

He abruptly stands up out of his chair and throws his arm out over the table. "Tristan."

"Olivia." I awkwardly shake his hand before shoving my stuff into my bag. "Do you often shake people's hands when you've just met them, or am I missing something?" I throw my bag over my shoulder and head out the doors before I feel him walk next to me. *What is his deal?*

"It's the gentlemanly thing to do. What class do you have?"

"Public speaking. I have a presentation that I'm going to have to do with my normal anxious thoughts and now a coffee-stained shirt." As I keep walking forward, I feel his hand snake around my wrist before he stops us both. "What are you doing?"

He drops his bag on the path we're on, takes his hoodie off—his shirt lifting with it and exposing part of his abs—and holds it out to me. "Take this."

My mouth falls open when he says those two words. "What? No, it's fine."

"Olivia, please just take it. It'll cover your shirt and ease my guilty conscience for running into you and spilling my latte." He shoves the hoodie—pale gray with what I assume is his last name on the back—in my direction again, and I sigh before taking it. It's not like I have much of a choice, and I'd rather be swimming in a hoodie during my presentation, than have everyone see through my shirt.

"Thank you, Tristan West," I say as I pull the hoodie over my head, and when I'm in it, I watch his eyes swipe over my body. *Did he just check me out?*

"You're very welcome, Olivia."

"Livvy."

He looks me up and down again before locking his eyes with mine. "*Livvy.*" He then turns around, heading back for the student center, and I yell after him.

"Where are you going, and how do I get this back to you?" I see a few heads turn as I shout after this guy I met fifteen minutes ago.

"I need more coffee. I spilled my last one on a cute girl." He smiles at me before opening the door to the student center. "And keep it. It looks better on you."

Before I can unpack what *that* means, I realize that I have ten minutes to get to my class and prepare for my speech. So, I adjust the hoodie that's definitely two sizes too big for me before walking briskly to class.

Chapter Five

— **SUNDAY BEST BY SURFACES**

"Do you want a beer?" Dom asks me as he waltzes into our apartment.

"It's two in the afternoon."

To that, he shrugs at me. "And?"

"And we have practice later." My other roommate and best friend, Harry Snyder, walks in, throwing his keys into the bowl we keep by our front door. "You know we can't get shitfaced before practice or Coach will kill us."

"What he said," I say from our couch.

"You guys are no fun," Dom slams the refrigerator door shut. "I wish Ethan was here. He'd be a good friend and drink with me."

"He's not an athlete on a rigorous workout schedule, Dom. We can drink this weekend if you have something to celebrate." Harry walks into his room, probably getting ready for our practice this afternoon. Ethan is also one of my roommates, and like Dom, he's not an athlete.

Ethan Perkins is our resident movie buff. His deep brown skin and hazel eyes that almost pop out of his face help with the ladies—along with his fucking charisma. He's getting a degree in film studies, and forces us all to watch weird indie films all the time.

Dominic Graves has black hair, golden bronze skin, and comes in at about 6'1". He has a dickish charm that's resulted in over twenty drinks being tossed in his face, but his ego hasn't ever taken a hit. He's getting a business degree so he can go into the family business after he graduates.

The two of them work out and shit, but Harry and I are the ones *on* a team. The four of us have been stuck together like glue since freshman year, and now we have our own apartment together in one of the buildings on campus. These three are a bunch of assholes, but I'd never dream of not having them as friends.

Harry and I are on the varsity baseball team here at Summit University, and since the semester started, practices have become a regular thing again. The season may not start until the spring, but Coach likes to practice outside as much as we can before the snow comes. Pennsylvania winters can be rough, and like the rest of my teammates, I prefer the dirt of a field over the turf of our indoor practice area.

Turf just isn't the same, but we make do with what we've got.

"Fine, but I'm holding you guys to that." Dom smirks at us as he takes a swig of his beer.

"Don't worry, Dommy. I'll pour the shots myself," I say as I latch onto his shoulder before heading to my room. I grab my bag that I always use, which has my practice uniform, water, cleats, tape, and anything else I might need in it before heading back out to grab a snack.

Before I can get entirely out of my room, Dom stands in my doorway with the weirdest look on his face. "What the fuck is wrong with you right now? Get out of my way, dude."

"Not until you tell me about the girl." He smirks at me.

"Girl?" Harry asks from behind Dom. *When did he get there?* "Tristan has a girl? Again?"

"Okay, fuck you, Harrison." I full-name him. "I don't know what the hell you're talking about, and you guys should know I don't have a girl."

"Not since last week at least, or was Jessica coming out of Ethan's room? I can't remember," Dom says to me. "I'm talking about the girl who has your hoodie, West. Care to comment?" He flashes me his phone, and I see a picture of Olivia—the girl I spilled coffee all over the other day—wearing my hoodie.

"Who the fuck sent you that?" I ask him.

"Maddie." *Fucking hell.* She's probably jealous. "She's pissed at you. Good luck with that, bro."

"Maddie doesn't mean anything to me. She's the one who throws herself at me when I've told her repeatedly that I'm not interested any-more." Not only is she not my type, but she's pushy. We've fucked a few times, but that's it. She wants more and I don't. "This picture is nothing."

"If it's nothing, then tell us who the girl is," Harry smirks. *I'm going to throw a ball at this fucker later if he doesn't stop smirking.*

"The girl's name is Livvy," I snap. *Where did that come from?*

"Livvy, huh? If she's so unimportant then why'd you get so pissed off?" Dom asks me.

"Fuck off. Her name's Olivia and I barely know her. I spilled coffee on her last week, and I gave her my hoodie because she had a big presen-tation. She looked nervous, and it was the least I could do," I confess. "I don't know her that well."

"Yeah, so? You still gave her the hoodie, and for Tristan West, that means something." Dom smiles. "You barely let Amanda in your room, and you *dated* the girl."

Dom bringing up my last girlfriend from freshman year is a dick move. Amanda and I only dated for a few months, before it fizzled out. There was no connection, and yeah, I'm weird about other people being in my space. I like things a certain way—neat and organized, and other people don't know how to honor that. Usually, if I need a quick fuck, it's never in my room. It's always at her place, in a car, or somewhere else. "I mean yeah, she's cute, but I was being nice, a gentleman even. You two should take notes." I shift my gaze to Dom. "Especially you."

"Me? I'll have you know that I *always* let a woman come first. There's nothing more gentlemanly than that," he smiles.

"Shut the fuck up, dude." Harry tells Dom. "I don't know how we haven't gotten sick of you yet."

"I keep things interesting around here, that's why." Dom lets me ease past him into our kitchen. "So, this Livvy chick, is she hot?"

"Fuck off, dude. I have practice," I say while grabbing water from the fridge. "Don't make this situation out to be more than it is. I was being nice. Now drop it."

"Do you want me to get your hoodie back from her? I'd love to meet—"

I cut off Harry. "Stop. I told her I didn't want it back, so no."

"So you're okay with this girl walking around with your baseball hoodie? With your last name and number on the back?" Dom asks me.

"Yeah. Why are we still talking about this?"

"Tristan, it's a little odd. Aren't you worried about other girls being jealous? You're never gonna get laid ever again when people catch wind of this," Harry tells me.

"Maybe I don't give a fuck what other people think. Ever thought about that?"

The two of them just stare at me, confused as all hell. "Okay, listen up, West." Dom starts, and I roll my eyes because I know whatever he's about to say is going to be ridiculous. "Girls take shit like that seriously. Exchanging clothes is more of a relationship type of thing, especially hoodies. Aren't you worried that she'll get attached and shit because of what you did?"

"He's got a point."

I roll my eyes. "Really, Harrison? You too?" *Why am I friends with these guys again?* "Livvy didn't seem like the type to cling. She would barely accept it in the first place, so calm down. Just because you guys have had bad experiences, doesn't mean that all girls or guys are the same. Livvy seemed nice, and I was the asshole who tried to help after I spilled coffee on her. That's all, as I've told you a thousand times."

Harry seems content with my answer. "Got it, Tris."

"Nah. Now I think you had an ulterior motive," Dom squints at me, but doesn't elaborate.

"You can think whatever the fuck you want, dude. That's called free will, congrats on discovering it," I look to Harry. "Ready for practice?"

"Yup."

✦

EVERY TIME WE WARM up with partner throwing, my mind always drifts back to when I was young. My dad used to be my throwing partner. He taught me everything I knew about baseball and was part of the reason why I loved it so much.

I loved the sport because he loved it. I was only in Little League when he died, but I kept playing because I knew he would want me to. It was also one of the few ways I felt him. Every throw, every at-bat, every caught ball in the outfield he was with me. I don't know how I could tell, but I just had that sort of feeling.

As a twenty-one-year-old now, I still feel his absence when I step on the field. He's the piece of this sport that I've always been missing. After he died, my mom kept me in baseball because she knew what it meant to me, and she knew how much it meant to my dad.

I've never been more thankful for her doing that. Even though I had to step up and become the man of the house, she still wanted me to have one thing for myself. One thing that I could turn to when I was missing him. His death was sudden, and it shook our entire family—being as close as we are. My mom kept going despite losing the love of her life, and as the oldest of three kids, I took on more responsibilities to help my mom out. All of us did, but I felt like I had to do more—it's what my dad would've wanted me to do.

Harry has been my throwing partner since freshman year, and now as seniors, it remains the same. I'm Summit's starting center fielder, and Harry plays left field. The two of us make a good team in the outfield, and we work well together. He's got sandy blond hair, green eyes, and a lean body from all the working out we do as part of the team. He's getting an education degree so he can coach in the future, and anyone would be lucky to have him as one. I'm going to miss playing with him when we graduate, and I leave.

I've always told everyone that I wanted to get out of Pennsylvania as soon as I graduated college. It's always been my plan, and I'll be sticking to it by getting a job as far away as I can.

I love my family and friends, but there's always been an itch to get out of here. With the degree that I'll be earning in software engineering, the job opportunities are pretty endless. Especially in Silicon Valley, that's my goal, at least.

I catch the ball Harry throws at my chest with my glove, before the fucker smirks at me. "What?" I yell to him, conversations from the other thirty-two players on the team drowning out my voice.

"You okay over there? You look lost in thought," he catches the ball as I throw it back. "Are you thinking about what Dom said?"

"No," I snap. "He's an idiot."

"I'm not denying that, but he did have a point."

I roll my eyes and continue warming up, not wanting to think about this anymore. *I was just being nice. Why is everyone making such a big deal about a fucking hoodie?*

Half an hour later, I'm with Harry and a few other guys doing out-field drills. Our coach makes the entire team know most positions; that way, if someone gets hurt, one of us can fill it. A few of the guys are specialists and only work on their positions, such as pitchers and catchers. The relationship between a pitcher and their catcher is important since they have to be able to read each other and work well together.

"Yo, West. I saw Livvy in your hoodie the other day," Bryce, our starting third baseman, says.

I sigh heavily. "Is there a question somewhere, Bryce?"

"Uh, yeah. Why was Livvy wearing your hoodie? Cassie texted me about it before practice, and I told her I'd ask you about it."

"Why does Cassie care?" Cassie is Bryce's girlfriend. They've been dating for a bit, and I've hung out with her a few times at the bar. She's cool. Pretty loud sometimes, but her energy is infectious. Fiery chick she is. It's funny how her hair matches her personality—red, bright, and all over the place most of the time.

"Cass is one of Liv's friends. They go way back."

"Oh," is all I say. "I gave it to her because I spilled coffee on her shirt, and she had a presentation. I felt bad, that's all."

"Yeah, but that's unlike you."

Jesus. "Since when is everyone so familiar with who I am? You guys need a life if mine seems so interesting. I promise it's not." I step up to where Coach wants us, and before I know it, he's hit the ball, and I take a few steps back, judging it. I always step back when I see a ball headed my way. It's easier for me to run up than to run backward and try to track it that way. It lands in my glove, and I throw it back to our assistant coach before heading to the end of the line.

"Livvy's been all hush-hush about it, and now you're getting defensive. That makes me think—"

"I don't care what you think. I told you what happened. It's not a big deal. Can everyone stop asking me about it now?"

"For now, Tristan. For now, I'll shut my mouth."

I don't even want to know what that means. Sure, I'm not one to lend my clothes to strangers, especially cute girls, but everyone is acting like aliens have landed and taken over my brain. Yeah, I guess I normally go for a one-night stand when I want to let off some steam, but that doesn't mean I'm incapable of being a gentleman.

I'm probably never going to see the girl again, so there's no harm in anything I've done. I want to move on and have people stop reminding me about it and thinking there's more to the story.

I was just being nice.

That's all it was.

Nothing more, nothing less. Me—Tristan West—being a nice guy.

That's *all*.

Chapter Six

— BUTTERFLIES BY KACEY MUSGRAVES

As I remove Tristan's hoodie from the dryer, I silently hope that I didn't accidentally shrink it. Getting the damn thing from him was embarrassing enough, I'd hate to give it back and learn it no longer fits him.

Though he did tell me to keep it...

No. I'm giving it back. Final decision. I've had enough weird looks to last me a lifetime after I gave my presentation wearing it. A few girls snickered during my speech, causing me to falter a little bit. Then, when I was leaving class, I saw them pointing at me as I walked out the door. I brushed it off, but this hoodie has bad juju surrounding it or something. I don't like being noticed. I don't like being the center of attention, and this hoodie makes me both of those things—therefore, I'm giving it back.

I do need to find out where he is right now, which is easier said than done. The only things I know about him are that he plays baseball for Summit, his number is thirty-one, and his name is Tristan West.

That's it.

As I get back to my room, I drop my laundry basket onto my floor and throw his hoodie over my desk chair. My room is notorious for being neat, my bed is always made, with my light brown comforter and forest green blanket neatly on my bed. A few plants surround my room, and I make a mental note to water them later. A bunch of prints line my walls—most of them being book quotes, character art, or song lyrics that I relate too deeply to. My bookshelf stands next to my desk, filled to the brim with my favorite books that I brought here. The rest of my own little library is at my parents' house about fifteen minutes away. My desk holds the minimal makeup I own, as well as a few of my current reads. My journal sits in the drawer, and flashcards for a book I want to write eventually, but probably will never have the guts to.

As I start to put my laundry away, my front door slams open. "Olivia Hart! Get out here this instant!"

"Cassie, what—"

She beelines for where I stand in my room. "You! Get over here. We need to talk. I saw a picture of you wearing—" Her yelling stops as she notices his hoodie thrown over my chair. "Oh shit, it's real. I thought it was photoshopped."

"What the hell are you talking about?" I ask her, confused.

"There's a picture going around of you wearing Tristan's hoodie, and I thought it was fake, but this being here is proof that it's not."

"What do you mean there's a picture going around?" *Fuck.*

"Someone sent it to me. Everyone's talking about it. Did you not know?" Cassie asks me as she pulls out her phone and shows me.

"Why is *everyone* talking about this? It's barely pressing news..." My body is starting to go into panic mode at the thought of the entire school seeing this picture, all eight thousand students.

"It's like a huge deal, especially with Tristan. Livs, he's one of the most popular guys on campus, and he's not one to share clothes with anyone—especially you."

Ouch. "What does that mean, especially *me*?"

"I didn't mean it like that, fuck. Liv, this is a big deal. How did you get this? Did you fuck him? You can tell me, this is a safe space."

"You look way too excited at the prospect of this. No, Cass, I didn't sleep with him."

"Okay, but then how did you get this?"

"It was last week before my presentation. I ran into him and he spilled his coffee all over me. He then continued to follow me around until he offered to help. I declined, and he kept pestering me—he literally followed me out of the student center." I pause to breathe. "Then he ripped it off of his body, held the hoodie out to me, and I took it because it was either that or give my presentation with a giant stain on my shirt."

Cassie looks less than impressed. "Okay, next time you tell it, you fucked him. Start using that smut writing brain of yours to think of a story to tell next time someone asks you about it."

"Absolutely not. He was being a nice guy, that's all."

She rolls her eyes. "Tristan West is not just a nice guy, Liv. He's notorious for only having one-night stands, and Bryce told me that he's weird about people being in his space, which is why him giving you this"—she grabs his hoodie and raises it—"is extremely out of character."

"That's probably why he told me to keep it," I say, and her eyes pop open.

"He told you to keep it, and you're going to bring it back to him? Dumb move, girl. He very clearly wants *you* to have it."

I shake my head. "Cassie, enough. It doesn't mean anything. Don't make out a simple kind gesture to be something that it's not." *Although he did call me cute as he was walking away...*

"He did what?!"

I didn't realize I had said that out loud. Fuck. "Don't start," I say as I exit my room and head to the fridge.

"Don't deflect! He called you cute? What did he say? I need the exact words, Liv."

"Why?"

"Because Tristan fucking West called you cute, and I know you don't realize how much of a big deal that is, but I do. Let me be excited enough for both of us. What did he say? Word for word, Olivia."

"I asked where he was going since he walked away from me, and how I'd get this back to him. He told me he was going to get a new coffee since he spilled his other one on a pretty girl." My cheeks *unintentionally* heat as I recount that day. Why does any type of compliment make me all flushed? God, I've read smuttier things in romance books, but a compliment from a stranger I barely know makes me weak in the knees. *Am I pathetic?*

"Interesting."

"After all that, you have one word to say?" I question her because it's very unlike Cassie to be speechless. I think I might've broken her. "You had more to say when you found out about that guy getting murdered at that one college."

"Listen…it was suspicious circumstances and at a small-town college. That could've been us, Livs! Our dean of students could've been slaughtered too!"

I roll my eyes again. "Okay, now that our gossip session is over, do you know where I can find him to give this back? Does Bryce know?"

Cassie's mouth turns into the biggest smile I've ever seen. "Bryce is at practice right now, and so is Tristan." Before I know it, she's grabbing the hoodie and fleeing. "We should wait for them at the field and that way you'll ensure he gets it! Let's go."

She heads for the door while I'm stuck standing in one place. "Cass! I'm *not* doing that. Ask Bryce where he lives, and I'll leave it outside of his door with a thank you note."

Cassie tilts her head at me and scolds me. "A thank you note, Liv? Really?"

"What? It's the nice thing to do..." I trail off while wrapping my arms around myself. I suddenly feel self-conscious and I don't know why.

"Yeah, but I want to see the look on his face when he sees you again. I want to confirm my suspicions."

"And what might those be?"

"That he likes you, or wants to fuck you."

I sigh heavily. "That won't happen until pigs fly, Cass. If what you've told me about him, and his status on this campus is true, then I'm the last person on his radar. He was being nice."

"I'll see for myself what he was being." She holds her hands out to me. "Let's go."

The two of us have a stare off for a few seconds before I crack. "Let me grab my keys and some shoes." I turn around and head for my room.

"Don't even think about climbing out the window and escaping! I'll drag you there if I have to."

I stifle a laugh as I put my Converse on, and the two of us head out the door and toward the field.

<hr>

"WHAT THE HELL ARE they doing?" I'm so confused as I watch them throw the ball around in some weird pattern.

"Oh, babes, I have no clue what they do at practice. It's confusing as fuck sometimes with the amount of drills they do. I just like watching Bryce in his uniform."

"It's like foreplay for you two at this point." I smile at her and she returns it.

"Yeah, basically..." She laughs and a few minutes later we see them all head to the bench, or dugout, or whatever. I'm not the biggest fan of any sports, so I don't know much about baseball. Only that there are four bases and a pitcher. That's as far as my knowledge goes. My dad was never a big sports fan, and my mom never put me or my sister into any as kids. My parents are bigger fans of watching the stock market and the news over anything recreational.

"Oh! Look, there's Bryce." Cassie's boyfriend barely emerges from the dugout, before she runs and jumps on him in front of the team. I slowly make my way over, wishing I could shrink into myself rather than be around all these sweaty athletes. I have nothing against them, but big crowds of people—especially dudes—are my worst nightmare.

I'm standing around for what seems like forever when I hear a voice in front of me. "Olivia?" I look up, and there he is. Standing in his purple uniform, with gray pants, black socks, and black shoes—cleats, according to Cassie. His baseball hat is hiding part of his face from the sun. "What are you doing here?"

"I, uh, came to give this back to you. I didn't know where I could find you, and Cassie suggested that I try here." I point over to where Cassie and Bryce are standing and talking with a few teammates. His hand is curled around her waist, and she's pulled flush to him. It's adorable, but I silently hate her for leaving me alone over here.

Tristan just smiles at me, that same pretty boy smile he flashed me when he gave this to me. "I told you to keep it, and I meant it."

"Look, I know you're weird about sharing clothes with people, so take it, please." I shove it at him, and he doesn't move to take it.

"Have you been asking around about me?" He smirks, and I suddenly can't think of anything to say. I *didn't* ask around about him. All my information came from Cassie about an hour ago. Before I can formulate an answer, a few of his teammates come over and give him a pat on the back. One of them looks over at me and smiles.

"Now, who might this pretty thing be?" the guy to Tristan's left asks him, getting a glare in response.

"Olivia. I was—"

He cuts me off. "This is Olivia?" Tristan doesn't dignify the guy with a response. "My, my, my. We've heard so much about you in the past few hours."

Tristan locks eyes with me. "Don't listen to him. Harrison is being an idiot."

"Noted. Now, can you take this, and we can go back to never speaking again? I even washed it, so every trace of me should be erased." I shove it at him again, and he stares at me. "Can you take it? I don't have all day."

"Yeah, Tristan. Take it. It's not like it's weird you gave it to her in the first place. So take it." The guy—Harrison—smirks at him, obviously trying to get a rise out of him.

"Look, I know you're weird about certain things, but I can't bear to get another odd stare from some girl, and I want the whispers to stop about why I wore it. Feel free to tell everyone on campus what happened so I can go back to not being the center of attention." I throw the hoodie over his shoulder. He's taller than I am, but I have no trouble getting it to stay. I turn to walk back to my apartment, but I feel a presence next to me as I do.

"Cassie, I'm going to kick your ass for making me—" I turn and realize that it's not her, but Tristan instead. "Do you have a habit of chasing after girls you barely know, or is it just with me?"

"Walk with me, Livvy."

"Technically, I should tell you that. I was the one walking away from you and that horrible situation back there." I look over at him, and he smiles.

"Is it that horrible being around me? You didn't seem to mind at the student center."

I sigh. "No, it's not. I just hate all the eyes that have been on me since you gave me that thing." I point to his hoodie. "I'm not blaming you. You helped me out a lot, and I appreciated it, but I didn't know wearing

your hoodie would come with a side of whispers and girls staring at me."
I swear I see his jaw clench at that last phrase, but I could be seeing things.

"I'm sorry. I didn't mean to make anything hard for you. I just felt bad." He sounds genuine right now, and after all, Cassie told me about him, I didn't think he'd be like this. Granted, I don't know how most athletes or men act, so I had nothing to go off of.

"It's okay. You were being a nice guy." He smiles at that, and the two of us continue walking across campus and away from the baseball fields, or stadium, or whatever you call it.

I take this time to really study him. I've only seen him once before, and I didn't get to take him in, especially not up close. His hair is dark brown, like mine, and it curls slightly at the ends around the baseball hat he's currently wearing. He's only a few inches taller than me, but I'm above average height at five foot seven. His brown eyes match his hair, and a stubbly beard is present on his face. I've never been a facial hair girl—only certain people can pull it off, and he most certainly is. His uniform practically molds to his body, and his muscles are on display since he's wearing short sleeves. *He's beautiful.* That's the only way I can think to describe him. It sucks that he's a nice guy, too. Normally if a guy looks how he did, I'd expect him to be an asshole. It's the proper balance of things, but with Tristan, it's different. He helped out a random girl that he spilled coffee on, which tells me all I need to know.

"Are you checking me out, Olivia?" His gravelly voice breaks me from my thoughts, and I realize I'm still looking at him as we walk.

"Sorry, I'm not swooning over the fact that I'm talking to you. I assume most girls come up to you and kiss those rings on your hands." I just noticed those because he started putting them on, and holy shit. Is it possible to be attracted to someone's hands?

His face falls a little, but he quickly masks it. "There's usually not much talking going on when I'm near another girl."

Oh. I get the insinuation he's making. "I must be special."

"You're different from most, Olivia." *Different.* I can't decide if that's a good thing or a bad thing, and I secretly hope that it's good. "And you didn't answer my question."

I search my brain for whatever he asked, but find nothing. "What question?"

"Have you been asking around about me? You seem to know a *whole* lot more about me than I do you." He arches an eyebrow at me. "I'd like to fix that. It's only fair, after all."

"Okay, first, I didn't ask around about you. Cassie told me a bunch of stuff earlier after she freaked out about me having your hoodie. I didn't *ask*; it was more like she blabbed about you." I pause. "And ask anything you want. You've already spilled something on me. I think we're past all the awkward first impressions by now."

He laughs at that. "Got it. My first question is, why did you give this back to me when I told you to keep it? It seems like you're not very good at following directions."

I scoff and roll my eyes at him. "I know you told me to keep it, but I was never going to wear it again, and I didn't want it to sit at the bottom of my closet."

"Okay, my second question is, why would it be at the *bottom of your closet?* Seems a bit rude. I was hoping for some sort of shrine dedicated to the guy who saved your ass before that presentation."

I can practically feel him smiling from here. "Oh, I'm sorry. I'll make sure to get a nameplate engraved to put in front of your hoodie. Did you want it to read 'guy who saved my ass,' or 'Tristan West, baseball God?'"

He ponders that for a minute, and I wonder where the hell all this banter is coming from. I'm never this outgoing or one to joke around with someone, but it seems to slip out around Tristan. "I like the second one the best. Being known as a God in your eyes is doing wonders for my ego." He throws a cocky smirk in my direction. *Oh, dear God.*

"It's easy to be known as that when I've never watched a game of sports before, so I don't know how *lucky* that is for you."

"What do you mean you've never watched sports? None of them? I find that hard to believe."

"Never seen anything but snippets. My parents preferred other things when I was a kid."

He doesn't press on that; instead, his mouth lifts up into a smirk again. "My final question, as we are now at your building, is, would you consider us best friends after this conversation? I would say yes."

"I'd say no. Now I have a question for you: how did you know this was my building?"

"You're not the only one who can do a little bit of research, Olivia Hart." He beams at me, having found out my full name, and I stifle the smile that's trying to creep up my face. "Take this. I was serious when I said you could keep it." He throws his hoodie at me, and I catch it before it can hit the ground.

"I'll see you never, Tristan," I say as I head to my building.

"I'll be seeing you, Livvy. You can count on that, bestie."

I throw him my middle finger, and the last thing I see before I close the door is Tristan smiling and waving at me.

Chapter Seven

— IT WILL COME BACK BY HOZIER

As I walk into my coding class in one of the computer labs on campus, I notice a familiar presence to the left of where I usually sit. "I'll see you after class."

"Dude, what are you doing?" I hear my friend Steve ask, but I don't answer because my sights are set on a girl who looks extremely out of place. *What the hell is she doing here?*

"You seem lost," I say, and she looks up at me, dumbfounded.

"Not lost, but nervous that you're going to spill that on me again." She moves her chair back away from me as I sit down at the computer next to hers. "Should I grab my jacket now or...?"

Instead of answering, I reach over and grab her chair, pulling her back near me. She rolls her eyes, but the flush creeping up her cheeks tells me something different. "You don't have to worry, and my latte will stay where it belongs this time. I promise."

"Good. I'd hate to ruin another shirt."

"Ruin a shirt or gain a hoodie? The world may never know." I smile at her. "So, why are you in this class? I think I'd remember if you were in my field of study, but I've never seen you in a single engineering class."

"Does it matter?"

"To me, yes."

"I'm taking this as an elective. I needed a few other classes, and I chose this one. It sounded cool, and I needed something different."

"Coding seems interesting to you? You're going to be regretting that when Python makes you want to rip your hair out." I love this field, don't get me wrong, but coding makes me want to punch a wall sometimes. You can have one piece of script wrong, and your entire code fails to run. It's the fucking worst. Especially at three a.m. when you're on your fortieth try, and it still doesn't work. I like the challenge, though.

"At least that gives me something to look forward to."

"Have you been in this class since the semester started? I feel like I'd remember seeing you," I ask.

"I signed up before the cutoff. Today's my first class."

Huh. This girl seems to be popping up everywhere now. "Well then, I guess I should say welcome."

"Thanks," she smiles at me.

"So, you're taking this as—" I'm cut off by the professor coming in, a new guy who joined as an adjunct this semester. He seems alright. "Did you get the syllabus already?" I whisper to her as the professor starts to talk.

"Yeah, it was online, so I read it over last night."

"Good. Our first project—"

"Mr. West, care to share something?" The professor calls me out, and I paste on a smile.

"I was just making sure Olivia was getting caught up with everything she missed the first two weeks."

"I'm sure you can take care of that after class. Now, back to the presentation..." I tune his voice out and feel Livvy smack my arm and slide something across the table. It's a piece of paper.

Nice going. You really pulled that asshole charm out. It almost looked too easy.

I stifle a laugh, not wanting to be called out by our professor again. I take the sheet of paper and write down something back to her.

What can I say? I'm a natural. If this is an elective, then what's your major?

I pass it back and see her smile. I figure that if Liv's going to keep popping up everywhere, I might as well get to know her. Plus, she's a pretty cool girl. She's quiet and shy but challenges me. We barely have a relationship past me spilling something on her and her badgering me about my hoodie, but I find myself constantly wanting more after every conversation. Albeit only a few, it's how I feel now. I'm kind of bummed that after this class, I don't know when the next time it is that I'll see her.

English literature with a minor in creative writing.

A writer, then, huh? I'm guessing a book lover too...favorite genre?

I hear her scoff before she slides it back to me. *What was that for?*

I'll always be a classics girl, but romance is by far my favorite.

Why did you scoff at me when I asked that question?

I don't know. You've been asking me a lot of them lately. I guess I just don't understand why.

I shake my head. Has nobody ever wanted to know anything about this girl? Surely, I can't be the first, and Livvy's cute—I didn't lie when I told her that the first time we met. Her dark brown hair always seems to fall in the right way. Those blue eyes have a sparkle in them, or whatever, and when she catches me looking at her, her cheeks turn as red as a tomato. It's cute. She's cute.

It's called getting to know you, Liv. I want to, so let me, okay? What's your favorite book?

I don't have one. Too many to choose.

Okay, so which one do you reread the most?

Persuasion by Jane Austen. It's timeless. I reread it once a year every fall. Why do you want to know me so badly?

Do I need a reason?

No, but you're you.

What does that mean?

You're Tristan West, big man on campus, notorious for one-night stands and no relationships. You don't have many friends that are girls besides everyone who kisses your ass on campus. You don't share your clothes or space with anyone, yet you gave me your hoodie. It doesn't make sense to me. Everyone knows you, wants to be your friend, and I'm just me, so why do you care?

Seeing what she wrote kind of makes me pause. Is that really what she thinks of me? That I'm just a popular athlete who doesn't care about people?

I don't have an answer for you. I'm sorry if I confuse you, but ever since I ran into you, you've been everywhere, and yeah, I guess I don't have many friends that are female, but it's not like I've never tried. Most girls only want one thing from me, and when they get it, they leave. Who told you all of this?

Cassie, but I should've learned not to trust anything that comes out of her mouth. I'm sorry. I guess I wouldn't mind getting to know you, either. You're not that bad, sans the coffee incident.

Oh, it's an INCIDENT now?

The two of us start to laugh quietly to ourselves and continue passing the paper between each other. I don't know what the professor taught for the entire class, but I don't care. I learned that Livvy loves reading, and she doesn't call herself a writer, but that's her goal one day. Her favorite color is champagne, which I looked up on my computer, and when I told her that it was just beige, she rolled her eyes at me. I then got an explanation about how beige is more of a cream, and champagne is a mixture of yellow and orange that *resembles* beige. I still don't get it, but I found out that she's very passionate about the things that she likes. Livvy has one younger sister, and we bonded over the fact that we're both the oldest siblings in our family.

By the time class was over, I'd learned a few new things about her, yet I wanted to know more. She seems to give me enough information to answer my questions but never anything extra. I think that's why I'm itching to know more. She's like a half-closed book that I want to read from cover to cover.

"I'll see you in class on Thursday?" I say to her as we leave. I feel Steve come up next to me since we usually walk to our next class together.

"Yup. Hopefully, this time, we'll actually pay attention. Although, don't feel like you have to sit next to me."

"Is my presence annoying you already?" I joke with her.

"No. Just don't feel like you *have* to."

"You're not forcing me to do anything, Olivia. You're semi-cool, and since we're besties—"

"We're not," she says to me, but her smile says otherwise.

"*Since we're besties*, you get to enjoy me annoying you in class and probably outside of it too when you beg me to help you with these projects." I throw a wink at her, and she tilts her head at me. *Always a challenge.*

"I don't beg, Tristan."

I turn and walk away from her. "You will when Python crashes on you for the thousandth time. That you can count on, Livvy!"

I hear her sigh as I pull out my phone. Talking with Livvy about our families has made me miss my siblings, so I send them a text to FaceTime soon, before I head to my next class.

Chapter Eight

— NORTHERN ATTITUDE BY NOAH KAHAN FT. HOZIER

THE SOUND OF MY ringtone breaks me out of the brain fog that comes with my data analytics homework. As I close my textbook, I answer the call from my computer.

"Wow, you look like shit."

"Thanks, Teags. It's nice to see you too," I tell my younger sister, and she laughs. Typical Teagen. She may be a few years younger than me, but we couldn't be more different. She doesn't quite have a filter, which she blames on growing up with three older brothers, and I can't say I disagree. It's probably our fault, especially since we've been teasing her all her life.

"Teags, leave him alone. How's the studying going?" My younger brother, Theo, asks. Again, he and I are different. He's the nice one in the family. At least, that's what most people say.

"Thanks, Theo. At least someone cares about me enough to ask. It's going great, but Dom is making me take a break in a few, so I don't have long."

"You? A break? Pigs must be flying."

"Hilarious." My brother Tobias has always been a pain in my ass, but he and I get along the best since we're closest in age. "How's life in North Carolina?"

"It's okay. Classes might be kicking my ass, but at least parties exist to take some edge off." Tobias is like me. He wanted to get out of Pennsylvania as much as I did, but where I chose to stay close for college, he went off to an entirely new state and got his fresh start. I would've done the same thing if I didn't feel like I still had to be around if Mom needed me. Tobias is two years younger than me, so he's in his sophomore year of college. Theo is four years younger, so he's now a senior at my old high school. Teagen is five years younger than me, and she just started her junior year.

They're starting to make me feel old, yet I'm only twenty-one—twenty-two in January. I remember when I was younger and having to take care of them, especially after our dad died. I remember helping all of my siblings with their homework as we got older. I remember helping my mom out by cooking dinner and doing what I could to help keep the house clean. I remember holding all my siblings up when we found out what happened. It feels like just yesterday I was helping my mom tuck them all into bed, me being last, and now they're all older.

It feels like it happened in the blink of an eye. *How did we get here?*

"Tristan, I should let you know that Mom keeps asking if you have a girlfriend. I don't know where she got the idea, but she keeps asking."

"Why isn't Mom on the call with us? Isn't she home?" I ask, wondering where she is. She's not the type to miss our family phone calls.

"She's probably asleep in her room. She's been going to bed a lot earlier these days," Theo tells me, and Teags nods her head, agreeing with him.

"Is she okay? I can come home this weekend and check on it." Mom never really came back from my dad's death. She used to sneak away from us kids and cry in her room by herself, and one time, I caught her crying in our pantry, but she tried to cover up what she was doing. I think she didn't want us to see her break, which made me upset. Why were we allowed to show our emotions all over the place, but my mom felt like she needed to hide? She was a great mom, and I'll always be grateful for her, but part of me misses who we all were before it happened. *Happy.*

"Tris, it's fine. Don't put too much on your plate. We know you have practice and a fuck ton of difficult classes. It'll be fine," Theo reassures me, but I still feel uneasy.

"Don't forget that girlfriend he supposedly has," Teagen teases while Tobias laughs.

"Tristan isn't the type to have a girlfriend. He's a lone wolf, remember?"

The rest of my siblings laugh at that nickname, but I don't. Ever since high school, that nickname has stuck. I've never really dated, and ever since Teagen coined the nickname, they won't let it go. "Hilarious. You guys realize that maybe I don't have time? I have practices, workouts, homework, tests, and a social life. Not to mention that I'm adding a job to the mix soon."

"Did you get the one you interviewed for?" Theo asks me.

"I still don't understand why you needed a job. You're on a thousand scholarships," Tobias scoffs at me.

"Yes, I got the job. They called me yesterday to confirm, and I already sent in the paperwork. I wanted to have some extra pocket change, and it's close to school, so it's perfect. I want to start saving for my big move now so I can—"

"Get the hell out of here," all my siblings say at the same time, and I roll my eyes.

"Exactly," I say as my door flies open.

"Tris, get your ass out here, the shots are ready." Dom enters my room as fast as he exits.

"Hi, Dom!" Teagen yells, but Dom doesn't hear her.

"Teags, I love you, but Dom will never notice you, so stop trying so hard." Tobias laughs, as do I. My sister has had a girl crush on Dom ever since she met him when we moved into our apartment. I keep telling her that she's too young for him and to move on, but she's as stubborn as I am. Also, that's disgusting. Dom and my sister are not something I want to actively imagine.

"Tobias, I will fly to North Carolina just to kick your ass if you don't shut up," she threatens, and he keeps laughing.

"Stop provoking our sister, Toby. You're not the one who has to deal with the fallout," Theo gripes at him.

"Okay, well, I have to go. I'll talk to you guys tomorrow. Tell Mom I say hi, will you?" I ask, and Teags nods at me.

"Congrats on the job, Lone Wolf. I hope it's fun," Theo says.

"I'm sure it'll be something. I love you guys," I say as I get up from my desk. They all say their goodbyes and log off. I shut my computer off, shove my books to where I don't have to see them and head out to the living room.

Dom, Ethan, and Harry are all sitting around the couch, and I see a few shot glasses spread out. "Dom promised me shots, so are we doing this or what?"

"Damn, princess, we're the ones waiting on you." Dom smiles at me and I throw him my middle finger as I sit down on the couch next to Harry.

"I didn't think my presence was needed to enjoy drinking. Why didn't you guys start without me?" I ask, wondering why these three would ever need to wait to have a drink. *Something isn't right here.*

"Tonight's drinking comes with a twist," Ethan explains. "Every shot you take, you have to answer a question."

What the fuck? "Just me?"

"Yeah," they all say in unison.

"This sounds like an interrogation," I say, taking a shot of something that was on the table. *Vodka.*

"Yeah, but it's a fun one," Dom smiles, and I'm starting to think this was his idea. "Now, what's going on with the girl?"

There it is. "Really? That's what this is about? You don't have to get me drunk, you know. You could've just asked me."

"Anytime someone asks you about Livvy, you get all defensive," Harry says, and as I open my mouth to protest, he speaks again. "Even Bryce noticed it, dude."

He's got a point. "Fuck you," I say, downing another shot.

"Okay, so that's two questions," Ethan smirks.

"He hasn't even answered the first one..." Harry trails off, while Dom keeps refilling the glasses.

"Nothing is going on with Livvy and me. There's your answer. Now start drinking because me sitting here drinking in front of you guys is weird as fuck, and kind of sad."

"Why did Steve tell me that you sat next to her in one of your classes the other day?" Dom smiles at me. *Fucking Steve and his big ass mouth.*

"Because I did, and it's not a big deal. I was helping her," I say, downing another shot. "Why the fuck do you guys care so much? You never cared about any of the other girls I've been around. Why start now?" I ask, wanting to know why they won't shut the fuck up about this topic. I wanted to have a chill night and drink with my friends since I don't have practice tomorrow, and they're fucking the vibes up.

"Well, it's just—" Ethan starts.

"I mean, it's weird that—" Harry stifles.

"She's hot as fuck and you haven't even—" Dom says.

"Holy shit, someone finish a fucking sentence," I say, and Dom opens his mouth. "Not you, asshole."

"I got this," Harry says. "You're different with her, and we've all noticed it."

"Fuck off, you guys. I'm being nice to her. I spilled coffee on her and gave her my hoodie. Now she's in one the hardest coding classes with me, and I know she'll need help because it's difficult as fuck if you don't know what you're doing. That's all, so fucking drop it so we can drink together and have a good time." They're all silent for a few seconds as they look at each other, and then they all grab glasses and down the shots that Dom laid out.

Thank fuck. I'm glad they're finally dropping the topic. Sure, I've been seeing Livvy more than any other girl that I've hung out with, but it's not a big deal. She's fun to talk to, that I can admit, but there's nothing else going on with us. She's a casual acquaintance, and that's all we'll ever be since I'll be out of here by the end of senior year.

There's no use getting attached to someone right now, only to leave them when I go. It's pointless, therefore, nothing will ever happen between us, and I'm okay with that.

It's nice having her as a friend. Most girls just want to fuck me for bragging rights, and it pisses me off. Livvy has been a breath of fresh air, and the two of us will remain the way we are—content with friendship and nothing more.

Chapter Nine

— IVY BY TAYLOR SWIFT

You look really concentrated.

Tristan slides the note over to me, and I stifle a laugh. For the past two weeks, whenever we have class together, he's sat next to me and helped anytime I was confused or had a question. We only have it twice a week; Tuesdays are lecture days, and Thursdays are computer work days. We have one mini project a week using Java or Python or whatever program he wants us to use, and Tristan has been my saving grace. Today is a work day, and I've never wanted to smash a computer more than I ever do now.

I want to stab my eyeballs out, but I guess concentrated works.

I slide the paper back to him and notice his lips turn up as he scribbles something else on the paper.

Told you so.

"Fuck off," I whisper, and he shakes his head as he continues working. This has sort of become our thing—passing notes back and forth in class. It's fun and way too easy since we sit all the way in the back of the lab. It feels weird to say that Tristan and I are slowly becoming friends rather than him just being the guy who spilled coffee on me. It's...weird, but I don't exactly hate it. He's a pretty funny guy, and he's been helpful anytime I've needed it during this class.

A few minutes later, as I grab my stuff to leave, I notice that Tristan is lingering at his seat rather than getting up and heading out with his friend Steve. "I'll catch up with you," he tells him before turning back to me. "I wanted to ask you to get coffee with me after my class, but I forgot I have a thing tonight."

"It's fine. I would've said no anyway."

"I doubt that, Livs. You'd never say no to your best friend."

"You'd be surprised. I have work later, so I couldn't even if I wanted to," I tell him.

"Oh, so you wanted to?" He smirks.

"No," I say as I pat him on the arm. "But then again, our last rendezvous with coffee didn't end so well, did it?"

"Are you ever going to let that go? If you forgot, I was also the one who saved your ass, and I deserve some credit there."

"Yeah, sure, but the spill overpowers the nice gesture," I say as I move past him. "I'll see you next week, Tristan."

"See you then, Livs."

I walk into work, almost late because of Parker talking my ear off about some girl that stole all her notes from her and see Eliza getting ready to leave. "Hi, and bye, I guess."

"Hi, and bye, Livvy. Don't forget that the new guy starts today. He did all his computer training already, so he should come right over here when he gets here at four."

"Got it. Have a good night." I wave to her as she exits the department, hoping to leave before someone else stops her from going home. Eliza is one of the best managers I've ever had. Granted, she and I are pretty similar. We've bonded over a few shared interests, and I silently thank her for letting me have a shift where I can leave earlier than normal. I have loads of homework to catch up on.

"Livvy! How the hell are you?" Joe asks me. It feels weird closing with him tonight. Normally, I'm with Cal, but since someone new is starting, Joe is here. This job is fairly easy, but it takes a second to get into your own routine with customers and all their dumbass questions.

"Hanging in there. How about you?"

He launches into a whole spiel about stuff that's been happening around the department—Jackie somehow got crazier, Megan's dog is pregnant again, and one of the cases went down earlier, but it's fixed now. "I'm going to fill it back up so we can start to sell some of this stuff tonight."

"Sounds good. I'll get started on cleaning."

"Don't do too much. Save some for the new guy!" he yells as he goes into the cooler.

"I will!" It takes around fifteen minutes to straighten up the department. By then, Joe is done filling and back in the department. "So, what did Eliza tell you about the new employee?"

"Not much. It's a guy, and his name is Tristan. That's all I know."

Huh. That seems like a funny coincidence. *What is with me and that name lately?* First school, and now we have a new guy at work with the same name. "Interesting. I guess we'll find out more when he gets here."

"Save your interrogating for then, Olivia," he jokes to me.

"I don't interrogate," I say, and all I get is a scoff.

"Yeah, right. You're as bad as Cal when we get a new employee." Joe says as he gets sidetracked by a customer at the counter.

"I am not," I say under my breath, knowing that it's a lie. Cal and I like to know what we're getting into when we get a new hire. We scope out the vibes of the person, and it's usually pretty easy to tell if they'll fit in here or just be another pain.

Leah, another closer, made a terrible first impression on me, so I haven't liked working with her, but I make do. I'm usually the type to keep my work and regular life separate. I don't like hanging out with coworkers outside of work—Cal is the only exception to that rule.

After the afternoon rush comes and goes, I hear Joe talking to someone as I help a customer. "It's nice to meet you. I'm Joe, the full-timer in this department. Is this your first job in customer service?"

"No, I used to be a barista before I came to college."

There's no goddamn way. I recognize that voice. I know that voice. I talked to that voice mere hours ago. I give the customer their stuff, and when I turn around, I see him. "Fuck."

"Livvy?" His eyes widen as he takes me in. The uniform that we have to wear isn't the hottest thing ever—today I'm wearing a pink polo, black pants, and my no-slip shoes, like normal. Somehow when Tristan takes me and my outfit in, goosebumps travel all across my skin. I'm prickled with an awareness that he's here. He's fucking everywhere at this point, and part of me wants to laugh. How is it that I went three years barely knowing of his existence, and in a few short weeks, he's infiltrated every corner?

"Wh-What are you doing here?" I ask, already knowing the answer.

"I work here."

"No, *I* work here."

"Sorry, do you two know each other?" Joe asks, and I forgot he was standing there for a second. The world seemed to disappear when I was looking at Tristan.

"No," I say.

"Yes," he says at the same time.

"I have a feeling this is going to be fun." Joe smiles awkwardly as a lady waves at him from the counter. "Livvy, why don't you take him to get some gloves while I handle the counter?"

"Fine," I say as I look at Tristan. "Let's go, newbie." I walk out of the department and feel him slide next to me.

"Newbie? Really?"

"What the hell are you doing here?" I ask, confused as to why he suddenly decided to get a job here.

"I work here, Olivia, as I said earlier."

"But why?"

"I needed money to pay off my dealer. Why do you think? I wanted to have some extra pocket change so I could save more money. It's the smart thing to do. You should try it sometime." He winks at me. Fucking *winks* at me.

"You're infuriating. I've been doing that since sophomore year when I started here." We reach the customer service desk, and I smile when I see Jenna working. "Hi, Jenna. We need a few pairs of cut gloves."

"Nice to see you, Livs. What size?"

"Uhhhh." I turn to Tristan. "How big are your hands?"

"Is that general knowledge that people have?"

"Oh my—" I'm cut off by Tristan grabbing my hand and putting it up to his. His rings aren't on because you can't wear jewelry here since it's a food safety hazard, but I hate that they still look good. I blame Mr. Darcy from *Pride and Prejudice 2005* for my obsession with guys' hands. That hand flex changed lives.

"I'm almost double your size." He smirks, and I quickly pull my hand away from his and turn to Jenna. *Why did that make me feel weird?*

"Two extra-large pairs, please," I say to her, and she moves over to the stock closet behind the counter. She hands them to us, and we head back to the department.

"You never told me where you worked, so this isn't completely my fault," he says.

"You told me you had a thing today!" Although remembering our conversation from earlier, I never asked him about what he was doing. We walk into the department in silence, and Joe has a huge smile on his face. "What?"

"This seems like a fun dynamic," he points between us.

"We have a class together, and he's been popping up everywhere lately. If I didn't know any better, I'd think he was stalking me," I say to them.

"First of all, I could say the same thing about you. Second of all, I spilled coffee on Livvy a few weeks ago. That's how we met," Tristan tells him.

"Can we get to work rather than talk about this all night?" I ask, and the two of them nod their heads at me.

"You're not getting off that easy, Miss Olivia, but you're right. Tristan, let me show you how we do things." Joe smiles, and before the two of them leave, Tristan flashes a smile at me and walks away.

This is going to be fun.

AFTER THE MOST WEIRD and confusing shift of my life, I'm finally headed out at around seven. Our department closes at eight every night, but since there were three of us, I was scheduled to leave early. The sun is just starting to set, and when I get to my car—a gray Honda Civic—I grab my phone and take a picture of it. I throw it onto my Instagram story before I slide into my car.

Tonight was confusing, to say the least. *Why do our paths keep crossing?* It's the question that's been nagging at me all night. I spent three years on campus without interacting with him. I barely knew of his existence because I don't tend to watch sports, but in the span of a few weeks, Tristan has invaded my life.

And I don't hate it—that's the weird thing. I'm not great at making friends, so when I find my people, I keep them. I've known Parker and Cassie since freshman year, and I even have a few close acquaintances who have classes similar to mine. That's all.

But Tristan is someone I never really saw coming, and I don't know how we got here. I don't even know what to call us half of the time. Friends? Acquainted? Classmates? Coworkers?

I could ask him, but he already thinks we're best friends—although I was sure that was a joke, but now I don't think it is. He seems to like being around me, and I don't hate being around him either. Maybe as we see each other more, we'll actually become friends. I can't say we are yet because I barely know anything about him besides the crumbs he's told me while we pass notes in class.

Tristan's a good guy, and part of me is looking forward to getting to know him a bit better. It's not like we'll ever be more than friends, so it'll be fine. Plus, he'd never date someone like me, anyway. It doesn't help that I find him attractive. I'd be an idiot not to with the way his hair falls perfectly on his head every time I see him, with the way he commands a room simply just by walking into it. *Those rings too...*

No. I'm not going down that road. Tristan and I will be friends, and that's all. I'm sure he's never thought about me in that way, so I'm shutting that out of my brain before it becomes a thing.

Friends. I can be friends with Tristan. That's easy enough for me.

Chapter Ten

— I THINK I LIKE YOU BY THE BAND CAMINO

I'M ABOUT TO LEAVE the student center and meet up with Ethan at the library, but a familiar brunette halts my footsteps out the door. What I should do is keep heading in the direction I need to, but something about Livvy has me pulling toward her. She's sitting at a table with someone I don't know, and before I go sit down and interrupt them, I text Ethan.

Tristan: I'll be late. Something came up.

Ethan: What could've come up in the last fifteen minutes?

Tristan: A thing. I'll meet you in half an hour?

Ethan: Are you perhaps seeing a certain someone? Name rhymes with trivia?

Tristan: Fuck off. I'll see you later.

Ethan: Whatever man. I'll be here.

God, sometimes I want to punch my friends. They will not let this whole thing with Olivia go, and all three of them are convinced that I like this girl, which of course I do.

As a *friend,* and nothing more.

I shake those thoughts out of my head and stride over to her table. I don't say a word as I slide into the chair next to her, and when I look over at her face, it's all pinched together. "Oh, I'm sorry, was this seat taken?"

"No, but what are you doing here?" Olivia asks me, and I hear her friend chime in before I can answer.

"Hi, Tristan. I'm Parker Owens, Liv's roommate, and I've heard *so* much about you these past few weeks."

"It's nice to meet you too, Parker," I shake her hand because she offered it. "So, you've been bragging about me, Livs? I hope all good things."

Parker goes to answer, but Olivia shoots her hand up at her. "You say a word, and I will dog-ear all your books."

"You wouldn't dare, Olivia." *Oh shit, the full name...*

"I would," she threatens, and damn, this is some serious shit.

"I didn't mean to cause a rift, but Livs, don't do it. My sister hates it when people crease her book pages. She told me once that it physically pains her." The two of them look at me, stunned, and I raise my eyebrows at them. "What?"

"Oh, he's too cute, Liv," Parker says as she gets up. *What does that mean?* "It's a pity that I have class soon, so I have to get going. It was nice to meet you, Tristan. I'm sure I'll see you around at some point."

"Bye, Parker. I'll see you at the apartment." Livvy says as Parker waves bye to her. I shift from sitting next to her to across from her. It's easier to see her facial expressions this way. "You're avoiding me."

"I am not!" she counters, and man, she is horrible at lying.

"You know your eye twitches when you're lying, right? You weren't in class yesterday. I emailed you the lecture, but you didn't respond."

"I got your email, and thank you, by the way. I hate that he doesn't post them online. It's a pain. I was...busy yesterday."

"Doing what?" I ask, and I can see the wheels turning inside of her head. "That's what I thought."

"Okay, fine. Maybe I felt a little weird after seeing you at work and didn't know how to handle this going forward. I'm a coward, I know."

"Livvy, you're not a coward. Also, why did you feel weird? I thought we worked well together. Joe also seemed to think so too. At least, that's what he said to me after you left." Joe asked me about a thousand questions about Liv and me after she left work last week, and it rattled me a bit. He also explained a lot about the other people that work in the department and how much everyone loves Livvy. It was adorable. She's the youngest member of the department—even still with me there now—and everyone's protective of her, according to Joe.

"You keep popping up everywhere, and it's making my head feel weird. I guess I'm just confused as to what our relationship is. Are we coworkers, acquaintances, friends, or nothing?" she asks me, and I take a second to think about it.

"I've already claimed us as best friends, but I'm willing to get to know one another so that can reign true. Are you okay with that?" She nods at me. "Okay, so we have a deal."

"Coworkers and friends, yes," she tells me.

"Exactly, so what are you working on?" She's got a ton of papers spread out around the table while she writes something down in a notebook.

"Oh, nothing important," Livvy says as she closes it.

"Judging by how fast you closed that thing, it seems like it," I joke.

"What did you want to be when you were a kid?" She changes the topic.

"Like job-wise?"

"Yes."

"A professional baseball player. What about you?"

"Well, that could still happen. Have you ever thought about going pro?" she asks me, completely deflecting from answering what I asked.

"A few times, but I don't think I'd like it. I love baseball, but I couldn't see myself going pro. I basically played it for the scholarship money and to make my dad proud." I have no fucking idea how that slipped out so easily. Sure, I talk about my dad a normal amount, but usually with my siblings and closer friends, but with Olivia, things seem to be slipping out of my mouth.

"That's nice. Is your dad a big baseball guy?"

"He taught me how to play when I was a kid," I say. "He's not around anymore."

"Oh. I'm sorry," she says, looking uncomfortable.

"It's okay," I tell her. "What did you want to be when you were younger?"

"I wanted to be an author," she says, a weird tone to her voice.

"You're studying creative writing and literature, right? I'd say that dream isn't too far out of reach for you." There's something about her body language right now. It's like she's trying to look relaxed, but her tense expression says otherwise. *Should I change topics?*

"I am, but I—" she cuts herself off as if not wanting to say what she originally wanted.

"What?"

"Nothing, I just—"

"Olivia, say whatever you want to say. We're best friends, remember?"

She smiles, and I see her relax. *Score.* "I closed my journal because I was writing down an idea that popped into my head for a book I've been wanting to write."

"Can I read it?"

"What?" she asks, stunned. "You—You want to read what I wrote? I barely know you."

I scoff at that. "So? Call it an outside perspective."

"I don't know..."

"Livvy, you can trust me. Plus, my opinion means shit since I don't read a lot. What genre do you like writing?"

Her eyes light up when I ask her about that. I find myself wanting to see that glint in her eyes all the time. "Romance, mostly. Fiction sometimes."

"My sister loves romance novels. She's practically got her own library at home."

Livvy smiles at that. "I understand that. My room here and at home has books all around it."

"You and my sister would probably get along great," I say to her, knowing that would be true. Nothing unites two people more than similar tastes in books—according to Teags.

"I bet we would," she says as she pushes her notebook toward me. "Go ahead."

"Are you sure?" I double-check.

"Yes, and you should feel really special right now because I don't let anyone else read stuff that I've written."

"Why?"

"I don't know...It's a vulnerable thing for someone to read words you created and strung together. I always feel cracked open when someone reads something I wrote. It's hard to explain, but it makes me hyper-aware that *I* wrote what you're about to read. It kind of fucks with my head."

"Do you want me to turn around?"

"No. It's okay, just read it. I promise I won't freak out or anything." Livvy smiles at me, and I turn open to the page she has bookmarked. She started writing something in the middle of a scene, and I began to read.

It's short, so it only takes me around five minutes to read it. I almost feel transported into the mind of this character when I read it. There's something about the way Livvy writes that fully captures my attention, and I'm not a huge reader. There's an ease to her words, and when I finish reading it, I read it over again because I want *more*. "Wow."

"Is that good or bad? Actually, don't tell me. I don't wanna know," she stutters, and I can tell she's nervous.

"Livs, you're fucking talented."

"You don't have to—"

I cut her off. "I'm not just saying that. I want to know more, and I've only read a short snippet. Is there a mystery element to the story?"

She smiles at that, the glint in her eye is back where I like it. "Yes. It's technically going to be a romantic suspense novel. I haven't figured everything out yet, and I probably never will—"

"The fuck you will. I need to know what happens, so you better write the damn book, Olivia," I snap. Why's she being so weird about this?

"I–I don't know, Tristan."

"Livvy, you have talent. Why don't you—"

"My parents think that being an author isn't a good way to make a living. It's something they've told me ever since I was young. They think I need a more stable and secure job, and they're probably right. I'd never be good enough, anyway. It's stupid of me to even try."

Hearing her say that makes my heart lurch. *Her parents don't think she's good enough?* Can they even fucking read? "They're not supporting your dreams? Isn't that what parents are supposed to do?"

"Maybe some, but not mine. My dreams are useless in their eyes. They just want me to be successful like my sister is."

"Isn't your sister younger than you? Why is there so much pressure?" I ask. I remember Livvy telling me at work the other day that her sister is two years younger than her, but that's all I've heard about her family.

"She's twenty right now, and not in school because she does social media full time. She already makes decent money through brand deals and such, so they consider her more successful than me. In their minds, it's me against Bree, but in ours, it's us against our parents."

"You two must be close then."

"Very. My sister is my best friend." She smiles when she says that, and I think about my own siblings. I can't imagine not having them in my life, and I'm sure she feels the same way about Bree.

"That's sweet. Does she think you should try to chase your dreams?"

"She does. She practically begs, but…I don't know if I could." Livvy's shoulders drop, and I try to think of another topic to latch onto.

"Well, consider me the second person who thinks you should go for it. Even if nobody else will read it, just write for yourself or for practice or something."

"That's not a bad idea, but all I have are snippets that come to me every now and again. I technically have like three books in my mind at the moment." She closes her notebook, bookmarking the page using a string. "So, what do you want to do with your life?"

"Anything that gets me out of Pennsylvania, but software is my bread and butter," I tell her with a smile. "I've always been naturally good with computers and different programs. I took a class in high school that really upped my interest, and here I am four years later."

"That's nice. Some days, I wish I had that—the feeling of direction you do. I've always been a little lost." Livvy glances at the table as if she didn't mean to admit that to me.

"Lost isn't necessarily bad. I think it's okay to not have everything all figured out. I'm mostly rolling with the punches every day as is. Same goes for most of the population from ages eighteen to thirty."

"Yeah, but I feel like when I look around, everybody else has at least an idea if not a full-fledged ten-year plan, and I don't." Her eyes lock with mine. "I'm sorry for the dull conversation. I didn't mean to dump all of my insecurities on you in one afternoon."

"It's no problem, Liv." I find myself wanting to hear about everything that's weighing on her. I want to know why she feels so behind and fix it for her. *What's going on with me?* "What's your favorite time of day?"

"My *favorite* time of day? That's an interesting question."

"Has nobody ever asked you that before?"

"No."

It feels good knowing I'm the first. "So, what is it?"

"I'll tell you if you tell me yours."

"The split second you wake up in the morning having forgotten who you are," I say, her eyebrows cinching together.

"Why?"

"That wasn't our deal. What's yours?" I'm too afraid to tell her that I love that time of day because I always seem to forget the weight of all the responsibilities I have and feel for my family. I will *always* love them, but some days, it's hard being the oldest and feeling like I have to constantly check in for my own piece of mind. I wish I could rewire my brain to just be a sibling to them and not another parent.

"Whatever time the sun sets."

"You prefer sunsets over sunrises?"

She nods her head at me. "I love all the colors the sky makes, and I have an entire folder of sunset pictures in my phone. It feels so...final, but also not because you know the sun will be back the next day."

"All the light goes away, but knowing it will come back is what you love about it?" I ask, making sure that I caught where she was going.

"Yeah. It's like there's always light at the end of the tunnel. That the dark won't last forever, you know?" It seems like there's a double meaning to that, but before I can press on it, her eyes widen. "Fuck, I'm gonna be late for class."

Livvy scrambles to get all of her stuff into her bag before throwing it over her shoulder and meeting my eyes one last time. "It was nice running into you, Liv."

"Yeah, you too. It was nice talking to you."

I smile at the fact that she finally gave me a compliment and also because she can't take her eyes off the rings on my hands. *Is she checking out my hands?* "Contrary to popular belief, I'm capable of holding a good conversation."

I watch her walk away before she turns around at the door to the student center. "I never said you weren't, Tristan. I'll see you at work tomorrow." And then she's gone, and I can't wipe the fucking smile off of my face. *What is up with me?*

I had fun talking to Livvy. Time seemed to fly as we sat here like old friends chatting after a long day, and I didn't hate it. Normally, conversing with girls is such a chore since I have an end goal in mind, but with Livvy, it just flows out of my mouth. I have no control over what I say around her, and I enjoy it. It feels easy, and I've never had that before.

Most girls like to skip the talking, but Livvy seemed genuinely interested in me and my life. It was refreshing, actually.

She might deny that we're best friends, but by the end of the semester, it might be true. Especially since we'll be seeing a lot of each other—at work, in class, and any other way the universe seems to want us.

Chapter Eleven

— DON'T BY ED SHEERAN

WHY THE FUCK DID I agree to go out tonight? I'm sitting at a bar near campus with my three idiot friends, but now that I'm here, I'd rather be doing anything else.

"Tristan, stop wallowing and drink. It'll make you feel better," Dom shouts at me.

"I'm fine. Just tired. Work and school combined with practices have worn me out," I tell him. That's not a lie. I knew taking on a job would make my plate extra full, but I didn't realize how drained it would make me.

"Maybe you need to get laid. Let off some steam, or whatever." Ethan tells me, and he's not wrong. It's been a few weeks since I've hooked up with someone, and I could use a distraction right now. From what, I have no clue.

"I've been saying that for days, yet nobody listens to me!" Dom exclaims, taking another shot.

"What did you say?" Harry jokes and Dom smacks him in the arm.

"You guys are ridiculous," I mutter. "Are you excited for indoor soon, Harry?"

"Not really, but it is what it is," he tells me, and I raise my almost empty beer to that. Snow is rapidly approaching, and practices are slowly starting to move inside to turf. It'll be fine, but I find myself already missing the warm weather, even though it hasn't fully disappeared yet.

"I'm getting another drink. Anyone want anything? It's on me."

"I'll take another beer," Harry says, and I see Ethan shake his head. I don't really care about Dom since he's now trying to pick some girl up, so he's on his own. I head over to the bar and flag down a bartender. I tell him my order and put it on Dom's tab as he hands me the bottles. As I'm about to grab them, another hand reaches for them and brings it to her lips.

"That tastes about as gross as I remember," she says, and I have to stop myself from rolling my eyes.

"That's why you shouldn't touch things that don't belong to you, Maddie." I look over at her—straight blonde hair, too much makeup, and an outfit that makes *me* cold, and I think about how I ever hung out around her without leaving immediately. Just her presence right now makes me feel itchy.

"You never minded before, Tristan. Why don't we take this conversation somewhere private?" she asks, putting her hand on my arm.

"I'm not going anywhere with you, Maddie. Not now, not ever!" I snap.

"Is there any way I can persuade you? I'll get on my knees right here, right now—" I grab her arm as she starts to sink down and yank her back up.

"Stop embarrassing yourself. We might've fooled around a few times, but that was it. It'll never happen again. Go fuck someone else and stay away from me." A little harsh, but I don't like how this makes me feel. She's trying to get under my skin, flirt, and fuck me because she wants to say that she's had me more than once. I see right through her motivations, and it pisses me off that it took me this long to see it. Of course, I knew, deep down, but one of these days I want a connection that means something. I want someone to want me for me, not what I am, the sport that I play, or the status that I have on campus.

"Tristan, why are you denying this connection we have?"

"It must be one-sided." I look at her. "Whatever we were doing is over, Maddie."

"Is this because of that slut with your hoodie? Is that why you don't want me anymore?"

I thought I was pissed before, but Maddie calling Livvy what she did has me seeing red. Where the fuck does she get off calling her that? She doesn't even know Olivia. "What the fuck did you say?"

"You heard me. Is she warming your hoodie or your bed too? I'd put all my money on both. The whore—" I've heard enough of this. I push off the stool, leave my drinks behind, and head for the table.

"Woah," I hear Ethan say.

"Are you good, man?" Harry asks me, but I don't respond as I grab my jacket and head for the exit. I feel an arm on my bicep as I'm almost out the door, and I don't bother looking over.

"Hate sex is always on the table for me, just say the word."

"I wouldn't touch you again with a twenty-foot pole," I say as I shake her arm off. "If you say another word about Olivia or even breathe in her direction, you won't like what I do."

"Oh, really?" There's a spark of challenge in her eyes, and it feels like she wants to keep pushing my fucking buttons.

"Really. Don't fucking push me, Maddie," I snap. "Just because she's a thousand times better of a person than you doesn't give you the right to judge her before you even know her." I don't stay to listen to any of the bullshit that comes out of her mouth, and as I head out of the bar, I find myself heading toward the batting cages to blow off some steam.

I'm angry. Fucking pissed off and smacking some baseballs is about the only thing that will keep me from punching the next person I see. As

I walk toward campus, I pull my phone out and start a new message with a girl that I can't stop thinking about. She gave me her number after work the other day in case I needed to get in touch with her about anything. This isn't necessarily an emergency. More like me just wanting to talk to her—as a friend, of course.

> Tristan: Hey. Are you up?

I don't know why I'm doing this. I don't know what possessed me to text her, but hearing her name out of Maddie's mouth made me feel weird. It pissed me off hearing her saying Olivia's name with all that jest.

> Livvy: Yeah…It's 9 p.m., Tristan. Of course I'm awake.

> Tristan: Did you see the sunset earlier?

> Livvy: No, I've been studying all night. Was it a good one?

> Tristan: *One attachment* Solid 8/10.

> Livvy: Wow, that's beautiful. I'd say 8.5/10. I love the blend of yellow and orange.

> Livvy: Thanks for the picture.

> Tristan: Well, I couldn't let you miss your favorite time of day, now, could I?

Livvy: I can't tell if you're joking or being serious.

Tristan: 100% serious, Livs.

Livvy: Did you take that earlier just to send it to me?

Tristan: No, I took it because it reminded me of you, but two birds with one stone, I guess.

Tristan: Do you want to hang out?

Livvy: Right now? I don't know, I still have a lot to do…

Tristan: Livvy, it's Saturday. Live a little.

Livvy: Ugh, fine. I'm only doing this, so you'll stop calling me boring.

Tristan: Those were only jokes.

Livvy's the least boring person I've ever met. How could the girl who captivates my mind most of the day call herself boring? *You've never told her that, dumbass.*

Tristan: Meet me outside the athletic building?

Livvy: Okay. See you in a few!

My heart races at the thought of seeing Livvy, and I find myself looking over my actions from tonight. *Why didn't I try to pick someone up like I always do? Why did I get so disgusted at Maddie's advances?*

The realization hits me in the chest. It's her. It's Livvy. Her genuine friendship means a lot to me. I've never had a connection with someone like I do with her, and the fact that we've crossed paths so much has made me think that some part of the universe wants us to know each other. I've never believed in that sort of thing, but with Livvy, everything is starting to make sense.

I like her. She's engraving herself into my skin, slowly but surely, and I don't hate it. In fact, I want more. I want to know more about her, about who she really is.

I like Olivia. She's the most genuine friend and person I know. "Hey!" Her voice interrupts my thoughts, and I look up at her. She's wearing that signature Livvy smile that makes the dimples on her cheeks shine, along with yoga pants, a light brown crewneck, and some vans.

"Are you ready to swing, Hart?" I ask her, and her features narrow at me.

"What are you talking about?"

"Come on. I'll show you." I hold the door open for her, and the two of us step inside. I lead her down a hallway before I grab my bat and helmet from where the spare equipment is. I hand Livvy a helmet that should fit her head. "Take this."

"Is this a torture device? Did you bring me here to whack me?"

I chuckle because, of course, she would ask me that. "No, Livs. You're gonna watch me hit a few, and then I'm gonna teach you how to hit some baseballs. Are you up for it?"

"I was born ready," she tells me as she slips the helmet onto her head. *Damn, that was kind of cute.* Fuck. I might be screwed.

"Good. Let's go, Hart."

"I'm right behind you, West." I take us over to cage one and set my stuff down before I step into it. I click the button so the machine can turn on and take a few deep breaths. I originally wanted to come here and let off some steam, but all of that seemed to disappear when Livvy walked in.

I take my stance in the box and relax my body as I wait for the first pitch. I set the machine to eighty-two miles per hour, which is the average speed of a Division two pitcher. I swing my head over to where Livvy stands behind the cage, staring right at me, her eyes wide as she takes all of this in. "Like what you see?"

"Maybe I do, but you'll have to impress me first."

"I plan on it," I say as the first ball whizzes past me and hits the padding.

"Not off to a great start," Livvy laughs as I try to focus again. This time I'm ready, and I hit a line drive back at the machine right off the sweet spot of my bat. *Damn, that felt good.* We do batting practice twice a week, but it's been a while since I've come here to hit and not worry about anything else. I hit a few more good ones and a few shitty ones when my focus gets caught on someone else when the machine turns off. "You're up, Livs."

"Oh God. I'm definitely not going to be as good as you, but I'll try." She tucks her hair behind where the helmet rests on her head while I reset the machine to around twenty miles per hour.

"Nervous?"

"A little."

"Don't worry. I'll be in here the whole time, and it won't be that fast."

"You're not gonna leave the cage?" she asks me.

"No," I say as I move to stand across from her rather than behind.

"What if I accidentally hit you?"

"I'll be fine, Livs. Trust me, I've had worse hits. I once got a line drive to the face during a game."

"How did that happen?"

"I used to play shortstop in high school, and a batter nailed one right at my face. It hurt like a bitch."

"It sounds like it."

"Okay, let me teach you how to hold a bat." I then briefly explain to her how to hold it, and when she holds it up, I smile to myself. *She's a natural.* "Looks good, Livvy. Now step up to the plate. I won't turn it on yet. Just get comfortable being in the box."

She steps in and tries to mimic my stance, but she's too tense. Her legs are too close together, and her shoulders are too hunched over. "Like this?"

I stifle a laugh. "Can I help?"

"Yes, but stop laughing at me. I have no idea how to baseball correctly."

"I'll try, but you just look so...adorable," I say as I move closer to her. "Do you mind if I touch you?"

"If it'll stop your laughter, then go for it." I move closer to her and lean down to where her legs are. I tap her front leg, and she moves it farther forward, so it's a little past her shoulder. Just that small contact has me wanting to trail my hand up her legs. I wasn't even touching her skin, but I felt a zap of electricity when I tapped her leg. As I stand up, I notice her eyes watching me intently. Her cheeks look redder than before, and I wonder if she felt the same thing that I did.

"Can I touch your shoulders?"

"Yes," she says, quieter than before. "You don't have to ask every time, you know."

"I'm being a gentleman, Livs," I say as I move around her. I grab her shoulders with my hands and roll them back so they're more relaxed. *God, all these little touches are driving me fucking crazy.* "That's more like it. I'm gonna turn on the machine now, okay?"

"Okay. How do I know when to swing?"

"You'll see the ball come down the chute. It's all about timing. You'll find a groove once you get used to it."

"You'll be behind me the whole time?" she asks, excitement and a little bit of fear showing in her eyes.

"I'll be right here, Livvy."

"Okay, good," she gets into her stance. "You can start it."

"I like when you're bossy," I say as I click the button and hear the machine start-up. I lean against the side of the cage and take her in. This girl continues to surprise me. I've never had as much fun with someone as I do with Livvy. Just being around her always seems to lift my mood, and I like breaking her out of her shell. I know it scares her, but she's braver than she thinks. Fuck, I definitely like her.

I'm rattled out of my haze by a few balls hitting the padding. "Try to keep your head tucked into your chin when you swing. That'll keep your eye on the ball."

"Okay." She does what I tell her to, and she tips the next ball that comes down the chute. "It made a noise!"

I smile like an idiot at her excitement. "You're doing great, Livs." She keeps trying to hit a ball, and there's only a few more left before the machine shuts off again. Two more misses and the red light comes on, signaling the last ball is coming. "If you hit this one, I'll owe you anything you want."

"Are you incentivizing me, Tristan?"

"Yes."

"Then this one's for you," she says, and as the ball comes toward her, I see her connect with it, and as soon as she does, she starts celebrating. "I did it! Oh my God, I hit a baseball!" And before I know it, she drops the bat and her arms are around me.

"I'm proud of you, Livs. That was a great hit." I rest my head on top of hers, and just hugging Livvy has me never wanting to let her go. She and I seem to fit perfectly together, my head on top of hers, her hands around my waist—it's a complete fit, the two of us.

"I had a good teacher," she mumbles into my shirt. "Thank you for teaching me."

Then her eyes lock with mine, and I'm sweating all of a sudden. It feels like the temperature went up in here. I'm fighting the urge to pull back because I don't want to make her uncomfortable, but I simultaneously don't want to let her go right now. *Can she feel how fast my heart is beating?* "You're a natural at this, Liv. You did that all on your own."

Her gaze burns into mine, and she doesn't bother pulling away either since her arms are still wrapped around me. *If I leaned in to kiss her, would she kiss me back?* I want to kiss Livvy more than I've ever wanted to kiss someone else before. Usually, I'd kiss a girl just to get to the other part of the night, but with Livvy, it would mean something, and I don't want to do anything that would scare her. I want the moment to be right, and even though I want to right now, I feel like I should wait. My head doesn't listen to what I'm thinking because my face leans down anyway but halts when Livvy's breathing picks up.

"Are you okay?" I ask her.

"I'm good. Just a little warm," she whispers.

"It's probably cooler outside. Wanna head out?" I ask, and she smiles up at me.

"Sounds good to me. Lead the way."

The tension dissipates as quickly as it arrived as we head out of the athletic center and into the cool autumn air. I had more fun here with Livvy than I did with my friends at the bar.

I'm fucked. Only I would start to fall for the first girl that I only think wants genuine friendship from me.

Chapter Twelve

— WHEN EMMA FALLS IN LOVE BY TAYLOR SWIFT

IN THE PAST FEW weeks, I've become well and truly fucked in the head. That's the only way that I can feel all the things that I have been.

The weather has turned into a chill. Autumn is in full force around here, and winter is on its way. The forecast says it's supposed to snow next week.

Snow is not the only thing that's moving in. My feelings for Tristan have rented a U-Haul and parked themselves in my heart. I feel like a crazy person. Sure, I barely knew the guy before this year, but ever so slowly, he's wormed his way into my skin. First, with the coffee incident, then finding out we had a class together, and now working together, he's just *everywhere*—and I don't hate it.

In fact, as I realized this, I found myself looking forward to spending time with him. The two of us have started hanging out on our own time. We've studied together, gone to the computer lab after hours to work on projects, and even eaten together in the dining hall.

When I realized that I looked forward to all this extra stuff with him, I practically screamed. Oh, and the fact that he almost kissed me a few weeks ago when he taught me how to swing a baseball bat.

The *almost* part of that sentence still pisses me off because I wanted him to kiss me, but we both pulled away. Almost has always intrigued me. A word that means so much, yet so little. It's a sad word. It represents being so close to something happening, yet it didn't.

Tristan and I *almost* kissed.

Tristan leaned in and *almost* touched his lips to mine.

I've spent *almost* every night dreaming about what would've happened if we kissed. What would he taste like? Would he take control like he does while swinging a bat? Would he kiss me with passion, unlike my past boyfriends who only kissed me as a formality? God, I want to know so badly, and it's been hard to be around him with those questions swimming around in my head.

Though this realization has slightly taken over my mind, our friendship has remained the same. It's become a lot stronger since our almost kiss, and I admit that it's nice to be around him, even if just in this capacity. Tristan's a great friend.

A friend I think about kissing at least once a day...

But a friend nonetheless.

Our little tradition of passing notes has increased to slipping them underneath each other's doors. We still text all the time, but the notes feel more personal, and I like exchanging them with him. He slid the first one underneath my door about meeting at the computer lab one night, and now it's become our thing—writing and passing notes.

I've always loved writing notes. I keep a journal, and there's something about handwritten notes that feels so romantic to me. The fact that someone would take the time to write something with another person in mind is so intimate. I'm the type of person who keeps every birthday card or note anyone has ever given me because I appreciate someone taking the time to do that. I know the power that words have, and I'm grateful to have people who think of me.

Does he think of me as often as I think of him? Did he want to kiss me as much as I did that night? Does he like me? I feel like a stupid teenager with the amount of yearning I'm doing for a guy who probably doesn't want me back.

My thought spiral broke when Cassie and Parker came into the apartment. "We have wine! Stop studying and get out here, Liv!"

"Coming!" I yell as I leave my room. When I got out to the kitchen, I saw Cassie uncorking the wine and Parker grabbing some snacks to lay out on the counter.

We normally have wine night at the end of every month as a palate cleanser, and we watch a random movie while we get drunk. It's quite a fun time, and since Halloween is right around the corner, we decided to move it up. We don't have plans yet, but I'm sure Cassie will drag Parker and me to a party. It's happened every year since we've been friends, and I'd expect nothing different from our last year at Summit.

"Here's your bottle, Liv. Moscato for my favorite sweet girl." Cassie slides the bottle to me, and I grab it. I'll forever be a sweet wine lover. Parker usually goes for a Riesling, and Cassie loves a pinot noir. "Maybe if we get Liv drunk enough, she'll finally tell us the truth about her and Tristan."

"Cass, I don't think there's enough wine on earth for that to happen," Parker tells her, and I roll my eyes.

"I've told you a thousand times to drop that subject. We're just friends! Nothing untoward has happened, and nothing ever will." I grab my bottle—a little aggressively, but whatever—and head toward the couch.

"Every time you give us that same rehearsed speech, it slowly convinces me that either something almost happened or you want something to happen. Keep denying it, Livs, but I can see right through you. You're as easy to read as one of those romance novels you love so much." Cassie pats my thigh as she sits down while throwing me a pity smile.

I take a big sip of my wine before I cross my arms in defiance. *I should just tell them the truth.* I don't even know what *the truth* is. I definitely like Tristan, but I don't know if I like him or who I am when I'm around him or both.

I'm bolder, and I find myself feeling a bit braver when he's around. He's a nice presence to have around, but maybe we're destined to be friends and nothing more. *Almost* lovers, but not quite. It would probably crash and burn like every other relationship I've had, and Tristan almost exclusively has one-night stands. He's also told me that he's never had someone who wanted him for who he was, and that's why he strays from relationships. I always found that odd—how no girl on this campus wanted to get to know him. It kills me that he feels used like that, and I hate that girls want to fuck him just to say they fucked *the* Tristan West. That's shitty, and nobody deserves that. That impression is the last thing that I want to give off, and part of me hopes he knows that I'm different from the others. His friendship means a lot to me, and I would never want to ruin that with something as stupid as my feelings.

"Livvy, all we're saying is that you could tell us if something happened. We won't judge or make fun of you. Life has become really boring since Cass got a boyfriend. I miss hearing stories about her conquests. They kept things lively around here."

"Ah, good times. But Bryce and I have our own conquests if you guys want to—"

"Nope. I'm good," I say.

"Forget I said anything," Parker says, as she takes a drink.

"Parker is right, though. We need some action around here, and your new relationship with Tristan is a hot topic right now, especially across campus."

My eyes shoot to where Cassie sits. "What the hell are you talking about?"

"Yeah, Cassie, what?" Parker questions, and Cassie moves uncomfortably in her seat.

"Bryce has heard some things..."

"Care to elaborate?" I ask her, my voice moving up an octave.

"Apparently, he told off Maddie after she said something mean about you at the bar one night. And according to Bryce, he hasn't picked up a girl in weeks. The guys were worried about him. They thought he was depressed."

What the fuck? "Depressed? Tristan seems fine to me."

"Then why hasn't he fucked someone else since you two started hanging out more?" Cassie questions me as if I would know the answer.

"Yeah, Liv, that's interesting, isn't it..." Parker trails off.

"Well, I wouldn't know! Maybe he's going through a dry spell or something! I don't even care about this, someone change the subject." Silence envelops the three of us for a few seconds after I say that, and I'm mentally kicking myself. Is there really nothing else interesting going on other than Tristan and me? I hear something slip under the door, but before I can get to it, Cassie beats me to it. She doesn't even bother grabbing the piece of paper, but instead, she rips the door open and yells down the hallway. "Tristan!"

"Oh my...Cassie, stop!" I say as I pocket the note he slid underneath the door. *This is the most embarrassing moment of my life.*

"I knew this was bound to happen at some point." Parker slips an arm around my shoulder as she slips me my bottle of wine. "You'll probably need this."

"Thanks." I take a long sip before I see Tristan in my doorway, my heart feeling all weird seeing him leaning against the door frame. He's wearing black sweats, a *Summit Baseball* shirt, and a baseball cap even though it's dark outside right now—and it's backward. *That shouldn't look as good as it does.* The same rings are still on his fingers, two on his left hand and three on his right. I spend way too much time looking at his hands before I hear someone clear their throat.

"Hey, Livs."

"Hi, Tristan." His gaze shifts to Cassie after a few seconds of looking at me, through me, or whatever the hell he was doing to my body just now.

"Cassie, it's always nice to see you. How's Bryce been lately?"

Part of me forgot that they know each other through Bryce. "He's been great. He told me how good you guys look at practice. I'm excited for the season next semester. It's gonna be a good one."

"Damn right, it is," his eyes shift back to mine. "Maybe the two of us can convince Olivia to go to a game or two."

My cheeks heat at his use of my full name. There's something about the way that he says it, his voice low, and how it rolls off his tongue so easily. God, it makes my knees weak, or maybe that's the wine...

"I'm sure you could be more persuasive than I could be, Tristan."

"Cass, hush." Parker says. "Nice to see you again, hotshot."

"Thanks, Owens. You too." Did he just use her last name? What is with the nicknames being flung around tonight?

"So, can I assume your answer was yes?" Tristan asks me, and my brows pinch together because I have no idea what he's talking about. Did he ask me a question, and I missed it because I was ogling him like a freak? "The note I slipped under the door. Did you read it?"

"Oh!" I slip it out of my pocket and read it over. Tristan was inviting me to a Halloween party at the baseball house on campus. "Is this invite for me, or can they come too?"

"If that's an invite to the baseball party, I was already going to go with Bryce. Well, all of us were because I would've forced you guys to come with me like always. This is the first time I've seen an official invitation, though." Cassie smiles at Parker and me.

"I'm in," Parker agrees too quickly.

"Livvy, what about you?" Tristan asks me, and I find it odd that he came all the way over here to ask me to this party if I technically didn't need an invite. "I'd love to see what you'd come as. I have a few guesses in mind already."

"Of course you do. I don't even know what I'd go as," I tell him.

"I'm sure you'll figure something out, Livs."

"And you have us to help, dumbass," Cassie smiles at me.

"I don't know how helpful you two would be," I joke as I take another sip of wine.

"Will I see you there?" His voice shakes at the end of his sentence. *He's nervous.* Am I making Tristan West nervous? Is he scared of what I'm about to say?

"I guess you'll have to wait for my next note to find out," I say to him, and he pushes off the door frame and throws his head back, clearly stressed about the answer I gave him. I shove his chest into the hallway, and I follow while shutting the door behind me.

"I'm looking forward to our next correspondence, pretty girl," he smiles at me.

"Why did you invite me if this party isn't invite only?" I ask him, wanting to know why he made a big fuss out of all of this.

"Damn, drunk Livvy is a lot bolder than sober Livvy."

"She is. Now answer my question, please."

"I want you there, and I want to see you all dressed up in whatever costume you choose. I want to see you on Halloween, and I'll be up all night thinking about your answer and hoping that it's a yes." Before I can say anything else, he leans down, and just when I think he's about to almost kiss me again, he pecks my cheek and leaves. I stand rooted in my spot for a few seconds, trying to take in everything that he said. When I get back inside, Cassie and Parker are looking at me like they're my parents, who caught me sneaking back in after a wild night out.

"That was a very sexually tense conversation," Parker says.

"No, it wasn't," I counter.

"He looked at you like he wanted to devour you, Liv. And vice versa. I saw you check him out and linger on those hands of his for way too long," Cassie tells me.

"I think Liv has a hand fetish."

"Both of you just quit it. Can we watch a movie now?" I ask, trying to steer the conversation.

"I think you should write that boy a note. It seems like he's on the edge of his seat waiting for your answer."

"Parker, haven't you figured out that those notes are basically foreplay for them?" Cassie points out. "It's so obvious."

"You're both ridiculous," I say as I grab the remote and turn on Netflix.

"The only ridiculous one here is you if you turn down that guy who so obviously likes you, cares about you, and wants you around, but don't listen to me or anything. What do I know?"

"Cassie, let's table this for now and enjoy wine night. I don't want Livvy writing characters like us in one of her future books only to kill us off," Parker laughs as she grabs a cracker from the table.

I smile at that thought. "That sounds like a great idea."

Chapter Thirteen

— FALLING BY CHASE ATLANTIC

I'VE NEVER REALLY CARED for Halloween before. It never stood out to me as one of my favorite holidays to celebrate.

But the fact that I know Livvy is coming to this party has put an unnatural pep in my step as I walk around the house, surrounded by drunk people dancing. It used to bother me, all the noise and annoying fucking people, but knowing that she could walk through the door at any moment makes it all seem worth it.

I am fucked. Absolutely fucked. Over the past few weeks, the more I've been around Liv, the stronger this invisible pull has been. It's taken all my strength to chill the hell out when I'm around her because I don't know how she feels, and I'm too scared to bring it up. I don't want to ruin any shred of a relationship we have. Our friendship has been great so far, and I almost don't want to risk losing that, losing her.

Plus, it's been a while since I've done the whole relationship thing. Part of me doesn't even know if I remember *how* to be in one. I've become so used to one-night stands that I don't think I'm capable of the relationship gene anymore.

But for her, I'd try my fucking hardest.

Someone knocks into me as I make my way to grab a water, and my cowboy hat falls off of my head. "Sorry, dude."

"You're good, man," I say to the guy. I feel like I should be used to this by now. Whenever Jeremy—the captain of the baseball team and current resident of the house—throws parties here, they're usually this packed. Baseball is one of the biggest sports here at Summit, and when we play games at home, the stands are usually packed full, and the student section, too. The makeshift dance floor in the living room is packed with people, and the music is blaring so loud that I can barely hear myself think.

As I'm grabbing my water bottle, I hear Cassie's voice barely coming from by the entrance. "Livvy, you look great. Just come inside, and I'll get you a drink to loosen up!"

Upon hearing that, I head in their direction and take in the group of them. Parker seems to be dressed as an angel, wearing all white and a halo above her head. Bryce and Cassie are Fred and Daphne from Scooby-Doo, and I laugh because it fits them too well. Livvy is wearing some sort of long skirt, blouse, a vest of some sort, and a blazer. Even in costume, I can't take my eyes off of her. There's something so captivating about her, and I don't mind getting sucked in every fucking time I look in her direction. I don't know who she came as, but I'll find out soon enough. "Tristan!"

I reach my hand out for Bryce, and he meets it with a clap. "Bryce, you look great. As do the rest of you," I let my eyes linger on Livvy for a second longer than the others and notice how uncomfortable she looks. She's told me before that she hates being around big groups of people, so this is probably her worst nightmare, but I'm determined to make her have a good time tonight.

"Thanks, West. Now, point me in the direction of some drinks," Cassie says, and I tilt my head to the right and signal to her where the table is.

"Pick your poison, Cass," I say, and she practically drags Bryce away. Parker then makes eye contact with someone behind me, and I hear her whisper something to Livvy before she excuses herself, leaving the two of us standing here like idiots.

"You look two seconds away from running right back out the door," I yell to her, the music still blaring.

"That's because I am!" She yells back to me, and I smile.

"Don't worry, I'll be by your side all night. Consider me your fun manager for the night. I'm determined to make this the best Halloween of your life."

"Those are some pretty high expectations, Tristan," she eyes me with curiosity, moving her eyes up and down my body as she takes in my costume. "Why a cowboy?"

"I just wanted to wear the hat, blue jeans, and a flannel. What are you dressed as?"

"Jo March from Little Women. One of my favorite female characters ever," she smiles.

"Not Anne Elliot from Persuasion?" I ask, mentioning the book that she told me was her favorite.

Her lips turn into a smile before she speaks again. "I went as her a few years ago."

"Gotcha," I say as I notice her pulling at her clothes, a habit I've seen and deduced that she does when she's nervous. "What's your drink of choice?"

"Anything sweet," she tells me.

"I'll make you something. Any no-go's for alcohol?"

"Tequila, anything not sweet, basically. No whiskey."

"Got it," I say as I grab her hand and lead her through all the people.

"Livvy!" I hear from behind us as we get to the table. Dom comes over and grabs her from behind before spinning her around. I start to make Livvy's drink as I try not to punch one of my best friends in the face. He's definitely drunk already since he started pregaming at the apartment, but the way he just grabbed Livvy has me feeling all sorts of pissed off. Dom, Ethan, and Harry are all dressed up as the Shelby brothers from Peaky Blinders—wool knit caps, long coats, and fake guns adorn the three of them. "You shouldn't be with him. Give me one chance, and I'll make you laugh all night."

"I'm not afraid to go full Wild West on your ass, Dom. Stop making Livvy uncomfortable," I snap at him.

"Pardon me for trying to get to know your girlfriend, West. I'm showing her another option if she gets bored with you." He smiles at me. I know he's doing this to unsettle me, and it pisses me off that it's working.

"Oh, I'm not his—"

I cut her off. "Yeah, Dom, she's not my girlfriend. We're friends. Have you ever tried being friends with a girl? I think it'd do you some good." He puts a hand to his chest as if I hurt his heart and pretends to faint before someone else steals his attention.

"Is he okay?" Livvy asks me.

"Just a normal case of being a dumbass," I hand her the drink I made, and a smile graces her lips as she tastes it. "Like it?"

"Love it. What do you have?"

"Water. I told you I was your fun manager tonight, so I'm not drinking."

She smiles at me, and I barely have time to say anything before Cassie pulls her away from me and onto the dance floor. Dom comes back over to me, along with Ethan, and the two of them look like they could be my bodyguards with how they're dressed. "How's your girlfriend?"

"Ethan, shut the fuck up," I snap. "Have you guys seen Harry?"

"It's a touchy subject tonight, Ethan. Although, it's kind of fun to see the murderous look in his eye when you glance in her direction," Dom laughs as he sips his drink, vodka most likely. "And no, I haven't."

"I'm sure Harrison is around here somewhere," Ethan says.

"We're friends. It pisses me off that you guys keep bugging me about it. I swear nobody understands the concept of friendship between a guy and a girl. It's possible, people!"

Ethan and Dom laugh at me as I say that. "Yeah, it's definitely possible, just not for you two." Dom pats me on the back before leaving and heading off somewhere else. Ethan stands next to me as he pours himself another drink.

The song switches to Falling by Chase Atlantic, and I see Cassie hand Livvy a shot, and before I think she won't take it, she downs it in one go. *Damn.* I smile to myself, happy to see her loosening up and enjoying the party. Maybe all she needed was some liquid courage. Cassie and her start dancing, and I can't take my eyes off of Liv. She and Cassie are mouthing the words to each other as they smile and dance. Bryce comes up behind Cassie a few seconds later, and they start dancing her back to his front. Livvy smiles at the two of them as she continues dancing, but her eyes fly back to where I'm standing and lock with mine.

Suddenly, it's just the two of us in this giant room. All I can see are her eyes latched onto mine, her hips swaying with the beat, and her lips moving with the lyrics of the song.

Is she singing to me, or am I being insane? All I know is that I can't fucking stop looking at her right now. She's loosened up, and the smile that's on her face is lighting up this entire dark room. Fuck, I need to get out of here before my body temperature burns it down. If Livvy keeps looking at me like she is, I don't know what I'm going to do about it. Those eyes...God, they reel me in so quickly. I barely stand a fucking chance when she looks at me. Before I know it, my feet are moving in her direction, and I'm suddenly pressed up against her. "I'm going to the bathroom, just so you know where I am. I'll be right back."

"Pity, I thought you were coming to dance," she says to me.

"Do you want me to dance with you?" I ask, wanting her to say yes.

"Unless you forgot, you owe me one." Her eyes sparkled, and I remembered the night at the batting cages when I incentivized her to hit the ball. "You promised me anything, and I want you to dance with me. Plus, I love this song, so it's a win-win."

"Your wish is my command," I say as I press myself against her. Not like I have a choice because of how packed it is. Shake It Out by Florence and the Machine plays, and I applaud myself for putting the playlist together earlier.

"Am I doing this right? I've never danced before."

I lean down toward her ear so only she can hear me. "You always look perfect, Liv."

The two of us are facing each other as the song plays, and I like seeing Livvy like this—loose, carefree, and uncaring of how many people are here. She's finally getting more comfortable, and I hope she's having as much fun as she looks like she is. "Having fun?"

"It's more fun now that you're over here. I thought I was gonna have to pull you out here myself if you kept staring at me."

"All you have to do is ask, Livvy, and I'll do whatever you want." I grab her arm and spin her around, catching her waist with my other hand. She laughs, the best sound I've ever fucking heard in my life, and I find myself smiling like a fucking idiot. The song's almost over, and I catch her as she loses her balance. The two of our faces are so close to each other that if I leaned down ever so slightly, I could taste her. I could find out if she tastes like that berry lip balm she's always carrying around, or if she tastes like the drink I made her earlier—vodka and watermelon punch. My dick strains against my jeans as I think about finally capturing her mouth with mine.

"Tristan," she whispers against my mouth, causing my undoing. *I want her. I want her bad, and it's killing me to keep this distance between us.* But what if she doesn't want me back?

The song slowly fades out and into the next one, which seems to break our focus from each other, and before I can say anything, Parker reappears and drags Livvy away from me, citing girl problems.

Fuck. I shake off all my thoughts, wanting them to go anywhere else before I head outside to the backyard. It's quieter out here, and this is where I find Harry hiding. "Where the hell have you been all night?"

"Around, you know." He waves his hand in the air. Harry isn't the biggest fan of parties either, the joint in his hand signaling that he's probably been out here for most of the night.

"I've barely seen you all night," I tell him.

"I've seen you, dude, trust me. Did you get all your drool off the floor when you were watching Livvy dance?" He laughs at me, and as I turn around to go back inside, he speaks again. "Okay, you looked stressed, so I thought a joke would help, but clearly that wasn't very funny."

"Not really."

"What's on your mind, dude? Is it her?"

Of course, it's her. Lately, she's all that's been on my fucking mind, and it's driving me crazy. I feel like the two of us are on this weird line between friendship and more, but neither of us wants to cross the tightrope that hangs between them. "Yeah, it's her."

"I fucking knew it, bro. You're shit at hiding your feelings. They're all over your face, especially when you look at her. Anyone with eyes could see it except the two of you, apparently."

"I like her, but I'm scared to make a move and ruin something we have by misreading things." It terrifies me—losing what I have with Livvy right now.

"I think you should go for it."

"Harrison, really? That's some shit advice," I say to him as he blows smoke in my face. "Fuck you."

"Don't tell me my advice is shitty. Remember that you came to *me* and not one of the other two idiots. You clearly trust me more than them, and I don't blame you."

"Okay, but why would I make a move when I don't know how she feels? Shouldn't I talk to her first?"

Harry shakes his head. "Well, you'll find out the answer to your question if she kisses you back. Won't you, Tris?"

"I guess?"

"So, what the hell are you waiting for then?"

Fuck, he's right. I'm losing momentum here. I head back inside and quickly search for her, immediately finding her laughing with Parker, Ethan, and Dom. I head to where they are and slip into the conversation. "Can I steal Livvy for a moment?"

"Tristan! Livvy was just telling us how you taught her how to swing a bat. Is that true?" Dom asks me, a hint of something in his voice.

"They don't believe me! Tell them!" Livvy insists.

"I did. This one's a natural when it comes to the cages." I smile down at her, and she cocks her head at my friends, shoving in their faces that she was telling the truth. God, how does she fit so fucking perfectly in every aspect of my life? She already gets along with my idiot friends, easily keeping up with their stupid ass jokes. She wants to learn my interests and get to know me. Every time I hug her, it's like she was always meant to be in my arms. I've created a habit of resting my head on top of hers, and we just...fit. *She's fucking perfect.* "Livvy?"

"Oh, yeah. Be right back!" She shouts to them, and I grab her hand and interlink our fingers as I start to take her outside and away from the noise of the party. I hear some people say hi to me as I pass through them, but my entire focus is on kissing Livvy in a few minutes. I've never been so nervous to kiss someone before. I can hear my heartbeat in my ears as I take Livvy to a spot away from the house. "What did you need me for?"

"I just wanted a second away from all the noise. I figured you could use one too. It can get a little overwhelming sometimes," I smile at her, still holding onto her hand with mine. She hasn't made a move to pull away, and I take that as a good sign. "How are you feeling?"

"Me? I'm good. Not quite drunk yet, but definitely tipsy."

"Tipsy enough that you won't remember this tomorrow?" I ask, wondering if I were to kiss her if she'd even remember it.

"Oh no, I'm fine. I know my limits."

"Good. I want you to remember everything about tonight," I say. "Having fun?"

"Lots of it. My favorite part of tonight was watching Dom and Ethan take shots without trying to move a muscle. It was hilarious."

"Yeah, Ethan always loses. We do that at the bar sometimes," I tell her. "What if I tell you that I have a way to top your favorite moment from tonight?"

"I don't think anything could top that, Tristan. You should've seen them, it was hilarious."

"I bet it was, pretty girl." *Fuck, I'm so fucking scared.* "Do you want to know my favorite part of tonight?"

"Of course I do. I want you to have as much fun as me, silly." She lightly smacks my arm, and I take the opportunity to grab her wrist and pull her toward me. Before she can say anything else, I lean in and lightly graze my lips against hers. When she doesn't pull away but instead sighs against my lips, I press my lips against her mouth and kiss her the way I've been dreaming about. One of my hands is around the back of her neck, the other is cupping her face, and both her hands are fisting at my shirt as if she can't get close enough. *Fuck, this is everything and more.* Kissing Livvy is better than the image I had in my mind. I was right in one aspect—she tastes like that berry lip balm she's always putting on, and fuck if that isn't my new favorite taste on the whole fucking planet.

I pull away for a second and give her a second to catch her breath. "Was that okay?"

"Y–Yeah, yes." She reaches up and touches her lips as if she can still feel me against her, and I take another opportunity to capture her lips again. When I pull away, I snag her bottom lip in mine and bite it softly. The breathy moan she lets out practically crumbles me.

"Fuck, Liv."

"Did you not like that?"

"Are you kidding me? I've been wanting to do that for weeks," I admit, and her cheeks flush.

"Kiss me again," she says. Feeling like it'd be rude to make her wait, I give in, and before I know it, my lips are on hers again. I take this moment to memorize every little sound she makes, the way her hands feel against my shirt, and by the end of it, I take my hat off and put it on her head. "What's this for?"

"Kiss the cowboy, you wear his hat. It's the rule."

"I guess I'm a cowboy like you now, right?" She smiles up at me, and fuck if I don't want to kiss her again. One taste wasn't enough. I'm officially addicted.

"You wear the hat better than I do, Liv. Do you want to go back inside?"

She nods at me, and I grab her hand and interlace our fingers again before we step inside and rejoin the party. "That was my favorite part of tonight."

"Me too."

Chapter Fourteen

— GLUE SONG BY BEABADOOBEE FT. CLAIRO

"Wait, you guys kissed? Oh, I totally called this. I need every detail right this minute, Olivia!" Cal practically screams when I tell him what happened on Halloween.

I go into detail about when we were dancing and how I was practically grinding all over him. I tell him about how he kept staring at me all night, his gaze heating me from the inside out despite me being dressed like Jo March.

Then I get to the kiss, and I practically stall. *I can't stop thinking about it.* How do you describe a kiss that consumes your entire body? How do you describe the feeling of floating outside my body and watching from the astral plane? There are not enough words in any language to describe how the kiss made me feel.

Possessed. Maybe that's it. I felt possessed by Tristan in that moment and in every moment since then. I can still feel him on my lips like he's a ghost that haunts me every time I open my mouth to speak—all I feel is him. Him kissing me. Him grabbing the back of my neck. His hand on my face, my hands against his shirt, his hat on my head, him grabbing my wrist and pulling me toward him. All my thoughts are covered in Tristan.

It's been two days since Halloween, and I've seen him in class once. I was a bit hungover from the party since Halloween was on a weeknight, but we still passed notes back and forth, just like normal. Neither of us brought up the kiss. At first, I thought he regretted it, but I'd be an idiot to think that. *He* kissed me, not the other way around. He wanted to kiss me as much as I wanted to be kissed by him. Tristan doesn't normally do relationships, so I'm giving him—and myself—a bit of wiggle room here. Neither of us is really good at this, I assume. I know I'm terrible with relationships—my longest one was seven months—and Tristan hasn't dated at all in college.

"Okay, so what happened with the kiss? Was it bad? Is that why you have that look on your face?" Cal asks me, shaking me out of my Tristan-induced haze.

"No, no. No, Cal." A customer coming up to the counter makes our conversation pause as I help them out. That's the one thing that sucks about customer service jobs—the customers are always interrupting the good conversations you're having. One minute, you're talking about all the drama in your life, and the next, someone is interrupting you to ask where the bananas are—at the *deli* counter. This job has only proven one thing to me over the years I've worked here: some people *really* don't have common sense.

I see Cal start to do some of our closing duties from my peripheral vision as I help the person at the counter out, and when they leave, I turn back around. "It was the best kiss of my life."

"I *knew* it. He looks like a good kisser." He smiles at me. "And what happened after?"

"We went back inside to the party and danced. His friends and mine were with us for the rest of the night." I continue to tell him about that and how Tristan insisted that he walk me home, even though Parker was with me. He told me he wanted to make sure that we were safe, and then, as Parker went into our building, he kissed me again. Stole my fucking breath out from under me for the fourth time that night—or however many times, frankly, I lost count after the first two.

"That's it? I was hoping for some big confession of feelings or whatever."

"Yes, that's it." I sigh, knowing Tristan and I will have to talk at some point. I'm not great at talking about how I feel. I find that it's easier for me to write down my feelings than to say them out loud. It's probably why I've always been drawn to creating fictional universes in my head.

"Are you going to talk to him at some point?"

"You're just full of questions tonight, aren't you?" I joke with him, and he rolls his eyes at me as he grabs the broom.

"Obviously. This is the most interesting thing to happen to you...well ever since I've known you. Excuse me for wanting all the details, Liv." He jabs the broom head at my feet. "Also, my life isn't that interesting, so I have to live vicariously through someone, and I don't feel like doing that through Joe and all his wife's cats."

I smile at that. Joe told us the other day that he and his wife have a cat on their porch that's been pregnant a few times. He's got a whole family of them now, and he's not an animal person. "Cal, your life is more fun than mine."

"Not as of late. But, back to you. What happens now?"

"I don't know. I doubt Tristan wants anything to change between us, and that's fine by me," I say, the ache in my chest strengthening. Just the thought of staying the same makes me want to hide in my room all day, but I don't know what he wants. Until we talk about it, it'll hang over my head like a dark cloud.

"Yes, but do *you* want anything to change?"

"I think so."

He rolls his eyes at me as he sweeps. "Livvy, it's a yes or no. Not an *'I think.'"*

"Yes, I do. I want things to change between us, even though he's always told me how badly he wants to get out of here after college. I still want him."

"He's told me that a few times, too. Maybe this will change his mind."

I shake my head. "But I don't want it to. I want him to chase after what he's always wanted, and I want to see him succeed, but I also want him. I want the parts that nobody else gets to see," I look over at Cal with a smirk on his face. "I've always felt lost in every single aspect of my life, but I've never been surer about something. Tristan makes me *feel*, and I like how I feel when I'm with him, so yes. I want things to change."

"God, you're such a writer."

"Cal! What the hell does that mean? I basically poured my stupid heart out at you, and now you're being mean?"

"Yes. You need to get cracking on that book, Livvy. I'd love to read it one day, and you surely have the talent for it."

"You're the one who asked. Now, can you go do the dishes while I straighten up over here? Or are you gonna ask me a thousand more questions about Tristan only to make fun of my answers?"

"I'll go, but remember that *he* kissed you. He wouldn't have done that unless he felt the same way that you do. Just talk to him about it," he smiles. "And then tell me everything about that conversation when I see you next."

I throw a paper towel at him, but he dodges it before heading to the back to do the dishes. Cal is probably right, and I'll talk to Tristan at some point.

Just get through tonight and leave tomorrow's worries for tomorrow. I repeat that about a thousand times throughout the rest of my shift with Cal, and when I leave work, the sun is just starting to set. I take my phone out, snap a picture of it, and open Tristan's contact picture. He has practice tonight—at the batting cages—so he'll probably miss this one.

Livvy: *one attachment*

Livvy: 5/10, not enough color, but still beautiful.

I pocket my phone, not expecting him to answer it soon, but I find myself smiling as I do. I've never been so sure about my feelings for someone as I do Tristan. That information both scares me and thrills me. I constantly second-guess myself and every decision I make, but something about Tristan feels right. He's wrapped himself around me—his presence, his cinnamon scent that I've memorized since he gave me his hoodie—but part of me is still confused as to *why* he kissed me.

I'm nothing like the girls that he's gone out with, and I never will be. I'm not popular like he is, and I prefer staying in most nights. *He knows that already, Liv.*

I shake the thoughts out of my head, and drive home with my playlist loudly blaring and my windows down since it's still warm out. I think about how to bring up the fact that I want more from our relationship without scaring him off. By the time I park in the lot by my building, my phone buzzes.

Tristan: 6/10, but I'd rather see the beauty behind the camera.

Livvy: I never look too hot after a shift, so absolutely not.

Tristan: You better take that back, Liv.

Livvy: Or what, Tristan?

Tristan: You don't wanna know.

Livvy: You don't scare me.

Tristan: Scary isn't really what I'm going for…

Livvy: *one attachment*

Tristan: There she is :)

Livvy: That was a forced selfie, just so you're aware.

Tristan: And now it's your new contact photo, bite me, Liv.

Livvy: If you're not careful I might.

Livvy: Goodbye, Tristan.

Tristan: Bye, Livs.

Chapter Fifteen

— HEAVEN BY NIALL HORAN

Tristan,

I figured that this was the easiest way to do this, with our tradition of passing notes in class and around school. I'll just cut right to the chase because I'm chickening out as I write this.

Meet me under the stars in your favorite place. I want to watch the sunset with you and talk about some things, if that's okay.

See you in a few,
Livvy.

It's been exactly a week since Livvy and I have kissed, and this note has me on edge. It was slipped under my door a few minutes ago, and as soon as I opened the door, there was nobody to be found. Either Livvy is as quick as a mouse, or she had someone else deliver it so she wouldn't get caught.

The past week has been exactly the same as all the other ones, except the kiss looms over the both of us. I've been wanting to kiss her again ever since I got a taste of her, but I've held off because I don't want to cross any boundaries.

I'm wrapped around this girl's finger, and I don't even give a fuck.

Not wanting to wait any longer for this talk, I throw my shoes on and head out of my apartment. None of the guys are here right now. They're all at the library, except Ethan, who's on a date. Her note told me to meet her at my favorite place, and I only have one favorite place—the baseball field. I would be surprised if she remembered, but Livvy is one of those people. If you tell her something about yourself, she'll remember it for later.

My feet carry my body toward the field, and as I get there, my heart rate picks up. *I'm nervous.* I'm fucking terrified. I don't think I'd ever be able to handle seeing her date someone else, but as long as she's still around, I think I'll be okay. Well, I'll have to be. If this is what she wants, then I'll do it, but fuck if it won't hurt like a bitch.

The sun has started to set, and I'm grateful that I brought a jacket because she might get cold if we're out here for a while. As I look onto the field, I see her lying down on a blanket, looking cute as all hell in my fucking hoodie. God, giving her that was one of the best decisions I've ever made. It's about two sizes too big for her, and as I walk across the grass and toward her, I realize that Livvy and I were never destined to be friends.

Ever since I spilled that coffee on her, she was mine. I just didn't know that at the time.

I'm not one to share my stuff easily. I always thought guys who gave their clothes to their girlfriends were weird, and I could never imagine doing that with anyone because I like my stuff a certain way. I don't let people into my space because it's *my* space, and I like it how it is. I didn't want anyone to change that for me.

Except her. Livvy could steal all my clothes and never give them back, and I'd buy an entire new wardrobe with a smile on my face if it meant seeing her wear all my stuff. She could take every single one of my hoodies and I'd let her, just to see the smile that's on her face as I lay down next to her. "Hi, Livvy."

Her face turns to mine, with a shy smile and red cheeks. "Hi, Tristan."

"What's a girl like you doing out here by yourself on a night like this?"

"Waiting for this guy. I'm in his favorite spot, waiting for the sun to set." I like that she's continuing the joke, and I'm still smiling like an idiot as my eyes shift back to the sky.

"He sounds like a good guy. What's he like?"

She takes a shaky breath before she speaks. *She's nervous.* "He's the best guy I know."

"Is that all?" I can feel my mouth turn into a smile as I speak.

"Well, he makes me feel like I can take on the world. I like who I am when I'm with him."

"I bet this guy feels exactly the same way about you. He'd be stupid not to, Liv. You're one of a kind." I reach my arm over and cup her face, wanting to feel her. I'm scared that this is a dream, and I'll wake up to realize that it's not really happening.

"Do you think so?"

"Okay, before this goes on, I'm stopping the ruse."

She starts to laugh. "I was trying to see how long it would go on."

"I know, but if I'm going to tell you that I like you and that I want more with you, I want you to know that I'm talking to you. Not anyone else," I say, and her pupils dilate.

"You what?"

"I like you, Liv. I really fucking like being with you, around you, and anyway I can have you. I want more from this, from us," I pause, nervous to say the rest. "Isn't that why you left me that note?"

She nods her head, and we both sit up on the blanket. "Tristan, I like you too. God, why is this so damn scary? I'm practically sweating through this hoodie right now."

I laugh at her nerves before I reach over and pull the hoodie off of her body. "Better?"

"Much better. Now, where were we?"

"Being idiots while confessing that we want more out of this relationship, but what else is new?" I smile, and she smiles back, and I swear I've never felt so euphoric before. Not even after winning championships have I felt this good. It's just her. Only Livvy could make me feel like I won the fucking lottery in life by confessing that she wants to be more as much as I do.

"You want me? You want this?"

"Yes, Olivia. I want you. I want your clothes all over my apartment. I want you to steal all my hoodies while you think I'm not looking. I want every fucking sunset with you that I can get. I want to carpool to work on the nights that we work together." I grab her chin and make her eyes look into mine. "I want *you*."

"Then you'll have to ask me."

"Olivia Hart, will you be my girlfriend?"

She taps her finger on her chin as if she's thinking about her answer, and before I know it, her arms are around my neck and she's tackled me. "Yes. I will."

"Fucking hell," I say as she pulls back from me. "Say that again."

"Yes, Tristan, I'll be yours. And you'll be mine."

"You bet I fucking will." Livvy surprises me by leaning down and pressing her lips softly to mine. *God, I can do that whenever I want to now because she's mine.* Olivia is officially my girl. *My girl.* I'm her boyfriend, and I wish I could shout that off of a rooftop right now. I've never felt so excited to call myself something before.

Every other guy on campus will know soon enough too, after I parade my beautiful girlfriend around. I can't wait to introduce her to people as such. Fuck, this feels good.

"Parker and Cassie are gonna kill me," she says as I lay us back down on the blanket and snuggle her into my side.

"Why?"

"I told them a thousand times that we were just friends, and they didn't believe me. They insisted that this would happen."

"Funny enough, Dom, Ethan, and Harry said the same thing. But they've been saying that since I gave you my hoodie."

"Tristan, that was in August, and it's November."

"I'm aware, Livs. They thought it was weird that I gave you my hoodie since, well, you know I don't like sharing my shit with people."

"Why *did* you give me this if you're so weird about people having your stuff?"

"Honestly, I don't know. It just felt like the right thing to do. Your face looked so worried, and I wanted to help ease that, so I did what I thought was right." I look down at her—my beautiful girlfriend—and press a kiss on her head. "Best decision I've ever made, if I'm being honest."

"I agree." Livvy smiles against my shirt, and I feel like I'm soaring. "Look how pretty the sunset is tonight."

"It's beautiful," I say as I take it all in. The sky is filled with mostly pink spreading through it, but on the edge of the top, it looks almost purple. The part closest to the sun is orange and just barely peeking through. It's captivating, but nothing could steal my attention away from the girl in the crook of my neck, eyes wide as she takes in the sky above us.

Livvy is more beautiful than any sunset I could see, and as long as she exists, that statement will always be true. Livvy throws my hoodie—her hoodie—back on. "Cold?"

"A little. Can I take a picture of us? I want to remember this moment."

"Of course, Livs. Take all the pictures you want. I'll even pose for you. Just give me a second to figure out which side is best right now."

"Tristan, every side is your good side. Have you seen yourself?"

"Of course I have, but I'd love to hear you describe me, so do tell," I say, and she smiles as she hits my arm. She settles back into my embrace, and takes a few pictures of us, which I tell her to immediately send to me. I want to make one of these my lock screen, and when I open my messages, the guys texted me.

> **Dom: Tristan, where are you? I thought we were gonna watch the Equalizer tonight when we got back. Are you with Livvy?**

> **Harry: This note just says you'll be "out." How does that equate to Livvy?**

> **Dom: Notes are their form of communication, so why else would he leave one?**

> **Ethan: Are things finally official or what?**

> **Dom: He's not answering, so he's either busy fucking, or doing something else.**

> **Tristan: You guys suck, you know that?**

> **Ethan: He lives!**

> **Harry: Or he's texting mid-fuck.**

Ethan: Disgusting, Harrison.

Dom: You guys have never done that?

Ethan: Disgusting, Dom. Truly the worst. Please never text me mid-fuck, or I'll cut your dick off.

Harry: I don't like the picture that's painting in my mind.

Tristan: Can you guys stop texting? My girlfriend and I are trying to watch the sunset in peace.

"I like that phrase," Livvy says as she watches me type. "Are they always this nosy?"

"Unfortunately, yes, but they mean well."

"I know. They told me at the party that they thought you liked me. It was hilarious the way they all talk about you."

My phone buzzing a thousand times cuts off our conversation.

Dom: I FUCKING KNEW IT!

Harry: Oh, we all saw this coming.

Ethan: Tristan is a sappy fucker now. Everyone get ready.

Harry: I, for one, am gonna love having Livvy over at our place. She's cool as fuck.

Ethan: Yeah, Tristan, when can we do game night? Or movie night?

Dom: Livvy better like action movies, or I'll have a serious problem with her.

Tristan: Hi, it's Livvy. I love action movies, and I'm down for game night, just let me know. Do you guys like cookies or should I bake something else?

Dom: OMG Tristan gave her his phone!!!!

Harry: You guys are adorable already. I need to throw up, or something.

Tristan: We'll see you guys later. Now, fuck off.

Dom: Put Livvy back on, she's much nicer.

Livvy's laughter distracts me from sending another mean message to my stupid fucking friends, and I pull her closer as we continue watching the sun go down in the sky. "Best night ever."

"With the best girl ever," I tell her as I lean down and kiss her again. I savor the feel of her lips, her ChapStick, the way her mouth feels on mine because, sitting here right now, we have all the time in the world.

I've got more than enough time to memorize every inch of her and commit it to memory, but with this kiss, I'm taking my time. I want to be in this moment with her—the girl who lives rent fucking free in my head.

God help me. I never want her to leave my mind, and now that I have her, I've got all I need. My girl kissing me back in my favorite spot in the world will always be enough for me.

Chapter Sixteen

— NOTHING NEW BY TAYLOR SWIFT FT. PHOEBE BRIDGERS

"WAIT, MOM AND DAD did what?" I ask my sister as she updates me on all things Bree from her vacation place in Florida.

"They told me that they want to start managing my social media accounts, and I told them hell no."

"Good for you. Why did they bring that up in the first place?"

"A few weeks ago, I told them how overwhelming it can get sometimes. Even though I know I can handle it if I'm organized, they didn't think so." My sister tells me about how my dad was going to start handling one of her accounts and my mom the other. They want my sister to focus on the biggest one and keep it growing—her YouTube channel.

"Dad can't even figure out Facebook. How's he going to run your account?"

"That's exactly what I said, Liv! And they started arguing with me! I swear they don't even hear me anymore. They just talk and expect me to agree like a robot."

"I'm sorry, Bree. If it helps, I've been watching your videos, and they get better every time."

She smiles at me, and I can't help but feel like a proud sister anytime I talk to her. "Which one was your favorite? Was it me rating all my reads from last month or the one of me rearranging my bookshelf? That was a fun one, especially with all the little trinkets I have."

"The ratings one. I love how you don't bullshit with the ones you don't like." Bree, like me, loves to read, and most of her content involves books. Even if she doesn't like a book, she's not afraid to say it, but she's always respectful about it because at the end of the day, authors are people too. Ever since her YouTube channel exploded a few years ago, she's been invited to all sorts of book events, makeup launch parties, and even a few fashion shows. My younger sister is way cooler and more successful than me at the age of twenty, and I couldn't be prouder of her and how she's handled this newfound influence.

"I knew you'd like that one. Maybe one day I'll be reading and rating a book that you wrote?" she questions, and I roll my eyes like I always do when she brings the topic up. "I'm just saying, Liv. You should try, Mom and Dad be damned."

"That's easy for you to say. You've been defying them your whole life." Bree might be younger than me, but she's also bolder. "I can't, Bree."

"Livs, you're good. You're insanely good. I remember when you used to read me to sleep with stories that you created when I got sick of the books we had."

My face lights up at the memories she jogged in my head. Bree used to get sick of hearing the same stories over and over again when we were trying to sleep, so she always made me read her one that I made up. I like to think that's when I first fell in love with storytelling, and Bree will never let me live down that I started writing because of her. "It's been on my mind more recently. Tristan keeps telling me the same thing you do—that I should just write and see where it takes me, but part of me is still holding back, and I don't know why."

"I like this boyfriend of yours already, and I haven't even met him."

Boyfriend. I'll never get tired of calling him that. "You two would get along. That I know for a fact." Tristan and Bree are similar in a way. They're unapologetically themselves and way more extroverted than I am. It's a good balance if I'm being honest. I always knew I'd need someone to be more outgoing than I am in a partner, and Tristan checks all the boxes for me—hell, he created the damn checklist at this point.

"I wish I could meet him at Thanksgiving, but we both know that's not happening again this year."

"Yeah, I know, but I'll see you around Christmas, right?"

"Absolutely, Liv. I already have gift ideas brewing in my mind for you." I smile, knowing my sister's love language is giving gifts because she always goes all out. I wish I'd see her sooner than next month, but I'll take all I can get of her. My sister is usually gone, and my parents' decision to work has made it a holiday I dislike.

I've never had much to be thankful for, except that my sister was okay. Now, there's an ache because I have a lot to be thankful for this year, yet nobody to celebrate with. My family has never been as close as most, but I've always wished that we could be.

My sister and I are attached at the hip, but when it comes to us and our parents, sometimes it feels like they're distant aunts or uncles. It sucks, but it also sucks to say that I'm used to it by now. I slid to the back burner when my sister got famous. My parents only get in touch if they need me for something, despite my living so close to home.

It sucks, but both my sister and I are used to it. I'm more forgotten by my parents than she is, but Bree hates having all their energy and time on her, too. It's a double-edged sword—Bree hates that my parents smother her all the damn time, and I hate that I've been left behind. I'm in college studying an artistic field, and that will never be good enough for them, no matter how much I tell them that it's my dream.

"I can't wait to move out."

Bree's sudden change of topic has me confused. "You're thinking about getting your own place finally? I've been telling you to leave for months. You're never home, anyway."

"I know, sis. I know. It's been hard to leave them. They don't think I'm safe out on my own."

"I always worry about your safety, too, but when you're in Pennsylvania and under their roof, you're not happy."

"I feel suffocated. The only time I feel like I can breathe is when I'm away," she admits.

"I know, girl. How about this? Next time you come home, we'll start to look for a place around here. That way, you're still close but still on your own."

Her smile practically lights up my laptop screen. "I'd love that. I'm not too picky, but if you send me some places, I'll look at them and tell you what I like and what I don't."

"You've got yourself a deal."

"I know how much you love browsing Zillow in your free time, so it's a win-win." I start to laugh, and a knock on my bedroom door has me pausing. "Oh my gosh, is that him?"

"Relax, Bree. It could be Parker." But when my door opens, and Tristan walks through, I hear my sister gasp through the computer screen.

"Olivia Willow Hart, you downplayed the fuck out of that man! What you've done should be considered a criminal offense!"

"I, for one, would *love* to hear what Olivia has said about me to who I assume is Bree. It's nice to meet you." Tristan tries to go out of frame, but I grab his arm and pull him toward me.

"Did you want me to describe every ridge of his abs, or what Bree?"

"No, but I didn't want to have to poke and pry out every detail from you. Tristan, it was like pulling teeth, I swear." She holds her hands up in defense.

"Bree, I'll hang up right now. Don't make me do it."

"I totally get that. I had to force her to take my hoodie the first time we met. My girl is stubborn, but I am too, so I can't say much." Tristan leans down and presses a kiss to my lips before he looks at the screen again. "You sound familiar, Bree."

"I get that a lot."

"She's a YouTuber," I tell him, and I see a switch flip in his brain.

"I prefer influencer, Livvy."

Tristan runs a hand through his hair, the rings he normally wears drawing all of my attention to those hands of his. "I think my sister watches your videos. She got back into reading and doing makeup looks after she started watching a bunch of YouTube videos. I'm ninety-nine percent sure my sister is obsessed with you."

"Oh, wow," I say. Even though my sister is sort of famous, I've never had anyone I know be a fan of hers.

"Aww, tell her I said hi. Or get my number from Livvy, and I'll send her a nice message or something," Bree tells him with a smile. She *loves* meeting people who watch her videos. She always tells me that it's because she wouldn't do what she does now without them, and I can always tell how much it means to her that they chose to follow her.

"Thanks, Bree. That's super nice of you," Tristan tells her. "I'll be on your bed, Liv. Take as much time as you need. Don't cut the call short just because I'm here." He presses another kiss to my head before sauntering over to my bed and hopping onto it.

"That was so disgustingly cute. I can see your red cheeks from here, Liv." Bree smiles at me. It's only been two weeks since Tristan and I made it official, and I'm still waiting for a time when I don't feel like my legs are jelly after he kisses me. I'm hoping it never goes away because I love how his kisses make me feel—how *he* makes me feel. "Do you guys have plans for Thanksgiving since we're not doing anything?"

"You guys aren't having dinner with your parents?" Tristan asks me from my bed, and I shake my head.

"Unless we're doing family dinner after years of doing nothing, then no."

Tristan's eyes narrow at mine, and I see some sadness behind them. I assume he's going to be with his family—they're all super close, and I bet they're the type of family to have a thousand traditions together. I've seen Tristan always texting and calling them. Even though he's away from home, he's always checking in on his siblings and making sure they're okay. His mom texts him once a day just to tell him that she's proud of him, and that fact alone makes my insides melt.

I wish I had that. I yearn to have that one day, but for now, this is how it is. All I've ever wanted is for my parents to be proud of me, and that's partially why I'm afraid to go after my dreams and write the damn book.

I feel like no matter how many books I write, no matter how successful I become, it will never be enough for them.

"I have to go, but one of these days, I'll be back in town, and we can all meet up properly. It was nice to meet you, Tristan! And Livs, I'll talk to you tomorrow, okay?"

"Nice to meet you, Bree," Tristan says from behind me.

"Sounds good. I'll start house-hunting for you," I say as I click end on the call, only to see Tristan's face turned down in the screen on my laptop. "Is everything okay?"

He doesn't say a word, but instead, he leans down and wraps his arms around where I sit in my desk chair. I can feel his breath on my neck before he presses a kiss to the same spot. His head pops up, and his eyes meet mine on the computer screen. "You haven't celebrated Thanksgiving in years?"

"My parents prefer to work, and since my sister has been busy most years, we canceled the holiday altogether." I pause, willing the emotions in my throat to go the fuck away. "It's fine. It's not like it would be fun or anything, even if we did celebrate."

"Yeah, but...everyone deserves to celebrate and be thankful, Liv."

"It's not a big deal, Tris. I hate being home anyway." I can tell he wants to press me about it more, but instead of asking anything else, he slips his hands underneath my legs and lifts me off of my chair. He carries me over to my bed before laying me down and pulling me to his chest. "I thought we were going for a walk?"

"I'd rather hold you, Liv."

"But—"

"Please just let me hold you, pretty girl."

And I let him because I can tell that he needs this. All I know is that I feel safe in his arms. I feel comfortable here, where it feels like nothing in the world can touch me.

As I start to drift off, I swear I imagine Tristan saying something in my ear, but I can't quite make out what it is as I fall deeper into sleep.

Chapter Seventeen

**— CONEY ISLAND BY TAYLOR SWIFT FT. THE NA-
TIONAL**

As Livvy puts the closed signs up for our department, I finish up all the cleaning we have left to do so we can get the hell out of here. It takes us fifteen minutes to be done, and before I know it, we're heading out the employee door. I grab her hand in mine as we head toward my car.

The two of us have started carpooling to work most nights since we often work together, and it's been yet another tradition that we've started doing.

I feel like a selfish son of a bitch, but I want all of Livvy's traditions. It seems like her family doesn't have any, and I want all of them with her. I want to show her that she's worth having all the little things she never had when she grew up.

I've always been one to run away from most things—feelings, emotions in general, and anything serious. But now, I want to run toward all of that with Livvy by my side.

"I only had one weird old man flirt with me tonight. I call that a win." Livvy smiles at me as we walk through the parking lot.

"It's not a win, Olivia. It's ridiculous. Some of these people are gross, and you shouldn't feel creeped out while you're at work." My shoulders tense up because I don't get how it can be okay for all these creeps to openly flirt with my girlfriend. Why do some people act like they do in public? A lot of people really don't have any semblance of common sense or respect these days. It's fucking annoying.

"Tristan, it's part of working with the public, you know that."

"I know. I just wish it wasn't. I don't like how it makes you feel."

She leans into me and presses a kiss to my hand. "That's why you're different from most." Her eyes shift to the sky as we get to my car. "What do you think?"

I study the sunset tonight. It's not very prevalent, but it's still there. The sky is a dark shade of blue, but where the sun disappears on the horizon, the sky is illuminated in orange and yellow hues. "Six out of ten. It's pretty, but I think we missed the main event."

"I agree. It probably looked stunning when it was just starting to set." Livvy's eyes sparkle as she imagines what it must've looked like. That's another thing I appreciate about her. Her imagination is so vivid, her mind so active, that she can get emotional just at the beauty of things like nature and such. Her mind fascinates me, and no matter how much I steal glimpses of her writing, I still can't convince her to take the leap and write her book. Maybe one day.

I open her door for her, and she slides into the passenger seat only after giving me a quick kiss. She always does that when I open her door for her, and if it were up to me, she'd never touch a single door again.

I lock the doors as I walk around to the driver's side and unlock them again before I can get in. Livvy always asks me why I do that, and when I told her I wanted to make sure she was safe, she laughed at me.

"So, I wanted to ask you something," I say as I turn my car on.

"That doesn't sound terrifying at all."

"It's nothing bad, I promise."

Her eyes are shooting all over my body as if she's terrified. *Shit.* "Just talk faster, please."

"I want you to come to Thanksgiving with me. And before you say no—"

"Yes."

Well, that was a lot easier than I initially thought. "Oh, okay. I thought I would have to convince you more. I had this whole speech planned about wanting to introduce you to my family and shit."

"Tristan, I'd love to spend Thanksgiving with your family. I'm really excited. I was originally going to do a watch party with my sister like we normally do, but she's going to a party. Now, instead of being by myself, I'll be surrounded by you and your family."

God, this fucking girl is going to be the death of me. "They're very excited to meet you. When I told them I was thinking about bringing my girlfriend, I was basically threatened to get you to come. I'm glad you agreed, because I don't want to face my little sister or my mom's wrath." I hear Livvy laugh under her breath. "You'll find out soon how terrifying they are. Consider this your only warning."

"Whatever you say, babe. Can we go now? I'm freezing my ass off in this parking lot."

"Of course we can. I'll turn the heat up. I can't have my girl getting frozen," I say as I place my hand on her thigh. The roads were slick on the way in, but overall it was okay. The drive back to campus is normally only ten minutes, but with the ice and snow, it takes around twenty now. I'm not complaining, though. I'll take any extra time around my girl that I can get. I could watch her lip-sync to the songs she plays in my car for the rest of time—and even that might not even be enough.

A few minutes into the drive, Liv keeps changing the song because she can't find one she likes. "Are you good?"

"No. I think I need a new playlist because no song is matching the vibe right now."

"Then make another one. It's not like you don't have a thousand already. What's one more—" My sentence is cut off by my car skidding on a patch of ice. "Fuck, fuck, fuck," I say as my car slides on the road. I try to pump the brakes like you're supposed to do in these conditions, but it's not working.

"*Tristan*!" Livvy shrieks from beside me.

"It's okay, Livs. You're okay. We're okay," I say as my car keeps sliding. I wasn't going too fast, so it should slow down. I glance around and notice that there aren't many cars on the road right now—in fact, I don't see a single one. My car runs into a snowbank, and I shoot my arm out across Liv's body. *Fuck.* The two of us take a second to slow our breaths, and when I look over at her, she's in shock. "Are you okay?"

She nods, but I run my hands all over her body to double-check for my own sanity. It's not like we were in some huge accident, but still, that scared me. "Are you alright?"

"I'm fine, pretty girl."

"We must've hit black ice." Livvy tells me, and I silently agree with her. "God, my heart is beating so fast."

I reach over and put my hand over her heart, just to see if it will slow down. "I'm sorry I scared you so bad."

"It's not your fault, babe. You can't control the weather. Shit like this always happens in Pennsylvania, anyway."

She's right, but that doesn't mean that I want to put her in danger or make her feel unsafe in my presence. I didn't think we were going to die, but that could've gone a lot worse than it did. I've seen snow accidents that ended fatally before, and I don't know what I would've done if one of us got really hurt. I've heard that some people see their entire lives flash before their eyes in near-death experiences, and while this wasn't really one, I did see something in my mind.

Her. Livvy. I was only focused on making sure she was okay as my car skidded out. All that crossed my mind was her face, and I swear this girl is the light whenever things get too dark or scary for me. Tonight just solidifies that for me.

"How are we going to get your car out of here?"

Oh shit, I forgot about that. "Ethan has a truck with a tow hitch. I'll call him and see if he can get here. We're not too far from school."

"We should probably get out of the car so that he can see us."

"Yeah, true. Put this hat on, though." I give her one of my spare hats, and she looks at me like I'm crazy.

"Tristan, I'm already wearing a hat."

"I know, but put it on anyway," I tell her, and she does. She might look ridiculous with two hats on right now, but I need to *do* something. I feel all out of whack, out of control, and I need to take my mind off of how crazy I feel. I grab my phone and dial Ethan's number. He picks up after the second ring.

"What's up, man?"

"I need your truck. My car spun out on the way home."

I hear his keys jingle in the back of the call, so I know he's probably rushing out the door. "Where are you? Are you guys okay?"

"Livvy and I are good, I think. Just cold and shocked, is all." I tell him where we are, and he says he'll be here in five. I guess we were closer to school than I thought. I feel Liv wrap her arms around the back of me, and before I know it, she practically tackles me to the ground that's covered in snow. "Liv, you're gonna get cold, and if you get hypothermia and die on my watch, I swear I'll—"

She cuts me off with a kiss, which stops my rambling. *I should ramble more often.* "Make a snow angel with me."

"What?"

"A snow angel? It's when you lay down and—"

"No, I know what it is, but why do you want to make one right now?"

She shrugs. "I don't know. We have time to kill before Ethan gets here, and I figured why not make light of a shitty situation by making snow angels?"

God, this fucking girl. Only she would want to make snow angels thirty feet from where my car spun off the road. But with the way she was looking at me right now, I'd do anything she asked, even if I felt like my mind was about to spiral out of control.

One of my biggest fears is not being there for someone I love when they need me or not helping them in a situation they need my help in. Almost hurting Livvy tonight has me feeling all out of sorts, but I can tell she's trying to take my mind off of all this. "Okay."

She practically jumps off my back, and in her work clothes, big puffy jacket, and the two hats she's wearing, she makes a snow angel. I smile as I watch her arms and legs slide up and down, a smile branding her face as if this is the happiest she's ever been.

I take my eyes off of her—not knowing how I did that because I could look at her smile forever and never get tired of it—and start to make my own. It feels silly doing this, but I find myself smiling and even laughing. *I'm having fun.* This is the weirdest night ever, but I don't want it to end. By the time we're done making our snow angels, she looks over at me. "Feel better?"

"Surprisingly, yes."

"I knew that would work. My sister and I used to do that when we were little. Our parents never used to let us play out in the snow because they hated how we would track water through the house when we were done. So, the two of us used to sneak out when they worked late and secretly make snow angels."

"That's simultaneously adorable and upsetting."

"It was a long time ago. It was Bree and I's first tradition when we were young." Her eyes sadden, and I know that she misses her sister a lot right now. They talk as much as I do with my family, but Liv and her parents don't seem to talk all that much. The thought pisses me off—the fact that they ignore Liv and put all their focus on Bree. Can't they see what they're doing to their kids? Bree has mentioned that she feels suffocated and how she can't wait until she can leave their parents' house, and Liv feels like she doesn't even have parents. I'm not usually one to judge people before meeting them, but Liv's parents don't count.

I already don't care much for them.

"Don't worry about me, Tristan. I'm okay."

"I'll always worry about you," I say as I press a kiss to her lips. She sighs into my embrace, and it takes all of my self-control to pull away from her.

"What the hell are you guys doing?" I hear Ethan's voice as he shines a flashlight on us.

"Nothing, Officer, I swear," I joke with him as he puts down the light.

"Hilarious. Nice to know that Livvy finally gave you a sense of humor."

"Awww, I did?" I can hear the smile in her voice right now as the two of us get up and off the snow.

"No," I say.

"Yes," Ethan says at the same time.

"Fuck you."

"Do you want my help or not?" Before I can back out and say no, Livvy interrupts.

"Yes, we do. Thank you for dropping everything, Ethan." Livvy elbows me, signaling me to say the same, I assume.

"Yeah, thanks, man. I appreciate it," I say in the most monotone voice I can muster.

"Anything for you two. Now, let's get your car out of a ditch, shall we?"

"Let's do it."

Chapter Eighteen

— HOLOCENE BY BON IVER

I CAN'T BELIEVE THAT I'm about to go into Tristan's childhood home in about two minutes. Tristan just parked the car after picking me up, and my nerves are on fire. When I agreed to spend Thanksgiving with his family, I was excited, but now I'm terrified. My orange dress is making me think that I look like a pumpkin, and I feel itchy all over. I've never met the family of someone I was dating because nothing was ever that serious, and my thoughts won't stop running all over the place.

I don't do family gatherings. I don't know how to act around other people's families—especially when they're so different from mine. Tristan told me that his family dinners are often loud and rambunctious, while mine are usually full of me sinking into the background as my parents berate Bree with questions. I was never the focus of my family, and I prefer it that way, but I have a feeling that's not what today is going to be like. Tristan told me how excited his family was to meet me, and I suddenly felt like my dress was too tight and that I looked ridiculous.

"Liv? Are you okay?"

Was he talking to me? "Yeah, sorry. Did you say something?"

"I've been speaking to you for like five minutes. Are you alright?"

I take a deep breath to calm my nerves, but it doesn't help. "Do you think they'll like me?"

"Is that what you're worried about?"

"Well, yes. That fact and about a thousand other things. Do I look okay? My dress feels like it's suffocating me." His eyes sweep over my body, and suddenly, I feel warm. It's crazy to me that with just his gaze, he can make me feel all sorts of ways. He adjusts the rings on his hands before he grabs both of my hands in his.

"You look like the most beautiful person to walk the earth, Livs. You have nothing to worry about. They're going to love you, babe. I promise. They're mostly excited that I'm bringing a girl home for once. My siblings thought I was going to be alone forever because of how allergic I was to relationships before."

"Before what?" I ask.

"Before you, pretty girl." He squeezes my hands a few times—three—and I already feel my heart rate slowing down. "I'll be by your side the whole time. Plus, it's only my immediate family. My aunt couldn't make it, and my dad's side of the family doesn't come around much anymore."

"Okay. That makes me feel better."

"Liv, you'll be fine. You don't need to impress anyone tonight. Just be yourself, and they'll understand why you're the perfect girl for me." He throws a wink in my direction before stepping out of the car and opening my door for me. "Take a few breaths, baby."

I nod as he takes my hand in his while grabbing the Tupperware full of chocolate chip cookies. I baked them yesterday because I thought it would be rude to show up empty-handed, and after burning the first batch because Tristan distracted me, the second came out flawlessly. I'm not a huge baker, but I enjoy it occasionally.

Tristan's childhood home is everything I thought it would be. It's light brown, with white shutters on the outside. The front door is a pale yellow that looks every bit welcoming, as well as the decorations on the outside of the porch. A few pumpkins adorn the doorstep, and I smile at the thought of Tristan growing up here. *It must've been great.* "Are you ready?"

"Yeah, let's do it." And then Tristan opens the front door after knocking a few times, and I'm met with the warmest feeling I've ever had. The house has all sorts of Thanksgiving themed decorations around it, and I can smell a few candles burning—cinnamon and cranberry, I think. To the left, up a few steps, is the family room, where I spot his siblings around a table, arguing over something, which stops when they see Tristan come in.

"Tristan!" His younger sister runs over to him and practically jumps into his arms. Her long chestnut hair practically flows all over the place and over Tristan's eyes so much that he has to move it out of the way. I've seen pictures of all his siblings—they all look identical besides a few distinguishing features—but seeing them in person is much better. They've all got the same hair color as Tristan, except Tobias's, whose hair is a lighter shade of brown. The four of them have the same eye color—brown, with flecks of orange around them. Tristan told me he's the tallest, then Tobias and Theo, who are the same height, and Teagen is the shortest. She's only slightly shorter than I am, so she might be around my height one day. It feels weird looking down at people since I'm normally looking eye to eye with my friends and up at Tristan.

One of his brothers rolls his eyes as he comes over to us. "She didn't miss me that much." *That must be Tobias.*

"She definitely doesn't like me that much, and I live here. Guess we know who the favorite brother is." *That's Theo, then.*

Tristan wraps his arms around his sister in a hug. *Adorable.* "Hi, Teags. Guess you must've missed me, huh?"

"Even though you're like half an hour away, it's too far. Of course, I miss you, dummy." Her eyes shift to mine. "You must be Olivia. I'm Teagen. It's nice to meet you."

"You too," I say before she pulls me into a hug.

"Teags, let us get in the door first, okay?" Tristan tells her as he pulls my jacket down my shoulders and puts it in the closet for me.

"Sorry. I'm just excited." Her eyes bear into mine, and she smiles. "You're prettier than he mentioned. You and your sister look a lot alike, too."

"Teags..." Tristan warns her.

"Sorry. No fangirling, I know."

"It's okay. I'll do anything to bring up my sister most of the time."

"Can I just say that I'm so glad that you're here? It sucks being around all these idiot boys all the time."

I stifle a laugh at her admission. *She's bold.* I think I like her already. "I'm glad to be here."

"Tristan? Is that you?"

"Yeah, Mom, it's me and Liv."

"Ah, Olivia! Get her in here!" I laugh when she says that, and I can tell by her voice that she's probably one of the sweetest people I'll ever meet. She just has the type of voice that you feel safe with, and I can't explain why.

"Mom's been cooking and cleaning all day. Saying she's excited would be the understatement of the century. I'm Theo, Tristan's favorite brother. It's nice to meet you, Olivia. Welcome to the chaos."

"Thank you, and I'm quite enjoying it already." I smile.

"King Tristan is home," Tobias says as he punches his brother in the shoulder. "It's good to see you, dumbass."

Tristan pulls his brother in for a hug. "You too, idiot." Tristan looks over at me. "This is Tobias."

I hold my hand out to shake his, but instead, he grabs it and presses a kiss to my hand. "I'm Tobias, the nice one."

"Easy, kid. Just because we're brothers doesn't mean I won't punch you if you touch my girl like that again." Tristan punches his brother in the shoulder before walking toward what I can assume is where his mom is.

"He's territorial over you," Tobias states.

"He is. But something tells me you knew that's how he would react," I say to him, and he raises his eyebrows at me.

"I was just seeing something. He never used to care about much when we were kids. I used to steal all his shit to see if I could get a rise out of him, but nothing ever worked." Tobias smiles at me. "Until you."

"You guys seem close. It's how I am with my sister."

"Is your sister cute?"

I roll my eyes. "Yes, but before you go down that road, forget it. She's in a relationship with her job."

"Gotcha. Well, if you need anything while you're here, ask any of us. It's nice to have you here, Livvy." As he walks back to where his siblings are, he shoots me a smile that lights up the entire room, as if it wasn't already bright enough to begin with. *They're all so adorable.* I walk forward into the main living area and notice that the fireplace is going, and everything looks so cozy. There's a mix of browns, beige, white, and orange going on between the couch, loveseat, and curtains. It *feels* like Thanksgiving here, and I find myself loving the vibe of this room.

"Livvy, come try this." Tristan's voice interrupts my thoughts as I look up at the kitchen and see him helping his mom with something.

"She's not allowed to lift a finger, and neither are you." Tristan's mom says as she walks down the steps and pulls me into a hug before I can properly introduce myself. "It's so nice to meet the girl who Tristan won't shut up about."

"Oh, won't shut up about, huh?" I say as I lock eyes with him, a smile gracing his features.

"My name is Tabitha. Welcome to Tristan's childhood home that he's probably told you nothing about."

I laugh out loud at that because he didn't tell me much. "Mom, really?"

"It's my job to embarrass you, you know that. I hope you're hungry, Olivia."

Tobias enters the kitchen and pops something into his mouth. "Mom has cooked enough food for a small village, and trust me when I say that nothing will ever beat Mom's cooking. It's the best, Olivia. I say that completely unbiased, of course."

"Can I start telling embarrassing stories about Tristan, or is that not allowed?" Teagen asks as she comes to stand next to me and her mom.

"That's for later, Teags. I'm going to take Liv on a tour first." Tristan comes over to where I'm standing and grabs my hand. "No offense, but we can be a lot all at once, so since Mom banned me from helping, Olivia and I will be taking a tour of the house."

"Are you sure you want to do it? You can be kind of boring, Tris..." Theo jokes, and Tobias high-fives him for that comment.

"Eat a dick, Theo."

"Boys, what did I tell you?"

The three of them look at each other. "No fighting in front of guests." And before Tristan pulls me away, I hear them all apologize to their mom. *I feel like I just walked into an alternate universe.* I can feel how close they all are after being here for about half an hour. *Is this what normal families are like?*

"My family is far from normal, but yeah, I guess in the traditional sense."

"I didn't realize I said that out loud," I say to him as he steals a quick kiss from my cheek. "Sorry."

"Nothing to apologize for, Liv. Now, this is my mom's office and the place that was my designated hiding spot for hide and seek as kids. It's a boring room, so we'll move on." He takes me back to the entryway and to another door that I must've walked right past when I came in. "To the right is the bathroom, but to the left is the basement stairs." He flicks the light on and leads me down the stairs, his hand still in mine.

"Oh, wow." It's beautiful down here. It's fully finished, and there's a pool table, dart board, and some basketball contraption against one corner. There are a few weight sets and equipment in the right corner. As I look past the stairs, I notice the basement continues to what looks like some sort of storage area with a bunch of boxes all around.

"That part of the basement used to be my dad's area. Mom never cleaned it out, and I never wanted to, so it just sits there."

I walk into it and see all sorts of baseball memorabilia all around. A few signed baseballs sit in glass boxes on a stand, and a bunch of trophies line the walls.

"Your dad really loved baseball."

"About as much as he loved us. He always told me that baseball was third on his list of things he loved most in the world. My mom was first, me and my siblings were second, and baseball was third."

"What was on the rest of the list?" I ask, seeing him lean against the frame of the room, with his hands stuffed into his jeans.

"That was the whole list." Tristan's jaw tenses, and I can tell he's trying not to get too emotional about all this. *How long has it been since he's been down here?*

"That's sweet," I say, going over to him and putting my arms around him. "Can I see your room?" I want to take his mind off of all the emotions he's feeling because today is a day to be thankful, not sad. When he grabs my hand and pulls me up the stairs, I know I succeeded. We round the corner, and he takes me upstairs to the last room at the end of the hallway.

"Here we are. My room isn't that special, but I still have some shit from high school all over the place." His room is painted light gray, and his bed sits against the wall with a black comforter on it. It's about as simple as his room in his apartment, but this one has more of *him* in it. More of what makes him who he is—a personal touch, I guess. Photos of his siblings and who I assume is his dad fill the frames on his desk.

I smile as I take in all the posters around his walls and how neat it is. *I guess some things never change.* "Care to explain why you have every single *Paranormal Activity* poster up?"

He laughs at my question. "Nope. They will always be my favorite movies, and I'm not ashamed to admit that."

"Understood," I say as I drag my finger across his dresser with all his baseball trophies on it. There's a bunch here, from MVP to simple team awards like the ones I saw in the basement. "It's adorable to see you interact with your family. I can tell how close you all are."

"It's nice being home with them. I miss them all, especially my mom."

I can tell he and his mom are close, and it's making emotions climb up my throat. I've never had any type of relationship with either of my parents, and seeing Tristan with his mom makes me happy for him. But, it also makes me yearn for something I could never have—a childhood growing up with my parents caring about me. "What was it like growing up here?"

He takes a deep breath as he sits at the edge of his bed. The sleeves of his henley are now pulled up, and his arms are on display, causing my mouth to water. *Livvy, calm the fuck down. They're just arms.* He pats his leg, signaling me to sit on his lap, so I do, and he wraps one of his arms around me so I don't fall.

"It was a typical childhood, I guess. Lots of laughs, even after my dad died. My dad is the one I got my love of baseball from. Me and my siblings used to play catch after dinner during the summer. He taught us all how to swing, how to throw, and we used to practice sliding when it rained.

We'd get all muddy, and my mom would be furious when we would all come inside and make a mess, but she kept letting us do it, anyway." He smiles at the memory that popped into his head just now. "My mom always wanted us to keep smiling, laughing, and playing, even through our grief as kids. None of us knew what it was like to grieve at that young of an age, and my mom always put on a brave face. I took it upon myself to step up and help because I knew my dad would want me to, and I didn't want my mom to do it all on her own. I helped out anywhere I could."

"You were eleven, right?"

"Yeah. It was hard, don't get me wrong, but I was happy to help take some responsibility, even though my mom pushed back anytime she could. She became both parents for us, and I don't know how she kept us and herself afloat after that. I didn't want to pick up a baseball after he died, but one day, she came home from work early when it was raining and took all of us outside to play in the mud. It felt like I was falling in love with the sport all over again, especially since Dad was gone. I didn't want to continue, but my mom changed my mind."

I have to hold back a few tears because even though Tristan had it rough growing up without his dad, he still smiled, and was able to be a kid despite him wanting to help raise his siblings. "That sounds...nice. I remember moments like that with my sister growing up, but not as prevalent. When she started to gain more followers, everything changed in my house."

"What do you mean?" Tristan asks me as one of his hands traces my thigh where I sit.

"My parents were always busy with work and stuff that we barely saw them, except for meals. They weren't there when Bree and I were kids, and it was fine for the most part, I guess. I don't know how to describe it, but I can't really remember most of my childhood. I only get flashes of the good parts that Bree and I shared."

"Oh."

"Yeah, but then my sister blew up online, and suddenly my parents were interested. They put all of their attention on her, and I faded into the background. Most days, they forgot I existed. I remember trying to do anything that I could to get their attention, but none of it worked. I'd set the table every night, and wash dishes until they were spotless and they'd say nothing. I even got first place in a short story contest when I was in high school, and they didn't even glance in my direction when I mentioned it to them. I was never the favorite, but Bree always felt smothered, so it was a double-edged sword."

"I'm sorry, Liv."

"It's okay. I'm thankful for it in the long run because Bree and I have always been close. At first, we bonded over how we hated how our parents were parenting us, but now I can't imagine not being as close as we are."

"Well, you're *my* favorite, Livvy. You'll always be my favorite person on the planet."

My eyes start to mist, and I blink away the tears, but one falls. "You're my favorite, too, Tristan." I lean in and press a kiss to his lips before the door opens suddenly, and I turn my head into his neck.

"Mom says dinner's almost ready." Teagen says as she waltzes into his room. "I didn't mean to interrupt."

"It's okay, Teags. We'll be right down." The door shuts softly behind her, and both Tristan and I start laughing.

"I bet it's not the first time someone has caught you in here with a girl, is it?"

"Actually, it is. I've never had a girl in here before."

"What?"

"You know I don't like other people in my space, Livvy. That's been my deal ever since high school."

"Then why am I in here?" I ask, wondering why the hell he's changed all his rules for me.

"Because you're not just *people* to me, Liv."

"Now, you all know the drill. I want to hear one thing you're thankful for this year. Teagen, you're first since you're the youngest." Tristan's mom—Tabitha—says, and I swear my face is going to hurt from smiling so much. Before dinner, Tristan's siblings told me a thousand different stories about him as a kid, and all of them made me laugh so hard that my stomach hurt. Needless to say, Tristan was a rowdy kid, and part of me wishes I could have known him back then.

The table is stacked with all the appropriate Thanksgiving foods—turkey, stuffing, baked potatoes, cranberry sauce, mashed potatoes, and gravy. It all smells amazing, and my mouth is watering already.

"Okay, I'd have to say that I'm thankful for books, so I can leave reality when shit gets tough."

"Language, Teags!" Tabitha yells at her.

"That's a great answer," I say to her as I raise my fist for her to bump. That answer is something both my sister and I would say. Sometimes, I prefer books to people, and that will probably never change.

"I'm most thankful for finally being able to watch college hockey. I hated bootlegging it, so thanks, Mom." Theo throws a big smile towards his mom.

"I, for one, am thankful for our cabin. I like leaving the loud big city for the quiet mountains. It's a nice reset on life." Tobias smiles softly, and I find myself wondering what that looks like.

It's my turn since Tristan is older than me by a few months, and I don't even have to think about what I'm going to say. "I'm thankful to be surrounded by you all for Thanksgiving. I've never had this type of holiday before, and now that I've experienced it, I never want it to end, so thank you for having me here. I appreciate it more than you'll ever know." Tabitha reaches over and grabs my hand while I feel Tristan squeeze my thigh under the table.

"We're so glad you're here, Olivia," His mom says to me. "Tristan, you're up."

"That's easy. I'm thankful for spilling my six-dollar latte on a cute girl and forcing her to take my hoodie."

My cheeks heat as he says that, and I can feel my smile bursting off of my face. *He's thankful most for me?* God, I'm going to burst into tears at this table if more shit like this keeps happening tonight. Being surrounded by Tristan's family and hearing all about how he grew up is making me feel like I've been missing out on this beautiful thing. I feel like I'm finally a part of a real family, and it's only the first time I've been here.

"You two are adorable," Tobias says, and I can't tell if he's making fun of us or being genuine, but the smile on his face says genuine.

"You'll have that someday, Tobias. Then you'll realize how *adorable* it is. I can't wait for that day," Tristan tells his little brother.

"I'm also thankful for our new addition this Thanksgiving. It's been way too long since we've had a newcomer, so thank you, Olivia."

"There's no need to thank me. You raised a wonderful son," I say as I look over at Tristan and smile.

"Can we eat now?" Theo asks, and we all laugh as we dig into the food and trade stories about anything and everything in between.

Best Thanksgiving ever.

"DID YOU HAVE FUN?" Tristan asks me as he takes me back home.

"The most fun I've ever had on Thanksgiving." He squeezes my thigh a few times as if he's glad. I've never seen Tristan smile as much as I did when he was with his family. It was nice to see that side of him. I've enjoyed peeling back all the layers that he hides from the rest of the world. It's like some parts of him are just for me, and I like that. There are definitely some parts of me that only he sees, and I want to keep it that way.

"Good. It makes me happy that you got along with them so well."

"Me too. All my nerves have disappeared, and now I feel all fuzzy inside. Your family is the best, Tristan. I'm glad I could finally meet them."

"Me too."

Tristan keeps driving, his hand on my thigh the entire time as we let the music from my playlist fill the car on the way home. Tristan got his car fixed after the accident, and it's like it never happened.

I glance over at Tristan, and everything disappears for a moment. I can't hear my music playing or any other sounds because he fills up all of my senses when I'm around him. I carefully study his features as the light filters through the car every few seconds. Those glimpses of his face in the light make me smile. *He's beautiful.* Inside and out. I don't know anybody else who could make me feel like the only girl in the world like I'm worth everything that I never had.

Before Tristan, I never had family dinners or holiday meals surrounded by people who cared about me. Before him, I never knew I could have half of the emotions that I do now.

I don't ever want to go back to who I was before. I want to feel everything that he makes me feel. I want to experience all of these new things and laugh until my ribs hurt alongside him.

I don't know why I'm having all of these realizations right now in his car, but it's taken me this long to realize it—that even in the silence,

I want him. I'm falling even harder than before, even harder than I thought was ever possible, and I'm not scared. I feel whole, and Tristan is the piece that completes me.

Chapter Nineteen

— YOU, LOVE (INTERLUDE) BY LIZZY MCALPINE

My girl,

Merry Christmas! If you're wondering how this got to you so quickly, it's because I dropped it in your mailbox last night after you fell asleep. Mail doesn't normally get delivered on Christmas, so I figured, as a little surprise, I'd drop this off.

I hope you're having a great day so far, even though you're home with your parents. I know Bree is with you because my sister watched her video, and I saw you walk around in the background a few times. (Yes, I did eavesdrop on my little sister while she was watching your sister's video. Don't judge. I'll take any glimpse of you that I can get, Livs.)

Anyway, I'm hoping that you'll accept my invitation to come to a New Year party that my

brother is throwing at the house. It's probably
going to be mostly high-schoolers, so we'll be
considered old, but I'd do anything to kiss you
at midnight and ring in the new year with you.
Just let me know if that's something you're
interested in.

I hope you got everything you wanted this
Christmas. I didn't, but that's only because
you weren't wrapped underneath the tree when
I came down this morning.

I'll see you soon, pretty girl.

Yours,
Tristan

TRISTAN,

I, too, didn't get what I wanted since you
apparently came by my house and didn't inform
me about that. You'll be paying for that sooner
or later.

Merry Christmas! And yes, today has been
alright since Bree is here. I'm so glad to see
her. We've been looking over some houses and
places that she can check out at some point.
It would be nice to have her here and not at my
parents' house anymore. I understand her need
to get the hell out from under this roof. Even

after being here for a few weeks has already felt…weird. I feel like I don't exist in this house sometimes. Does that even make sense? Whatever.

I was glad to get this letter from you. I missed hearing your voice in my head as I read them. I'd be glad to come to you for the new year. You're not too far from me, but I miss you.

Bree is currently trying to convince me to do a haul with her, but I told her for the tenth time that I do not want to be on the internet.

I miss you, even though you're so close. I can't wait to get back to school. I don't sleep well when you're not with me—my bed feels like a rock.

I look forward to our next correspondence, sir. It was good to hear from you in true Tristan and Livvy fashion.

I'm excited to celebrate your birthday in January. I already have the perfect gift in mind…

Until next time, my love.

Yours always,
Livs

Chapter Twenty

— BODY TALKS BY THE STRUTS

SITTING IN MY KITCHEN and watching my beautiful girlfriend bake cookies is something I would never consider a hobby.

Until now, at least.

Livvy has been spending a lot of time over at my place lately, and since she feels bad for intruding all the time—which she doesn't, the guys and I love having her around—she's been baking a ton of things. Brownies, cookies, and I think she even made pie once that I didn't get to have because they ate it all before I could.

I tell her all the time that she doesn't need to do this, but she won't quit. Hell, I'm not complaining. Livvy is a great baker.

Dom practically moaning breaks my thoughts. "What the fuck kind of noise was that?"

"What? It tastes good!" He smiles at me. *Fucker.* Dom won't stop flirting with Livvy, and I know he does it to get a rise out of me, but it's become rather infuriating over the past few weeks. I think it's because this is uncharted territory for us—I'm the only one in a relationship at the moment. Normally, at least two of us—Harry and Ethan—have partners at the same time, but senior year has not been kind to my friends in that department.

Sucks for them, though. I'm happy as fuck with my girl, and it'll stay that way.

"I think I'm going to miss Livvy more than you while you're at spring training, Tristan. Her cookies are the fucking best." Ethan tells me, and I honestly can't blame him.

"Aww, you guys are too nice to me," Livvy says from the kitchen.

"When do you guys leave?" Dom asks.

"Third week of February."

"Oh shit, so in two weeks. Livvy, if you want to come over while they're gone, I'm sure Tristan will be okay with—" Dom's sentence is cut off by me throwing a binder at him.

"I don't want your creepy ass around my fucking girlfriend, especially since you won't stop flirting with her."

"Baby, he's just being nice," Liv says.

"Yeah, *baby*, I'm just being nice."

"He's never that nice," I say as Livvy comes over to me with a cookie in her hand.

"Eat this, and you'll stop being grumpy." I take a bite, and these cinnamon things are fucking good.

"He's just sad that he won't see you for three weeks, Liv. He'll deny it all he wants but—"

I cut off Harry. "I'm not denying shit. Yeah, I'll fucking miss my girlfriend while I'm away." I love spring training. It's fun to get together with a bunch of other Division two teams and play, but I've never had someone to miss before, and now I do.

It's got its pros and cons, but not seeing Livvy's fucking face for three weeks? I think I'd rather die or something. "Okay, the cookies are done, but let them cool because I don't know how hot they're going to be."

"Thanks, Livvy," Harry says as he swipes a few from the rack.

"You're the best, Liv," Ethan says.

"If I knew getting a girlfriend had perks like this, I would've gotten one a while ago," Dom says, and the rest of us laugh. "What?"

"Yeah, because that's why you don't have a girlfriend. Not because of all the other red flags that you give off."

"Well, you're right about one thing: I *am* a giver..." Ethan throws a towel at Dom, and I take in the state of my apartment. My girlfriend is hanging out with my three idiot friends, and she looks as happy as can be as she watches them horse around. I'm living the fucking dream.

"Okay, I'm going to clean up. I think I'll start with—" I don't give her time to finish before I throw her over my shoulder and head toward my room.

"The boys will clean up for you, baby. Since I won't see you for three weeks, I want you all to myself as much as I can."

"But, the mess—"

"We got it," I hear my friends say from behind me. *Good.* Livvy keeps making them shit, so they should clean it for once. I set Liv on my bed, and I'm so glad that we finally have a moment alone together. It's been weeks of practice, the adjustment to our final semester, and closing shifts together, but I've barely seen her besides when she sleeps in my bed or me in hers.

"Hi." I smile at her.

She smiles back. "Hi, Tristan."

"What has my beautiful girlfriend been up to lately? I feel like I've barely seen you."

Liv laughs at that. "Tristan, I see you all the time."

"Yeah, I guess, but around other people. How's the book coming?" I ask, noting a conversation we had the other day about Livvy getting her writing kickback.

"It's nothing, as of right now." Her eyes grow sadder. "I'm scared that when it turns into a real thing that it won't make sense, or it'll be a big jumbled mess." She hops off of my bed and starts pacing around my room. My body is off the edge of my bed, and I swear she looks adorable when she does this. One thing I've learned about Livvy in the past few months is that when her brain is a mess, she paces. My girlfriend is a pacer. I think it helps her body have something to do when her head is too loud. *There are other ways I could help her, though...*

"You never know until you try, Liv. You know your characters, and you know the story. Just let it come to life. I know it'll be amazing."

"Yeah, but where do I start? How do I get it to be something other than the scattered flashcards in my desk drawer?"

"Liv, it doesn't have to be anything, if you don't want it to be. Just write and get it all out. It only has to make sense to you, but I think you should go for it. Especially if it's taking up a lot of space in your mind as you say it is."

"But what if it's not good enough? What if I'm not good enough? God, my head hurts."

I grab her from where she's pacing and move her in between my legs. I put my hands on her temples and start to massage her head like I always do when Livvy has a migraine flare-up. I learned over break that she often gets migraines when her head gets too full—with anxiety, stress, schoolwork, her own expectations, or, more recently, the book she wants to write but is too afraid to. "Is this helping, baby?"

"A little bit."

I lift her off of her feet and set her down on my bed. "Don't move," I tell her as I head into the kitchen. Dom, Ethan, and Harry are still cleaning up. Dom is on dish duty, Ethan is drying, and Harry appears to be supervising.

"Need a condom?" Dom asks me, and Ethan hits him for me.

"Dom, shut the fuck up," I say as I grab Livvy's extra migraine ice pack from the freezer that she leaves at my place and some Advil before heading back to my room. "Here, Liv. Put this on and lay down."

Before she can put it on, I do it for her, wanting to help in any way that I can when an idea strikes my mind. "So, tell me all about this book you want to write. What ideas are in that pretty mind of yours?" She slouches against my headboard, the ice pack over her eyes, before she tries to move it. "Leave it there and tell me about it, okay?"

"There's this character that's been in my mind for a while, and she's the complete opposite of me."

"Is it a romance novel? Or more toward fiction?" I ask her as I trail my finger down her arm, just gentle enough to see goosebumps spread over her skin.

"Uh, it's mostly romance, I guess." I move closer to her and keep repeating the motion up and down her arm and even trail down her legs. She shivers as she tries to continue. "She's feeling lost, so she cuts all ties and moves to a small town for a fresh start."

"And then what happens?" I whisper against her neck as her body erupts in goosebumps again. *That's it, baby.*

"She gets a local job and falls in love with herself again. She meets a sweet guy who deals with all her quirks. It's mostly her story, but romance is pretty prevalent in it."

"Is there smut?" I ask, wanting to see her cheeks turn red like I know they will.

"There probably will be one or two scenes," she says as I continue kissing her neck before I slide my hand up to her throat and lightly squeeze. She lets out a breathy moan that's so quiet I think I imagined it. "Tristan."

"Yes, Livvy?"

"What are you doing?" she asks me, her voice strained, but her pink cheeks tell me that she's turned on. *Good.* That's what I was going for.

"I'm helping to get rid of your migraine. Do you want me to stop?" I ask her before moving my other hand down toward her pussy.

"No, please..." Her head rolls back, and I slowly press on her clit.

"Tell me what you need, pretty girl. Tell me, and I'll do it."

"Touch me, please. I need you." Her hand reaches out for my shirt, and before she can pull me to her, I slide back, grabbing her legs and pulling them toward the edge of my bed. "Woah."

"Keep the icepack on. If you take it off, I stop. Do you understand?" She nods at me, and I trail my fingers into the waistband of her pants, teasing her until she tells me what I want to hear. "Tell me you understand, Liv."

"I—I understand, Tristan."

With that, I yank her pants and underwear down and throw them to the floor beside me. "Look at you, Liv. All spread open for me."

"Tristan, please—"

"Patience, Liv. You have no idea how much I've dreamed about tasting you, and I'm going to take my fucking time enjoying you, okay?"

"Okay."

"Good, now show me how you've been touching yourself when you think of me. I want to know what makes you feel good, pretty girl."

"Tristan, why can't you just touch me?"

"I'm a visual learner. Now, show me, please." I kneel down so I'm closer as she drags two fingers over her clit, her breath hitching as she does. Then she dips one finger into her pretty little pussy, and I'm a goner. She looks fucking perfect like this. This right now is Livvy at her most vulnerable, and fuck, I can't get enough. I know as soon as I get one taste of her, that I'll be ruined.

I was always hers to ruin, and my God, if I'm not excited to fall to my knees in front of her. Livvy and I have had some intense make out sessions, but I never pressured for more because I knew she'd let me know when she was ready. But now, seeing her like this, I have to tell myself to calm the fuck down. I want this to be as good for her as I know it'll be for me.

One taste of her is all it'll take. I'll be *done.* Ruined. Fucked.

Livvy starts to pump her fingers—she must've added a second one while I was mesmerized—and I lift her legs onto my shoulders. "That's it, Liv. Make yourself come, baby. Get yourself ready for me."

"Tristan, fuck," she breathes, a moan slipping out of her mouth after. *God, that sound is enough to make me fucking explode.* Everything about this girl is perfect.

"Do you want my fingers or my tongue?"

"A—Anything, please, I—" I grab her hand from inside her pussy, and bring her slick fingers to my mouth. She tastes like my fucking undoing, and when I see her eyes watching me lick her off of her fingers, I get annoyed.

"I told you to keep it on, Olivia. Put it back on so I can taste you again. Don't make me starve, pretty girl." Her breath hitches before she pulls the ice pack over her eyes again, and leans back. *Good fucking girl, listening to me.* I lower my mouth to her pussy. I can smell her fucking arousal from here. "Do you want my mouth?"

"Please."

"Beg," I say, and her face twists underneath the ice pack. *God, she's beautiful when she's pissed at me.* "If you want to come, then beg, Olivia."

"I told you before that I don't beg, Tristan." Her voice is straining, and her legs—which are currently on my shoulders—start to squirm.

"Baby, I want to make you feel good, so give me what I want, and we'll both be satisfied."

She's silent for a few seconds until her resolve breaks. "Tristan, I need you, please. Fuck, I need to come. Make me come."

"Good fucking girl," I whisper as I finally fucking taste her properly. I swipe my tongue through her pussy, her legs squirming where they rest on my shoulders. I flatten my tongue against her clit and realize that my girl needs more. With that, I remove my mouth and before she can yell at me to keep going, I thrust two fingers into her pussy, which fucking squeezes my fingers. "Fuck, Livvy, you're so perfect."

"Tristan, harder, please." Her pleas turn into a moan as my mouth lowers and I suck on her clit. She's so fucking loud, and I'm having a hard time being in control. I find myself wanting to say fuck it and bury my cock inside of her right now, but I don't. Only when Livvy wants it will I give it to her, but until then, I'm fine with devouring her in other ways. "Fuck, baby."

"Shut yourself up, Livvy. I don't want any of my friends hearing your moans that belong only to me." I thrust my fingers harder, and I can feel her start to unravel. "Are you gonna come for me?" I peer my eyes up and see her nodding, and before I can say anything else, her legs shake, and she comes all over my fingers and face. *God, what a beautiful fucking sight she is.*

"*Tristan,*" she says as she finishes, and it takes all my strength not to blow inside my fucking pants. Hearing Livvy say my name like that means it belongs to her and only her now. I don't want to hear my name any other fucking way other than moaned from her lips. "Fuck, I'm tired."

"Do you want to go to bed?" I ask as I taste her off of my fingers again. I'm never gonna get enough of her—her mind, her body, her laugh, her taste. *Her.*

"Please?"

"Whatever you want, pretty girl." I don't just mean that for right now. Anything she wants, I'll give it to her. She's given me the greatest thing of all—a reason to stop running away from everything.

"My headache is gone." She blushes as she says that.

"Livvy, the fact that you're acting shy when my mouth was on your pussy five minutes ago is so fucking adorable. And I'm glad your headache is gone. I'll put the ice pack back in the fridge." I grab it off of her head before I press a long kiss to her lips. Her tongue presses against my mouth, and I let her in. All my senses are her, and I think they always will be. She invades every corner of my life, and fuck, I *love* it. "I'll be right back."

"I'll be here," she says before grabbing one of my shirts, throwing my sheets back, and crawling into my bed.

Our bed.

By the time I'm back from the kitchen, she's fast asleep, and I find myself wanting to freeze this moment. If only time worked that way because if given the choice, I'd stay here forever with Liv wrapped in my arms, fast asleep, looking more peaceful than I'd ever seen her.

Chapter Twenty-One

— SINK BY NOAH KAHAN

As I open my door to an empty apartment, I realize that I forgot Parker wasn't going to be home tonight. I sigh before taking the two pints of ice cream that I bought for us to the freezer. *There go my evening plans.*

I clean up our apartment before I go shower, wanting to wash the smell of work off of me. That's the one downside to working with food—you constantly smell like it. Cal and I had a pretty typical shift. It's a Friday night, so it wasn't too busy besides a few people and college kids doing their weekly shopping—like me. My shift ended early, and I stocked up on some necessities for Parker and me, including all the snacks Cass loves to steal when she comes over.

As I get into my room, I notice that part of my drawer is open, and when I go to close it, my flashcards catch my eye. I stare at them for a few seconds, wondering if the itch to write will come, but it doesn't. I shake my head, disappointed in myself, and head for my bathroom.

After my skin-burning shower, I do my skincare routine before settling on my bed with my latest read. It's a romance about a ghostwriter who can *actually* see ghosts, and I'm loving it so far.

About an hour into reading, my phone starts buzzing, and I already know who it is before I see my phone. "Hi, Tristan."

"Hi, pretty girl. I fucking miss you."

"I miss you, too. Only one more week, and you can handcuff us together if you so please."

He's silent for a few seconds. "That's pretty tempting..."

"Tristan, I was kidding!" I laugh. It's been weird ever since he's been away. I didn't think I would miss him as much as he would miss me, but that's not true. It's weird not having him around all the time, and it's even weirder sleeping alone. I thought it would be no problem going back to how I slept before, but it turns out my bed doesn't quite feel right when he's not in it.

Nothing feels quite right without him.

I even sniffed his pillow like an absolute creep the other day because I missed how he smelled. It's so strange how he's become my person after all this time. I didn't think it was possible. I thought I was going to keep floating through life, feeling lost as ever, but Tristan, I've realized, is my tether. His brightness, his smiles, his support, it's all tethered me back to earth.

I ghosted my way through the first three years of college, and now I feel like I missed out on everything else. I was so busy wrapped up in my head that I missed things that were right in front of me. Tristan did that, and I'll forever be thankful that he made me *feel* again after a few straight years of trying not to feel at all. "Livvy, did I lose you?"

"No, sorry. I got wrapped up in my head for a second."

"What are you thinking about?"

"You." I smile as if he can see it. "What are you thinking about?"

"Always you, Liv," he whispers as I get a text. "That was me. The sunset earlier was absolutely beautiful. I wish you could've seen it."

I pull up the photo after placing Tristan on speaker. And when I pull up the photo, I let out a gasp. "Oh my, Tristan. It's stunning."

The sky is filled up with orange, pink, and some yellow as the sun goes down. The top of the sky has some blue hue to it, and all of them together look...otherworldly. I've always loved that the sky could look like a painted canvas when the sun rises and sets, but they'll never look as good to me unless Tristan sees it, too. "I took one earlier after work that I forgot to send you."

I send the photo through and hear muffles of him shifting how he's sitting. "Wow, Liv. It's so pretty."

I took a quick picture of it as I left work, but it was beautiful. The sky looked pink and almost purple in some parts, with the glow of the sun illuminating an orange ring. "Just pretty? I thought it was beautiful."

"Well, I've seen prettier things."

"Okay, then send me a picture of a prettier sunset that you've captured." I hear a shuffle again and note that he's probably scrolling through his sunset album in his photos right now. "Come on, West. Conceding isn't going to tarnish that win streak of yours."

"I don't need to concede because I'm going to win. There. Those are by far the most ethereal things I've ever seen. Those top your sunset by miles, Liv."

I'm about to throw back another quip, when twenty photos come through my phone—and they're all of me. Every. Single. One. "Tristan, that's cheating."

"Nope. You asked to see something prettier than the sunset, and I sent just that."

My eyes fill with tears as I note the pictures he sent. A few of me that I took when I stole his phone while he wasn't paying attention. A few of me in his hoodie. Two from our first date that he took of me while I wasn't looking. One from Halloween after he kissed me for the first time—from when we went back inside. My cheeks are red, and my smile is the widest I've ever seen it. The last one is of both of us, but I don't know who took it. I've never seen it before, but it's of Tristan and

I walking hand in hand toward a building on campus. It looks like I'm laughing, and he's looking at me as if I'm the only thing in the world. "Tristan…"

"You'll always be the most beautiful thing I've seen, sunsets be damned, Liv."

It's then that I think about it for the first time. It's on the tip of my tongue, and I have to stop myself from blurting it out while he's miles away from me. *I love you. I've never loved anyone like I love you. You're the person I think about when I think of the word love.* "I don't know what to say."

"You don't have to say anything, Liv. But it's late, and I should get some sleep before tomorrow. We have an early practice."

"That's a good idea."

"Are you heading to bed soon?"

"I might. I'm not sure yet."

"Well, goodnight, Livs. I'll see you soon."

"See you soon, baby." I smile as I hang up the phone and immediately jump over to my desk, throwing my computer open. *I can do this.*

As I migrate to Microsoft Word, I take the flashcards out and pin them onto my corkboard above my desk. I lay out all the ideas I've had over the past year, and I begin plotting out a book that's lived in my mind for a while.

The first draft just has to get written, Liv. It's not going to be perfect, and for the first time ever, I block out everything else and write.

Chapter Twenty-Two

— GOLD RUSH BY TAYLOR SWIFT

SITTING IN THE STADIUM, I wonder how people do this—play their sport while a giant crowd watches them. I certainly couldn't write with an audience around me, but having to focus on a game like baseball while all these people look at me would scare the shit out of me.

I took tonight off of work to be here to watch one of Tristan's games. Cassie is to my right and currently trying to get a good picture of Bryce to post to her Instagram. She's struggling, and I keep hearing her moaning and groaning about the lighting. I'm about to interrupt her when my phone buzzes.

Bree: Hey, what are you doing right now? Can you talk?

Livvy: I'm at Tristan's game, but what's up? I'll always make time for you.

Bree: Oh, then never mind.

Livvy: Is everything okay?

Bree: Yeah, it's fine. Having a bit of a situation, that's all, but don't worry, it's not that important.

Livvy: Are you sure?

Bree: Yeah. 100%. Enjoy his game! Go Summit! Who are they playing?

Livvy: Grand Mountain, or something.

Bree: Oh, cool. I'm sending winning vibes from here!

Livvy: I'll call you tomorrow?

Bree: Sounds good! Love you.

Livvy: Love you too!

That was weird. My sister has been acting off lately, but I haven't pressed because I assumed it was burnout, but I make a mental note to ask about it later.

"Did he give you another hoodie?" Cassie asks me, grabbing my sleeve and looking at the back of it.

"I stole this one from his closet the last time I was at his place. It's comfy, and I knew I was going to be watching him play a lot."

Cassie's smile graces her face instantly. "You guys are too cute. I'm also glad that now I have someone to talk to while we watch our boys. It's boring watching one of these by yourself."

"I bet," I tell her as the game starts, and I see Tristan run out to center with two of his teammates—Harry included because he plays left field. I joked with Tristan that I was going to paint Harry's number on my face, but he told me that if I had his number on my body, there would be consequences.

I *almost* showed up with Harry's number on my face, just to see what he would do, but I didn't want to tamper with his focus.

Bryce plays third, and he's currently throwing back to the first basemen. It's this thing they do while the pitcher warms up, or so Tristan told me. Tristan stands in the outfield and is talking to the other two players before his eyes find mine, and a smile falls over his face. He pretends to throw something at me, and I pretend to catch it.

"That was so cute, I might cry," Cassie tells me, faking some sniffles next to me.

"Oh, hush."

"Never, Livvy. That man has it bad for you, and I, for one, have loved seeing this relationship blossom from the sidelines."

I roll my eyes at her before turning my attention back to the game. The first batter is up, but my attention is locked on Tristan in the outfield. His pale gray uniform molds to his body and the purple lettering on it really pops. Light gray, purple, and black are our school colors. The combination looks good on the uniforms, but I'm far too focused on the way Tristan commands the outfield while he's out there. *I never thought a uniform could look that sexy.* I'm about five seconds away from drooling over his arms and all those muscles on display.

Or what those arms and muscles do to me a few times a week... No. I need to chill out. I can't get turned on over a baseball game—that's ridiculous.

Something happens and the other team now has two people on base. I must've been too busy fantasizing to notice what happened. I'm not a big sports girl, but I will say that I love the contrast of the colors on the field. The other team—Grand Mountain—has dark green uniforms, and I'm not as confused as I thought I would be. The next guy comes up, and on the first pitch, the ball goes high up into the air. *I thought Tristan said you're not supposed to hit the first one?* Some people have already started cheering—probably because it looks like it might be a home run—but I see Tristan tracking the ball in the air. He's so focused, and before I know it, he jumps up on the wall and catches it. He throws it to another member of his team, and our section cheers. "What was that?"

"He robbed that guy's home run!"

I start clapping, and watch as Tristan points at me from the outfield. *That's my man.* I can't help the smile that bursts off of my face. I knew he was good because you have to be at a certain level to play college sports, but damn, he's *good.* He told me yesterday that he was worried about the game today, but from what I can see, all those nerves have seemed to disappear.

Tristan has been working himself to the bone during our last semester. On top of baseball and the regular school load, he's still working part time, and now he's been doing virtual interviews with a few job prospects already. I'm super proud of him, but I can tell he's getting burned out, and I don't know how to help him.

I also don't know how to help myself. When I look around at my own life, I feel so far behind everyone else. I have no job interviews lined up, my resume is lacking in about every way, and I still have no concrete plan for when college is done.

I keep telling myself that I'll be fine, but everything feels so out of my control, and I wish I knew what the next few months would look like. I hate feeling like this—lost, with no clear path forward. I know I'm young, but I thought by the time I graduated everything would magically fall into place.

It hasn't, and I don't know how to make it that way. I've tried to talk to Tristan and my friends about it, but they tell me not to worry—which is hard because how can I not? Tristan still reiterates how he wants to get the hell out of here in May, and I don't know where that will leave us if I get a job in another state or something else.

I feel so uncertain about everything at the moment, and I hate that I have all these questions and no answers.

This is not the time to think about this, Liv. Right. Let's save the breakdown over my future until after Tristan is done playing. Summit is now up to bat, and Tristan isn't on the batting roster today, so he gets a break in between innings. I see him and Bryce peek their heads out of the dugout and point in our direction. It looks like Tristan is showing Bryce where we are, and he throws a wave to Cassie.

"God, they're so fucking hot. Those uniforms really are nice to look at." Cassie giggles, and I shake my head in agreement.

"Agreed. I wish Tristan were allowed to wear his rings because those make my knees weak, and that combination could be lethal..." I joke with her.

"Okay, but imagine the rings and some tattoos. Bryce has a few, and I swear an inked man is somehow hotter than a normal one." Cassie fans herself as if she's getting warm.

"Tristan told me that he doesn't like tattoos, at least not on himself."

"Did he say why?"

"He doesn't want anything permanent on his body. I joke that he's scared of needles, but he hates when I say that."

After a few more innings pass, Summit is up 6-2 over Grand Mountain. It's been an exciting game, and I find myself hooked on watching it. It's mostly because I like watching Tristan do his thing in the outfield, but even when we're hitting, I enjoy myself. Baseball usually goes seven innings—according to Tristan—and we're in the bottom of the fifth right now. Each inning has a bottom and a top—which I laughed at because I thought it was funny at first—and Tristan explained that each inning has two halves. We're in the second half of the fifth inning—also known as the bottom of the inning. Summit is currently batting, and as I'm watching the game, I feel something hit my head from behind.

"What was that?" Cassie asks me, popping some candy in her mouth.

I bend down, grab the balled-up piece of paper that hit me, and look around, wondering where it came from. When I lock eyes with Maddie—a girl Tristan used to hook up with—she smiles and waves at me. *That's weird.*

"Just some paper, I think."

Cassie looks to where Maddie is sitting, and her eyes narrow. "Did she throw that at you?"

"I don't know. Let's watch the game. She's not worth our attention." A few more pitches get thrown before I feel something else hit me in the head. I ignore it, but then I hear the murmurs behind me.

"I still don't understand why he's with her."

"She's not even that cute. I don't understand what he sees in her."

"You're much hotter than her, Mads. He fumbled the bag, losing you."

"She's just your replacement. Tristan will come crawling back after he's done with her."

I blink away the tears that are threatening to come up from all the things I'm hearing. I might have those insecurities sometimes, but hearing them out loud makes them ten times worse. It feels like my thoughts are manifesting in the form of mean girls. "Liv? Are you okay?"

"I'm fine," I say, but I can tell she doesn't believe me because she wraps an arm around me like a shield. "Let's just focus on the game, okay?"

"Okay." Cassie squeezes my shoulder, and I smile at her, trying to seem okay when I don't feel it.

"What's the secret, Olivia? Do you have something on Tristan? Is that why he's with you? It can't be because of your looks." Maddie is now directing her insults at me, and I do all I can to ignore her and not let her see she's affecting me. "There's no way he's pussy whipped for you as much as he was for me. Does he still do that thing with his tongue? I always *loved* when he did that to me."

"Maddie, shut the hell up and crawl back to whatever trash can you came from. We're here to watch baseball and support our boyfriends. Tristan being Olivia's. It's funny how you never got to call him that, huh?" Cassie snipes back at her, and I giggle into her shoulder when she turns back around.

"Thank you, Cass."

"Nobody talks about my friends like that right in front of me. God, she's such a bitch." I'm about to agree with her when Maddie interrupts me.

"He always liked when I wore his jersey when we fucked. Have you two done that, or was that just for Tristan and I?" My eyes mist again, because hearing that Tristan had some sort of tradition with this she-devil is making me upset. *Why is she doing this?*

"I'm gonna go grab some water, Cass."

"Do you want me to go with you?" she asks, and I shake my head before I book it from our seats. I find the nearest bathroom and quickly wash my hands, as if I can scrub off all the insults that she threw at me. I've been secure in my relationship with Tristan, and I knew that this could come with the territory. But hearing Maddie throw some of the things Tristan and I have done in my face hurts like a bitch.

Tristan's one of the most popular guys at Summit. Practically anywhere on campus we go, someone's always saying hi to him or patting him on the back about something or other. I always felt proud of him, especially when he would introduce me as his girlfriend to all those people, but now I feel insecure.

I don't like the fact that all of these people think they know him. I don't like the fact that he's the most beautiful person I've ever seen. It makes me jealous—the fact that other people get to look at him and all of his perfect features—and I've never been one for jealousy. I hate what that emotion does to me, but I can't help it.

If given the chance, most girls on campus would give anything to brush one of his hands or run a hand through his hair, and that makes me want to cry. I've never had to compete before, and I constantly feel like I'm competing with every other girl on campus for Tristan.

But he's yours, Livvy. I know that. I know that down to my bones, but just thinking about some girls imagining how he is in bed, even though he's with me, angers me. I shake off all these thoughts before I drive myself crazy, and as I exit the bathroom, I run into someone standing directly outside of the door. "Sorry."

"Whatever." Maddie says as she flips her hair.

"Do we have a problem? Because last time I checked, I've never said two words to you."

"How did you do it? How did you lock a man like Tristan down? I tried for months, and he barely looked in my direction."

"Huh, let's see, I wasn't a bitch, and I actually care about him. Maybe try that next time instead of jumping into bed with someone just to brag about it. Best of luck!" I smile as I decide to head back to my place and not watch the game, feeling proud that I stood up for myself but equally off-kilter about this entire afternoon.

— MARGARET BY LANA DEL REY FT. BLEACHERS

WHEN I GET TO the outfield after we scored two more runs and look into the stands, Livvy is nowhere to be found. *Where did she go?* I shake off all the bad thoughts that are in my head—she's in pain, hurt, or in trouble—and focus back on the game. Throughout the remaining innings, I steal glances at Livvy's spot and still only see Cassie sitting there. She doesn't look nervous or scared, so I assume that everything's fine. By the time we reached the last inning, Livvy still hadn't come back. The team lines up at the plate so we can high-five the other team on a good game. I'm last in line, so I stop to talk to one of my friends who plays for Grand Mountain. "Hey, Nick. Nice pitching today. If I were hitting, you probably would've gotten me, man."

"You bet your ass I would've gotten you, West. You guys look good. Are you dreaming of the post-season yet?"

"Not quite, but you never know. It was good to see you on the field again." He smiles at me as he claps my hand, and we bring it in. Nick and I have gone to a few baseball camps together around here. He used to live up here until he moved to Virginia. "Does it feel weird being back up here?"

"It's like coming home, Tristan. I've missed this place. Grand Mountain's great, but nothing compares to Pennsylvania. Especially since I get to see your ugly ass face on the field again."

"I'm just on a different side now, bro. Best of luck on your season."

"You too," he says as I rush to the dugout to grab my shit and hopefully find where Livvy went. Coach tells us to be at practice early tomorrow so we can watch over some game footage of our win, and we all agree before he dismisses us. *Thank fuck.* I miss my girl, and the weird feeling I have in the pit of my stomach is unsettling me. When we get out of the dugout, I only see Cassie standing by herself. My Livvy is nowhere to be found.

"Good win, you guys!" Cassie says as Bryce spins her around.

"Where's Livvy?" Cassie's face falls as she looks at me. "Why did you make that face?"

"She went back to her apartment. She told me she didn't feel good, but..."

"Cassie, did something happen? Is she okay? Fuck, I have to go—" I say, but she stops me from leaving.

"Maddie was saying a bunch of shit to Livvy, around Livvy, and about you. She went to get some water, but she texted me saying that she was leaving and to tell you that she's at her place."

Fuck. Why the hell was Maddie running her fucking mouth here? "What did Maddie say?"

"A bunch of shit. I know Liv probably tried not to let it get to her, but Maddie just wouldn't stop. I yelled at her because she was being a bitch, but that didn't stop her."

"I have to go. Good game, Bryce. I'll see you guys later." I don't stop to hear what they say because I'm only focused on one thing—getting to my beautiful girlfriend's place to show her how much I adore her.

I DON'T BOTHER KNOCKING on her door. Rather, I burst into her apartment. I stopped at my place for a quick shower and change, and then I ran over here. It's not far—only a five-minute walk—but I need to see Livvy. I need to know what she's feeling, and I need to tell her that she's the only person I have eyes for, and it'll always stay that way. I don't know what she's thinking or what exactly happened, but anytime Maddie's involved, shit gets ugly.

I'm practically kicking myself for ever touching that girl. What the hell was I thinking? "Livvy, baby, where are you? Cassie told me what happened at the game."

I hear her door slowly open, and she walks into her living room, still wearing my hoodie that she wore to the game, her eyes puffy. *Fuck, she was crying.* "Hi."

I rush her and fall to my knees. "What's wrong, pretty girl? Tell me what happened," I say as I wipe a stray tear from her eye. *Fuck, this is destroying me.*

"Cassie told you what happened?"

I nod. "Yes, but I want to hear it from you. What the fuck did Maddie say to you?" Before I think she won't say anything, her mouth opens, and out comes all the shit Maddie said to her. Apparently, Livvy told her off before she left. *That's my fucking girl.* "Are you okay?"

"Yeah, I think so. All the shit she said just cut too deep, you know?"

"I know, Liv, but you know that it's all false, right?"

"I know, but it still hurt." She sniffles, and I get off my knees, pick her up, and carry her to her room. She buries her face in my shoulder, and every time I feel her breathe, a part of me dies inside. It kills me that she feels like this right now, and I can't do anything to solve it. *Besides warn Maddie that if she pulls something like this again, I won't be so fucking nice.* "Why me?"

"What?" I say as I set her on top of her bed. She lets her legs dangle off of it, and I stand in between them.

"You could have anybody you want, Tristan. Why did you pick me?"

"Livvy, baby, you're not just anybody to me. So get that thought out of your mind right now. It kills me that you think of yourself like that."

"Well then, what am I to you? Because some days I'm afraid that you're going to wake up and realize there are way better options out there." I see a few tears fall, and I wipe them away as I cup both of my hands around her cheeks. "I'm nobody, Tristan, and you're somebody."

"Livvy, I'll say this as many times as you need to hear it. You're fucking everything to me. *Everything.* There's nobody on this earth that

I imagine being with other than you. There are no better options, Olivia. There's just you."

"But I'm—"

"Call yourself a nobody again, Olivia. Do it, I dare you." I grab her legs and pick her up before I sit us both down on her bed. Livvy's legs are now wrapped around my center and behind my back. "You're someone to me, Liv. You're the only one for me. You're every molecule in my body, every atom in my cells, and I can't imagine not spending these past months with you." Fuck, why is this so hard? "You're the first thought I have every morning when I wake up and the last thing I think about when I go to sleep. You're everywhere, Liv, and damn, if I don't love every fucking second that I spend with you."

"Love?" she whispers to me, her eyes bulging out of her head as more tears fall. "You love me?"

"Fuck, baby, I thought it was obvious? Of course, I love you. I'd be the stupidest guy in the world not to love you." I smile, knowing in my heart that this was the girl I was meant to love. I press a kiss to her lips, and when I pull back, and she leans her head against mine, I know I'm ruined for the rest of my life. Olivia Hart has ruined me, and now I can't imagine a future where she's not in it alongside me.

"I love you too," she whispers against my lips.

"God, four words is all it took, Livvy. Four words, and I'm done for." The two of us laugh through our emotions as we realize what we just said. "You're the only girl I've ever loved, Liv. My first and last, as far as I'm concerned."

Her laugh surrounds me, and I can't help but take in the state of us right now. We've gone from panicked to crying to confessing our love, and now the two of us are smiling like complete idiots. This is the best day of my entire fucking life. "God, I feel like a mess right now. You have tear stains on your shirt."

"I don't care. Those are tears from the love of my life. They probably have healing powers, as far as I'm concerned."

"I'm sorry I left the game. I—"

I cut off her apology with a kiss because it's not necessary. I kiss her with all the emotions that are bubbling up in my body after all the shit we confessed tonight. Every time I kiss Livvy, I get an adrenaline rush. Olivia Hart is the only drug I want to take because she makes me feel like the happiest guy on the planet. I want to live in the emotions that she makes me feel. I thread my tongue into her lips, and she opens for me. *Such a good fucking girl.*

"Tristan," she moans as I take one of her nipples in my hand and pinch it. My mouth is still moving against hers, and Livvy has started to move her hips over my dick—which is growing increasingly harder every second.

"Fuck, Livvy, you feel so good," I say as I pepper kisses all down her neck and all the way to her nipples, taking one in my mouth. Before I let it go and focus on the other one, I bite it ever so slightly, and a moan falls from her mouth. *Fuck.* Her moans haunt my dreams. I can't get them out of my head. Those moans are mine. *I* do that to her. Me.

"Tristan, please, baby, I—"

"I know what you need, Livvy," I say as I capture her mouth again, getting a taste of the lips that I could glue myself to forever. As I kiss her, I flip her over so she's on her back now. Her hand reaches for my sweats, and she palms my dick through them. I'm hard as a fucking rock right now, and as she pumps me over my pants, I think of a thousand different things to not come right here, right now. "Livvy, baby, do you want my dick?"

"In my mouth? Yeah, I do."

Motherfucker, I'm gone. But tonight isn't about me. I move my right hand up her body and pinch one of her rosy fucking nipples before I wrap my hand around her pretty little throat and squeeze. Her pupils dilate—like they do every time—and I smirk down at her. She looks like a fucking angel. My hoodie is bunched just above her boobs, and all that she's wearing is tiny black shorts—well, she wears my hand wrapped around her throat pretty nicely too. "Not tonight, Livvy. That pretty pussy of yours is taking my dick. I'll take that mouth another time, though."

She smiles up at me as I grab her hoodie and yank it over her head. Her shorts and underwear are gone next, and she yanks my shirt off of me when I come back up to her. "It's not fair that I'm naked and you aren't."

"All you had to do was ask, pretty girl." I strip the rest of my clothes off, and even though Livvy and I have fooled around in the past, this is the first time we're having full sex. I've tasted her more times than I can count, and feeling her come on my face has been unreal.

I don't think I'm quite prepared to feel her unravel around my dick. I'm determined to last and make this perfect for her, but it's going to be fucking hard. She's just...perfect. "Are you sure about this, Livvy?"

"Positive. Fuck me, Tristan, please," she practically begs as I join her on her bed again. "How do you want me?"

My dick flexes when she asks me that. "Lay on your back and put those pretty legs on my shoulders."

She complies, and I grab a condom from my wallet, rolling it onto my dick. As I line up to her entrance, she whispers to me, "I love you."

Fuck. I'll never get tired of hearing that. "Say it again, Olivia."

"I lo—" And in one thrust, I'm buried. Her tight pussy is wrapped around me, and I can't think, breathe, or digest any thoughts because all of them are surrounded by her.

Livvy. Livvy. Livvy.

"Tristan...Fuck...It's too much."

I smirk at her. "I haven't even moved yet, Liv."

"Christ. I'm so full."

"You can take it, pretty girl. You'll take every inch of it like the good girl you are, Liv." She nods at me, and I start slowly thrusting in and out of her. "Fuck, you feel like a dream." Livvy's pussy was made for me. She's so fucking wet, my dick sliding in with ease, and I barely touched her before this.

"Harder, Tristan."

My girl likes it rough. "Are you sure? I want this to be good for you, and if I go harder, I probably won't last."

"I need you to go harder, please."

"Whatever my girl wants," I say as I deepen my thrusts. I reach down and press a finger to her clit, massaging it in slow circles as I pound into her pussy. God, I love seeing her like this—completely undone underneath me. I could come just from the sight of her alone.

"Fuck, yes, just like that, please," Livvy's pleas turn into an indecipherable moan before I feel her pussy squeeze my dick.

"Not yet, Liv."

"Oh my God!" Her angry yell turns into a moan as I lift her legs farther up so I can get deeper. Livvy's eyes practically roll to the back of her head when I pound into her over and over again.

"That's right, Liv. I love how you call out for me while I'm buried in your pussy."

"Tristan, I'm—"

"Come on my dick, Liv." Her pussy pulsates over my dick, and as she rides out her orgasm, mine practically blinds me. I can't think about anything other than how fucking amazing this feels—her underneath me, looking like a wet dream, as my dick flexes inside her. A few seconds—or years—later, after I pull out and dispose of the condom, I grab a warm towel and clean her up.

"Fuck, I'm already sore," she slurs as I throw the towel onto the floor where my clothes are. I grab her hoodie and throw it back on her so she doesn't get cold before I put my sweats back on and join her in bed.

"Come here, pretty girl," I say as I lift my arm up, and she slides right where she belongs into the side of my body, one of her arms draped over my chest and her head against my shoulder.

"I can't look that pretty right now, Tristan."

"I think I like this look on you best, actually," I say as I press a kiss on her forehead.

"What look?"

"Thoroughly fucked."

Her cheeks instantly turn red, as if I wasn't just seven inches deep in her pussy a few minutes ago. "I love you, idiot."

"I love you too, Liv. Now, go pee before you get too comfortable. I'll be here when you get back, and we can go to sleep."

She lifts her head and meets my eyes. "Promise?"

"I promise, Liv." *All my promises are yours from now on, and I don't plan on breaking a single one.*

Chapter Twenty-Three

— DOROTHEA BY TAYLOR SWIFT

"Why has this been going on for months, and I'm just now hearing about it?" I say—no, yell—at my parents for keeping something this huge from me.

"It was need to know," my father says as he continues glancing at his laptop, still not having looked at me since I burst through the front door.

"And you didn't think I needed to know? If it concerns Bree's safety, then it concerns me!" I'm fucking livid. It turns out that the reason my sister has been acting so off the past few weeks is because she's being stalked. *Stalked.* Apparently, it started off with a few notes from the same person—the police said the handwriting was the same after they analyzed the notes—and it's become increasingly worse with every letter.

At first, he told my sister how much he loved her videos and her aura. Lately, though, this person has been threatening to sneak into her room at night. I only read three or four of the notes, but my body went cold at some of the things that were said. "We're handling it."

"Mom, no offense, but you're doing a shitty job. Bree is fucking terrified!" I look over at my sister, who is staring blankly at her Kindle, clearly not reading. "The only reason I'm here is because she told me about the situation and wanted my help. Clearly, you and Dad aren't doing your fucking job as parents."

I'm being harsh. I know I am, but my sister is scared to even be in the house because of this. "What do you suppose we do? The police have already been notified, and they'll keep an eye on our mailbox if any more notes come."

"That's not good enough if Bree doesn't feel safe here!" I'm pacing through the living room, trying to figure out how to get my sister out of this fucking house. The housing market sucks right now, and I'm afraid that we'll never find anything good enough for Bree to get out from under my parents' roof. "What if you guys stay at a hotel for a few weeks?"

"A hotel? That's not possible. Your father and I have to work, and all our important documents are here."

"You can bring them with you, Mom. That's the nice thing about paper. It's flexible." I sit on the couch across from them and look over at my sister. *I should've asked her about all this sooner.* How did I not see that something was clearly wrong? She's lost her shine the past few weeks, but I brushed it off. God, I feel like I failed my sister. How am I supposed to protect her from things when I don't know they're happening in the first place? "What about getting Bree, a bodyguard? Celebrities have those all the time."

"Your sister does not need some burly man following her around just because of a few notes. She's strong. Isn't that right, Bree?" My mom smiles in her direction, and Bree continues looking at her Kindle as if the world around her doesn't exist.

"Mom, enough. Bree is strong, yes, but she needs protection. Or did you not read the letters that detailed everything they wanted to do to her without her consent?" Nausea overtakes my body as I think about something like that happening to someone I love. God, this situation is so fucked, and my parents don't seem to give a shit. "I'll ask Tristan if you can stay with his family."

"We're not going to send her off to some family we don't even know," my dad finally speaks up.

"Tristan is my boyfriend, Dad. His family is very welcoming. I'm sure Bree would feel safe there." I grab my phone to call Tristan, but then Bree speaks up.

"Liv, it's fine. I don't want to burden anyone else. Plus, I don't want anyone to be in danger because of me."

"Bree, I can't leave here knowing that this person knows where you live. I can't leave knowing that you don't feel safe in this house." I sit on the arm of the chair she's sitting in. "I'd feel better if you had some sort of bodyguard or something."

"I don't want anyone fussing over me. It's not like I'm famous. I'm just a YouTuber."

"A YouTuber with over six million subscribers, Bree. At least tell me you'll think about it."

She nods at me a few seconds later, and I don't feel any better than I did before, but at least it's a start. "Great. Problem solved. Now, your father and I have to get to the office. I assume you can let yourself out, Olivia."

My parents don't wait for my answer as they get up and are out the door in a few seconds. I turn to my sister. "Wow, they really don't care anymore, do they?"

"I've been telling them about how scared I've been for weeks, and they've brushed me off. I can't tell what I prefer—being smothered or ignored."

"Either way, it sucks," I say as I grab my sister's hand. "Why didn't you tell me sooner?"

"I thought I could handle it, but when that last one came yesterday, I just..."

I get up and pull her into a hug. "Bree, you can *always* come to me for anything. The next time you're scared or having any emotions that feel too big, call me. I'll be here in minutes."

"Okay, Liv. I will. I'm sorry—"

"Don't apologize, Bree. I'm the one who's sorry that you've been dealing with this by yourself." I squeeze her harder before we pull apart. "For the time being, I wouldn't post anything on your socials. Does your manager know about this?"

"Yeah, Connie knows. She's the one who flagged the correspondence in the first place. She's going as crazy as you are about this, but I told her that I'll be okay. I'm only allowed to post sponsored stuff that has strict deadlines and about books that are coming out this month. I won't do anything else, I promise."

"Good." Connie is only a few years older than I am, but she manages all the contact that my sister gets—whether through the mail, emails, or other things besides Bree's socials, which she manages herself. "Do you want to come hang out with me? I have the night off. We could have a girls' night with Parker and Cassie?"

Bree shakes her head. "No. I think I'll just go upstairs and read. Ellie is calling me soon, and I don't want to miss her." Ellie is Bree's best friend, who's also an influencer. They both blew up around the same time, and a brand collab brought them closer together. I'm glad she has someone who understands the craziness that comes with being on the internet.

"Okay, I'll head out then. Did Mom and Dad say an officer was stationed outside the house at all times, or do I need to arrange that?"

"He should be out there right now. If he's not there when you go outside, can you fix that?" Bree asks me, a flicker of panic crossing over her features.

"I'll text you when everything is set." I grab my purse off the floor from where I threw it when I got here. "Lock the door behind me."

"I will."

"And are all the—"

"Every entry point is locked, Liv. The cops double-checked when they were here." I smile, glad that she knew what I was going to ask before I said it.

"I'm telling them to upgrade the security system, too," I say as I hug my sister again. "You'll feel safe here, Bree. If it kills me, you'll be safe here. I don't care what Mom and Dad do, but I'll do whatever it takes."

"Thanks, Liv," she whispers in my ear, her breath shaking as if she's about to cry. "I'm glad I called you." I pull back from her and notice her already red eyes are all misted.

"Next time, I better be the first person you call after the police."

"You will be. I promise."

"I love you, Bree."

"I love you too, Liv." I smile at her before I pinch one of her cheeks and then hold my hand out. She grabs my pinky finger with hers, a tradition from when we were kids that's carried us into adulthood.

Pinky promises are the most iron-clad agreements one can make. I remember saying that to my sister when she asked me to promise that I would never fully disappear from her as a kid. "Try to get some rest. I'll see you soon."

"See you." I shut the door behind me, and when I hear her lock it, I leave our porch. I look around and sure enough, an officer is posted in an unmarked car on the other side of the street. *Good.* At least some people are taking this situation seriously, even if my parents aren't. I used to think that they could change when we got older, and maybe they would miss being here for my sister and me, but now I see them as who they are—human. They're just two people who coexisted in the same house with me for so long.

I've always felt that as a kid, you see your parents in a certain way, and when you grow up, you see them for who they really are. Time can do that to you—shift your point of view as you get older. I hate that they don't care about Bree's safety. You'd think after reading some of those notes that they would snap out of it, but if that doesn't do it, I don't know what will.

I'm scared to think about all the outcomes of this situation. Before I spiral out of control, I get into my car and immediately dial Tristan using my Bluetooth as I drive back to school.

"Hey, pretty girl. How's Bree holding up? Does she need anything?"

I love this man so much. "She's okay. A bit scared, but that's to be expected."

"The offer still stands if she wants to stay with my mom. My sister is practically foaming at the mouth for a chance to meet Bree in person."

"Bree declined again. She doesn't want to put your family in danger in case her location gets leaked. She appreciates the offer, though."

"Tell her she's always welcome at the West house. She's practically family."

My heart warms at the insinuation. I don't know how he always manages to make me feel like this. "I'll be back at school in about fifteen. Are you on for girls' night with Parker and Cassie? I think Bryce is coming over, too."

"What are we watching tonight?"

"*The Notebook*, I think."

"Oh, a classic. I love that movie."

"You've seen it?" I ask, almost laughing at the fact that he's watched it.

"With Teagen, yes. It's one of her comfort movies, which makes no sense because it's depressing as fuck. How can a movie like that be comforting?"

"Well, one of my favorite books turned into a movie is *Dead Poets Society*, so I can't even talk. That book makes me sob profusely every single time. Don't even get me started on the deleted movie scenes, either."

"One day, someone will be crying over one of your books like how you do sad movies." The thought of that makes my stomach drop. *Maybe one day.* I try not to think too far into the future, but it would be cool if I could make someone feel like that—connected to my characters so much that they feel big emotions.

"Maybe, Tristan. Let's not get ahead of ourselves."

"You have the talent, Liv. I can't wait to say I told you so when it eventually happens." I can practically hear him smiling through the phone. "Drive safe. Text me when you're home."

"I will, Tristan. I love you."

"I love you, too."

Chapter Twenty-Four

— ROBBERS BY THE 1975

"Do you want me to do anything else before I leave?" I ask Cal as I tap the butler out over the garbage can.

He stops cleaning the counter and looks at me. *Why does his face look like that?* "Yeah, just answer a question for me."

"Okay?" I question, scared as to where this could be headed. Cal may be friendly with me, but he was Livvy's friend first.

"How are you and Liv doing? I know graduation is coming, and I was curious about your plans for then."

Oh. It wasn't as scary as I thought. "Honestly, that's a good question. I guess I haven't thought too much about it," I say as I throw my jacket on. "Why?"

"Liv has always told me that she's never known what she wants to do after college. I guess I was wondering if that's changed recently." He throws out the paper towel he was using as he comes closer to where I'm at and leans against the counter. "You told me when you started that you wanted to leave here and never look back."

"I've always said that, Cal. Ever since I started college, I've been itching to leave."

"Is that still your plan?"

Why is he asking me all this shit? "I don't know. I have a few job prospects and stuff, but I haven't really looked too in-depth at them." I narrow my eyes, suddenly seeing right through him. "Look, Livvy and I have been taking it one day at a time. I know how she feels about the future, and I never want to pressure her to align hers with mine."

"I just think that you two should probably get on the same page. If you're going in two different directions or states, I think it's important to let her know that. Because I swear, Tristan, if you break her heart, I will end you."

"Yeah, you and me both, Cal. That's not my plan. Whatever future I have only works if Liv is still in it." I mean that. She's the only person I can imagine going through life with. "If that's all, I'll leave now."

"Remember what I said, Tristan. Talk to Livvy sooner rather than later. Get on the same fucking page, and all will be fine. I want to see my girl happy, and if she's happy with you, then so be it."

"Got it. And here I thought we were starting to become friends," I joke with him as I grab my bag.

"We *are* friends. That's why I'm giving you advice."

"Noted. I'll see you at some point," I say as I head to go punch out. On my entire drive back to school, it's all I can think about. What am I going to do now that Livvy is with me? Do I cancel my plans to leave and stay here with her? Do we leave together? If I asked her to do that, would she?

All of my future plans have taken a back seat to Livvy and I's relationship, and I'm not even mad at that. I've been having the best few months with her, but would it be too soon to move in together in a whole new state, or even here? I don't think it would be for me because that means more time around my girl, but maybe she would think it's too soon.

By the time I'm putting my key into my door, it's all I can think about. All of my thoughts have spiraled, and I can't stop them from going in every fucking direction possible—including to the one where Livvy decides that she doesn't want me anymore. I keep reminding myself that she's not like that, and she's as much in this relationship as I am, but once the thought entered my mind, the seed was planted.

All I know is that I need to talk to Livvy before my thoughts eat me alive. It's late tonight, but this is definitely a conversation we need to have soon.

My apartment is quiet when I get in, but I notice my door is slightly open, and I remember closing it before I left for work. I sigh as I head over. "Dom, I swear to God, if you took my condoms again—" My voice dies out when I see my beautiful girlfriend asleep in my bed.

I didn't know she would be here when I got off of work, but now, seeing her like this, I've never seen anything better. Her brown hair is sprawled all over my pillow, and she has one of my old *Summit Baseball* shirts on and her normal black sleep shorts. Her laptop is slightly open and off to her side as if she fell asleep with it on her legs and it slipped off. I grab it off of my bed and place it on my desk, and it turns back on when I do. I go to shut it off and notice that she appears to be writing. I'm so fucking proud of her, I could scream, but I don't want to wake her. I grab my pajamas and head to take a shower.

Fifteen minutes later, I get back to my room, and Livvy's holding onto my other pillow as if it's a human being. *God, she's so fucking cute.* I notice her phone is plugged into my charger on my nightstand as I go to charge mine. God, my girl is taking over all my stuff, and it's the greatest thing I've ever seen. I want Livvy's fingerprints all over my shit, and I'm glad she feels comfortable enough to crawl into my bed and make it hers. Hell, it's hers now. She owns it, just like she owns me.

I crawl into bed beside her, feeling a sense of comfort at her being here right now, but still tense about the conversation we have to have soon. I think I'm scared of all the outcomes that could happen because of this conversation. There's too fucking many, and it makes me all itchy just thinking about it. I shift around as my thoughts race, and Livvy stirs beside me. She's a light sleeper, so I should've known that she would wake up. I'm practically tossing and turning. "Baby?"

"Hi, Livs. I didn't mean to wake you. Go back to sleep." I try to lean her head back, but she pops back up.

"You're so tense, Tristan. Are you okay?" she asks as she massages my arm and shoulder. "Was work stressful tonight?"

"No, it was dead at the store."

"Then why does your body feel tight?"

"A lot on my mind, I think." That causes her to sit up fully. "What?"

"Want to talk about it? I don't know how long I've been asleep, but I'm awake now."

I guess now is as good of a time as any. "Liv, I don't want to scare you, but I think we need to talk about what happens after graduation." After I finish my sentence, she smacks me. "What was that for?"

"The next time you start a sentence like that, it better end differently. I thought you were about to break up with me or tell me you were dying or something!"

I stifle the laugh that's about to come up because I don't want to get smacked again. "I'm sorry! It's been on my mind for the past few hours, and I know the future scares you, so I didn't want you to run in the opposite direction when I brought up the topic."

"Tristan, out of the two of us, you're the one that likes to run, not me. I prefer being stagnant, apparently." *Good point.*

"You've got me there. Now, can we talk about it?"

"Of course, you idiot." She smiles at me, and even when she's mad at me, she's adorable. I shift, so I'm sitting up, too. Livvy's leaning against my wall, and I'm against my headboard, hoping that this conversation won't end with our relationship having an expiration date of graduation.

"So, do you have any idea of a plan for us?" I ask her, wondering if she's given any thought to it.

"Not really. I love you, Tristan, but I haven't thought of the next chapter yet. I've been living in the moment with you, and it's been great. I know we have to decide, though."

I fucking love this girl. "I think we have a few options. One being that we both stay here and see where that takes us. The second being that you come with me to wherever I end up. The third being long-distance if I end up getting a job somewhere else."

Her wheels are turning. I can tell because of the face she's making. "So, I guess it all depends on your job offers and stuff."

"Well, no. It's about what you want to do, Liv. It's not just me here, it's you too." That earns me a smile, and I consider that a win. "So, if I get a job out of state, what do you think you want to do? Go with me or do long-distance?"

"Long-distance isn't the goal. I think I'd want to go with you, but is it too soon for that? We haven't even been dating for an entire year yet."

"So?" I say to her, and her eyebrows shoot up. "What, Liv? There's no timeline to the way I feel about you. I love you. I love your presence around me at all times, and I can't imagine not having all of your clothes on the floor of our first apartment together. Call me fucking batshit crazy, but that's something I want."

Her cheeks flush as that beautiful smile of hers graces her face. "You want that with me?"

"I don't dream of it being with anyone else, Liv. Just you." I lean across my bed and take her hand in mine. "But only if you want to come with me. There's no pressure, Liv. You can take some time to think about it. We don't need to make this decision tonight."

"No. I want that, Tristan. I want it with you." Her smile illuminates the once-dark room, and I feel like the luckiest fucking guy in the world. *She wants me. She wants a future for us as much as I do.* "Even if I have no idea what I'm doing, I want to figure it out with you by my side. Is that okay?"

"Fuck, Liv. It's more than okay. It's fucking amazing." I swallow her laughter as I press my lips to hers. "It's you and me, pretty girl. Is that okay with you?"

"Me and you, Tristan. There's nobody else I could imagine doing this with."

"Likewise," I say as I drown myself in her lips for the rest of the night, neither of us getting a minute of sleep.

All my happiness comes from this girl, and the only reason that I know it exists is because she's shown me what it feels like.

Chapter Twenty-Five

— IT'S TIME TO GO BY TAYLOR SWIFT

WAKING UP TODAY HAS been one of the hardest things that I've ever done. Today is the day that I graduate from college.

Do I know what's coming next? Absolutely not.

I thought today could be normal. I thought I'd wake up, and Tristan would kiss me on the forehead like he always does, and we would go to class, and everything would be fine.

I thought I had more time.

Today is the day that I've been thinking about my whole life. When you're young, college graduation seems so far away—light years into the future in a decade you can't possibly imagine. When you're in elementary school, and your teachers tell you that you're the class of 2023, it's hard to imagine. You can't really wrap your head around it. Because when you're little, you feel like you have all the time in the world. You think about how 2023 is more than ten years away and how ten years is a long time—so much can happen in a decade. Then, all of a sudden, you're in high school, and you're graduating. It's bittersweet, of course, but you remember that you still have four more years before you have to figure everything out.

When you leave high school, you're a half-adult. You're about to embark on a big new journey on your own for the first time, but you always know that you'll still come home for breaks and the summer.

When you graduate college, you're thrust into the real world with nothing. Sure, you have your degree, but what good does that do when you have no idea what you want from your life? It also doesn't help that everyone else around you—friends, classmates, peers, and your boyfriend—have their lives mapped out and all ready to go.

I'm falling behind, I think to myself. I try to hold my head up and tell people that I'm looking for jobs and doing my best, but I feel like I'm not. I'm just starting the race when everyone else has already finished. I've been lapped before I've even started, and I hate feeling like this. I hate feeling like nothing has or will ever be clear to me when today is supposed to be a day of celebrating milestones and being proud of myself.

Nothing will erase the panicky ache that I feel. Today was my deadline—the day I was supposed to have everything figured out by, and I'm nowhere near that. I'm a big fucking failure, yet I still have to get up, wear the cap and gown, and pretend like I don't feel like my life is falling apart around me.

Now as I stand here and look in the mirror after going through the motions of getting ready, I don't recognize myself. Gone is the ten-year-old girl who shouted to everyone who could hear that she was going to be an author one day, and in her place is...nobody. I'm nowhere I thought I would be by now, and I was stupid to think that I could figure it out.

This is not how I thought life would be, but there's nothing I can do about that.

"Are you ready to go?" Parker asks me as she comes into my room. "You look beautiful, Liv."

I chose a white mini-dress and simple heels that match. My hair is curly, and I did minimal makeup because it's probably going to be hot in the gym. Parker has a strapless white dress and purple shoes to match our cap and gown. "Thanks, Parker. You look great, too."

"How are you feeling?"

I meet her eyes in my mirror. "Do you want the truth or a lie?"

She moves behind my chair as she runs her fingers through my hair. "The truth, but I think I already know what you're going to say."

"I feel disoriented. Confused. Excited. Terrified. I feel like I'm being sent out to sea without a compass." My throat closes when I say the last sentence, and I look away from the mirror before I shed more tears about my uncertain future.

"Sometimes routes change when you least expect it, and the map you once had doesn't work anymore." Parker tells me, and I digest what she's saying. *It's okay not to have a plan because life isn't something that can be planned.* "You'll be okay, Liv. I may not know what the future holds, but I know you, and you'll be okay."

"I appreciate that, Parker. Really, I do." I reach up and grab her hand from where it rests on my shoulder—giving it a squeeze. "Life can't be planned sometimes. I know that. It sucks feeling like I have no clue what comes next."

"I get that. But no matter what, Tristan, Cassie, and I will be by your side every step of the way. No state lines can break that promise, Liv."

"You're right." I may not know where I'm headed, but I do know that I'd rather take on this scary path with the people around me than alone. After all, it's easier walking through the dark with someone by your side than doing it by yourself.

"Are you ready to graduate?"

I take a deep breath, wanting to take in every moment of today as much as I can. "I'm ready."

FOUR HOURS AND A thirty-foot walk later, and I'm officially a graduate of Summit University.

What now? Honestly, the whole graduation thing felt kind of anti-climactic. As soon as my name was called and I walked across the stage, I thought I'd feel a little bit better, but nothing has changed for me.

I do need to find Tristan. He graduated with all the other engineers, and I want to get some pictures. I might feel like I have no idea what I'm doing, but one thing will always remain the same—I'm so proud of him. He reached his goal, and now he's going to Silicon Valley to achieve his dream. I'm looking around for any one of my friends when arms reach around my waist, pick me up, and spin me around. That familiar cinnamon scent wraps around me. *Tristan.*

"Hi, pretty girl." He presses a kiss to my lips as he sets me down. "Did you hear me yell when you walked? I tried to be loud enough."

A smile graces my lips. "I did. I heard Bree say something, too, and a few other voices."

"That was probably my family." I smile, feeling overwhelmed all of a sudden. Tristan and I have spent so much time at his house since Thanksgiving. I took Bree over to meet Teagen, and they're now attached at the hip. I've never seen two people become instant friends after one conversation, but it makes me happy that they've gotten closer. Theo and Tobias—when he's home—have also taught me how to kick Tristan's ass at Xbox. Tristan claims it's because he never had the chance to get good as a kid since he was helping his mom out. I went easy on him after that.

"Where's everyone else?" I ask, wanting to see all of our friends.

"I'm not sure," I say as I sweep the auditorium, seeing Bree waving at me like a madwoman, a bouquet in her hand. I rush her and squeeze the hell out of her. Even when I've seen her a lot over the past few months, I can never get enough. I've had to remind myself that she's safe and okay, but *seeing* her is a lot different. I see my parents heading this way, neutral expressions on their faces as always. "Hi, Bree."

"I'm proud of you, sis. Did you hear me when you walked?"

"I did, and thank you." My parents flank Bree on both sides, and I retreat back to where I know Tristan is still standing.

I've tried to keep him away from them, but I always knew this moment would come. *Deep breaths, Liv. It'll be fine.* "Mom and Dad, this is Tristan. Tristan, meet my parents."

Before Tristan's hand makes it out for a handshake, my mom speaks. "Olivia, have you received any job offers yet?"

That was rude. "You want to do this right now? Really?" Tristan's hand comes to mine, and he squeezes three times, signaling that he's here with me. "I haven't, but—"

"If you had known you were going to Silicon Valley at the end of college, you should've studied something other than creative writing. It feels like a missed opportunity," my dad states, malice in his tone.

"To be fair, I didn't know what my plan was for after college. It sort of happened—"

"And that is *exactly* why we've told you that your degree was useless, Olivia. You need something sustainable, not—" *Don't cry. Do not cry, Liv.*

Tristan cuts in, halting my mom's disappointments. "I'd appreciate it if you'd stop talking to her like that. It's quite rude, especially when Livvy just accomplished something that you should be proud of."

Oh my God. He's standing up for me. "Excuse me, but who are—"

He cuts in again. "As Livvy stated previously, I'm Tristan—her boyfriend. If you had listened to what she said, you would know that. I'd say it's nice to meet you both, but that's not quite what I'm feeling."

Bree and I lock eyes, scared as to where this conversation could go, but I'm also feeling other things. Nobody besides my sister has ever stood up for me before. It feels nice knowing that I have someone like Tristan in my corner.

"Well, that's quite ill-mannered to say," my dad scoffs, clearly thinking he's done nothing wrong.

"I don't know how it's possible for me to be impolite when you two are the ones insulting your daughter's accomplishments right in front of her."

"How we talk to our daughter does not concern you, boy," my dad spits out. I have the sudden urge to flee, but Tristan's hand is anchoring me to my spot.

"It does, actually, when you're making her feel like garbage. She's your daughter, for crying out loud. You're supposed to build her up, not knock her down."

"I second that," my sister says. "I'd quit while you're behind, Mom and Dad. Head off to the airport for your next trip." *Trip?*

"Are you guys leaving?" I ask them.

"We have a business conference to attend for the next two weeks." My mother juts her chin out, as if she's trying to remain confident.

"Well, have fun. When you get back, I'll be gone," I say, not feeling sad that I probably won't see them very much anymore. All the emotions in my body right now are overwhelming me, but one comes out on top—relief. Hopefully, I can get Bree a house of her own, and the two of us can finally be free from them. My parents walk away, not sparing a glance back at the three of us.

Tristan turns his eyes to mine. "Livvy, Bree, and I are so proud of you."

My teary eyes start to grow. "Damn right, we are." My sister says.

"Thanks. Can we go find our friends now?"

"Of course we can." Tristan leans down and captures my mouth again. He pulls back, inches from my lips, and whispers at me. "I'll always be proud of you, Livvy. Never forget that."

I won't. I smile against him as we pull apart. "You guys are so cute it makes me sick."

I stifle a laugh into Tristan's body. "Bree, we're having dinner at Tristan's place with everyone. Are you coming?" Everyone being Tristan's roommates, Parker, Cassie, Bryce, and Tristan's family.

"I have an early morning tomorrow. I'll stop by for a few and then go back home. I'm so glad I drove separately from them because I'd hate to be a fly on the wall in that car."

"They have really shitty first impressions." Tristan says.

I lean into his embrace. "I'm sorry that they treated you like that."

"Don't apologize for them. I'm just thankful that they gave me you."

There's so much I want to say to him right now.

Thank you for standing up for me when my parents made me feel less than.

Thank you for making me feel like the luckiest girl in the world.

But none of that comes out because I know I'll start crying. Today marks the end of one chapter, but I've never been more excited to turn the page and start a new one with him. Even though it hasn't been written yet, I can tell that this part of our story is going to be my favorite. "Bree, you know how to get to campus, right?"

"Yup. Congrats again. I'm so fucking proud of you. I'll wait for you guys if I beat you there." We hug for a few seconds, and then she leaves. I'm glad she was here today. I know college was never in the cards for her, but she will always be the only family member that I want here for the big moments.

"Let's go surround ourselves with people who deserve our time." Tristan says to me before grabbing my hand and pulling me through the crowd of people.

AFTER A HUGE DINNER and Dom drinking his weight in whiskey, most of us have congregated in Tristan's living room. His family and my sister left an hour ago since it's now around ten PM, and as I sit on his lap, he's running a hand through my hair. Tristan hasn't stopped touching me all night, and you won't find me complaining about it.

"So, where is everyone headed now, and how do we all stay in touch? Slack channel? Carrier pigeon?" Dom asks the group of us.

"I'll be a research assistant for a lab around the corner." Parker says, and I'm glad she'll still be here even though I'm leaving. She's always loved Pennsylvania, and I'll be sure to visit her when I come back to see Bree.

Cassie and Bryce are moving in together. Cassie got a job in New York as a childhood therapist, and Bryce is going to be an athletic trainer for some college where they're headed.

Ethan is headed to New York City to start work at some film company. Dom's parents are getting him a place here before he starts working for them in the family business. Harry has decided to stay around here, too, and teach at a local high school where he's also coaching the baseball team.

"So, California for you two lovebirds. Are you excited?" Harry asks Tristan and I.

I nod my head, a huge smile gracing my face. "I might be slightly nervous, but I'm very excited to travel out of state."

"I couldn't be more thrilled. It's even better now that this one is coming with me." Tristan presses a kiss to my shoulder.

"Is this someone's Cartier bracelet, or can I steal it?" Cassie asks from the kitchen. *When did she get over there?*

"Where the hell did you find that?" Ethan asks, probably thinking of a few ways to sell it.

"Attached to the flowers in the vase."

"It's probably my sisters. It must've dropped by accident," I say, walking over to grab it and check if there's an inscription on the inside of it. "It's hers."

"But how can you be so sure, Livvy? Maybe it's not, and I can make a bunch of money off of it." Dom nudges my side, and I roll my eyes. *He's lucky he's cute.*

"The inscription. She practically never takes it off." I don't know who gave this to my sister—I assumed it was a friend of hers—but the inscription on it makes me think that it might be someone important. Combined with the fact that she never takes it off is making the wheels in my head turn. *Has my sister had a boyfriend before and not told me?*

"Speaking of Bree..." Tristan says as he holds my phone up to me, my sister's caller ID showing up on the screen.

I shuffle over and grab it from him. "She's probably going crazy looking for this thing," I answer her call. "Don't worry, sis, I have your bracelet. It must've—"

"Livvy, there's someone in the house." My sister whispers over the line.

"Bree, what are you talking about?"

"There's someone in the house with me, and I don't know who."

My stomach practically bottoms out when she tells me that. "What? Where are you?"

"I'm hiding in my closet. I heard the door slam open, and I thought it was Mom and Dad, but when I looked downstairs, I saw someone." Her breathing escalates as she recounts the memory. "I—I think they had a kn-knife, Liv."

"Stay where you are. Call the police, and they'll come in from outside. Hang up and call them, Bree. I'll be there soon."

"The police?" I hear Parker say behind me.

"Livvy, what's going on?" Tristan asks me, but I don't answer.

"Okay, I will. Liv, I'm scared."

Fucking hell. "Bree, you're going to be fine. It's just someone trying to scare you." *Or it's her stalker.*

"Wait, I hear footsteps."

"Bree, call the police right now." She doesn't have time to say anything else before I hear a scream, and the line goes dead. "Bree! Bree? Fuck!"

"Baby? Are you okay?" I turn to see everyone staring at me, confused as to the one-sided conversation they overheard.

"There's someone in my house. Bree's hiding, I—I need to go home."

"What the fuck?" Dom says.

"Keys, Tristan," Harry says as he throws them our way, Tristan helping me put my jacket on.

"I'm sorry to leave like this, but—"

"Liv, just go to your sister. No apology necessary." Cassie gives me a quick hug before Tristan and I are out the door and speeding to my parents' house.

⁂

TRISTAN MAKES IT TO my parents' house in ten minutes—no doubt breaking a few traffic laws on the way—but I can't find it in myself to care. I need to make sure that Bree's alright. I need to see her and confirm that this was all a bad dream and that she's safe.

But when we pull onto my street, red and blue lights surround my house, and my heart lurches more out of place than it felt previously.

Bree's okay. It's just a formality that this many cop cars, ambulances, and fire trucks are here. It's fine, right? Everything's going to be fine. I even notice a few news trucks, and there's not a doubt in my mind that this is going to be all over social media by tomorrow morning.

Tristan parks the car, and the two of us get out in a hurry. I think he's just as worried as I am. His knuckles were completely white from how hard he was gripping the steering wheel. I walk up to the police line, and an officer tries to stop me. "Nobody is allowed to cross."

"This is my parents' house. My sister called me while she was hiding."

"Do you have any identification?" the officer asks me, and I pull my wallet out and hand it to him. He looks at it for a few seconds before waving me through. "He's with me."

"Let's check the ambulances first," Tristan suggests, and I nod my head, not really wanting to see my sister hurt. "Wait, I see her. She's over there."

I turn to see my sister sitting in the back of an ambulance, a blanket wrapped around her as she talks to a female EMT. I practically sprint toward her, and as I reach her, she flinches. "Livvy?"

I throw my arms around her and squeeze. "Bree. Oh my God, are you okay?"

"Y—Yeah. I'm alright, I guess." She's crying, and it takes everything in me to keep my own tears in. *I hate seeing her like this.* I notice some bruises and cuts on her thighs, and my stomach bottoms out again. Her neck is red and starting to bruise, her voice comes out thick and coarse, as if she has something stuck in her throat.

"What happened?"

"Try not to overwork your voice," the lady says.

"I was working on a promotional post when I heard the door slam open. I thought Mom and Dad came back because the alarm code was entered after they came in. I went to yell at them for how they acted earlier, but when I peered over the banister, it was someone else."

"Fuck, Bree," I hear Tristan mutter under his breath.

She coughs before she speaks again. "I—I went to hide in my room, and then I called you."

"Yeah, the call hung up, but I'm glad it was you calling the police."

"I did—call the police, I mean, but I didn't talk to them." *What?*

"What do you mean?" I ask her, scared of what she's about to say.

"I called, but before I could say anything, the closet doors opened." *No.* "H—He dragged me out, and I—I tried to kick him a few times, but he was too strong. He threw me on my bed...It was him, Livvy. I know it was." *Him.* Her fucking stalker. My sister trails off as more tears come, and I wrap her in my arms, afraid that what she'll say next will break her more than she already is. *She's strong.* My sister is a strong fucking girl. A fighter.

"You don't need to explain right now, Bree."

"Th—Thanks. They told me not to talk because my vocal cords might be damaged." She wipes a few tears from her eyes, and I release her. "They're taking me to the hospital."

"That's probably for the best." Tristan says from behind me, his voice as hard as a rock.

"We'll follow you to the hospital," I tell my sister, slightly wishing that I could ride in the ambulance with her but knowing that's not an option. "I love you, Bree."

"I love you too. Thanks for coming so quickly. I didn't mean to ruin your night."

"Bree, don't."

"We're just glad you're okay." Tristan tells her. "Did they catch the guy?"

"No. He ran off after—" My sister cuts herself off. "He ran off before the cops finally got here."

After what? God, I'm not gonna press her for more, but my parents aren't around, and I feel helpless right now. I can't make my sister's pain go away, no matter how many hugs I give or how many kind phrases I throw at her. She'll tell me when she's ready. I just have to be patient. "We'll see you at the hospital, okay?"

She nods at me as she gets inside, the doors closing behind her. "She's alive, Liv. She'll be okay."

"She's alive. But what the hell happened to her in that house?" I ask, my knees weakening and giving out altogether as emotions overcome me. He lifts me up and carries me bridal style to the car, and I silently thank him for that because I can barely feel my legs. *I couldn't protect my sister.* I'm a fucking failure. I'm her older sister. I should be the one who looks out for her and makes sure she's okay, and I failed.

I wasn't here. Fuck. The guilt is eating me alive. *If I had found her a house of her own, this might not have happened.*

Silence envelops Tristan's car as he drives from my house and toward the hospital. I feel like I can't breathe as a thousand different thoughts race through my mind. I try to call my parents, but they must be on their flight because it goes straight to voicemail. Just fucking great. I leave both my mom and dad a message about what happened and urge them to call me back as soon as they land.

What the hell am I going to do? My parents are gone for two weeks and there's no way that Bree is staying in their house after what happened.

Fuck. Tristan and I are supposed to leave next week for California. Maybe we could postpone? Or maybe I could postpone?

The questions with no answers flood my mind until Tristan parks at the hospital. Somehow, we get to where Bree is—well, outside of where she is. Tristan and I are sitting in the waiting room of emergency, waiting to hear what's going on. "The crew sends their love to Bree. My family, too."

"How did they find out?"

"Twitter. My sister texted me and asked if Bree was okay. I told her she was hanging in there." *Of course, it's on Twitter.* Fuck the Internet. Can't Bree have one moment of privacy when she's going through something?

"Fuck." This is a nightmare, and I don't know how to handle it. I'm breaking apart, piece by piece, and I'm realizing that maybe my parents were right—I'm not cut out for real life. I'm not good at anything. I can't protect my sister. I can't handle the shitstorm that's coming, and I sure as hell can't handle moving to a new state with nothing lined up in advance.

I'm in over my head in every aspect of my life right now. I'm fucked. Where am I supposed to go from here? "Liv, it's okay."

"What is?"

"I can see those wheels turning in that pretty head of yours." He grabs me from my seat and pulls me onto his lap. "What's on your mind?"

"Everything, I think. The move, my sister, my parents." I shrink into his shoulder. "What do I do, Tristan?"

"You stay."

My head shoots up, and my eyes meet his. "What?"

"Liv, come on. It's the only right answer. If you leave with me next week, all you'll be thinking about is Bree. Plus, she needs you more than I do right now."

I can't believe he's saying the words coming out of his mouth. Sure, that was an option, but I didn't think he would tell me to stay. "You want me to stay here while you go off to California on your own?"

"It's not like I want you to stay, Liv. If I could erase this entire night and drag you to California, I'd do it in a heartbeat. But this is where you *need* to be. Not just for your sister, but for you. I want you with me, but she needs you. There's a big difference." He presses a kiss to my forehead as tears fall from my eyes. I don't know what to say. He's right, of course. If I left with him, I'd be a wreck. But if I stay, he'll be gone. "It's not forever, Liv. It's just until your sister gets back on her feet."

"But, you're okay with long-distance?"

"As long as I have you, I'll be okay. We can still write to each other, and FaceTime and all that. We'll make it work, Liv."

"You're not mad or upset about our plans changing?"

He smiles at me as if that thought never crossed his mind. "I told you to stay, remember? It was my idea. It sucks that you won't be with me, but I know it's the right decision, Liv. My question is if you're okay with it?"

"It's not ideal, but it's not forever, right?"

"Right, Liv. You have a lot going on, and the one thing I don't want to happen is you being scared that we're not okay because of a blip in our plans."

"We'll write, and we'll text and call. We'll be okay, Tristan." I press a hard kiss to his lips as some tears fall from my face. "I can't lose you."

"We've got time, Liv. A whole life ahead of us to spend together. I'm not worried about a few months or however long. You're the only one for me, of that, I'm sure." This man is trying to kill me, I think. How is he so perfect? How did I get so fucking lucky to run into him that day at the student center? God, that feels like forever ago, but he's right. We have all the time in the world. He runs his hand on top of my head and through my hair, tears misting his eyes. "So, next week, I'll leave."

I sniffle. "And I'll stay here."

"And it'll all eventually work out how we want it to. We just have to wait a little longer for our happily ever after."

"We'll be okay, Tristan," I whisper as he kisses me again. Our next chapter has started rockier than I thought it would, but no matter what, Tristan and I still have time. Time to live together, time to sleep next to each other, and time to be with each other.

I can't leave my sister. She needs me, and I need to make sure that she's truly okay, or else I won't be able to sleep at night.

No matter what, we'll all be okay. No matter how long it may take, there will come a time when everything will fall into place for us, and I can't wait for that to happen.

But for now, I need to be here. Of that, I'm sure.

Chapter Twenty-Six

May

— SKINNY LOVE BY BON IVER

PRETTY GIRL,

I know your first letter is probably going to be wishing that you came here with me. I miss you more than I thought I could miss anything, but you made the right decision, and you shouldn't second guess that. We'll make this work, and I know if you left Bree, you'd be kicking yourself every single day about whether she was okay or not.

I've always wanted to get the hell out of Pennsylvania, and I never thought I'd have a reason to miss it again. I thought I'd leave and never look back. You've become that reason. You've become who I look back to.

I know these next couple months, or however long, are going to be tough, but I wouldn't want to do it with anyone other than you.

If you get anything from this letter, I hope it's this: it's okay to stay. You don't have to leave town and never look back after college like I did. I know lots of people pride themselves on starting their lives somewhere other than where they grew up, but there's nothing wrong with staying.

I'm damn proud of you every day, and I love you, but you already know that. I'll dream of you tonight and every night like I always do.

Give Bree my love. I can't wait to hear that beautiful voice of yours on our call later tonight.

Yours forever,
Tristan

PS. The sunsets out here aren't the same without you. Be on the lookout for pictures. I have a few saved up that are coming your way—all 8/10. (they would have been ten's, but you're not here, so I deducted two points.)

TRISTAN,

God, I miss you. I really fucking miss you. Life feels incomplete without waking up next to you every morning, but I know I made the right decision. I'm glad I'm here for my sister. I don't think I would've survived the trip, so, thank you. Thank you for being the best boyfriend ever and doing long-distance so I could stay.

A few updates that I saved for this letter are as follows:

My sister is slowly opening up and coming back to herself. I still don't know what happened, but she's been talking to her therapist a lot. She and her new bodyguard are getting along, I think. He doesn't really talk, but Bree seems to trust him. He's with her every time she leaves the house. I'm happy she's not bottling it up, but I hate that she thinks she can't talk to me, so I'm being patient. I don't want to press. Teagen came over the other day, and we all had girl time. It was fun hearing about you from her.

Seeing you on FaceTime is one of my favorite sights every night. That's not an update, but I wish I could reach into the screen and kiss you until I stop breathing.

I enjoy our letters. It gives me something to look forward to every week. I can't wait to show you where I'm going to keep all of them. Bree and I decorated a box, and it looks so ridiculous but adorable. (There might be a cutout of your face on it…I'll neither confirm nor deny.)

Bree and I are still house-hunting—mostly for her, but also me. We figure that if we find a place, we'll share it so we can get the hell out of my parents' house. I still can't believe they kept it after what happened. Bree can't even step near her room without crying, so she's been sleeping on an air mattress in my room. I can't wait until we find somewhere she feels comfortable in, but until then, I'll be right here where you know you can find me—still under my parents' roof.

That's all I have for now. Oh, wait, I forgot something. I love you. I'll always love you no matter how far apart we are, so remember that if times ever get tough. You've always been in my corner, and this is me telling you that I'll always be in yours. I love you.

Yours no matter the distance,
Livvy.

PS. The sunsets aren't the same without you, either. I practically cry every time I see one, but happy tears, knowing that you're under the same sky that I am.

September

My Livvy,

Hi, pretty girl. I see that you sent me part of your book, and I know you're anxiously awaiting to hear what I thought so…

I loved it, Liv. Of course, I fucking loved it. I sent copies to my mom and sister via email, they loved it as well, and they hate you for pulling at their heartstrings in the prologue. Teags even told me that she annotated part of it with Bree when they had a sleepover at my mom's house. I'm glad Bree is finally getting out of the house. I remember you telling me that baby steps were still steps with her, and I'm glad she's slowly coming back.

I'm super proud of you, my beautiful writer girlfriend.

I'm also sad that by the time this letter gets to you that you'll be a year older and I won't be able to be with you on your birthday. Just know that I'm currently at home after work trying to bake something for our call later.

I'm thinking that you could blow the candles out through the camera.

I'm definitely coming home for Thanksgiving because my mom is already threatening me, so I'll see you then, but God, it still feels like an eternity. I've been okay with all this, but it's still hard.

I miss your face. I miss the way you laugh. I miss you pacing around my room when you're talking passionately about something you love. I miss my siblings and my mom, but I miss you most of all. I thought I'd be going crazy about them, but my head only seems to think about you all day.

What's Livvy doing? Is she at work with Cal, or did she just get off? (The time difference sucks, btw.) I don't feel the same without you. I don't feel like Tristan. I feel off, and my body aches every day that we're a part.

Again, I told you to stay, so you better stay in Penn with Bree. Plus, it's nice that my sister and family still have you there.

The job is going well, but it's keeping me busy, as usual. I really like my coworkers, and we've all started doing Friday lunches together. It's been…nice being here. I feel like I'm becoming my own person, but it scares me being here and changing without you. I get scared that if I change too much, you won't like this me, but I'm just blabbering at this point, when these letters are supposed to be romantic.

I love you, Liv. I'm so damn proud of who you are and who you're becoming. Your writing never ceases to amaze the shit out of me, and I can't wait to have all your books on shelves in our house one day.

One day, right?

I love you. Send all the sunset pics.

Yours for however long you'll have me,
Tristan.

PS. No distance will ever make a difference for my love for you. Just in case you needed a reminder…

PPS. The boys won't stop calling me whipped when I text them updates about you. They might think they're funny, but when they fall in love, I'll be giving it right back to them.

TRISTAN,

No matter who you are or become, I'll love you, regardless. I fell in love with you, remember? Not just that version of you, I promise. Also, those candles never stood a

chance against me. Thanks for making my birthday one to remember, even though you're miles
away. It was one of the best birthdays ever.

Also, Bree is doing a lot better. I still
don't know what happened fully, patience is
key, but she's starting to become more confident in her body, and for that I'm thankful.
If I'm being optimistic, I could probably go
back with you after Thanksgiving. Bree seems
to be sticking to her routine, and even though
they haven't caught her stalker yet, he's been
quiet. The police are working nonstop on it,
but every trace of him vanished into thin air.
Her bodyguard, Vince, has still been around.
He's slowly become friends with us. He talks
more, so I guess it's a win.

We're going to look at two houses next
week—both huge—for my sister, and I can't wait
to send you pictures because I think one of
them could be the one. I want to get her settled
before I leave so I'm not worried about her.
Bree and I fell in love with it online, and I
think it could be a winner.

These letters keep me going, Tristan. I can
hear you in my head when I read them, and it's
like I have a piece of you with me even though
you're so far away.

This distance won't be forever, baby. We just
have to do it for a little while longer, and
everything will finally fall into place. We've
had too many speed bumps to count, and I'm

anxiously waiting for the day when you can come home to me in my office writing, kiss me on the forehead, and tell me about your day.

We're almost there, Tristan. We're so close.

I love you more and more every day. I can see a crack of light in the distance, just waiting for us to get to it.

I love you, I love you, I love you. All of our progress the past few months won't be lost. I love you. I'll see you soon.

How about forever?
Livvy

PS. I had a dream yesterday that you were in my room last night. It felt so real and I woke up and cried that it wasn't. I forgot to tell you on our call last night, but I know one day I'll wake up and you'll be sleeping soundly beside me. This distance isn't forever. Repeat that until November, and we'll be safe and sound.

PPS. Attached is a picture of me so you don't forget who I am or what I look like. I'm wearing one of your shirts in it because I miss you.

Chapter Twenty-Seven

— EVERMORE BY TAYLOR SWIFT FT. BON IVER

AS MY LAPTOP RINGS from my desk, I practically trip over myself, trying to get to it.

"Hi, pretty girl." God, three words is all it takes for my stomach to bottom out.

"Hi, baby." I smile as if I didn't talk to him last night. Even long-distance, it feels like an eternity between calls, and our letters only come about once a week. It's been months of them back and forth, and not once have I felt forgotten or unwanted by Tristan. He *always* makes time for me, even if our calls are short and we only talk for a few minutes. "How was work today?"

He yawns before answering. "It was good. We're still working on the software development for that one big company I told you about. I have to work the entire weekend to meet our deadline, but I'll be fine."

Tristan has been overworking himself a lot lately, but he wants a promotion that his company said he would get if he did well on this project. "Make sure you're taking care of yourself, drinking enough water, and sleeping a good amount. I don't want you to get burned out since you're burning the candle at both ends. As a matter of fact, we can end our call early—"

"Don't you dare finish that sentence, Liv. These calls are all I look forward to every day. I sit at work knowing that I'll see your beautiful face at night, and it keeps me going. *You* keep me going, Olivia, so there's no way I'm cutting our call short. And I want a book update, so hit me."

I smile widely before I launch into a discussion of all the things I wrote today—including a scene that Tristan has been waiting for since I started the damn book. I've been feeling in a creative high lately, and writing has been the only thing that I feel good at. Job hunting has been a no-go since I still feel a little lost. For now, I'm writing and working part time at my same job. My student loans are looming over my shoulders, practically begging me to get a full-time job that will sustain me, but I can't get myself to start applying. "I'm excited to see where the story goes in my head."

"I'm on the edge of my seat for the next few chapters." He smiles at me, and I wish I could kiss the corners of his mouth through the screen. "How has Bree been lately?"

"She's alright, I think. She's back to a regular routine and posting schedule—which she's ecstatic about. Apparently, she and Teags have been planning some sort of video with one another, and they're both excited about it. Connie is still on her about telling her followers about what happened, but Bree won't do it."

"I don't get why her manager wants her to tell the entire internet about something vulnerable when she hasn't even told you about it. It's pushy and rubs me the wrong way."

"Yeah, you and me both." I sigh, noting the heaviness in my chest over the past few weeks. The police *finally* caught Bree's stalker. After months of living on edge, my sister finally took a full breath when she got the call last week. She had to go in and identify him—by his voice because she didn't see his full face—and when we got out of the police station, she broke into tears. It *killed* me to see her like that, but it was the closure that she needed to start fully healing.

She's been talking to her therapist a few times a week—more than usual—but she's been smiling more, and for that, I'm thankful. Vince is gone, too, having moved on to another job. I was sad to see him go. He felt like a part of the family since he'd been with us for so long, but it was thankfully never going to be permanent.

"I'm just glad they caught him."

"Me too."

"I'm also excited that you can finally move her into her house. I know you both have been wanting to get out of your parents' house, and this past week feels like a step in all the right directions." Tristan's smile illuminates my room, and I already know what he's thinking about.

"I'm most excited to turn your apartment into *our* apartment."

"Me too. I love our letters, Livvy, don't get me wrong. But seeing your face when I come home every day is going to be the highlight of my year after not seeing you for months."

I can't fucking wait. Tristan comes home for Thanksgiving next month, and if all goes well, we'll *both* be on the first flight to California. There's a lot to be done before then, like packing up my entire life and moving my sister into her new house, but I'll get it all done as soon as possible if it gets me to him faster.

I've missed him, but we survived this. We got through it, and that means that we can do anything. "I love our letters too, and the fact that we probably only have a few left makes my heart soar, baby. You better make these last few count," I joke.

"Oh, I'll pull out all the stops, Liv. I'll try to channel my inner you, and I'm sure I'll come up with something book worthy."

"I'm sure whatever you say will have me falling more in love with you, baby. You're the only one for me, you know that."

"I'll always know that, Liv. Now, describe the sunset you saw for me tonight, and I'll do the same."

I launch into a description of it, and he does too, and for two more hours, we talk on the phone, not wanting to hang up even though we're both yawning. "Livvy, you have to work early, so you need to go to bed."

"Tristan, you have to work, too. So, you go to bed."

"Maybe I don't want to. Maybe I want to watch you fall asleep like I used to do when you crawled into my bed and made yourself at home." As Tristan says that, Bree comes into my room and plops onto the air mattress.

"Look, I know you two are in love and all, but I'm tired. Livs, can we listen to rain sounds again?"

"Of course we can, Bree." That's another thing that's changed for Bree. She used to hate having sound when she slept. She would sleep in dead silence, but now, she needs sound. Rain has been our go-to lately, but we've also listened to a few sleep stories. "I'll talk to you tomorrow, Tristan. I hope you sleep well."

"You too, pretty girl. I'll dream of you like always. I love you."

"I love you, too."

"Nice to hear your voice, Bree. Tell my sister that I miss her."

Bree just laughs, knowing that he probably texted Teags earlier today like he always does. I think he likes to make sure that even though he's gone, he hasn't forgotten his family. Hell, he even texts Bree to talk about his new skincare routine. It's absolutely hilarious. "I will, Tristan. I'm sure I'll hear your voice tomorrow like I always do."

"Bye, Hart sisters," he says as he ends the call, and I start to get comfortable on my bed. I'm wearing one of Tristan's shirts that he left me, and I'm fluffing my pillows when Bree speaks.

"I'll never get tired of seeing that look on your face."

"What look?"

"You're just…in love. It's written all over your expression when you're near him. I love seeing you happy, Livs."

My heart is bursting. "Thanks, Bree. I can't wait to watch you fall in love and say the exact same thing to you."

"I can't see that ever happening, but thanks, I guess."

My heart aches at the statement she made, but I decide not to press on it tonight. "Good night, Bree. I'll see you in the morning."

"Good night, Livs."

Four Days Later

As I RETURN TO the front entrance of my house, no letter from Tristan in my hand, I find myself disappointed. It's been days, and one still hasn't arrived yet, but the mail sometimes takes longer, so I chalk my disappointment up to the stupid post office.

I'm about to text Tristan back, when I start getting a bunch of messages and calls. "What the—?"

"What the fuck?!" I hear my sister scream from the living room. "Shit. Fuck. Shit!"

"Bree, what's going on?" I ask her, hoping that she can bring some clarity.

"Connie called to let me know that all of our numbers were leaked. Fuck!" she screams as she throws her phone against the wall. *Well, if she can't use it, then why not break it?*

"Why would someone do this, Bree? And what do you mean by *all*?"

"We have a family plan. Mom and Dad's numbers were also leaked on Twitter. Their phones are probably just like ours now."

"Well, like mine. Yours is broken now," I say as I pick it up, the cracked glass of the screen falling into my palm. "What the hell do we do?"

"Connie is already working on getting us all new phones and numbers."

"Wait, does that mean that all my pictures and texts are gone?" I'm the type of person who saves every picture and text message with people I love. *How am I going to talk to Tristan for the next few days?* If I don't answer tonight, he might get worried, and if I send a letter, it won't reach him for a few days. *And I never memorized his number.* Fuck, I guess a letter it is. A few days won't kill us, right? It'll be fine. He might be a little upset that he can't get a hold of me, but he'll know why soon enough.

"Yeah, sorry. Connie can't get the phones to us until tomorrow since she's trying to wipe the leak from the internet. I'm sorry, Liv. I didn't mean—"

I sit down next to my sister. "It's not your fault, Bree. It happens. Don't beat yourself up over it."

"I know, but Tristan—"

"Will be fine for a few days," I reassure her. "I'm going to mail him a letter today that will explain everything. He'll have it soon."

"Don't let me stop you. Go, Liv. Go write it." She sighs heavily, the weight of her number being leaked hitting her. I don't know how she deals with all this stuff—the fame, the no privacy even in the hard moments. I could never handle that, and I'm glad she at least has good people around her to keep her tethered.

I grab the cardstock that I always write my letters on and immediately explain the situation to Tristan. I apologize profusely for not memorizing his phone number but hope that when I can call him, it'll pop into my brain.

I shove it into an envelope before I put it in the mailbox, throwing the red lever up, but something already in there catches my eye.

It's from Tristan. His letter must've slipped out of my mail pile when I was rushing to grab all of it. My heart soars at the fact that I'll hear his voice in my head in a few seconds, and when I get back in the house, I excitedly rip it open. At first, I'm smiling, and then my heart sinks.

No. No, this is some kind of joke. I read the entire thing, and by the end of it, tears were pouring from my eyes and onto the paper. I'm mumbling some incoherent things, and I feel my sister's presence next to mine. She might be saying something to me, but the only thing I can hear is my heartbeat in my ears. *This is fake. It's not real. Tristan would never write this.* I read the letter over and over again, hoping it'll change.

```
Olivia,


I don't think I can do this anymore. Between
the long hours and the distance, it's getting
too hard for me to continue feeling like this
relationship is going in the right direction.
    I don't think we should see each other
anymore. It's too difficult.
```

Just a few days ago, he was telling me that no matter the distance that we would be together, that he was in it for the long haul. So, where did this come from all of a sudden? Did he fall out of love with me in the five days it's been since our last call? He told me he would be working late the next few nights and that he couldn't call, but we still talked all day. We texted and sent flirty messages like we always have. It's all been normal. *Where did this come from? What did I do?*

```
Cutting ties sounds like the best plan going
forward. You're here and I'm in California, so
a clean break is best, I think. I'm sorry to
```

do it this way, but I couldn't lie to you for
another day.

I'm sorry, Liv. You'll always be my favorite
almost.

Tristan.

That's it? That's all he has to say while he's ripping my heart to shreds is eight lines of absolute bullshit? The tears won't stop. I don't know how to get them to stop. I try to stand up and my legs give out. I'm crinkling the letter in my hands as more of my tears stain the page. I can barely read what's written anymore, but that doesn't matter because those eight lines will be forever cemented in my brain.

A clean break is best.

I couldn't lie to you for another day.

It's too hard.

You'll always be my favorite almost.

God, there's that word again—almost. I need to talk to him. I need to hear him say it—that he doesn't want to be with me anymore. The Tristan I thought I knew—would never say this to me. He promised me that we had all the time in the world. He promised me that I was the only one for him. Was all of that false? Was every memory that I have of him telling me all of these things only important to me?

Where do I go from here if I find out that he really meant this? Where do I go without him and our plan together? "Livvy? Liv, you need to breathe with me, okay? Can you do that?"

What is she talking about? I open my mouth to tell her that I'm breathing just fine, but I can't get any air in or out. My brain seems to catch up with my body, and my chest feels like it's on fire as the sobs keep coming out of me. "You're having a panic attack, Liv. Just look at me and breathe, okay?"

This isn't right. I'm the older sister. I'm supposed to have it all together. I'm supposed to be the one that helps my little sister through things like this. But now, our roles have reversed, and for the first time ever, I'm showing her all the tears that I used to stuff down in front of her.

All of a sudden, the front door opens and I hear two sets of footsteps come into where we are—my parents, home early from work. "What's going on here?"

My sister ignores them for a few minutes as they rant on and on about their phones not working and how they need them for important work. She pays them no mind as she helps my breathing come back to normal—well, as normal as it can be. My mind is still racing.

I need to call Tristan, but my phone is broken.

I need him. I need him to tell me that this isn't true.

I need our future together that he promised me.

He's gone, and I'm still here.

I need him to come back and hold me. I need him to tell me that everything is going to be alright.

My phone is broken. My number was leaked. My boyfriend no longer loves me. I have no job, no future, nothing. In one afternoon, my entire world has flipped upside down, and I'm more lost now than ever before. "Thanks, Bree," I whisper hoarsely at her.

"This isn't him, Liv. He wouldn't say this. He wouldn't do this," she reassures me, but more tears come as I think about the letter he wrote.

"It's his letter, Bree. He wrote it. He meant it," I whisper again, feeling like I lost my voice.

"Girls, what is going on? Why do the two of you look like that, and why is the house a mess?" My dad says as I fail to pull myself together.

Our front door swings open again as I hear more footsteps coming toward me. "Am I interrupting?" she asks as she hands the four of us new phones. I grab it out of her hands like a psychopath, ripping it open and turning it on.

"I thought you weren't coming until tomorrow?" Bree asks her manager, and she smiles at her.

"I'm a miracle worker, Bree. What can I say? Now, I'll be leaving now. Enjoy your new phone numbers!"

I hear all of this in the background as my phone powers on and I set it up as quickly as possible, tears still mulling my vision. I feel my sister come over and rub circles on my back, trying to comfort me in any way she can but unsure how to.

My phone finally works, and I find the phone button, hit it, and my fingers mindlessly type his number into the bar like I knew they would. I put it to my ear, hoping that I'd hear his voice come through the line to tell me that he still loved me, and he didn't write it.

But it never comes. The dial tone comes through after the third ring, so I immediately try again. I must try calling him a hundred times, hoping that one will eventually go through, but none of them do.

"Why isn't it working?"

"I—I don't know, Bree. Wh—What do I do? I need to talk to him, I need—"

"I know, Liv. Maybe I can ask Teags if she can get ahold—"

"No. Don't involve his family, Bree. This is between me and him." I don't want his family to comfort me after their son and brother just shattered my heart. If he wants a clean break—which he very clearly does from what I'm seeing—he'll get one.

"Goddammit, the press is outside," my mom scolds. I forgot she was home. She's barely said two words to us, or if she has, then I've become really good at tuning her out. "There are cars up and down the block."

"Why?" My sister asks.

"Because of you, of course. Why else would they be here?" My mom looks disdainful as she talks to my sister. What happened to the stars in her eyes when the press would be lined up outside? Has she finally had enough of the breach of privacy? I never thought I'd see the day. "Bree, your fame is too hard on us. It's all become too much this past year. Your father and I have decided to move houses in hopes that our address won't get leaked again. Our firm is threatening to let us go after all the press recently."

And there it is. Her precious job is being threatened. Meanwhile, my sister has been dealing with her own demons while being in the same house that gave them to her.

"I'm sorry my trauma has been such an imposition on you guys," I hear Bree snap at them.

I want today to be over. I want to crawl into the wall and disappear. I want to wake up from this nightmare that I seem to be living in and erase the past year from my memory. Maybe then it would hurt less. Maybe then the pain would stop, and I could exist without the weight of my feelings crushing me. Every step I take toward my room feels heavy, and I don't even care that my parents are getting rid of the house. I wish I was gone, anyway. I have no good memories here besides feeling like an insignificant human being and daughter. I know my sister feels relieved that this house will be gone—the memories of that night hopefully with it.

I have to hope that soon enough Tristan will see the letter that I'm sending, and maybe he'll rethink things. I have to hope that as soon as the letter gets to him, that he'll come to me and explain. But for now, I have to wait. I have to wait in the pain I'm feeling and see if it's true or not—that Tristan really doesn't want to be with me anymore.

I somehow get into my bed and sink into the covers, my tears staining the pillow as my swollen eyes shut and I dream of nothing.

Even in my dreams, he's gone.

— UNKNOWN / NTH BY HOZIER

Three Days Later

IT'S BEEN TWO DAYS since I got a letter from Livvy breaking up with me because it was too hard to be with me. Two days of trying to call her and have her explain who had a gun to her head when she wrote and sent it here. Two agonizingly fucking painful days where I haven't been able to get into contact with her.

It's been the worst two days of my entire fucking life.

Now, I'm standing in front of her parents' house after booking the first flight back here that I could. I explained to work that I had a family emergency, and while that's not the entire truth, they gave me a few days off since the project we've been working on just finished—successfully, might I add.

The only person I wanted to celebrate with was her, and then I opened that fucking letter, taking all my excitement with it as I read five lines of her explaining why she didn't love me anymore. About why she couldn't take it anymore—being with me over the distance.

I've never broken so many things like I did after I read that—plates, cups, anything I could. I ripped her letter to shreds, refusing to look at it or believe a single word written on it before I drank myself into a coma to try and forget every word she said.

It didn't work. I woke up yesterday remembering every painful word that slashed into my chest. Every word was like a knife dragging up and down my body, cutting me to pieces.

I've been standing in front of her house for minutes now, heartbroken and confused as fuck.

There's a sold sign in the front yard and no sign of Livvy, Bree, or their parents. It's not like I'd want to see them, but maybe they could've explained something, anything. Liv's social media is all gone—completely erased—and I haven't wanted to check Bree's.

It's like she vanished. She disappeared into the air like the ghost of someone I thought I knew. *How could she do this to me? To us?* She was in it for the long haul like I was. This letter came out of left field, and I want some fucking answers.

I just wish she would say something, anything else, to show me that this is all fake, a lie, a joke, no matter how cruel.

My Livvy isn't cruel. She's the most caring person I've ever met. Her smile lights up every fucking day that I walk this earth, and now she's gone.

What should I do? How the fuck do I fix this? Doesn't she know that she could've talked to me about this, and I would've come running back here for her? I would've done anything to keep her by my side—even if that meant quitting my job and dream to be closer to her. I would've driven across the country to prove to her that she means more to me than anything. No plane ride, no car ride, nothing could keep me from coming back to her—except herself.

But she was coming to you. She was, wasn't she? She told me that we would have our future by November if all went well, so why did she up and disappear? Why did she write this to me, seal it, mail it, and move on so quickly?

God, all the questions I have that I can't fucking answer.

How do I fix this? I can fix this, right? Yeah, I can fix this. How do I find her and make her love me again? How do I get this feeling that it's all over out of my mind, chest, and body?

It's not over until I see her. It's not over until she looks me in the eyes and tells me everything that letter said. Was I too much of an imposition to her? Does she really think that I'm better off without her? I'm nothing without that girl. Nothing else fucking matters except her, so how could she say the things she did? How could she break us in five sentences? How could she think she means so little to me when I tell her every day that she's not nothing—she's fucking everything.

I somehow get in my car and head to my house, slamming the door open as I enter. God, the memory of her is everywhere. I'm never going to be able to escape her if she really wants to break up. I swear I can still smell her fucking lip balm around me. "Tristan? What are you doing here?"

I turn to see Teagen sitting in the family room, staring at my disheveled appearance. I don't remember much about the past few days. I don't know how I got dressed, made it to the airport, got on the flight, and made it here. All I had in my mind was her—getting to her, seeing her, letting her explain, and finally being with her again. "She's gone."

"Who?" Theo asks me, clearly confused.

"I think he's talking about Livvy. Have you talked to her recently, Tristan? Bree's gone completely offline, and she's not answering my texts."

"What did you say?" I yell louder than I mean to.

"Bree hasn't answered me in days. I know her number got leaked the other day, but I assume she got a new—"

"Did Liv's get leaked too?" I ask, the pieces starting to fall into place.

"I think so." That must be why her old number isn't going through. *But why hasn't she called me with the new one?* "What's going on, Tristan? You look terrible, and you're supposed to be in California right now."

"Yeah, why *are* you here?"

"Liv's gone. She sent me..." I trail off, not wanting to think about that fucking letter sitting in pieces on my apartment floor. "I can't get a hold of her, and I think something's wrong."

"Give her a few days—" Theo says, but I cut him off.

"I can't. I need to talk to her now. Her house is empty. Her parents sold it. I don't know where the fuck she is, and since I don't have her new number, I can't talk to her." I can feel some tears start to mist from my eyes, but I'm unsure why they're suddenly here. The anger? Sadness? That fucking letter that won't stop floating around my head? The fact that she's gone, and we're over, and that I can feel my heart slowly breaking. I've never felt like this—completely broken beyond repair.

I guess all it took was the love of my life breaking my heart to do that to me. "I can ask Bree if she has it, but I doubt she'll answer me. I don't know what happened, Tristan. I'm just in the dark as you are."

"She broke up with me, Teags. She sent me a letter and broke up with me in five fucking sentences two days ago." Hearing that out loud makes it hurt more, and I want it to stop—no, I need it to stop, or I'm going to be crushed. Crushed under the weight of my failure. Crushed under the boulder that Livvy threw on top of me.

I gave her everything—every broken piece of me, every vulnerable moment, every laugh, every single thing I had to give was hers. How could she do this? How could she break us before we ever had a chance to be together in real-time? How could she erase us before our next chapter started?

"What? Livvy would never do that. She loves—"

"Loved, Teags. She *loved* me. Past tense." *God, it hurts.* It fucking hurts.

The love of my life is gone. She's gone. When things got tough, she fucking ran. I thought I was the one who loved running away from things, but it turns out that Livvy was a con artist that I never saw coming. She tricked me into falling for her, only to rip the rug out from under us before we ever truly started living.

I'll never love anyone as I loved her again, of that, I'm sure. She may have disappeared from everyone and everything, but she'll never disappear from my mind.

We could've been the best thing either of us had, if only she let us actually get there.

Every sunset I see will always be her. Every letter I send will always be to her. Regardless if she gets them or not, and regardless if she sees them or not, those two things will always be ours.

Our traditions. Our things. *Ours.*

But now, us doesn't exist anymore, and I'll spend however long it takes trying to figure out what the hell happened between us, and why she vanished from me like a fucking ghost.

Part 3
— Now —

Chapter Twenty-Eight

— GOOD GRIEF (REORCHESTRATED) BY BASTILLE

You know when you're driving and reach your destination wondering how you got there? That's how I feel now as I sit in the driveway of my childhood home.

How did I get here?

Not just here as in home, but here as in life. How did it all come to this? I left four years ago and thought that every piece of my future was falling into place, and now...now it's all broken. *I* am broken. My family is broken. It's like I put the puzzle together only for it to be shoved off of a table.

I can't bear to move from my car. It's still on as I sit in the driveway, building the courage to go in and face what I've been avoiding.

My brother is dead, and he's not coming back.

When I got the call from Teags the other day, I practically crumbled into pieces on my apartment floor. I thought she was kidding, and I hung up on her. I *hung up* on my sister, who was sobbing over the phone because I couldn't bear to believe it was true.

Death is the only thing that's permanent in life, and Tobias isn't coming back. I've officially outlived my younger brother. He'll never get married. He'll never be my best man at my wedding, like he always promised. He'll never fall in love again. He'll never joke around with me or my siblings ever again. He's gone.

How the fuck am I supposed to keep going, knowing that I'll never celebrate another birthday with him ever again? How do I do it? How the fuck am I supposed to keep my family afloat again?

And how do I focus on that when all I want to do is go back and talk to Livvy about what happened all those years ago? There are too many thoughts overwhelming my brain and I'm having a hard time focusing on any of them.

God, I'm a fucking mess.

She's still fucking here. After four years, she's still here. That was one thing I didn't prepare myself for when walking into the fucking store, but I always assumed that she left after it all broke apart. I assumed she ran from me, this town, and everything in it, but it turns out she's been here all along.

What the fuck.

She hasn't changed a bit. Besides the sadness that I saw deep in her eyes, she's still the same Livvy that I gave my hoodie to that first day we met. She's still the same girl that I fell in love with all those years ago. Hell, she's the girl I'm *still* in love with, even after everything, but it doesn't change the fact that I'm angry.

If she was here all this time, then why the fuck did she send that letter to me?

God, it hurts. Every emotion I'm having is like a punch to the gut, and instead of letting it out, I'm running in the opposite direction.

Fuck it all. Fuck the feelings, fuck being sad, fuck feeling like everything I've ever done was a waste. My mom, sister, and brother still need me.

Brother. Not brothers. Singular.

Punch.

I rest my head against the steering wheel of my Audi, feeling like I want to turn my car around, or run myself off of the road.

But I can't. They need me—no matter how much I dread walking back into the house that my brother once inhabited, too.

A knock against my car window has me flinching. "Are you okay in there?"

I unbuckle my seat belt and step out of my car, wrapping my arms around Teags. At twenty-two years old, my baby sister is the same age I was when I was graduating college, which she'll do next year. The thought of that scares me, but I'm glad both her and Theo chose to go to Summit. I know they were glad to have stayed close to home like I did—Mom would've been too lonely with nobody left in the house. Tobias was really the only one who ever wanted to get the hell away from here during college, and me after, but now it's him that's brought us all back here.

Punch.

"Tris, I asked if you were okay?"

"Sorry, Teags. I'm fine."

"Mhm, I bet," she mumbles into my shirt.

"How are you? How's Mom?" I ask, wanting to divert the topic off of my feelings—the ones I don't even know what to do with.

"Mom's okay, I think. She's putting on a brave face like she did when we were kids. Her eyes are red, though. Hell, my eyes are red as fuck, too." My sister's face breaks as she tries to laugh off her pain. "I miss him, Tristan. I keep going into his room and thinking that he'll appear from under the blankets, but he's gone. He's really gone, and my chest aches."

I wipe away a few of the tears that have fallen from her eyes before wrapping her in another hug. "I'm back indefinitely, Teags. We'll get through this together. One day at a time, okay?"

"One day at a time, no matter how much it fucking hurts." Teags pulls away from me and the two of us head towards the front door. My palms feel itchy all of a sudden. My clothes feel too tight, and I want to run again. I want to run far away from here, as far away from the thought of knowing that my brother didn't think he could come to me for help when he was struggling.

Fuck, how am I supposed to do this? How do I stay strong for everyone else while I'm crumbling inside?

As I step inside my childhood home, I expect it to fall apart beneath my feet, but it doesn't. It looks and smells exactly the same as I remember. Every room is still as it was, sparkling and dust-free since my mom has been cleaning all day, according to Teags.

The only difference here is that Tobias and his smile aren't around to fill the walls with laughter. He's not here to make it feel more like home. He may be in all the family pictures and photos that hang from our walls, but that's all he'll ever be again—a picture, a memory, a story being told. He'll just be past tense, while the rest of us grapple with the fact that he's gone in the present tense.

"Mom?"

"Tristan? Is that you? Did you get the groceries I asked for?" she yells from the kitchen as I hear her footsteps come closer.

"Yeah, I did. They're in the car, I'll go—"

"Nonsense, Tristan." My mom comes into view and immediately pulls me in for a hug. "You just got here, I'll go grab them, and—"

"Mom, I'll get them. Why don't you sit down and put some music on? Teags told me you've been cleaning all day." I motion to my sister to help my mom sit down, and she grabs her arm and pulls her into the living room. Typical Teags. I'm glad some things haven't changed.

After I unload all the groceries into the fridge and pantry, I take a seat next to my sister and remember that Theo still isn't home. "Have you talked to Theo at all?"

"No. He's read my messages, though."

Fucking hell. I grab my phone from my pocket and check his location, only to find that it's been turned off. *Fuck.* "Where do you think he is?"

"Not sure, but he'll be here eventually, I think. He's been having a rough time."

"We all have, and he promised that he would be here today." I'm pissed, but I try to calm myself down before I say something I don't mean. The house is silent as the three of us sit here. I don't think any of us really know what to say. A lot has happened in the past few weeks, and it's too much to dissect in one afternoon.

None of us wants to talk about the elephant in the room, and it'll probably stay that way for a while.

Tobias was silently struggling, and none of us seemed to notice. He never told us about it. In every text or phone call I had with him, he seemed fine, happy even. But isn't that what some people say about their loved ones before they take their own lives? God, I wish I could fix this. I'd give anything to go back to last month. He had called me to ask me a simple question, which then turned into a two-hour conversation about anything and everything. We laughed, we smiled, and the two of us just talked like brothers.

He had been struggling to find a new job after the last one laid him off, but he was optimistic about it, or so he said.

How he went from optimistic to taking his own life in our family cabin, I'll never understand. How he didn't think he could come to me for help, guidance, or a shoulder to lean on, I'll never understand.

He and Theo were there for me all those years ago when I lost Livvy. My entire family stuck around me while I was down and out over her, so why didn't he think I'd do the same for him? No matter how bad he felt, I would've been there. In a goddamn heartbeat, I would've been at his place with whatever he needed.

"Is someone knocking?" My sister asks as she gets up.

"It might be someone bringing food over, Teags. Open the door with a smile, and make sure you're polite!"

"I'm sure they'll understand if I'm not, Mom, but okay." Her voice quiets as I hear her open the door. "Are you drunk?"

"No, little sister. Are you drunk?" Theo's voice permeates the air, and I get up and rush to the door.

"Why the fuck did you turn your location off? The three of us promised to never do that after—"

"After the fourth one of us decided to do what he did? Forgive me for wanting any semblance of space for a few days while I coped." Theo smiles at me, and it's like every trace of my younger brother has disappeared. I have no idea who this person is in front of me. He's grown a beard, his hair is messy and unstyled, and I can smell whiskey on his breath. God, what I would give to have a drink right now, but I need to hold it together. One of us needs to have a clear head, and as always, it has to be me. It's always been me.

"Go sit down, and I'll bring you some water. Mom's in the living room."

"Yes, sir." Theo salutes me before throwing off his shoes and jacket and heading into the living room. Teags and I stand at the front door, shocked by what we just witnessed.

"I guess we all cope differently, huh?" she says, trying to break the tension.

"Yeah, I guess. I'm gonna get him some water to try to sober him up so we can all talk."

"Should I get him some food?"

"No. Just water for now." I grab my sister's arm as she passes by me. "I've got this, Teags. I'll anchor us through this."

"Tristan, you don't need to be our anchor anymore. You know that, right? You can grieve just like the rest of us, and we'll get through this together."

She makes a good point, but I don't know what I'd do if I chose to do that. It's become second nature to me to weather my family through every storm that comes our way. "I'll be fine, Teags. Just let me help us. Let me try to patch the pieces back together."

"I will. Just promise me that you'll patch yourself up in the process, too." A tear falls from her eye, and I don't think she even notices. I've never seen my sister so emotional before, and I wish I could take all this pain away from her. She's too young to know what all this feels like.

"I promise."

AFTER ONE CASSEROLE AND the most silent dinner we've ever had in the West household, we finally sit down to talk. All of us kids are on the couch in the living room while my mom sits on the chair that used to belong to my dad.

Used to. That phrase now works for two members of my family.

"I know it's been a difficult few weeks, and I don't want to make it any worse, but I'd go crazy if I kept these from you." My mom slides three white envelopes toward us before I see the fourth in her hand. Each has our names on it, and my siblings and I look at one another, all confused as fuck.

"What are these?" Teagen asks, never afraid to speak up.

"They're from your brother," my mom whispers, but it feels like a scream. Her words penetrate my mind, and as they seep in, I realize what it means.

Tobias left these. They're the last things he'll ever say to us.

"Wh—Where did you get these?" Theo asks. I'm unsure if he's blubbering because he truly doesn't understand if he's too drunk or too emotional to deal with this. It might be all three if I'm honest.

"One of the police officers gave them to me. They were found in the cabin…" My mom trails off, not wanting to say it out loud. "Excuse me."

My mom leaves the room, not wanting us to see her cry, before I hear her bedroom door shut upstairs. God, it feels like when my dad died, but a thousand times worse. She had a reason to stay strong—raising us. But now, we're all grown up, and she's lost one of her sons.

It's not fucking fair.

"So, he wrote these before he…" My sister trails off, more tears leaking from her eyes.

"Yeah," Theo says, not having moved his eyes off of the white envelope in front of him.

"I'm going to clean up dinner," I say as I shove the envelope into my bag where I can't see it and head into the kitchen.

After receiving a certain letter four years ago, I'm never in a rush to open them anymore. Knowing this one is one of the last things my brother did in that cabin before he left isn't helping. Part of me wants to lock it away in a safe, so I never have to hear what his last words to me are. The other part wants to rip it open and read it immediately.

But I do neither as I wipe the dishes down and place them in the dishwasher, running away from all the guilt, sadness, and anger I'm feeling and focusing on what I can do to help.

One day at a time. One agonizing day at a fucking time.

Chapter Twenty-Nine

— RIGHT WHERE YOU LEFT ME BY TAYLOR SWIFT

IT'S TOO MUCH. IT's all too fucking much.

He's here. He's back. *Indefinitely.*

I barely know how I finished my shift. I don't know how I drove back to my apartment, and as I unlock the door, I immediately slam it shut, wanting to keep all of my emotions out.

But instead, I break.

I can't breathe. Every single memory of us is rushing back into my brain, and it's making me sick.

Tristan is back. I saw him with my own two eyes. He's not just a figment of my memories anymore. I knew this day would eventually come. I knew he would be back, and I'd see him, but it still hurts. I thought I had shielded my heart after it broke into pieces all those years ago. I thought I was stronger than this, but all it took was one short and awkward conversation with him to fry my circuits.

All it took was one look at him, and I knew I wasn't over it. Over us.

He's back for a funeral, and I didn't even know about it.

I try to stand, but my legs feel like jelly. My breaths are short and constricted, and I'm still on the floor of my apartment. If anyone were to come in and see me like this, I think I'd look insane. My mind feels like a madhouse, and I'm trapped inside of it.

I somehow get to my feet and to the island in my kitchen, fetching a glass of water from the fridge before I pull my phone from my work bag. My sister picks up on the third ring. "He's back, Bree."

"What? I can barely understand you, Livs."

I take a steadying breath before I say anything else. "He's back. I saw him. He's here." She should know who I'm talking about. Bree was the one who picked up my broken heart off of the floor after I read that letter.

"You saw him with your own two eyes? Are you okay? Did he talk to you?"

"Yes, no, and yes. My coworkers practically forced us to have a conversation. It pissed me off, but he's back here for a funeral. Someone close to him."

"How did he look?"

God, what a loaded question. "Different, sad, annoyed, as beautiful as I remember." He looked exhausted, but I'd never seen someone as gorgeous as Tristan. He's grown up nicely over these past four years. His hair is slightly longer and more curled at the ends—probably from all the hats he loves wearing. He was dressed in nice clothes as if he got on a plane right from the office. The stubble of his beard was more prominent, and it suited him. Those same brown eyes still look right through me, as if he can see all the thoughts swirling around in my head. Tristan was always good at that—reading my facial expressions and emotions. For the first time ever, I couldn't tell what he was thinking. He just felt...cold.

Before all this time aged us, Tristan was always so light. He was the warmth that floated into a room every time he entered. He was the person who always had people laughing at his jokes. Now, he's the exact opposite of who he once was. It's like all that warmth got sucked out of him. I wonder if it happened when he ended things between us or if whatever funeral he's back for has him like this.

"I know you still have feelings for him, Liv, but don't forget how torn up you were when you got that letter. I don't want to see you like that again. Not if I have anything to say about it, at least." My beautiful, strong sister. The one I can always count on to be there for me when I'm down. "Do you want me to come home? This event is boring me anyway."

"No, Bree. I'll be okay. I'm glad I have you to talk it out with. My brain has never been more confused. Part of me wanted to punch him for what he did, and another part of me wanted to stay in his embrace for longer than ten seconds."

"Olivia Hart, you let him touch you? That's like rule number one of talking to an ex. Never embrace because then you'll think about all the other times and fall back into the trap!"

"I only let him because I was consoling him. He lost someone close to him, Bree. It was the right thing to do. The friendly thing to do." I'm saying it out loud, but I don't believe a word of what I'm saying. I wanted to hold him like I used to before, back when everything was perfect between us. I missed it. Nothing beats the feeling of being in the embrace of someone you love.

I blame the nostalgia of it all. That's all it is, right? I miss the thing that I can't have, and it makes me yearn for it more. "Who did he lose?"

"I don't know. I asked, and then I could tell he didn't want to answer it, so I told him he didn't have to tell me. God, the look on his face, Bree. It practically killed me. He's in so much pain, and he's trying to hide it." Tristan was always one to run away from his feelings and everything in between. I can tell he's back to doing that by the look I saw on his face.

My sister sucks in a breath over the phone. "It's Tobias."

The name hits me like a ton of bricks. "Tobias…His brother? No. No way."

"It was suicide, Liv…" I think she keeps talking, but I can't hear her through the ringing in my ears.

Tobias. Dead. Suicide. I feel my phone drop from my ear as my breathing picks up again. It's all too much. The past few hours are hitting my brain, and all my thoughts are scrambling together. I feel like I'm on fire. I need to get out of here, of my apartment, my brain, my skin, my body. Tears are leaking out of my eyes like a sieve, and they won't stop.

Tobias is gone.

Tristan was gone, and now he's back—for his brother's funeral.

He lost his brother, and I'm focusing on how I feel about all this. *God, he must be a wreck.* I can't even imagine how his mom or siblings are doing.

My tears keep coming, and I feel a hand against my face, picking my head up off of the floor of my kitchen. *How did I get down here?* I see Parker's face come into view, her mouth moving, but I don't hear what she's saying. Her eyes search my face as she takes the water I was drinking and throws it against my face, breaking me out of whatever brain fog I was in and bringing me back to the present.

"What the hell is going on, Liv?"

AFTER I BRING PARKER up to speed and put Bree on speakerphone, the three of us sit quietly as the information sinks into our minds. I hate that I'm breaking down over this. He lost his brother, for fuck's sake, and I'm over here panicking about seeing him again. I wish I could do something. I wish I could make all of his pain go away, but I can't, and it's killing me. It's killing me that someone I loved—maybe still love—is in pain, and I'm stuck watching him crack from a distance.

"I need wine," Parker says as she heads to her room to change out of her work clothes.

"You're home early. I thought you were staying late."

"I decided to not keep overworking myself. I still have a week, and I can work from here tonight. I just wanted to be home, and I'm glad I was Liv. You scared the hell out of me. You were having some sort of panic attack or out-of-body experience."

"I didn't mean to scare you. I'm sorry. It's all too much," I say as I slump against our living room couch, wanting to sink into the pillows. "Him being back has thrown me for a loop."

"That's normal, Liv. Seeing your ex—especially after four years, and how you two ended—would throw anyone for a loop." My sister says over the phone.

"I can't keep thinking about this, or I'll combust. I need a topic change," I say to the room. I can practically feel the blood flowing through my veins, and I need it to stop.

I can't bear to think about him for another second. He's practically flooded every waking thought I've had for the four years he was gone, and seeing him in person has amplified those tenfold. If Tristan and I were a book, all of our pages would be out of order and stuck together, all of our memories overlapping. *I guess, in a way, we kind of are...*

"Liv, how are your book sales? Have you hit five million pages read yet?" my sister asks, changing the subject to one I was already thinking about.

"Ooh, yeah! I'm curious too. We've barely talked about your book sales since I've been working so much the past few weeks."

That's not the only reason. I hate talking about the book I wrote and self-published two years ago. I never knew self-publishing was a thing until I looked into it online and asked Bree about it, but she was the one who convinced me to do it after she read my manuscript. So, yeah, I wrote a novel about a couple who *almost* made it. It's a twist on a traditional romance novel where the couple you see throughout the book doesn't end up together.

I'm officially one of those writers who sticks all of their complicated and emotional feelings into their characters and lets them figure it out rather than deal with it myself. "Yeah, I hit five million last week."

"Congrats, Liv! That's insane for your debut. I'm so proud of you." My sister cheers.

"I'm proud of you, Liv. You're a fucking author, and nobody can take that away from you." Parker grabs my hand and squeezes it, and I have to fight more tears from coming up.

"Thanks, guys." My mind flashes back to the book launch party that my sister threw for me at her house. She invited a bunch of her close influencer friends, Parker, Cassie and Bryce even showed up from New York, and I signed a bunch of my books for people. I think that's how it got so much attention. Not only was my sister promoting the hell out of it, but a bunch of the people from the party read it and loved it. Their promotion helped skyrocket it up into the Top 100 in the Kindle store. It was...insane, actually. The most unreal day of my life.

But I still felt like I was missing something, and I knew that something was him.

It felt wrong to publish a book loosely based on Tristan and I's relationship, but I did it anyway because my sister convinced me that people would relate to it—and many did. I still get messages from people who read my book and how much my characters make them feel seen. It feels good knowing that my book can reach people like that.

But I still wish he was here by my side rather than fictionalized in my book.

After I published that, the rest of my stories felt flat and uninteresting. I've barely written a word since, and I don't know how to get that feeling back again—where the characters speak to you, and the story writes itself. I've tried to go back to the ideas I had when I was in college, but I physically can't write them. Not without him. Not without the guy who believed in them when I would plan them out on his dorm floor while he worked on his homework.

God, I miss him. I never let myself admit it before, not out loud or in my head. Now, I find myself acknowledging it more than before.

"I think I'm gonna head to bed. I feel exhausted. I need to lie down, or sleep forever, or cry myself to sleep."

"Or all three!" my sister cheerfully says.

"Bree, don't encourage this," Parker says, taking a sip of her wine that I just now noticed. "Take a rest, Liv. We can talk more tomorrow. You have the day off, right?"

I nod at her. "I plan on rotting in my bed all day."

"Sounds like a plan. We'll have wine night. I'll update Cassie and get her on FaceTime." Parker smiles at me as I pull myself off of our couch and head to my bedroom.

"I'll talk to you soon, Bree. Enjoy your trip."

"Thanks, Livs. I'll see you as soon as I get back. Okay?" she asks, not hanging up yet.

"I'll pick you up from the airport like always, Bree. It's a date." I smile at her through the phone. She can't see it, but I bet she can hear it in my voice. *I miss her.*

"Good night, Liv. Get some actual sleep for once. I love you."

"I'll try. I love you, too," I say as I hang up and fall into my bed, tears, and sleep coming as soon as I hit my pillow.

Chapter Thirty

— ANCHOR BY NOVO AMOR

I'm finally sitting down after helping my mom around the house, and I still feel the need to be doing something. In the past few days, I've cleaned the gutters out, weeded the garden, mowed the lawn, trimmed the hedges, got the Halloween decorations out from the basement, and dusted the entire house.

Now I have nothing else to fucking do but sit here with my feelings, and I hate it. Free time has become my worst enemy lately. It gives me way too much time to think about Tobias, Livvy, and my fucked-up life. If my brain and body don't keep moving, then I'll sink further down into my feelings.

My mom has barely left her room in the past few days. Teags and I have been bringing her all her meals in bed, and it crushes me every time I see her red eyes. She's not even trying to hide her emotions anymore, which is good, I guess. Theo's stolen two bottles of whiskey from the liquor cabinet, opting to stay drunk most of the time. Teags and I have been dancing around the topic of Tobias for the past few days, but I can tell she's hurting. She might be the most outspoken West sibling, but she's been way too quiet the past few days.

I can't say I blame her. I've been distracting myself, but maybe I should check in on her.

I take the stairs two at a time, and when I get to her room, I notice she isn't in there. *Weird.* I check every room—including mine—and when I reach the last one, I take a deep breath before I push the door open. "Tobias would hate that we're in here, you know."

Teagen's eyes meet mine. "I know. He always used to hate other people in his personal space, just like you."

"Ouch."

"You guys were similar in that aspect." She smiles at me, unshed tears in her eyes. "I used to sneak in here when he was at college and use his desk. I always liked his chair more than mine. It was more comfortable, and I got less distracted here."

"That's because he has a gaming chair. Mom got it for him a few years ago."

"Ah."

The two of us are silent for a few moments, taking in the room that will never be used by my brother again. It feels like a tomb in some ways—all of his stuff still exactly the way he left it, and now he'll never touch any of it again. "How are you holding up?"

She rolls her eyes at me. "It's been like four days since you got here, Tristan."

"I know. Now answer the question."

"Horrible. I don't know what to do with all of my feelings, and I can't stop crying. It's pissing me off. I don't know what to do with all the loss. I don't know how to stop talking about him as if he's still around."

"What can I do?" I ask as I throw my arms around her.

"You can't bring him back, so nothing. We just have to keep going."

"These feelings won't be forever, Teags. Repeat that anytime you feel like shit."

She sniffles into my shoulder as I shove my emotions down further and further. "Thanks, Tristan."

I lead us out of his room before she heads back into hers, shutting the door behind her. A few seconds later, her music starts blaring. *She'll be okay.* Teags practically communicates through her playlists, and this one doesn't seem too sad. I guess I'll see as the day progresses.

I pivot to my mom's room, knocking softly before I enter her room. "Come in."

"Hey, Mom. Just checking in," I say as I move to the end of her bed to sit down. Her room is spotless, and besides the ruffled covers that she's under, you'd never think it was lived in. She still sleeps on her same side of the bed, leaving the other side that was my dad's as his. I always thought it was weird that she did that, but as I got older, I started to understand.

It's how I feel about leaving Tobias' room as his and not changing it. It's all we have left, and I want to remember him as who he was here, not how he chose to leave. "I'm okay, honey. Just feeling overwhelmed."

"Have you thought about the funeral at all?" I ask, wondering if she's even started or thought about preparations for it.

"Oh, no. I haven't even—"

"Mom, it's okay. I can handle that if it's easier for you."

"There's nothing easy about this," she says, her voice low and sad, and fuck, it's killing me to hear my strong mother like this. "I can help with some of it, but I don't want to step into that church until I have to. There should be a file by the door with everything you'll need."

"I know, Mom. I know. But we'll give him the funeral he deserves. It'll be great, okay? I'll make sure it's perfect."

"And you'll give the eulogy? I want to say a few words, but I don't think I could—"

"I'll do anything you ask of me, Mom. I'll head over there now, and if you could get a list together for when I'm back, that would be helpful."

I grab a few plates from her side table from the breakfast and lunch we gave her this morning and close her door softly behind me.

Okay, funeral planning. I have something to keep me busy now. I don't know if I could find any other surface in this house to clean, and I haven't found my old baseball stuff yet, so the batting cages have been off the table. I place the dishes in the sink, making a mental note to do them later so I can head to the funeral home near us before it closes.

It's around three in the afternoon, and I want to get there today, so I have something to do. I grab my keys, wallet, and the folder my mom put together a few days ago. It has his social security papers, birth certificate, and all the other documents I'll need to get the planning started.

Only when I open my door and see a familiar head of dark brown hair do my insides twist. Her eyes meet mine when she hears the door open, shock waving through her features. "Did you not expect to see me at my own house or what?" I snap, instantly regretting what I said. *Fuck, I'm an asshole.*

"No, I just wasn't expecting anyone to open the door. I was leaving these for you and your family—"

"Has it ever occurred to you that my family doesn't need or want anything from you?" *I am such a dick.* As soon as I say that, her face tightens as if she's in pain. *I did that to her.* I made her feel like that. I remember how I used to only want to make her feel happy. I remember feeling like the luckiest guy in the world every time Livvy laughed and smiled near me. I loved pulling all of her happiness out of her body like it was a contest, and I wanted to win first prize.

Now, I've changed. Both of us are different, and I'm the one hurting her instead of putting a smile on her face. God, I don't deserve her—not like this, anyway. I'm broken beyond repair, and I'm pushing away the only person that I know could patch my pieces up, just like she told me I did for her all those years ago.

Only she was the one who smashed us to pieces four years ago with that letter. Her. Not me.

"Tristan, I was leaving these to show my condolences. I saw the obituary online, and I'm so sorry—"

I cut her off, "Thanks, but no amount of food will change how shitty I feel."

"I know. Nothing could ever, but—"

"What are you really doing here, Olivia?" I don't even know why I'm so pissed off at her presence. She's doing something nice, and I'm yelling at her for it. I'm a fucking asshole, and my brother is dead, and I feel helpless. I need all these emotions to get the fuck out so I can think clearly again, but they won't leave. They're festering and now I'm taking it out on the one person that I want to get closer to. The one person I want to run toward so she can help me decipher why I can't seem to cry over my brother's death.

"Dropping off brownies, Tristan. I'm sorry for your loss and all, but that doesn't give you the right to yell at me."

I know. "You yelled at me when I saw you at work. Consider us even!" I say as I slam the door behind me and head toward my car. I can feel her following me. I can always tell where her presence is, and it drives me crazy that my body still knows hers so well. "Go home, Olivia."

"No. You don't get to do that. There's no getting even for us, not after what you did four years ago. And if I recall, you were the one who showed up at *my* place of work and demanded to talk."

"Oh, what *I* did? What about you, Olivia? You're not exactly blameless in the destruction of us. And forgive me for wanting to speak to you after four years apart. I guess I'll just forget that we ever existed. It's a hell of a lot easier than remembering everything the way that it was." God, I am an asshole. But to be fair, she is too. She's the one who sent that letter, so I don't know why she's bringing me into this. I didn't even get a phone call or a text message. Nothing. She broke every string that held us together. I had nothing to do with it. *Right?*

"I never wanted that, Tristan. If you knew me at all back then, you would know that." Her voice is so soft that I barely hear her say it, but the words invade my bones, cracking them even more than before. *What is she talking about?*

"I thought I knew you, Liv. I thought we were in it forever, but it turns out that it was just me. Now, if you'll excuse me, I'm going to go plan my brother's funeral." I unlock my car, and before I get into it, Livvy speaks again.

"As far as I'm concerned, we were forever, Tristan. Excuse me for wanting to be nice to you while you're going through a tough time, but maybe we don't work that way. Maybe we should both move on."

"Sounds great to me, Liv. I started moving on a long time ago." God, why did I say that? I hate looking at her face and seeing the blow I landed. Has she gone on dates? Has another guy touched her while I was in California? Did she move on with someone else that makes her happy? I never fucking did. Anytime I tried to go out with another girl, all I saw was her, so why did I lie?

"Good for you, Tristan. I hope you're happy with whoever it is because I clearly wasn't worth the effort. Stay the hell away from me." And before I can say something else I regret, she turns and walks away, not wanting to listen to any of the bullshit that spews out of my mouth. I hate who I've become. I lied about moving on because how could I move on from the love of my life? There's nobody on this planet that compares to Livvy, and I've just fucked any chance I had up because of my stupid mouth. There are so many things I've wanted to say to her, but this is only the second time we've seen each other since I've been back. I'm sure she's busy working, and I've been busy distracting myself from everything.

What happened to us, Livvy? Why did you send me that letter and break my heart?

I fucking miss you. I miss what we had. I miss us.

Do you miss me as much as I do you? Do you miss what we once had? Can we ever get that back?

What can I say to bring you back to me, to us?

Fuck. It all fucking hurts, and before I punch something and break my hand, I get in my car and head toward the funeral home.

Chapter Thirty-One

Two Weeks Later

— SUPERMARKET FLOWERS BY ED SHEERAN

IF ONE MORE PERSON comes up to me and offers their condolences, I'm going to lock myself in a closet.

Today is my brother's funeral. Today is the day I've been dreading since I left California to come back here. It's all too overwhelming. People that I barely know are coming up to me and telling me how sorry they are. The wake yesterday wasn't any better.

The worst part is that I have no control over my emotions. I want to cry. I want to feel the pain and the hurt, but I physically can't. It's like there's a wall in front of them, and no matter how hard I try to break it down, it won't budge.

My stoic mask is up, and as much as I try to tear it down, I can't. I know people are noticing that I'm seemingly fine, but the one person who could see right through that isn't here anymore.

I regret everything I said to her that day she was on my porch, and in the mess of planning the funeral, I haven't apologized to her yet. She deserves an apology from me. Liv was being nice, and I berated her for it because of how fucked up I am right now.

"Drink?" Ethan asks me as he hands me a flask. I don't answer before taking it from him and feel it burn down my throat. "I figured you would need a steadying shot."

"How are you holding up?" Dom asks me. It's been weird having him and the guys around the past few days, but I've missed them. We've all stayed in touch over the years—Ethan being the only one who went far besides me—and I'm glad they're here now. It just sucks that *this* is why we're all seeing each other again.

"I'm fine," I say, knowing none of them believe me, but they don't press. They just stand by me while more and more people come up and offer condolences. I look at where my sister is. She's talking to one of my aunts, tears in her eyes and a smile on her face. I bet she's being told some story about Tobias and her as kids. Theo is sitting up in one of the pews, looking just as ghostly as he did when I woke him up this morning and threw his suit on his bed. My mom is next to him, tissues in hand, black gloves going up her arm. I laid out her outfit for her this morning, too. I know she wouldn't have done it herself.

Teags and I have been helping them out. I thought I was going to be alone in all this, but my sister has made sure that I'm not shouldering this entire thing on my own, and I'm thankful for that.

I'm pissed off that she seems to be headed in the direction of healing, and I haven't even started yet. "Do you have your cards, Tristan?" Harry asks me.

"Yeah, I do." I'm saying a few words in honor of my brother, and it took me an entire week to write anything down on them. I couldn't think of much to say, but when I sat down to write it on my flashcards, nothing came. I stared at the blank cards for a week until I wrote down whatever came to mind. It probably makes no sense, but I'll say it. I have to stick to the script, or else I'll fall to pieces in front of the entire church.

"I think it's starting. Let's go sit down." Ethan motions for us to head to the front. The officiant walks out, and everyone makes their way to their seats as he begins talking. The guys all sit behind me, giving condolences to my mom and sister. Theo ignores them all, still staring blankly at the casket that my brother is in. I try not to look at it. I'm afraid that all this will turn real if I look at it. It's a closed casket, but just knowing he's in there makes me miserable.

Minutes or hours pass as I stare at the altar behind the officiant as he speaks. I see my mom get up and head to the front podium to say a few words, and I clench my fists, wanting my emotions to simmer. I can't get angry in a church and curse God for taking my brother away from us, not today.

My mom clears her throat before she speaks. "Tobias was my second-born son. He came into the world quietly, not wailing like my three other kids. My husband and I always called him the patient one because of how bright his smile shined and how calm he was. I never...I never imagined I'd be here doing this. As a parent, you expect that your kids will speak at your funeral, but nothing prepares you for having to speak at one of theirs."

Tears begin to creep up on me, and my sister hands me a tissue as one finally falls. Just one. My mom is one of the strongest people I know. She's lost a husband and a son in the time she's lived. I don't know how she's still standing.

"Tobias touched the lives of everyone he met, and I'm grateful to see so many faces here today. I would trade anything to be able to hug him again, to talk to him again, to walk into his room and see him sitting at his desk playing video games. I thought losing my husband was the worst pain I could've imagined, but this pain is different. I feel like I failed as a parent, but if he was here, he would tell me that I did my best. I know that for sure because Tobias was that kind of kid. He didn't tell you what you wanted to hear, but what he knew was true. Mom loves you forever, Toby. I hope you never forget that." She looks up, then over at the casket, and then walks back to her seat. My sister hands her a few more tissues as she intertwines their hands on her lap.

"Now, Tristan West would like to say a few words. Come on up." I feel my friends give my shoulders and back a pat as I stand up, button my suit jacket, and head to the podium. My heart pounds in my ears and through my body, but I feel like I don't exist. I feel like I'm not really here right now—my brother's funeral, my body, this church. None of it feels like real life. It feels like I'm watching it all happen from a different part of space.

I step up to the microphone and take a few calming breaths before I take the cards out of my jacket. I place them in front of me, but I don't speak. I can't. These words all feel lifeless, so I disregard them.

"Tobias' last words to me were that he wanted to be like me when he got older. He had called me for some random thing about a month ago, and we ended up talking for a few hours. That was a normal thing with Tobias. He would go off on eighteen different tangents when trying to tell a story or ask a question, and nobody stopped him because of how he looked when he spoke." I take a breath, looking out into the crowd and seeing a bunch of people nodding their heads in agreement. *God, look how many people he impacted.*

"My only wish is that he could know I've spent my entire life trying to be like him. I'm a few years older than him, and people used to tell me that I was too rigid when I was younger. He might've been my younger brother, but he was always the one I looked up to. He was always smiling, always happy, always going out of his way to help others, and I wanted to be like that—like him. I never told him that, and now I'll never be able to, but I hope that he can hear me wherever he is."

I lock eyes with my sister, brother, and mother, tears flooding all of their eyes as I continue to speak. And for the first time, I look over at where my brother lays to rest. The casket closed over him as I spoke. "Tobias, I'll miss you for the rest of my life. I hope you know how much we all miss your smiles and laughs around the house. You may have been my younger brother, but I'll spend the rest of my life trying to emulate even a fraction of what you made people feel. Rest peacefully, brother. I'll see you again someday."

As I sit back down in my spot, Theo throws his arm around my shoulder. "You did good."

"Thanks," I say as he hands me his flask, and I take a drink out of it, feeling worse now than I did before.

THE FUNERAL SOMEHOW ENDS, and my family and I drive home after, the car silent as we all take in the finality of today. There's nothing else to do to keep my thoughts from creeping up, and they practically flood my brain as my mom drives us all back home.

My brother is gone. All he'll ever be is stories and old photos now. What happens after a funeral? You just move on? I don't know how that's possible, but I guess it's all I have left to do. It seems insurmountable. It feels impossible to do. I don't know how or if I'll ever be happy again because how can I be without my brother? So many of our experiences growing up were similar and shared between all of us. We all took our first steps in the same house. They all loved the same family and mourned the same father that I did. Yeah, we fought over stupid things as kids, but at the end of the night, we were always sitting on the same couch to watch the same movies together—as a family.

We all grew up to be different people, but nothing can change the fact that we lived the same childhood. The four of us were pieces of our parents, all split up, but when we came together, we were whole again. And now one of those pieces is gone—missing forever from the puzzle box that we all were stored in. Nothing will ever fit the three of us the same again, but then again, did anything really fit after our dad died? Maybe it did. Maybe it didn't. But that doesn't change the fact that our puzzle will never be complete again.

There's an empty space in the shape of where my brother used to be, and no form will ever fit right, no matter how hard we try.

I hear the doors of the car slam as Theo and Teags get out of the backseat, but I find myself not being able to move from the car.

I can't go back there. Going back into the house where all those shared memories are is too much. It's too much after I just watched my brother get lowered into the ground, tossing dirt over his final resting place.

"Honey? Are you coming?" My mom asks me, but I can't muster the words to answer her.

"I—I—"

"Tristan, are you alright? You look pale." My mom's hands come over to touch my face, but I lean away from her touch as I open the car door, needing fresh air. When I try to breathe it in, it feels dirty. My lungs are seizing, and nothing feels right. It's as if the world has been flipped upside down and inside out because nothing fits. My brother is dead, and nothing will ever make sense ever again.

"I have to get out of here. I—I can't stay here. I can't. I won't," I say as I unlock my car and speed out of my driveway. The weight of it is too much, and I feel my breathing even out by the time I pull into a random hotel, deciding that it's easier being here than being back in my childhood home.

Always a runner, never a finisher.

Chapter Thirty-Two

October

— MEET ME IN THE HALLWAY BY HARRY STYLES

TODAY HAS BEEN THE longest day ever, and I can't wait to be home. Work was crazy busy for a Monday, and after running around all day, I had a date with a hot shower.

The drive home is normal. I've been listening to the playlist I made for fall since it's right around the corner. October has officially begun, and I usually make a new playlist each month, depending on the vibe I feel. This month features a bunch of slow and melancholy songs that match perfectly to my life.

In the past few weeks, life has gone from zero to one hundred almost too quickly. Tristan being back has shaken me, and after the short conversation we had outside of his house a few weeks ago, I've wanted to crawl into a hole and stay there.

I made him and his family brownies, and he told me he wanted nothing to do with me. He also told me that he moved on a lot while I was gone, which shouldn't have affected me as much as it did.

Anytime the ache of that conversation creeps back in, I have to keep reminding myself that he's grieving. Tristan lost his brother only weeks ago, and he's probably barely started to get through it, considering how fresh it is.

I wish I could do something to help, but he clearly doesn't want it. Harry told me that the funeral was the other day—the two of us have kept in touch over the years—and I almost showed up before I remembered what he said to me when I offered condolences. *Has it ever occurred to you that my family doesn't need or want anything from you?*

I swear it was like he stabbed me on the spot. I don't know if he forgot, but I was close with his family while we were together. Tobias and Theo always used to try to teach me how to play video games when I went over and they were home. I also hung out with Bree, Teags, and Theo while Tristan was in California. I stayed close to his family because I knew he would want me to be and because I loved them like they were my own. They all treated me better than my own parents.

The last time I saw Tobias was a few days before Tristan sent that letter. I keep replaying that conversation over and over in my head. He was as happy as ever, boasting about his new job. I'd never seen him happier—which is rare for someone like Tobias, who always had a smile on his face. I told him I was proud of him, and we hugged.

I'll never forget that day now—knowing it was the last time I would ever see him again.

I shake off all thoughts of the West siblings as I continue driving, switching my mind to my next book idea—which is a whole bunch of nothing. I have a bunch of ideas written down in my book journal, but I can't seem to flush any of them out. Every time I try to expand the little ideas I have, everything falls flat, and I give up.

Writer's block is a bitch, and maybe I was always meant to be a one-hit wonder—if you could even call my debut novel a hit. To me, it feels like profiting off my relationship troubles, and I definitely wouldn't call that a hit.

I park my car at my apartment complex but don't immediately get out.

I never thought I could feel more lost and confused than when I was in college, but I was wrong. I don't know how to feel lately. Part of me longs to run back into his arms and tell him that if he wanted to, we could fix us. I want to help him through this tough time and tell him that it's okay to feel things and it's okay to focus on himself for once and not everyone else.

The other part of me wants nothing to do with him. After all he did—break us up when I thought we were going to last forever and say everything he has to me now that he's back—he doesn't deserve my forgiveness.

But maybe he's moved on with someone else, and maybe she makes him happy—happier than I did. I never thought anyone could love him like I did, but maybe that was never true. I used to think that Tristan and I were writing the same book, with all the same chapters in the same order.

But we never were, I don't think. Maybe I was too codependent on him, and maybe he got tired of it. Love is one of the most complex emotions that one can feel. I've known that for a while now, but I also remember how I willingly fell for Tristan. I knew the consequences—that this relationship would either be the best or the worst thing to ever happen—but humans are inherently always looking on the bright side. I'm no exception. I thought we would make it, but he didn't think the same.

We're both two people who had two different ideas of the future. Now, here we are—both back in the same city we began in—and it's crushing me. The weight of our memories is creeping back up and making me feel again.

As I finally emerge from my car and swipe into my building, I trudge up the stairs like I normally do, only to trip over something in the hallway. I throw my arms out to break my fall, only to realize that I didn't hit the floor.

Two strong arms wrap around me, a familiar cinnamon musk washing over me. *No. No fucking way.* I lift my eyes, and my suspicions are confirmed. I scramble out of his hold, his eyes as shocked as mine probably are. "Tristan, what are you doing here?"

"Moving into my new apartment. What are you doing here?"

My eyes shift around, catching on the boxes that line the hallway. His door is propped open, and I can see partial silhouettes of furniture. "I live here. Why are you moving in when you have a perfectly good house to live in?"

His eyes cast down, and I immediately felt like shit because I clearly struck some sort of nerve. "I just couldn't keep staying there. It's not important. What floor are you on?"

"This one. I live right there with Parker." I point to the door next to his and hear him start to laugh. "I'm sorry. Is this funny?"

"Kind of, yeah. It reminds me of how, after I spilled coffee on you, you kept popping up everywhere—in class, at my new job. It's all so...familiar."

I feel a soft smile pop up at the memory of us. He's not wrong. Tristan suddenly appears at our old job after four years, and now we're neighbors. I'm scared to think of any other coincidences that might occur after this. "Okay, well, good luck. Let me know if you need anything—or don't. I know you no longer need or want anything from me."

"Olivia, I—"

"Save it, Tristan. I'll see you around." I shove my key into my door, slamming it behind me, suddenly not feeling like making neighborly chatter. As I get into my room, I realize that his apartment mirrors mine, and we share a wall. *Great.*

Could these few weeks get any worse?

Livvy: Parker, we have a new neighbor.

Parker: Ooo! Who is it?

Cassie: Is this person creepy? Just be careful…

Parker: Cass, not every person who moves in here is going to be a serial killer.

Cassie: I'm just saying!

Livvy: It's Tristan.

Parker: WHAT?

Cassie: Like…THE Tristan?

Livvy: Yes.

Cassie: Oh fuck.

Parker: I'm bringing wine home.

Livvy: Thank you. I'm going to need eight bottles.

Cassie: Oh we are SO having a chat tonight. Call me at your earliest convenience. I've cleared my entire night for you two.

Livvy: We will.

Parker: Love you, Cass. Come visit soon, please. We miss you.

Livvy: I second that.

Cassie: I will. Love you guys!

Livvy: Love you so much, Cass.

Chapter Thirty-Three

— OLIVIA BY ONE DIRECTION

"Where the fuck does this go?" Dom asks me as he throws a few kitchen towels I bought back into the box. "Why do you have all this shit?"

"It's called being an adult, Dom. Not all of us can pack a duffel bag and be set." Ethan says. When I told the guys I needed help unpacking, they dropped everything to come and help, no questions asked. Though they're walking on eggshells around me right now. I can tell. They keep shooting glances at one another, and Harry's eyebrows haven't fallen since he walked into my new place. They're all skeptical and most likely confused as fuck.

I found this listing on Zillow when I got sick of staying in the hotel I was at. Yeah, I fucking ran away from my family and childhood home, but if I'm going to be back indefinitely, I might as well have my own place. One where I can deal with the loss on my own and not drag anyone else down with me.

My job also allows me to work remotely. I'm glad to have something to fill all these days, and diving back into work will keep my mind occupied. "Thanks for the help, guys."

"How did you get all this furniture here already? Doesn't it take like weeks to get deliveries?" Harry asks me.

"I put a rush on it. It didn't cost much extra."

"You guys are forgetting that Mr. West here is loaded. He's got all that Silicon Valley money burning a hole in his pocket." Dom jokes, now having moved on to putting together a bookshelf I ordered.

"Dom, shut up and don't fuck up my bookshelf. It's the centerpiece of the living room," I tell him, wanting to make sure that it's perfect. I'm not a big reader, but I have some books packed away in a few boxes that I've accumulated over the years. Most of them come from my sister, who likes to give books as presents during the holidays.

"So, how are you holding up since...well you know," Ethan asks, the other two stopping what they're doing to hear my answer.

"You mean since I buried my brother and refused to go back into the house he once lived in? I'm alive. That's about the best I can do," I tell them the truth, fiddling with the rings on my fingers to distract myself. "I feel like a coward, but I know that I'd rather feel that instead of the crushing weight of responsibility that I feel over Tobias' decision."

"You'll get through this, brother. We're here for you, you know that." Harry pats me on the back, lightly squeezing my shoulder before he gets back to unpacking and opens my fridge. "Dude, there's no food in here. What have you been eating?"

Nothing. I've been so busy keeping my mind occupied that I've forgotten to eat. Taking care of myself has been low on my list of things to do. "Uh, nothing. I guess I haven't eaten since I got here."

"Tristan, you've been here for like three days!" Dom yells at me. "Harry, why don't you go get us all some food while we keep unpacking?"

"Why do I have to get it? Why can't you?" he argues.

"Because I'm building Tristan's focal piece, and it's very tedious work." Dom smiles at him, that same pretty boy smile he's had since I've known him.

"Fine. I'll go get bagels or something. It's too early for lunch." Harry grabs his keys and heads out. I'm about to ask for Ethan's help to put my dining table in a different spot when I hear a familiar voice in the hallway. Realizing my front door is still open, I look out and see Harry talking to Olivia—a huge smile on both of their faces. I lean against the frame of my door as I take in the woman I used to love.

The sight of her in a short red dress, heels in her hand, hair and makeup from the night before has my dick flexing against my pants and anger brewing in my body. *Is this a walk of shame?* I shouldn't care, but I do. Livvy's not mine anymore. She can fuck whoever she wants because we're not together, but thinking about her coming undone for someone other than me has me fisting my hands together. *She's not fucking yours.*

"Tristan, you failed to mention that you and Liv are neighbors..." He smirks at me, clearly knowing why I neglected to tell them that. I'd never hear the end of it. I can imagine the jokes that they would make, and I didn't want to hear it.

"Why the fuck are you wearing that?" I snap, ignoring what Harrison said. He's pissing me off. Why is she smiling at him and not me?

Maybe because you're a fucking asshole.

"Excuse me?" she snaps back, the smile leaving her face in the instant that she turns to me.

"I asked you why you're dressed like that? Long night?" God, I'm fucking pissed. Part of me wants to kill anyone who saw her in this dress, and the other part wants to put her over my lap and punish her. I've never been so confused in my life.

"Dude..." Harry says to me, clearly annoyed at my line of questioning, too.

"Yeah, it was a long night, but my life is none of your business, Tristan. Don't you remember that, or do I need to refresh your memory?" she asks, bolting for her front door. She should know she's not getting away that easily. I want some fucking answers.

"No memory refresh needed. Where were you last night?"

"Damn, she looks good," Dom says.

"Shut the fuck up, Dominic," I snap at him, eyes still trained on Liv.

"Leave me the fuck alone. I don't owe an explanation to you." Liv pushes her door open and before she can slam it in my face, I shove it open with my foot.

"You owe me every name of every man who saw you in that. Starting with whoever's place you just came from."

"Get the fuck out, Tristan!" She yells, not backing down. This is the first time I've been fully inside her place, and it reminds me of her college apartment. *God, the memories.* All the furniture is the exact same, just in a different layout.

"No. Names, Olivia." I stare at her, her eyes unmoving. *My Liv is a fucking fighter.* God, she's changed so much. She used to hate looking me in the eye when she was shy or mad. Now her cold stare doesn't waver as my gaze pierces hers.

"Cal." *Fucking hell.*

"Have you been sleeping with him this whole time?" I ask, my fists bunching again. To that, Livvy laughs—like full belly laughter. It almost sounds maniacal, in a way. "I'm sorry. I don't remember telling any jokes recently. What's so funny, Olivia?"

"You're jealous, Tristan. You're fucking jealous of *Cal*, of all people, when you should know he's just a friend." She turns to her fridge, grabbing a bottle of water out of it, and when she turns around, I'm behind her.

"Yeah, I'm fucking jealous. I'm jealous that you got all dressed up for Cal and went out somewhere where a bunch of half-assed guys could touch you. It fucking pisses me off, and I know it shouldn't, Liv. It pisses me off that all of them could touch you, and I can't. I might not be yours anymore, but you'll always fucking belong to me." Liv and I aren't anything anymore, but shit, I want to be. Being this close to her all the time has my blood boiling. I look down at her, pupils dilated, nipples hard and showing through her thin fucking dress, and her breathing has picked up.

"I'm sure if you called one of those girls you moved on with, they'd happily come over and help you with your little problem." Liv's hand reaches down—her eyes still glaring into mine—and she grazes my dick through my sweatpants. *Fuck.*

"Little? I bet it didn't feel so little when I was pounding into that pretty pussy of yours, you begging me to go harder." I snake my hand up to her neck, and her head lifts, expecting it, but I don't touch her. My hand floats between us, an unspoken challenge in the air. I want to kiss her so badly right now, but she'd probably slap me. "None of them compared to you, Liv. Not a single fucking one."

"I don't want to hear about your conquests, Tristan." Her voice is low as she grabs my now hard dick and strokes it a few times. "Now, get the fuck out of my apartment."

"I'll leave if you answer something for me."

She rolls her eyes at me. "Fine."

"How wet are you, Olivia?" I ask, squeezing her neck ever so slightly, my rings looking beautiful around her pretty little neck. "If I ripped this dress off of you and got on my knees right here and right now, how wet would you be? Is your pussy dripping just for me? Is it pulsing at the memory of us together? Are you aching for my cock as much as I'm aching for another taste of you?"

Her breath hitches as I drop to the floor, silently hoping that she'll give in to us. *Say yes, Olivia. We both need this. I need this. I need you.* "That was more than one question." She grabs my chin with her hand, yanking my eyes back to hers. "I'm not going to be a distraction from your grief, Tristan. Get. Out."

I comply, not wanting to piss her off more than usual, but taking in the state of her as I lean against the door frame, I notice she's as turned on as I am. *I fucking knew it.* Before she closes the door on me, I stop it with my hand.

"What?"

I take a deep breath before I apologize, my emotions coming back to reality. "I'm sorry I'm such an ass, and I'm sorry I yelled at you. You're allowed to do whatever you want. I know that."

"Cal dragged me to some club with him. I sat at the bar and read my book while he failed to pick up someone. We went back to his place, and I slept on his floor because I had a few drinks." Her eyes meet mine, sadness showing through them. "There have been a few guys, but none of them were you, Tristan. You'll never have to see me bring anyone back here. That I can promise you. Are we done?"

"As far as I'm concerned, the two of us will never be done, Liv."

"In my opinion, Tristan, the day you sent that letter and never came back for me was the day we were done. Have a good rest of your day."

Wait. What? "Liv, what are you talking—" Her door slams in my face before I can finish my question. What is she talking about the day *I* sent a letter? That I never came back for her? The last one I sent her was an entire week before I got hers, and it was five pages of me pouring my heart out. That can't be what she was talking about, so what fucking letter is she referencing?

I've always known something was off about that last letter, but this just confirms my suspicions. Something else happened, and I'll spend the rest of my life figuring out if that's what it takes. Liv and I are being played, and I'll be damned if I let anything break us apart again without our knowledge.

Whoever fucked with our relationship has a rude awakening coming, and when I find out who it is, they won't stand a chance hiding from me.

When I get back into my apartment, the guys are all staring at me. "What?"

"What's wrong, Tristan? Something is clearly gnawing at you." Harry asks.

"Geez, well, how much fucking time do you have?" I ask them before sulking onto my couch, my hands covering my face in disappointment. "I want her."

"I can't believe I'm saying this, but sex is the last thing you need with her right now. It would be way too confusing, Tris." Dom says to me.

"Maybe stop being such an asshole when you're around her? That seems like a good place to start." Ethan tells me, and I know he's right.

"She said something that has me confused, though. I'm having a hard time wrapping my head around it."

"Tell us, and maybe we can help unscramble it," Harry says before he and the guys sit around me. Most of the things we were working on were abandoned for this conversation.

And I tell them everything, and by the end of it, all of us are confused as fuck with no answers in sight.

— THINKING BOUT YOU BY ARIANA GRANDE

Dɪᴅ ᴛʜᴀᴛ ʀᴇᴀʟʟʏ ᴊᴜsᴛ happen? My mind is running at a rate of one hundred thousand miles per hour, and I don't think it's ever going to stop. I haven't felt that confident since...ever. I don't know where all of those stolen touches came from, or how I got the conviction to do what I did, but I liked it. In those few moments when I heard Tristan's breath hitch, I felt powerful. More so than I have in four years.

I never imagined that when I was coming home that I would run into anyone. It's early in the morning, so when Cal offered a change of clothes to me before I took an Uber home from his apartment, I declined.

I'm seriously regretting that decision. Though, Tristan probably would have reacted worse if he had seen another guy's shirt on me.

Tristan.

I'm still standing in front of my door, and our entire conversation comes back to me. How dare he say all the things he did to me? How dare he chastise me for how I dress?

And why did I like his jealousy so much?

Tristan and I are nothing. We're neighbors. We're two people who *used* to know one another. Two people who used to be something and now we're not. That's all.

All I know is that I need to calm down. When I heard Tristan speak in that low, gravelly voice I always remember, I had to will my body to stay standing. It pisses me off that my legs still turn to jelly around him.

We have a history. That's the only reason that I still react the way I do. Him getting on his knees in front of me, saying all those dirty things had nothing to do with it.

I need a cold shower.

I throw my purse on the counter, opting to deal with the mess in the kitchen later and head into my bathroom. Parker's at work, and thankfully, I have the day off because I feel a migraine coming.

Twenty minutes and a cold shower later, I feel worse. My body is throbbing everywhere, and my skin is on fire. I'm proud of myself for having some self-control when around Tristan, but God, I wanted him. I wanted him more than I've wanted anything lately, but I can't have him.

He's not mine. Not anymore. But judging by our conversation, he might still want me—my body, at least. But he's probably in his apartment calling some girl to come over and take care of him.

If I hear him through this wall, I'm going to need to invest in some noise canceling headphones. I always knew in the back of my mind that he was probably with other girls after he broke us apart, but I never thought I'd actually have to see him moving on with someone else. God knows I never did.

Sure, I've dated, but none of it stuck. None of them ever measured up to Tristan in my head, and they never could. I barely ever let them touch me when I was with them. In the past four years, I've never gone past kissing with another guy.

Pathetic. I'm pathetic. That's how I would describe myself right now. As I slump down onto my bed, I find myself reaching for my vibrator like I've done for four years, images of him still flooding my mind. This time, they're new ones of him in my kitchen just now, on his knees, asking me what he did.

Fucking hell, this man is the death of me. I remember the way I stroked him through his pants, his body reacting the same way it used to all those years ago. I turn my vibrator on and push it inside of me in one go. Tristan asked me how wet I was earlier, and I could barely breathe to be able to tell him that I was fucking soaked. The only thing I need to get turned on is him. He's the only one who can bring my body back to life, and it pisses me off.

God, I miss him. I miss every single thing about him, but we're too different from before. I don't think we could ever work again, but that doesn't stop me from remembering all the things from before.

My vibrator strokes against my clit as I thrust it in and out of myself. My breathing picks up as I think back on everything Tristan said earlier.

Is your pussy dripping just for me? Yes.

Is it pulsing at the memory of us together? Yes.

Are you aching for my cock as much as I'm aching for another taste of you? Yes.

Tristan always had a filthy mouth, and I *loved* it. I press down on the part over my clit, needing more friction, more pressure, *more* before my orgasm crashes over me, and stars flood my vision. "*Tristan.*" His name leaves my lips like it always does, the same weird feeling crossing my body after I say his name.

My legs are shaking, the orgasm more powerful than it usually is, and I feel *all* of it.

God, I miss how he used to touch me. He's right next door, and I could've asked him to help me, and I know he would've. He would've made me come all day if I asked him to, but that would make things even more complicated between us, and that's the last thing I want.

The last thing I want to be is a distraction from his feelings. I don't want to be someone he fucks just to get his mind off of all his shit.

As I come down from my high, my exhaustion hits me, and I feel my eyes start to droop as thoughts of the past swarm through my brain and sleep drags me under.

Chapter Thirty-Four

— SCOTT STREET BY PHOEBE BRIDGERS

"Why not take a step back from it, then? Get some space, a different perspective?" My sister offers advice, knowing damn well that I probably won't take it.

"It's hard to get a new perspective when I barely have one to begin with," I tell Bree as she sips her drink across from me. Bree has joined me at my favorite spot—a local coffee shop where I wrote most of my first book sitting at this exact table.

I came here to try to see if it could kick start any of the ideas I had in my mind for my sophomore novel, and I still have a whole bunch of nothing. It's like all my creativity has depleted from my body, and I don't know how to get it back.

"Were you planning on making it a series, or is it a standalone? You had some really fun side characters, and I'm sure people would love seeing your former main character again."

"Bree, the last book ended with her splitting up with who she thought was the love of her life."

"And? She also ended up choosing her own happiness for once. It was a refreshing take on the modern state of romance."

I smile, grateful for Bree's optimism. "Thanks, but that doesn't help my possible future career if I can't write anything else. I've been feeling shitty that I'm not writing every day."

"Liv, just because you're an author doesn't mean you have to be writing all the time. Life is about balance—especially when it comes to your job and having a social life. When's the last time you got out of the house?"

"Well, I—"

"Work doesn't count, Liv."

Shit. I guess it's been longer than I realized. I went out with Cal, but does that really count if all I did was read at the bar? "Besides the one with Cal, it's been longer than I intended."

"I know you've felt all this pressure to have your life together by now, but your twenties are for feeling like you're simultaneously headed in the right direction while you have no idea what you're doing."

I close my laptop, wanting to stop staring at a blank page on Microsoft Word. "Aren't I the one that's supposed to be telling you this?"

"You might be my older sister, Liv, but I was always the wiser one. We both know that and don't even try to argue with me."

"Hilarious, Bree. Truly. You should consider comedy as a backup career. You'd be wonderful at it." I stand up from our table, not wanting to hear whatever quip she has ready for me, and head to the counter to get another coffee.

"What can I get for you?" the barista asks.

"Iced white mocha, please."

"Name?"

"Olivia."

He smiles while writing my name down. "It'll be right up, gorgeous."

Okay... "Thanks." I turn to Bree, wondering if she heard that interaction at all when I see another person has pulled up a chair at our table. I can tell from the back of her head and Bree's bugged-out eyes who it is. I smile to myself, happy that Tristan and I's split didn't kill Bree and Teagen's friendship.

The ache that has been sitting on my chest is back, though. Does she hate me as much as Tristan seems to? She only knows his side of the story, if that, so maybe she feels bad for me? God, I have no idea, but I don't want—or need—anyone else's pity.

Though she just lost her brother, too. She's probably still trying to wrap her head around it like Tristan is. It's funny how the youngest and oldest West siblings are pretty similar. Both of them have a strong head on their shoulders, but Tristan used to tell me he hoped Teags wouldn't turn out like him. Don't even get me started on how stubborn the four of them are. It was always funny watching—

Oh. No. Not four anymore. Three. There are only *three* West siblings now. I hate that. I hate that so much. Lowering that number has split my chest wide open. I can't even imagine how Teags and them are doing.

I remember when Bree was trying to heal, she didn't leave her house for a while. She preferred being in her room and hidden away rather than try to face the world. When I was grieving the loss of Tristan, I forced myself into a new routine and focused on that. It helped me to have something to keep my mind occupied. The Hart siblings are fond of hiding or tricking our feelings, it seems. We prefer avoidance as our key way of survival after something tough.

Tristan was always a runner. He used to run from everything—feelings, things that scared him. The only thing he ran toward was getting out of Pennsylvania after college, and me once upon a time.

"Olivia," the barista from earlier says as he places my drink on the counter. I go up to grab it, thanking him before I head back to my table—not before I notice a phone number scribbled on my cup. *Wonderful.* I sit down, plaster a smile on my face, and brace myself for an awkward encounter, only to be met by Teagen's smiling face.

"Hi, Livs."

"Hey, Teags. How have you been?"

"I've been better, but one day at a time, right?"

Her optimism surprises me. "Absolutely."

"I'm glad I ran into you guys. I wanted to thank you for the brownies you made, Liv. They were a really good midnight snack when I couldn't sleep."

"I'm glad *someone* enjoyed them." My sister remarks, and I instantly want to kick her under the table for letting that slip.

"Bree!"

"It's okay, Livs. Tristan has been...off lately. More so than normal. I saw him eating one, though, and it looked like he enjoyed it even though tears were brimming." *Tears.* Was he crying over his recent loss or the memory of all the baking I used to do at his old college apartment?

"I get it, I do. He just said some hurtful things," I explain, suddenly wanting to crawl into the corner where the plants are and wilt away. "We're too complicated right now. He needs to focus on healing and I need to focus on me. Maybe someday we'll work it out."

Teagen's hand reaches over and brushes mine. "I hope you guys do. You two were the ones who made me believe in love all those years ago. I figured if the lone wolf of the family could find someone, then the rest of us weren't doomed."

"Thanks, Teags. I hope we do, too."

"How has the family been since the funeral?" My sister asks her.

"Things have been strained. Theo's drinking so much to stop feeling whatever he is. My mom barely leaves her room, and I'm trying to hold things together since I've barely seen Tristan since he left. It's hard, but we're all trying our best. The notes that Tobias left for us aren't helping, either."

Tobias left them notes? God, that must be difficult—knowing that someone took the time to write out their last words to family members. Yet another piece of information about Tobias and his death that rips my soul in half. "I've been seeing a lot of Tristan, and he's definitely playing the avoiding game," I say, taking a sip of my drink and stopping as the two of them look at me, dumbfounded. "What?"

"You two are seeing a lot of each other? How and why?" Teags asks, a giant smile on Bree's face because she already knows why.

"He's my new neighbor." And after a few seconds of painful silence, the two of them burst out laughing. "Great. Get it all out now, you two."

"I was wondering where he ended up, but I figured he was doing an extended stay at some hotel, not moving into your apartment building." Teags practically snorts as she and my sister grasp onto each other's arms, about to fall out of their chairs from laughing so hard.

"Okay, I've had enough of you guys. Enjoy your hangout session while I try to find a new perspective for my next book. I'll see you guys later."

"Bye, sis. I'll see you soon."

"It was nice to see you, Liv. Don't be a stranger, okay?" That phrase hits me in the chest. *Does that mean she missed me?* It's a strange feeling—reconnecting with someone you used to know and talk to all the time. The West family was such a big part of my life way back then, and when everything fell apart, I lost them, too. Kind of how Tristan lost Bree.

Sometimes, it feels like humans just can't help but become strangers after a while. Growing apart from people is a simple fact of life. As you age, you get busier with your own shit, and eventually, you stop hanging out with the people you always thought would be around you forever. All the conversations you had about where you'd end up ten years from then become you sitting in your car alone, reminiscing on who you used to be—who you wish you still were.

But life doesn't work that way. People grow apart and change, and sometimes your lives don't add up anymore. What once was a simple equation has turned into something far more complex and complicated, and you have to live with that. You have to live with the knowledge that the free flow of people in and out of your life will always happen. It's not something you can control, no matter how hard you try.

Tristan and I grew separate from one another. We grew up for four years apart from each other's lives, and no matter how much I want to help him through this tough time, I can't.

Because I don't know if he wants it, and I don't know how I can help him. I could try my hardest to heal him and patch up all of his pieces, but how do I do that for him when I can't even do it for myself? I've been falling apart at the seams for four years. I'm in no way capable of giving advice to someone else right now, especially with what he's going through.

If he wants my help, he'll have to ask. And if he does, I'll be right by his side through it all—no questions asked.

He believed in me back then, even when I didn't. He convinced me that I was good enough and that I should follow my dream because he thought I was talented enough to make it a reality. He was once my lighthouse, guiding my lost ship in from a storm that felt never-ending.

I'd do anything to be that for him because I know exactly how he feels—lost in the storm of his own mind.

All he has to do is ask me, but until then, I'll watch him from the end of the pier, waiting to pull him into calm waters, hoping I can get to him before he crashes.

Chapter Thirty-Five

— RENEGADE BY BIG RED MACHINE FT. TAYLOR SWIFT

"Cassie, calm down. It's not like we've kissed. We're not even anything. I'm Olivia, and he's Tristan. Nothing more and nothing less."

"Livs, you're in such deep denial that I can feel it over the phone."

I sigh heavily, knowing that she's right. We may not have kissed, but we've touched each other. We've been *close*, and I've been craving more of what I can't have. I've barely seen him over the past week, and I'm starting to get worried. I doubt he's taking care of himself, and even Harry texted me, asking about him yesterday.

I'm worried that he's shutting the world out and not letting anyone in because he's too stubborn to ask for help.

But I can't do anything about that.

"I'm not in denial. I want to help, but he doesn't want it." I stretch my back out and switch positions in bed to get more comfortable. "Can we talk about something other than Tristan and I? How's work and living with Bryce?"

Cass launches into a full recap of her workplace drama and how she and Bryce have christened every room in their new apartment together. "Needless to say we've been *very* busy."

"I forgot how much I—" A loud crash from next door halts my sentence.

"Livvy? Is everything okay?" she asks, but I hear another crash against my wall, and I know something is going on in Tristan's apartment. *Maybe he just has a girl over...*

"Uh, I think so. Sorry, what was I talking—" I hear a pained and guttural noise come from the other side of my wall, a bad feeling swirling in my gut. "Cass, I'll call you back. I have to go check on something."

I don't wait to hear her answer before I hang up, pulling a sweater on as I practically run and slip through my kitchen, my slippers scraping against the floor. *Is he hurt? Why do I have this feeling in my stomach that something is seriously wrong?* When I get to his door, I realize that if I knock, he could ignore me. Opting against that, I turn the handle of his door, grateful that it's unlocked, before I enter his apartment.

It's the first time I've fully seen his place, and it looks exactly how I expected it to be. It's basically the same layout as mine, just flipped. I look around, wondering what all the noises I heard were, as I see a knocked-over shelf, another small table flipped over, and papers scattered all over. It takes my eyes a few seconds to adjust to the darkness that envelops his place, but when I finally see the outline of his body against the floor, I rush over to him. "Tristan? Are you okay?" My hands scatter all over his body, looking for any signs that he's bleeding or hurt, scared to find any physical wounds on him. I lift him so that he's leaning against the wall so I can see him better.

When he realizes it's me, he slaps my hands off of his body as if I was hurting him. "Why are you here? Go away, Olivia."

"I came to check on you. I heard—" I cut myself off, not really sure what I heard. As far as I know, Tristan destroyed his place, but I don't know why. Looking at him all curled into himself has me terrified. I've never seen him so vulnerable. This seems like one of the bad nights. He can't keep going like this. It'll kill him.

"You always have great fucking timing, don't you?" His voice jagged, as if he's struggling to talk to me.

"I came over because I was worried about you. Forgive me for caring, Tristan." I grab his face with my hand, forcing him to look at me. God, he looks like a wreck. His stubble has grown into a small, unkept beard, his hair is messy as if it hasn't been washed, and his clothes are wrinkled. He's breathing heavily, and that's when I smell it. "You're drunk?"

"Not drunk enough."

"Why?"

"I can still feel things." He smiles lazily as if what he said was funny. "Are you really here or is this a dream?" He reaches up to cup my face, and I don't pull away, missing the feeling of his touch after all this time.

"Do you dream a lot of me?" The question slips out before I can stop it.

"Only every fucking night for four years, Olivia. You sweeten my dreams and haunt my nightmares." He takes another sip from the bottle of whiskey in his hand. *Is he serious, or is this just drunk talk?*

I swipe the bottle from him and dump it down his sink before I grab him some water. "You don't ever drink this much, Tristan. What happened to always staying in control of your feelings?" I hand him the glass, sitting back in front of him where he lingers against the wall.

"Maybe I wanted to lose control for once. Maybe I wanted to forget about the shitstorm that's my current phase of life for a night. Fucking sue me, Olivia. Sue me for wanting to have one night of peace—one night of forgetting about my brother dying."

"This is not the way to do that, Tristan. You need to grieve, not just forget about it and drink all your feelings away."

"I don't remember ever asking for your advice, Liv. So fuck off, okay? Leave me alone to do whatever I want. It should be easy for you since you did it so well four years ago." *Don't slap him. Do not slap him, Olivia. He's sad, drunk, angry, and grieving.* I know he doesn't mean them, but it still stings. Drunk words are sober thoughts, right?

"I know I shouldn't worry about you. I know you're not my problem anymore, but I can't help it. I can't help wanting to be there for you through the tough moments. Regardless if you like it or not, I'm not fucking leaving you like this. I'll sit with you all night if I have to because I know you'd do the same for me."

"So, you're not leaving, huh?"

"No," I say, standing my ground. "Drink the water and sober up."

"Whatever you say, Liv," he says as he stands up, wobbling over to his couch to lie down. "Welcome to my humble abode."

"Not exactly how I wanted to see it, but it's nice, sans the turned-over furniture." I head over to where his table is flipped over and put it back where I assume it belongs.

"I had nothing else to throw, so I went after the furniture."

"Do you often throw breakable things when you're pissed off, or is this something new?" I ask, walking over to where the papers are on the carpet and putting them back on his counter. I can feel his eyes on me as I put back all he destroyed, but I disregard the heat crawling up my back.

"It started four years ago with plates and glasses in my cabinets. I guess I've leveled up to furniture after all this time."

Four years ago. Was that around the time he sent me that letter? "Ah."

He doesn't try to make more small talk as I lift the shelf off of the floor, more books and trinkets falling off and hitting me as I raise it. When I feel like the shelf is steady, I go to grab what fell off of it. "You should invest in wall mounts for your furniture if this is going to be a recurring—" My eyes fall on a familiar book that currently lies on his floor.

All five copies of it.

I turn to face where Tristan is, hoping he's asleep so I can escape and not talk to him about this, but his eyes are glued onto mine, his expression unreadable. "Why do you have this?"

"I can't read for fun?" He's teasing me. I can tell by the stupid smirk on his face. There's no way he's read my book. No fucking way, because if he read it, then why didn't he reach out?

"You've read my book?"

"Of course, I have, Olivia." His low and vulnerable voice creeps under my skin. There are so many things I could say to that.

Then why didn't you call me?

Couldn't you tell that I wished we had ended differently?

Don't you know that I thought of you the entire time I was writing it?

Why did you support me from afar when you broke my heart?

What I end up saying is much more ridiculous. "I don't believe you. This is drunk Tristan messing with me. It has to be."

"'To my favorite almost. I loved you, but apparently that wasn't enough.'" He reiterates the dedication of the book to me. Word for word, and my heart drops. He actually read it. He read it and memorized the dedication, but he still didn't reach out after that. I never look at the dedication page anymore because it reminds me of the letter he sent me. It still hurts remembering what it said. I don't think those words will ever leave my mind. I've never wished I could unread something—except that.

My throat is dry, my heart is beating out of my chest, and I can barely breathe. *I need to get out of here.* This is too much, but I promised not to leave him in this state. "How do you want them set up?" I ask him, knowing that he likes his stuff to be in a certain way.

"Stack four of them up and lean one against it so you can see the cover." My heart constricts as I do as he says, looking at the book that helped and hurt me when I wrote it. God, it felt so easy back then, the words flowing out of me like a river, and now I've got nothing. "You're fucking talented, Liv. I've never read a book so fast in my life."

Feelings are slithering up my body, attempting to burst from my eyes, but I remain calm somehow. "Thank you. It helped that it was based on a true story. Living through something makes for really good writing."

"I bet," he says, his jaw suddenly tenses as if what *I* said hurt him. Doubtful. His actions inspired the entire fucking book. "Teags told me that it hit number one in the contemporary romance section and had that banner on it."

Teagen. This is all starting to make sense. He heard about it from her, who probably heard about it from my sister. "Yeah, it did."

"I'm proud of you, Livs. You turned your dream into a reality like you always wanted. I always knew you could do it. I always knew that your words would touch people like they did to me when I first read them that day in the student center." He yawns as he ends that sentence and gets more comfortable on his couch.

I gather my thoughts, unsure of what to say. I feel like I've been going through emotional whiplash—not just tonight, but since he got back here. One minute, I'm angry at him like he is at me, and the next, I'm cracking because of how nice he's being.

Back then, I was working on two different stories, my mind not staying occupied on a single one because of how overloaded I was with ideas. I eventually scrapped them both to write the book I published.

It's funny to me how I couldn't write the other two after Tristan left because they reminded me too much of him, only for me to publish a book based on what he did. The irony is not lost on me. "Look, Tristan—" I start to speak before I notice the faint rise and fall of his chest that I know all too well. *He's asleep.*

I sigh heavily before I pick the rest of the stuff I neglected off of the floor, placing them back on the shelf where I think he would put them. I spot a framed picture of myself, the one I sent him way back in the day.

He saved it all these years. I clean up the rest of his apartment, clearing the rest of the dishes in the sink and placing them in his dishwasher so it's one less thing he has to worry about. I straighten up the rest of the main area before my gaze catches on his sleeping form again.

God, he's beautiful. He's still as stunning as I remember. I haven't gotten the chance to look at him this close, undisturbed and vulnerable. His face looks peaceful for once. Every time I've seen him in the past few weeks, he's either been scowling, hiding the pain he's in, or sad. Those are the only three emotions that he seems to be capable of right now, which makes sense, but seeing him this unguarded while sleeping has me reminiscing.

To days when I would wake up in his arms, sunlight streaming through the curtains of his apartment. His voice was the last thing I would hear before I slept and the first thing I heard in the mornings when he woke me up with a kiss. My head on his chest as his heartbeat lulled me to sleep. His body was tucked against mine like it fit perfectly when we were curled up together.

I press a stolen kiss against his head. "I miss you, Tristan, but I can't do anything to help you if you won't let me. No matter how much you push me away, no matter how many times you tell me there's no room for me where you are, I'll stay. I won't take your pain away completely, but I'll help you carry it until you can hold it on your own."

Before I leave his place, I cover him over with a nearby blanket so he doesn't get cold. I lock his door behind me, silently reiterating the promise I made to him in my head.

And I know exactly where to start.

The Next Day

Livvy: Why is there a coffee outside my front door?

Tristan: Did you read the note?

Livvy: Oh. You didn't have to do that, but thank you.

Tristan: Coffee is the least I could do.

Tristan: I'm sorry about what I said last night.

Livvy: It's fine. I've already forgotten.

Tristan: No, it's not fine. I never want to be the cause of your anger or pain. I said a lot of stupid shit last night, and I'm sorry.

Livvy: Tristan, it's already out of my mind. You're grieving. It's okay.

Tristan: Not an excuse, Liv. I've been treating you like shit, and that stops now. I promise.

Livvy: Well, thanks. I appreciate the gesture.

Tristan: Have a good day at work.

Livvy: I'll try.

Chapter Thirty-Six

— ABOUT YOU BY THE 1975

It's been only a few days since I barged into Tristan's apartment and helped him through a tough night. Since then, I've been going back and forth on how to help him again, and I've landed on one thing that my sister and I used to do when we were upset.

So, now I'm standing outside of his apartment door, trying to force myself to move my hand and knock.

Just do it, Olivia. Raise your fist and knock on the door.

Two short taps later, Tristan opens his door, and I instantly regret doing this. He's standing in his doorframe wearing nothing but gray sweatpants and a black dri-fit shirt that practically molds to his abs. I remember dragging my hands down those another lifetime ago.

Stop thinking about that, Livvy. A hand waving in front of my face breaks me from my thoughts. "Livvy?"

"Sorry. Did you say something?"

His lips turn up in a smile. "I asked what you were doing here."

"Oh." *Right.* "Go for a drive with me."

"Is that a demand?"

"Yes. I know you were probably planning on hitting balls at the park or something, but my offer is way better."

He's quiet for a few seconds as he ponders my offer. This whole situation is weird. The fact that he's my neighbor, the fact that we still haven't talked about what happened four years ago, and the fact that his brother's funeral was only a month ago.

"Of course, you knew that. I'm not even surprised." He pauses for a second before giving me his answer. "Okay, but as long as you promise that you're not kidnapping me."

"Tristan, if I were going to kidnap you, I'd be much more creative than this."

"I'll go put on something comfier. You're welcome to come inside," he waves his hand out, but I instantly shake my head.

"I'm okay here."

"Suit yourself, Livs." He slightly shuts his door, and I continue to stand in the hallway. I don't know why I declined his offer. Maybe it's because seeing the inside of his apartment in the daylight makes me feel weirdly vulnerable.

Entering this new era with Tristan sounds terrifying because it feels like I missed so much of his life. It feels like I have to relearn all these new things about him, and the thought of that makes me ache everywhere. I wish I didn't have to. I wish I knew what makes him tick now. I wish he would talk to me about things again without having to be drunk to do it. I miss it. I miss *him*. But I don't know if we're headed down that road again. Sure we're acquainted, but how do I know things won't end the same as they did last time?

His door shutting breaks me from my trance. He's now wearing a long sleeve henley, the same sweatpants, and a backward baseball cap. *God, that was always a weakness of mine.* Does he remember that? Is that why he's wearing it?

No. It's probably a coincidence. "Are you ready?"

"Lead the way."

Since we both live on the second floor, we take the stairs down and head to my car. It's a pretty warm night; the sun hasn't set yet, so it still feels nice enough that I don't need a jacket. I opted for some mom jeans and a cropped long-sleeve shirt. My vans adorn my feet but will most likely come off as I drive since I hate driving with shoes on.

He opens my door for me, and I let him. *God, I hate how easy this is.* How easy it is to fall back into these old patterns from college. "Thank you."

He flashes me a smile—not a real one—as he shuts my door and makes his way around to the other side. After two songs played, he was the first one to break the ice. "So, where are we headed?"

"Somewhere."

"When did you become so..."

"Mysterious?" I finish his sentence for him.

"Yeah, I guess so."

"I'm not sure. I seem to only be like this with you."

"Oh, really?" I don't dignify his answer with a response, but instead, I turn up the music and pretend I didn't hear him.

"I'm sorry, I can't hear you over the music," I say as I turn onto the road leading up to my sister's place. Then the most beautiful thing happens. Tristan bursts out laughing. I know it's real because I can see the smile lines on his face, and it's a different timbre than the soft laughter that's fake. It reminds me of the days during college when I would watch him during his games, laughing before innings started while pointing at me from the outfield.

A pinch of longing hits my chest. *I miss those days.* Everything seemed easier back then. It felt like I had ample more time—time to figure out who I was, who I wanted to be, what I wanted to do. Looking back now, four years later, I wish that version of me was stronger. I wish she was more courageous. If she had been, maybe I would be in a different spot now, and maybe Tristan and I would've been together this whole time instead of spending years apart.

But that's the thing about time. You can't reverse it, no matter how hard you try. The past remains just that—dead and buried.

Tristan turns to look out the window as I park. "Where the hell are we?"

"My sister's place."

"Your sister?" he asks, a shock in his tone. "Bree owns this whole property?"

"Yes, she does. Or have you forgotten that Bree is the extroverted sister?"

"Well, I knew her channel was still growing. My sister watches her videos all the time."

"Teagen still watches her videos? They're best friends. Why not actually hang out?"

"I'm not sure. I've even seen you in a few of her videos talking about your book. Teagen used to send them to me, and I'd watch when I had time."

"I never knew you did that."

"Livvy, it's been four years. Of course, you didn't know that." *Don't cry.* "What are we doing here?"

"Right." I unlock the car doors. "Follow me."

The two of us get out of the car, and as he stands and takes in the view of my sister's place, I circle around to my trunk, where four dozen eggs are waiting for us. I silently hope none of them broke on the way over here. "Please tell me you didn't drive me here to egg your sister's house, Livs. I thought you two were on good terms?"

I stifle a laugh. "No, Tris, we're not going to egg my sister's house. She's not even here. She's at a launch party for some makeup brand or something in California. I texted her and asked her if we could borrow one of her trees, and she said yes."

"One of her trees?"

"Follow me."

I slam the trunk closed and head off to the tree at the very edge of the property. Her house here is big, but the surrounding property is even bigger. With the sun starting to set, a few of the path lights have turned on so Tristan and I aren't walking in the complete dark. "I'd give this sunset a solid eight out of ten. The orange and pink colors are some of my favorites to see up in the sky. What about you?"

Tears fill my eyes as Tristan brings back one of our traditions that we had back in college. "Seven out of ten. It's beautiful, don't get me wrong, but I've seen some better ones."

"Oh, come on, Livs. If there's one thing I've missed about Pennsylvania, it's the sunsets."

"You don't get sunsets out in Silicon Valley?"

"None quite like this, and none that have your eyes viewing the same one. That makes all the difference."

I shift my gaze back to the surrounding view, too afraid to let that statement sink into my bones. I've always loved this house. My sister has a few of them, but this one will always be my favorite. I helped her pick this out, and I miss the period of my life when I lived with her here before I moved back in with Parker. Many holidays and parties have come and gone, but some of my favorite memories are at the tree that has now come into view.

It's a large oak tree, its leaves just starting to turn and fall as autumn moves in. I'm hoping that this will help him let go of some of the things he's been carrying. If not, I'll keep trying. I won't give up on him because he never gave up on me.

"Livvy, what's going on?"

"I'm going to tell you a story. The story begins with this tree. Growing up, my family never had many traditions—you know that. But when my sister bought this house, we decided that we would start some of our own. I won't get into details about all the other ones, but the one I'm going to share with you is my favorite." I pause, willing the sudden tears in my eyes to go away. I don't know why I get so emotional talking about this. It makes me sad that Bree isn't here to do this with us. I've never found myself missing my parents this much, but I'll always yearn for my little sister. I want to hold her close and protect her from any harm that could come her way with being in the public eye, but I know I can't. She's twenty-three after all—almost twenty-four—and with a good head on her shoulders, I know she'll be fine. But that doesn't stop me from wishing I could spend more time with her.

Tristan's hand on my shoulder breaks me from my thoughts. "Are you okay?"

I take a deep breath. "Yes, I'm fine. Sorry. Where was I?"

"You were talking about your favorite tradition with Bree."

"Right. So, Bree bought this house when she was twenty. It was the first time she had something for herself, and she made it her own. This home became ours, in a way. And when things got too much, too loud, and too difficult to handle, Bree and I came up with something that helped us let out some frustrations." I lean down and open a cartridge of eggs that I sat on the grass. "We would grab some eggs—most often the expired ones—come out to this tree and throw them at it."

Tristan smiles as he stares at me. "You're not serious."

"I am. We've done it a few times. The first being after—" I stop myself before the rest of the words could come out.

"After we broke up?" His voice sounds strained all of a sudden, like it hurts him to get those words out.

"Yeah, we had a lot going on around then. Bree suggested that throwing eggs at the tree would help to get some of my feelings out." My eyes turn to his. "I brought you here today to do the same thing, but with a twist."

"A twist?"

I reach into my pocket and pull out a black marker. "Before you throw it, I want you to write down anything that weighs on you. Write it down, throw it at the tree, and watch it break into a million pieces."

"What's that going to do?"

"Maybe nothing," I say, grabbing his hand, suddenly feeling more courageous than I am. "Maybe everything, Tristan. You're being weighed down. I can see it, and I know you feel it, too. You've got the weight of the world on your shoulders, and it's crushing you. I saw it the night I came over after your rampage. You're silently struggling, and it kills me to watch you do this to yourself. You can't hold on to that forever. Part of the healing process is letting go of the hard stuff, and this might be able to help you get to that point."

His eyes have unshed tears in them, and as soon as I feel like I went too far in saying that, he grabs the marker from me and picks up an egg. I see him write something on the egg and lightly toss it at the tree, only it doesn't break.

"Oh, come on, Mr. Baseball Player. I know you can throw better than that. I've seen you throw from center to home plate and barely break a sweat. Throw it like you mean it."

"Oh, taunting me, are you?"

"Is it working?"

His mouth lifts into a smirk. "Kind of."

"Then throw it like the baseball player you are."

"*Used* to be. I'm retired now."

"Doesn't matter," I smile at him, and again that pang of old-time feelings hits. I remember when he first taught me how to throw so we could play catch together. I remember how he used to bring me out to the baseball field at school so we could watch the stars on those warm nights. I remember *everything* about us, and it still hurts—all those memories that I have, not knowing if they meant the same to him. Has he been thinking about us these past few weeks? Has being in proximity with each other again made him feel the things I am? I could ask him, I should ask him, but part of me doesn't want to know that answer.

Tristan picks up another few eggs, and I see him write 'expectations' on one of them, and then he chucks it at the tree. "There you go. How does it feel?"

"Surprisingly good."

A soft smile slips from my lips. "Good, now keep going. I've got four dozen eggs, and you're going to throw three dozen of them."

"Why?"

"I figured you needed it, and I wanted to throw some too," I smirk. "I can't let you throw eggs by yourself. That would be rude."

"Well, I'm not going to stop you." He smiles at me as I pick up a few eggs, palming them in my left hand before I chuck one at the tree, watching the yolk spread down it.

I see Tristan to my left, writing something down on it before he throws it at the tree. The way he throws reminds me of how I used to watch him in the outfield during college. He might be retired or whatever, but clearly muscle memory has taken over.

Neither of us talks as we continue throwing eggs at this tree. The only sounds that I can hear are them breaking against it while the wind rustles the leaves and Tristan's deep breaths as he throws. I can't tell if this is helping him, but I find myself feeling better as I throw my last egg.

I look over at Tristan's cartons, and he only has a few left too. I watch as he writes something down on the egg that looks a lot like my name, but I quickly turn my head as he throws it, not wanting him to see what I saw.

Is my presence weighing on him? Or is it our past that haunts him as much as it does to me? God, maybe this was a horrible idea. After our big talk the other day, I should've known that he needed space.

As he continues throwing, I sit down on the grass, wanting to watch him throw to see if it's helping. I don't think I can keep doing this. It all hurts too much. I know Tristan and I need to have a big talk at some point, but I'm too scared to bring it up with everything he has going on. Our past mistakes should be the last thing on his mind right now. His brother is dead, for fucks sake. Our stupid and petty relationship problems should not be at the forefront of his mind.

After his last egg is broken against the tree, he falls to his knees as if he can't bear to stand. I go in front of him, making sure that he's okay when I notice he's looking right through me. "Are you okay?"

"I—I think so."

"I don't believe you. Was this too much? We can go back home, Tristan. It's okay—" I try to stand us both up and walk away, but he catches my wrist before I can, yanking me back to where I sat in front of him. "Tristan—"

And then he kisses me. But it's not how it used to be. Tristan used to kiss me with all his confidence, all his power. I felt every kiss in my bones when his lips touched mine all those years ago.

This kiss feels more tender. His hand comes up to cup my jaw, the other one remaining at my hip, squeezing me tight as if he's afraid I'll disappear into thin air. It's simultaneously just how I remember it and brand new as if Tristan's lips had never touched mine before.

I should stop this. Neither of us is in the right state to be kissing one another right now, but I can't seem to find the strength. The way his lips thread with mine, the way he tastes like cinnamon and whiskey. I practically melt into his touch as his kiss gets harder, more urgent. It's overwhelming me—all the emotions that we've experienced in the past few hours. "Tris—"

"Livvy, please just let me kiss you. Fuck, I've missed the feel of you so bad, please—"

I've missed this too. "Okay."

That word is barely out of my mouth before he pulls me onto his lap, adjusting from being on our knees to me straddling him on the grass.

God, I never want this to end. It's like Tristan and I exist in our own bubble out here. Right now, we can be just us—no emotions, no sadness, no past mistakes haunting us.

That's what tonight was about—letting go of some of the shit that's been over our heads. I feel like my walls should be up, but I can't help but want to get lost in the memories of us, lost in who we used to be and how good we used to make each other feel.

He continues to kiss me before he flips me onto my back, pinning my hands above my head so I can't touch him. "That's not fair."

"You still tasting like that berry lip balm I loved so much is what's not fucking fair, Olivia." His mouth moves from my lips to down my neck, his teeth locking on the part of my neck that makes me squirm. Having my hands pinned underneath one of his while the other roams around my body has all my senses waking up. This is getting heated way too fast, and I don't ever want it to end. "Good to know how crazy that spot still drives you."

"Tristan, we should stop," I say as his free hand moves to my nipple, slightly pinching it through the fabric of my shirt. My nipples are hard as a fucking rock. My pussy is throbbing too, and I can feel Tristan's dick against my leg, hard and ready. God, it would be so easy to fuck our feelings away. I wish we could, but I don't want any shred of a relationship we have left to be torn into pieces. It feels like I just got him back—just got through to him again. I don't want to ruin that, and sex could really complicate things, no matter how much I want to rip his sweats off and feel him push into me in one thrust.

He presses one final kiss to my lips before he pulls away. "I'm sorry. I got carried away, I—"

"Tristan, I wanted it as much as you did. You don't need to apologize." I meet his eyes and see that his pupils are dilated as much as mine probably are. He stands up, reaching his arm out, and I take it. He hauls me to my feet, and I stand next to him, suddenly not knowing what to do with my arms.

"Careful, Olivia. If you say you want me again, I'll throw you over my shoulder and the two of us will mess up one of Bree's guest rooms." Fucking hell. My cheeks heat at the memory of his body against mine a few seconds ago. His muscles up against me, his one hand wrapped around both of mine, pinning me to the ground. God, I might not want to mess us up again, but I want him. I want him badly.

"Maybe we should head back."

"Yeah, that's a good idea," he says as he collects the cartons from off the ground. We silently walk back to the car. The tension in the air between us could cut the windows in half. My body feels wound up, and I don't know how my legs are moving. They feel like they're not attached to my body anymore.

I play music in my car as we head back, the sound acting like a barrier between us and what happened. Not even just the kiss, but the emotions that Tristan felt when he was done throwing eggs. I don't know if it helped, but his shoulders seem less tense than before, and his jaw isn't as tight.

About halfway home, Tristan is the first to speak. "Liv, you know at one point we're gonna have to talk about it, right?"

It. I hate that he refers to the destruction of us as that. Is it because it hurts him to talk about it or because he's angry? I know I still have some unresolved feelings about that time of my life, but did he forget that he was the one who sent that note to me? Did he forget that he never came back to me, even after I sent him a letter explaining everything?

"I know," I say, my voice suddenly quiet. "Let's just remember tonight as it was. A friend helping another friend through something difficult. That's all."

I look over at him, but he's already looking at me. "Is that what we are? Friends?"

"Friends, yeah. Or acquainted, if you prefer that. I don't really know this version of you and the same goes for you."

His eyes narrow at mine before I turn back to focus on the road. The rest of the ride is silent, and as the two of us unlock our apartment doors, he speaks.

"I don't know if we'll ever get back to what we used to be, Liv. But I want to. I want us to be something. Kissing you tonight just solidified that for me. I'll never be over what we had, what we *could* have if we talked about what happened. So, let me know if you ever want to know this version of me, and I'll happily oblige." He pushes his door open, and I find myself rooted to my spot as he stalls before fully entering his place. "And you sure as hell still moan my name when you come, so I know you still feel for me, too. You might want to be quieter next time because if I hear my name moaned through my wall again, I'll fucking break it down."

Oh my God, he heard me? He fucking heard me moan his name while I used my vibrator. Fuck my life. "I—"

"It's okay, Liv. You always were a screamer. Don't stop on my account. I love hearing my name on your lips. You know that." He fucking winks at me before he shuts and locks his door behind me, leaving me in the hallway feeling like the biggest idiot in the world.

Chapter Thirty-Seven

November

— LOVER, YOU SHOULD'VE COME OVER BY JEFF BUCKLEY

As I SLIDE THE letter underneath Liv's door, I know I'm in for a long night. It's been two weeks since I've seen her. Two weeks since we've kissed, and not knowing what happened between us is driving me insane. She kissed me back. She still wants me. So, why did she do what she did all those years ago?

This is the only thing I'm capable of controlling, and because of that, I want answers. And if this is the only way to get them, then so be it.

A knock on my bedroom door wakes me from the accidental nap I took. I remember sitting down after work in my comfy clothes—black sweats and brown baby tee—and wanting to rest my eyes for a second. When I check my phone, I realize that I've been asleep for two hours. It's around seven PM, and Parker peaks into my room, a weird look on her face. "What's that face for?"

"I—I found this when I came home. It must've been slipped under our door. It's for you, Liv."

What? She hands me a slip of paper, and as I read it, my heart drops. *What the hell is this?* I grab my copy of the letter Tristan sent me from where it resides in the box in my closet and storm out of my room. There's only one place this could've come from, and seeing nothing but red, I march over to his place and aggressively knock on the door. When he doesn't immediately answer, and I notice his door is unlocked, I invite myself in. He doesn't get to do this. He doesn't get to play games with me after all this time.

Looking around, I find him sitting in low light on his couch—in no shirt and gray sweats—holding a drink that he looks to have just poured. "What the fuck is this, Tristan? I've had enough of all these mind games. Why did you slide this under my door?"

"It should look familiar to you, Olivia. You wrote it, after all," he says, bringing the drink up to his mouth.

I scoff at him, feeling equally pissed off and confused. "No, I didn't. I'd never say this in a million years. If this is your idea of a joke, then it sucks. This doesn't sound like me at all. So, why did you write this and slide it under my door?" I'm full-on yelling now. I want answers. Why is he saying I wrote this when it's not true?

"Lying never looked good on you, Olivia. It might not be the original—I tore that one up immediately after reading it—but I recreated it word for word." He stands up, leaving his drink on his coffee table, and stalks over to me. "Just own up to it. We both have nothing left to lose, so come clean, Liv. Tell me the fucking reason you wrote that and sent it to me four years ago."

"I never sent this to you! You were the one who sent me eight lines on a piece of paper breaking up with me!" The two of us have moved to arguing across the island in his kitchen. There's *literal* space between us, along with the rift that's been there for four years. I feel like I can't sit still. My skin is itchy, and if I stop moving, I might collapse from how angry I am.

"Then why did it show up at my place four years ago?! Addressed to me, from you!" He's yelling at me, too, and I feel like I've crawled into a different dimension. Tristan raising his voice is not something he does often—if ever.

"I have no idea why because I didn't send it! I wasn't the one who broke us apart! You were! In eight lines, you broke us." I don't understand what's going on. We're both yelling at each other over the exact same accusation. "Here. Read what you wrote to me all those years ago." I practically shove the letter across the island and watch his face. His eyebrows pinch together as he reads it, and my stomach instantly drops. *He doesn't remember.*

"Olivia, I didn't write this."

"Then how did it show up in my mailbox? I realize my number getting leaked really fucked things up, but I tried calling you, Tristan. I called for days, and you didn't answer. I left voicemails with my new number, but you never called me back!" Tears are starting to fall from my face as I remember the days after I got the letter. My sister barely left my side as I crumbled to pieces, not wanting to pick myself back up.

"I never got any voicemails from you. I don't know how it showed up because I would never fucking write this, Liv. It looks like my handwriting, but it's off. The last letter I ever sent you was five pages, not eight lines of complete and utter bullshit!" He throws the paper from his hands as if it's on fire. He brings his hand up to his face and pinches the bridge of his nose—clearly as confused as I am. "God, what the fuck."

"You didn't get the letter I sent explaining what happened? I wrote and sent it that day, Tristan."

"What letter, Liv?"

Are we admitting to what I think we are? That neither of us sent them, and someone else did? That's not possible, though. Right? Why would someone want to break us up, and for what reason? None of this is making any sense. Tristan grabs his drink from where it rests as he comes back over to the island, his body a little more relaxed than before. "Tristan, if you didn't send this to me, and I didn't send that to you, then what the fuck happened?"

He takes a deep breath before he throws his glass against the wall, and it shatters, the whiskey dripping off of the paint. The shattered glass represents what my heart has felt like for four years. I assume the same goes for him. Both of our hearts were glass, and those letters were like a high-pitched scream that shattered them.

For four years, I've waited anxiously for an answer to why he did this, and it turns out he didn't. Someone else did.

We could've been together this entire time. God, it hurts. The two of us are silent for a few moments, and when I lift my eyes to where he stands and off of the shattered glass, he's already looking at me. His angry gaze pierces mine, and my entire body shutters. "You said it was too hard."

"What?" I whisper.

"The letter said that it was too hard loving me from a distance, so I got on a flight, and I came back here prepared to fight for us. I was ready to leave my job and life in California if that's what it took." His voice is strained, and if I weren't already crying, I would be.

"I always thought you never came back for me." I take a breath in between my tears. "Loving you was the easiest thing I ever did. No matter the distance, it was always the one thing that came naturally to me." I admit it because it was. He made it so easy to love him. No matter how many miles apart we were, I never felt like an obligation to him. I felt like his choice, and I was lucky to be chosen to be loved by him.

"Of course, I came back for you. When I got to your house, I found a sold sign in the front. I tried calling you, Liv, and none of them would go through. Teags told me your number got leaked, and I thought I'd wait a few days in case you called and wanted to meet somewhere. Nothing ever came, so I left. I left with no explanation and assumed it was over for us. Nothing ever showed up at my apartment in California either."

"My family's phone numbers and address got leaked. It was too much for my parents, and they decided to sell the house and move. They disregarded Bree's trauma for months, but when their jobs were threatened, it became too much. It took them one day to pack our house up. Bree and I moved into her house after that because it seemed pointless to stay under their roof." My parents moved twenty minutes away from where we used to live, and I haven't seen them since that day. They text every so often, but I tend not to answer. I have guilt about that, but I know it's what is best for me. Bree has always been the only family I've needed, and it'll always stay that way. "My letter said that you couldn't do it anymore—us. That we weren't going in the right direction in our relationship." More tears leak out of my eyes as I restate what he already read.

"I don't know what to say, Liv." He takes a deep breath. "This is so fucked up."

"Everything that could've gone wrong did. I still don't get why my calls wouldn't go through. It haunts me, Tristan. I wanted to call you all these years, but I was afraid that you either wouldn't pick up or you wouldn't miss what we had. I really thought you sent that fucking letter."

"I missed you every single fucking day, Liv. Every breath I took felt like agony, not knowing if you really meant what you said. For four years, I didn't look at other women because all I could see was you. All I wanted was you."

What? "But you said that you moved—"

He practically runs around the island and invades my personal space. His body is inches from mine, and I have to crane my neck to look at him. "I lied. There was no moving on from you, Liv. I meant it when I said that there's nobody else for me except you."

"I dated, but none of them ever compared to you. It was one failed relationship after another," I admit in a whisper, embarrassed that I had the audacity to move on while he was still thinking about me. Guilt washes over me, but I remind myself that neither of us knows what we do now. God, this is so fucked up.

His hand finds my waist, the weight of our confessions over us like a black fog. "I'm sorry."

"I'm sorry, too." More tears fall, but this time, Tristan takes the pad of his thumb and wipes them away. "Where do we go from here? How do we fix this?"

"You want to fix this? Fix us?" he asks, a look of uncertainty crossing his features. "It's been four years, Liv. We're different. I'm a fucking mess, and you deserve someone better than me right now."

"That letter may have crushed me, but not once did I stop loving you. I tried. I tried so hard not to think of you or look you up online and see how you were doing. When I released my book, the only person I wanted there was you. I might not have admitted that to myself, but I always knew. You lingered in the back of my mind every day. I have journals filled cover to cover with thoughts of you, memories that I never wanted to forget about us. I thought it was for the better—us breaking up. But that doesn't mean I stopped loving you."

His hands come to my face, cupping it like he used to do all those years ago, and then he pulls me into him, wrapping me in a hug. His head still rests on mine like it used to back then, and I break. I sob into his chest, feeling the weight of the past four years come to the surface and explode, and he lets me. I feel his chest heave, tears probably spreading down his face, too. His hand comes up to the back of my head, and he rubs it up and down my hair, soothing me. "It's okay, pretty girl. I've got you."

"I wish I fought harder for us," I say through my sobs.

"I wish I did, too," he tells me, the weight of our admissions lifting off of my shoulders and disappearing into the air. I feel his arms move to my legs as he lifts me up, carrying me over to his couch and setting us both down, my legs around his back, our faces aligned with one another. "You still love me?"

"I'm not sure I ever stopped," I tell him, the imaginary ice that has surrounded my body slowly melting off of me. "Do you still love me?"

"Always, Liv. I always will." He presses a kiss to my forehead before I throw my arms around him, wanting to be as close as I can to him. The two of us sit like this for a few minutes, soaking in the intense conversation we had. He's the one who breaks the comfortable silence. "What do we do now?"

"We take a few days to think. Both of us said a lot of things tonight, and I need time to sort through my jumbled head. We can't just jump back into what we were. Too much time has passed. Things are different now, and there's nothing we can do to change that. I think space would do us both some good."

When I meet his eyes, he nods at me. "Okay."

I smile, feeling a real one bloom from my face for the first time in four years before my eyes catch on Tristan's collarbone. I trace the lines of his tattoo and feel his eyes burning a hole into my head. "I thought you didn't like tattoos."

"This one is different. It's special to me," he whispers, his words making tears come back to my eyes. I trace the lines over and over again.

It's a sunset. Tristan got a tattoo of a sunset on his collarbone. "I meant it when I said you were always close to me, Liv."

"It's beautiful. When did you get it?" I meet his eyes again, emotion spreading through my chest.

"Halloween. Three years ago." *Halloween.* Our first kiss was on Halloween.

"Do you regret it?" I ask, scared of the answer. Tristan never wanted tattoos. He always told me he would never get one.

"Not one fucking bit," he says as he gets up, places me to the side, and goes to his bedroom, a stack of envelopes in his hand when he returns. "You wrote about me in your journal, and I kept writing letters to you that I never sent. I didn't have an address to send it to, so they sat in a drawer. Take them, please. You don't ever have to read them, but they're yours."

My shaky hand reaches out and grabs them, the stack of unsent letters so thick that it feels like I'm holding a textbook. There must be fifty of them in this pile. God, what I would give to go back and warn my younger self that it was all a lie. So much of our pain could've been avoided if we both tried a little harder not to believe the bullshit that was in front of us.

Instead of spending four years how we did, we could've been together—happy. Sure, there's no guarantee that we would've lasted this long, but Tristan and I would've fought tooth and nail for one another—of that, I'm sure. "I should get back. Parker is probably worried about me."

"Of course. I'll walk you out." Tristan places his hand on the small of my back as we leave his place and walk the fifteen feet over to my front door.

"Thank you for these, Tristan."

"Of course, Liv." Silence engulfs us as neither of us knows what else to say. "We'll find out who did this. Together, Liv. And then I'll spend the rest of my life making up for all the time we lost. I lost you once, and I'll be damned if I lose you again."

"We both need time, Tristan. But I won't lose you again either." *I wouldn't survive it a second time.* Now that I have a tiny piece of him back, I'm clinging onto it for dear life. I press a quick kiss on his cheek before I turn my door handle. "Good night, Tristan."

"Good night, Liv."

Chapter Thirty-Eight

— BOYS OF FAITH BY ZACH BRYAN FT. BON IVER

IT'S BEEN A WEEK since I gave all my letters to Livvy, and I've barely seen her. I'm worried that I might've scared her off. My head has been spinning for the past few days, and even the boys taking me to the batting cages isn't helping. We just got back to my place to decide what to get for lunch, but I speak before anyone can say anything. "Thanks."

"For what?" Ethan asks me, the guys' faces all looking confused.

"For sticking around here for so long to make sure I'm okay. I know we're all busy with our own lives and shit, but it means a lot that you guys have been here for me through all this. I never thanked you properly, so I'm doing it now."

"No need to thank us, buddy." Dom slaps me on the back. "You'd do the same for us."

"Anytime you need us, Tristan, we'll be here," Ethan tells me.

I look at Harry. "What he said. You're stuck with us for the long haul, so get used to it."

"Even though my freak-out is still happening, I'm grateful you guys are here."

"Okay, so you're still freaking out. Can I suggest something that might help?" Dom says, circling the kitchen island where the four of us reside. Ethan and I are on the stools while Harry and Dom stand across from us.

"I'm scared," Harry says.

"Me too. He could either suggest something ridiculous or illegal." Ethan jokes, but not really, because that describes Dom in a nutshell.

"Smash therapy, and no, it's not what you're all thinking—"

"Dom, we all know what that is. You rent a room and smash a bunch of shit," I tell him, considering the idea in my head. Smashing a bunch of shit sounds fun. *Maybe we should look into this...*

"Oh, well, good. That's my idea for our next outing. I love watching the two of you hit in the cages, but I want to be the one smashing some shit next time." Dom smiles before grabbing some water from my fridge.

"That's not bad, D. We might actually take one of your suggestions," Harry says.

"I feel like pigs are flying because Dom said something helpful for once," Ethan jokes, punching him in the arm.

"Hey, I can be helpful sometimes. Remember the time I helped Tristan realize his feelings for Liv? I flirted with her all night that one Halloween, so he'd finally own up. And it worked! They kissed that night for the first time if I remember correctly."

And now he's back to being the same old Dom we all know and love. "You were *flirting* with her all night, asshole. You weren't helping, you were being a dick."

"Yeah, and Tristan came to *me* for advice that night, not you," Harry tells him, always holding that one fact over his head.

"This is ridiculous. I've just about had enough of you guys. If you're not careful, you'll lose me," Dom jokes, heading toward the door as if he's leaving.

"Oh, and what a day that will be when we finally get rid of you!" Ethan yells at him, again joking because we all love Dom, deep down. Our group would be a lot less lively without him around to spice things up—even if he is an asshole sometimes. Dom opens the door but doesn't leave.

"Hey, Miss Livvy," I hear him say, and my head shoots to the door. Sure enough, I see her familiar fuzzy socks and a bun in her hair as she stands in my doorway.

Did she read my letters? Did she come over to check on me?

Part of me doesn't care about those questions I just asked myself. The only thing I care about is that she's here. *Liv is still here.* And somehow, she still tolerates me despite how much of a mess I've been.

— THIS IS WHAT THE DRUGS ARE FOR BY GRACIE ABRAMS

Tears fall from my eyes as I read another one of Tristan's unsent letters. I haven't cried this much since I got the letter that broke us apart the first time, but finding out that he's still been writing to me after all this time...I feel crushed.

Nothing makes sense. I've had a thousand different questions rummaging through my head since we talked this all out, and I'm not finding any answers.

These letters aren't helping either because Tristan poured his entire heart out to me, and I never knew until now. I never knew he could write anything like this—all of his emotions jumping off of the page at me. I can tell when he's angry when he's yearning, depressed, or confused.

Livvy, why did you do this to us?

You lied to me. I left my heart with you in Pennsylvania, and you mailed it to me in shreds.

I remember watching you read with your head shoved low in the book and how you were practically crawling inside the pages. I remember loving how your eyes would tear up when you read something that you connected with. Did you know your book did that for me?

I'm so proud of your book, Liv. I knew you could do it, and I'm proud that you thought you could, too.

You were always my favorite sunset, Liv. It turns out my sun doesn't rise anymore, though.

The lines of all his letters swim around in my head, and I can't get them out. There are at least thirty here, and I've been slowly getting through them, but it's hard. Every time I read one, I have to stop myself from having a breakdown because of the guilt I feel.

He was always afraid of the distance being too hard, and he almost canceled, leaving a few times because of it. I had to convince him day after day that I was okay with it, but in the end, his biggest fear was used against him by someone he loved.

God, I feel sick. All of this is fucking horrible. *But who would've done this?* I've been racking my brain to try to figure out who could've double-crossed us, but nobody's jumping into my mind.

All I know is that I can't spend another second not knowing what happened. After four years, I want answers. *Real* answers. Since Tristan is the only one who can help me figure them out, I head over to his place, hoping he's home.

I take in my outfit before I leave—large crewneck, flared yoga pants, and thick fuzzy socks—and opt not to change. Why do I need shoes to walk fifteen feet?

Before I can knock on his door, it swings open, and Dom looks down at me, my fist raised to his chest. "Hey, Miss Livvy."

I smile, the familiarity of the boys punching me in the chest. "Hi, Dom. I didn't know you guys were still around."

"Yeah, we're all still kicking it around here for that one," he says as he points to Tristan sitting at his kitchen island, Harry and Ethan staring at our interaction. "What are *you* doing here?"

He throws a wink at the end of that, probably knowing all about the adventures of Tristan and me over the past few weeks. "I came over to talk to Tristan, but I can come back later if—"

"Dom, let her in, you asshole," I hear Tristan say to him, a smile beaming from Dom's face. *He always did love fucking with him.* It's nice to see that some things never change. He moves from the doorway, allowing me in, and I head over to where the three of them reside.

"Hi, guys. It's nice to see you all again," I say, trying to break some of the awkward tension.

"Likewise, Liv. It's good to see you." Ethan hugs me from the side, and another smile slips from my mouth. *Just like old times.* "I like your socks."

I look down at my fuzzy socks—pink with otters on them—and laugh. "Thanks." I have an extensive fuzzy socks collection because my feet are always cold when the weather dips. I remember leaving them all over Tristan's apartment and having the guys make fun of him for it.

"Since you guys are reconnecting, does this mean you'll make us more brownies? I swear, yours can't be topped," Harry tells me before Tristan punches him in the arm. "What?"

"Shut the hell up," Tristan snaps at him, and I laugh, already feeling better than I did before. Tristan's eyes swipe down my body, and just from that, I feel goosebumps erupting under my clothes. His eyes linger on my face for a beat too long before his gaze turns concerned. *Is there something on my face?* "What's up, pretty girl?"

My heart skips a beat at how easily that slipped out before I center myself. "Can we talk?" I ask him, holding up the stack of letters that he gave me.

"Yeah, of course." Tristan's gaze lingers on mine as if we're the only two in the room.

"We'll see you later, Tristan." Harry lifts his head at him before he exits, Dom and Ethan following close behind him.

I hear a few murmurs of goodbye at me, and before I know it, the door is closed.

Tristan and I are finally alone to talk through the final piece of the puzzle—who the fuck broke us up and why?

Chapter Thirty-Nine

— HAPPINESS BY TAYLOR SWIFT

Anxious silence covers the room as each of us waits for the other to speak. I don't even know where to begin, so I say the first thing that comes to mind. "I read them. *All* of them."

He sits frozen in place, as if all of our feelings aren't spread out all over the counter, poured out like a spilled carton of milk. "And?"

"And what?"

"What are you feeling?"

"Guilt. Anger. Sadness. Guilt. Confusion. Did I mention guilt?" I chuckle anxiously. "Tristan, I'm sorry. I'm so fucking sorry about all of this."

"It's not your fault, Livvy. Someone else carries that blame, not you."

"I know, but the letters—" My voice cuts out at his chair scraping against the floor.

"I gave them to you because they were yours. I wanted you to know how I felt while you were gone, not because I wanted to make you feel guilty. I needed everything to be on the table. No more secrets will come between us again. Not if I have a say in that, at least."

Oh. That makes sense. We've spent the past four years practically hiding from one another. "I agree. No more secrets, Tristan."

He smirks, an underlying tone to it. "Good. Are you single?"

"What does that have to do with anything?" I question, annoyed that I fell for his little trap.

"Answer the question, Olivia."

"Why?"

"Teags told me she saw a phone number on your coffee cup once. I was wondering if the guy had a chance or not."

Feeling a little braver, I step closer to him. So close that I can practically hear his heartbeat. "Do you think I would've kissed you back that day if I wasn't?" A smile graces his face as he gets the answer that he was hoping for. "And you, Tristan?"

"There was nobody after you, Liv. Nobody else will ever come close to how I feel about you." He reaches for a strand of my hair, taking it between his fingers before he tucks it behind my ear. "Do you want to sit on the couch and talk?"

"That sounds good," I say as I make my way over.

"Do you want a drink?" he asks me. "I've been a terrible host. I should've asked sooner."

"Tristan, it's fine. Water would be great." I hear his fridge open and shut before he sits next to me on the couch, his elbow propped up on the back of it as his eyes stare into mine. "So, I've been thinking, and I don't think Bree, Parker, or Cassie left me that letter. They all loved you, and since they're the only ones closest to me, that's all I've got."

"Yeah, I eliminated all the guys, too. They like you more than me, so it wouldn't make sense for it to be them. I wish I hadn't ripped the original letter, so I still had it. Maybe we could've gotten something from it."

"I don't have mine either. Bree hid it from me after I kept re-reading it and crying until I passed out. It's probably buried in my old backyard, for all I know." I stifle a laugh, but when I look over at Tristan, his face has fallen.

"I'm sorry, Liv. God, I'm so sorry. I'd do anything to erase that letter from your mind. I know it's still up there. I know every word that was written is still floating around your brain, and I'd erase it if I could." His hand is on my leg now, stroking softly up and down while he speaks to me.

"It's neither of our fault, Tristan. That's why we're here right now—to figure out who the hell wanted to break us up so bad."

"I know. I just hate that I hurt you. I hate that I caused you so much pain."

"It wasn't you, though. I may have thought it was for years. The same goes for you, but it wasn't. I know that letter wasn't you, Tristan. I *forgive* you, even though there's nothing to forgive."

He nods at me before we get back to the subject at hand. "The only other person I thought of was Maddie."

Maddie. "That's a name I haven't heard in a long time. It would make sense, though. She didn't like us together, but why go through all the trouble?" I ask him, confused as to what she would gain from breaking us up.

"That's what I can't figure out, either. Also, I looked her up on Instagram and she's been happily married for two years to some rich guy. They live in Seattle now."

"At least someone has been having a good time since graduation," I sarcastically say, hating that we've come to another dead end. "Maybe I could ask my parents to see the security footage from our old house—so I could see who put it in the mailbox. I asked back then, but with everything going on, they never gave it to me." God, my memory is so scrambled from back then. I did too good of a job blacking out that first year after Tristan and I fell apart, and now I can barely remember anything about it.

"How much of that day do you remember?" He asks me, a weird look I can't decipher on his face.

"From that day? Mostly everything, I think."

"Walk through it with me. I want to know every detail."

I nod, hoping that this can jog my memory, and curious to see if Tristan's perspective on that day might be able to put some pieces together. "I remember checking the mail and being disappointed that nothing from you had come yet. I threw the pile on the side table before my phone started blowing up, and Bree told me our numbers had been leaked. It was a shitshow. I was mostly worried about what would happen if you couldn't get in touch with me. Bree told me to write you a letter since I wasn't gonna have a new phone until her manager could get us new ones."

"Why didn't you call me from your computer?" he asks me.

"The thought never crossed my mind. I was overwhelmed, but my leaked number was connected to my laptop. It wouldn't have worked. My phone was blowing up, and I didn't know what to do, so I did the one thing I knew—I wrote a letter." I'm up and pacing around his living room now, all the thoughts rushing back to me. "I went to put it in the mailbox for the post office to pick up the next day, but something sitting in it already caught my attention. It was a letter from you. I just assumed it fell out of the pile when I excitedly grabbed it the first time."

Tristan has moved from his relaxed position on his couch to standing behind it, arms against the back, watching me pace. "Keep going, Liv."

"I brought it inside after I put mine in the mailbox and ripped it open with a huge smile on my face, only for my heart to sink through the floorboards. I collapsed in tears, and Bree caught me. I started reading the letter over and over again, wishing the words to change before I had a panic attack. Bree helped me down from it, and at some point, my parents came home and—"

"Wait. How long after you got the letter did your parents come home?"

"I don't know how long it was. It could've been minutes or hours. I barely knew what was happening. I felt like I was suspended in time when I read what the letter said. I was a goddamn mess. But they came home and told us that they were selling the house because Bree's fame was too much for them..." My voice trails off, and when I look at Tristan, he has the same exact thoughts that I do. "My parents?"

"It appears that way, Liv. It makes sense. They didn't like me, and the timing of their arrival home and when you found the letter is too coincidental." He runs a hand through his hair, balling his fists at his sides, but it does nothing to hide how pissed off he is.

"They barely knew you, Tristan. They barely knew *I* existed most of the time. Why would they break us up?"

"I don't know, Liv. But they're the only people who make sense. Maybe they didn't like how I acted toward them at graduation and decided to get rid of me."

I'd like to think my parents weren't that petty, but I never really knew them. They were two ghosts that coexisted in the same house that I grew up in. I don't want it to be them, but I think my gut already knows that it was. "I don't even talk to them anymore," I whisper to the room.

"I think you should, Liv. Ask them if they did it, and if we're wrong, we'll go back to the drawing board. But if we're right, then we can finally move forward for once rather than live in the past like we have been."

I meet his eyes, tears threatening to fall before I shove my emotions down. "I don't want to believe they did this, but I'll talk to them."

"Soon, Liv."

"Tomorrow. I'll go over to their house tomorrow."

He comes around the couch, putting his hand in one of mine. "Do you want me to go with you?"

"I think I need to do this alone. I know they broke us apart, but for once, I need to confront my parents on my own, with no backup."

Tristan nods at me as he brings my hand to his mouth, pressing a quick kiss to my knuckles before lowering our hands. "I understand, Liv. I'll be on standby if you need me. I'm only one call away."

The phrase hits me in the gut, a tear escaping from my eyes. "Thank you, Tristan."

He wipes the tear and cups my face with both of his hands. "I told you I'd always answer if you call. That promise will stand no matter what happens tomorrow, okay?"

"No matter what, Tristan. We'll be okay."

"We'll be okay, pretty girl," he says, pressing a quick kiss to my cheek before he walks me back to my apartment, the weight of what I have to do tomorrow pressing heavily on my chest.

I know it will all be worth it eventually, but I was never good at standing up to, or even talking directly to my parents. I was so good at fading into the background when I was younger that I've never had to do something like this before—confront them.

All I know is that if they had something to do with breaking apart the only good thing I've ever had, they'd never see or hear from me again.

Chapter Forty

— TOLERATE IT BY TAYLOR SWIFT

You can do this, Liv.

I've been repeating that phrase for the past twenty minutes. Now that I'm here, sitting in their driveway, I feel like I absolutely cannot do this. I know they're home—one of the debates is on TV tonight, and they wouldn't dare to miss it. But there's a voice in the back of my head that's telling me I can do this. *Tristan.* Without thinking, I dial his new number, and he picks up immediately.

"Liv? Are you okay?"

"I need you to tell me that I can do this because I'm a few seconds away from backing out of this driveway and never looking back." I'm panicking. I know the two of us need answers, but suddenly, I feel like a little kid begging for her parents' attention again, and I hate it. I hate how it's making me feel like I'm doing something wrong by wanting to know if they ruined Tristan and me.

"Livs, you're one of the most resilient people I've ever met. I *know* you can do this. There's never been a doubt in my mind that you deserved better growing up. You've got this. Don't let them throw you aside again. We deserve answers. *You* deserve answers."

I take a deep breath as what he says sinks in. *He's right.* "Okay. Thank you. I just needed to hear someone else say it. I'm going in." I turn my lights off before I exit my car, softly closing the door behind me.

"Call me after. Okay?"

"I will," I tell him as I pocket my phone, my keys dangling off of the ring they sit on. I get to the front door, and without knocking, I head in.

I've never been to their new house before, but it's bigger than the last one. A staircase greets me ahead. Two rooms that look like they connect in the back of the house are on either side. I opt forward, hoping to find them somewhere. "Mom? Dad?"

"Olivia? Is that you?" I hear my mom say, no clear emotions in her voice. As I head deeper into the house, I see a flatscreen TV playing something above the fireplace and the back of both of my parents' heads.

You can do this, Livvy.

I take a deep breath before I head into the room. It's an open space. It seemingly connects to the dining room, and the kitchen is probably just off of that. The blacks and grays of this room don't make it feel welcoming at all. As I sit down on a chair to the side of the couch, an eerie feeling crosses my body.

This entire house feels cold and unlived in. There's not a single sign of warmth in here, and I wonder if my childhood home was like this. Did I not notice if it was because of how bright everything looked when I was a kid? Did my childlike wonder cloud my judgment of the home I grew up in? Maybe. Probably, if I'm being honest. The world always felt brighter when I was a kid, and as I've gotten older, those colors have dimmed.

Until I found Tristan. He brought all of those colors back for me, and if they really did break us up, I don't know what I'll do. "Hi, Mom and Dad. I have something to talk to you about."

Neither of them looks away from the television, computers on their laps as they watch the debate. "Go ahead, Olivia. We're listening, but we have to get these quotes down," my dad says as he types fast on his computer.

"Can you guys stop for a second? It's important that I have your attention." I could tell them that the world was about to go up in flames, and they'd still keep working. But for once, I need them to look at me. I need them to hear me.

"Fine. Make it quick," my mother says, slightly closing her laptop. My dad does the same when I look over at him.

"Do you remember the day our phone numbers got leaked four years ago? It was the same day I got a letter from Tristan telling me he wanted to break up."

"Yes, we remember that day quite fondly." My dad smiles over at my mom, and a weird feeling enters my gut. *Fondly?*

"Well, Tristan is back in Pennsylvania, and we've been reconnecting. It turns out he never sent me that letter. He also told me he got one from me that I never sent."

"Oh. Is that right?" my mother says.

"Yes, it is. Do you guys know or remember anything about that?" My leg is starting to shake, anxiety taking over as I wait for their answer. I'm not sure what I'm hoping they'll say. Either way, I feel like I'm screwed. If they confess, at least I know who did it, but if they don't, it's back to square one.

"We sent them, dear. It wasn't very hard forging your penmanship and his after we saw all the others he sent you. It was what was best for you, Olivia," my father says, shifting my world upside down. *They really did it.* I thought it was going to be a lot harder than this, but they confessed immediately.

"You sent them? Both of them? Why? Did you take the one I was going to send out of the mailbox that day, too?" I can barely get words out because of how angry I am at them. "You had no right to do that."

"Oh, Olivia, stop being so dramatic. We were only doing what we thought was best for you. Your mother and I did not like that boy. He was not good for you, and the way he talked to us was unacceptable."

"You were doing what was *best* for me? And how the hell would you two know what that is?" I yell, standing from the chair I was sitting in.

"We're your parents, Olivia. We will *always* know what's best for you. Now, if that's all—"

I cut my mother off. "No. That is *not* all. How dare you call yourselves my parents after you've pretended I don't exist for my whole life! Not once did you care about anything I did. The only thing you cared to tell me was how my degree was useless and how I would never get far in life."

"Well, we were right, weren't we? You're twenty-six and still working at that same job you've always had," my mother chides, a smirk forming on her face.

Tears flood my eyes, but I force them back down before I speak again. They don't deserve my tears. Not after what they did. "I would be in California and far away from you two if you hadn't interfered in my relationship! You had no goddamn right to do what you did. You had no right to meddle in anything of mine."

"Olivia, please, let's calm down. It's not that big of a deal." My father says, rolling his eyes at what he probably thinks is me being dramatic.

"I spent my entire life trying to get you both to notice me, to care about me, and you never did. Not once did I feel like you cared about something that I was doing. But the one time you take notice of me is when you break apart the only thing I've ever cared about."

"He was just a man, Olivia. Just a person. One day, you'll understand why we did it." My father says, opening his laptop up again, clearly done with the conversation that we're having. It's too bad that I'm not finished.

"No, he wasn't just a man—not to me, anyway. He was the first person that made me feel like my voice mattered, besides Bree. When I'm with him, I feel like I can do anything, *be* anything that I want. He didn't stifle my dreams like you guys did. He lifted me up and made me feel like I was worth something—that I was worth more than what you two thought of me and my decisions. Where you guys destroyed me, Tristan patched up my pieces. He carefully glued back together all the ones that you chipped off of my body year after year. All you two saw was me being happy and wanting to destroy it like you've always done."

"Always one for dramatics, she is," my mother whispers to my father, again proving my point that they never cared about me.

"I'm so tired of this. I'm tired of catering my life to your expectations of me. I feel sorry for you both. I feel sorry that you'll never know what it's like to be fully and unequivocally in love with someone. It's the greatest feeling in the world to be loved by someone, and all you two will ever love is yourselves." I leave the room, stopping at the door frame. "Consider this the last time you'll see me. I don't want to spend time with people who dim my light, and that's all you two ever do. I'm done letting you have that power over me."

I don't wait around to hear what they have to say—if they even heard me—before I get into my car and head back home.

— RUN AWAY BY CHASE ATLANTIC

I'M PRACTICALLY PACING AROUND my living room as I wait for Liv to call me back. It's been almost two hours since she called me before she was going to talk to her parents. She promised that she would call when she was done, but it's been nothing but radio silence.

Does that mean we were right? If we were wrong, it wouldn't take this long. Liv would never spend more time with her parents than she has to, so I can only assume we were right.

God, I knew those motherfuckers were shady when I met them. What kind of parents do that to their kids? Did they see how happy Liv was and want to take that away from her, or did they just not like me?

I try to turn on some music to help me take my mind off of every-thing, and as the first song comes on, I hear a few rapid knocks on my door. *Is that her?* I scramble over to my door and swing it open. Those blue eyes I know so well meet mine in an instant.

And before I have time to say anything, she pulls me in and kisses me. *Oh fuck.* I pull her into my place—without breaking the kiss—and slam the door shut with my foot before I press her against it. "Fuck, Liv. You're driving me insane."

"Not as insane as I feel. Now, is your shirt coming off, or do I have to rip it?" she asks, eyes on fire while she pulls at the bottom of it, wanting it off of me.

"Shouldn't we talk first?" I ask, wondering where this is coming from all of a sudden. *What the hell happened at her parents' house?*

"Later. I need you, Tristan. Please."

"Your wish is my command," I say, pulling my shirt off of my body, Liv's lips finding mine again as soon as it's on my floor. She nips at my bottom lip, grabbing it as she pulls away. I like how she's taking control right now. The old Livvy would never have done any of this, and I like it. I go to kiss her again, but she dodges it. "*Olivia.*"

"Yes?" she asks me before dropping to her knees, pulling at my sweats like she wants them off, too. God, the sight of her like this below me has my dick hardening in seconds. Liv was never the one to initiate any sort of physical contact like this when we were in college. All of this newfound confidence that she has is a hell of a turn-on.

Some guys would hate letting their girl take over during sex, but I'd do just about anything Liv asked me to. I'm at her mercy, and God, if I'm not loving every second of it. "What are you doing?"

"What does it look like I'm doing? Get these off. Now, Tristan."

"Whatever you say." I step out of my black sweats, tossing those aside too. Before I know it, Liv is pulling my boxers down, too, my dick standing straight out as she throws my last piece of clothing to the side. I'm standing here naked with my hands braced against the door, my last shred of sanity hanging on by a thread before Liv's warm, wet mouth wraps around my dick. "Fuck, Liv. Jesus."

Her mouth works my dick up and down, driving me absolutely fucking crazy, before she wraps one of her hands around me, too, squeezing and sucking in perfect sync. Her low moans vibrate around my dick as she keeps her pace. "Olivia, if you don't stop, I'm gonna come down that pretty throat of yours."

She removes her mouth and hand from me, and I groan at the loss of contact. "Not yet, Tristan." Liv moves her mouth back toward my throbbing dick, opening her mouth but not moving forward.

"You're such a fucking tease."

"Fuck my mouth, Tristan."

Holy shit. I could come just from her *saying* that to me. It's been a while since I've done this, but whatever Liv wants, she'll get. I move my dick into her mouth, and she stays where she is, like a "good fucking girl." I didn't even mean to say that out loud, but Liv is making me lose my mind. Motherfucker, I'm not going to last like this. I thrust into her, noticing her eyes start to tear up but continuing my pace. When I'm about to explode down her throat, I pull back. "As much as I love seeing you on your knees, Liv. I'd rather you be spread open on my bed." I remove myself from her mouth before I grab her, lift her up, and carry her to my bedroom.

When we get in, I throw her onto my bed. She tries to crawl away, but I drag her by her legs back to the edge of my bed. "Tell me what you want, Liv."

Her cheeks turn red, and I know she's getting shy on me again.

"Liv, thirty seconds ago, you got on your knees, and I fucked your mouth. I think we're past being shy, especially after all these years. Tell me what you want me to do." I hover over her, still fucking naked and waiting for her answer.

"I want you to fuck me, Tristan."

"Then fucked is what you'll get, Liv," I say as I flip her over, dragging her yoga pants down her body and underwear, too. Her ass looks as beautiful as I remember, and I smack it before I can stop myself.

"Fuck," she moans as I drag my hands and mouth all over her body. Liv takes her shirt off, and I take my time as I move my mouth all over her back—wanting to cover every inch of her body with me. My dick throbs as I lower my mouth to her pussy, wanting to get her nice and ready for my cock. "Tristan, please."

"Liv, don't rush me. I can't skip right to the main course, now, can I? Let me fucking savor you." I drag my tongue down her already dripping pussy before I grab her legs to steady myself. "God, you taste sweeter than I remember, Liv."

"Don't you dare fucking stop, Tristan," she threatens, a moan slipping out of her mouth as two of my fingers enter her aching pussy. "Oh, God."

"As much as I love feeling like a God in your eyes, it's actually pro-nounced Tristan," I say, pumping my fingers in and out of her before Liv starts grinding her clit against my bed, needing more friction. "That's it, baby. Help me make you come."

"Tristan, I'm close. Fuck, fuck, fuck." I feel her pussy clench on my fingers, and I remove them, replacing them with my tongue so I can feel her come all over my face. Her legs start to shake, and just as she's coming down from her first orgasm, I push into her in one thrust. "Fuck!"

Jesus Christ. "So much fucking tighter than I remember."

"You fucking asshole." Liv moans as I slowly start to move inside of her.

"Fuck, Liv. I forgot a condom," I say, pulling out before her arm snakes around to stop me.

"I'm on birth control, and I'm clean. Are you?"

"Yes, I am, but I don't want you to—"

"Tristan, I'm okay with this as long as you are."

"I'm clean too. I haven't slept with anyone since you, anyway," I admit, and feel her pussy clench when I say that. I stop a laugh from coming out before she turns her eyes to meet mine.

"Then what are you waiting for?" I pull fully out of her, flipping her around onto her back.

"Keep those eyes on me while I fuck you raw, pretty girl." And before she can say a word, I push into her. "God, you feel like a fucking dream, Liv. Do you know how many times I jerked off to the memory of your sweet pussy clenching around me like it is now?"

"Tristan, I—"

"Yeah, probably around the same amount as you and that vibrator of yours. Did you moan my name every time you came?" I say, picking up the speed of my thrusts and watching Liv's eyes practically roll to the back of her head.

"I did."

"That's what I thought, Liv. Because no matter what, you've always," thrust, "been," thrust, "mine."

"Fuck, just like that." Her pussy clenches hard around my dick, and I keep the pace I'm at as I lift her legs onto my shoulders, causing her to take me deeper. "Tristan!"

"Come for me, baby. Come all over my dick, please," I beg, and like the good fucking girl she is, she listens.

Her moans and screams sound like music to my ears as my release comes just as quickly, all the sounds we're making morphing together into cries and pleas for one another. "Fuck, Olivia."

Both of us come down from our highs at the same time, and I feel Liv's body go limp, exhaustion taking over. I take a moment to steady myself before grabbing a warm washcloth from my bathroom. By the time I'm back, Liv has officially fallen asleep. I clean us both up and throw a new pair of sweats on. I grab one of my shirts for Liv, carefully throwing it on her beautiful fucking body so as not to wake her before I press a kiss to her forehead. "Good night, baby."

I grab my pillow and head to the couch in the living room, but her arm pulls me back into bed. "Don't leave, Tristan."

How silly of me. "I won't, Liv. I'm all yours," I say, crawling into my bed, exhaustion from the chaos of the past few weeks hitting me.

And for the first time in months, I fall asleep in an instant next to the girl I've loved for four fucking years.

Best night ever.

Chapter Forty-One

— THIS LOVE BY TAYLOR SWIFT

As my eyes slowly open and I take in the room that surrounds me, memories of last night flash through my mind.

Seeing my parents.

Yelling at them and telling them I never want to see them again.

Getting in my car and coming back to Tristan.

Getting on my knees for him.

My core aches as I remember what we did. God, what the hell have I done? I wasn't even thinking last night after I left my parents' house. All I was focused on was getting back here to him so we could talk. But when he opened his door, the look of concern for me on his face, I didn't even think—I just kissed him.

And then we had sex. *Fuck.*

It's then that I notice his arm flung across my chest, his breathing even as he stays asleep. I'm hit with memories of us in college, waking up in tangled sheets, smiles gracing our faces before he would kiss my forehead and ask me how I slept.

I wonder if we could ever get back to that. Now that I know it was my parents who broke us up, and not either of us, I wonder if he feels how I do.

If he'll let me, I'd love him and make up for all the time we lost. But I don't know where he's at. He's still trying to work through his own grief, and I don't want to hinder that.

Tristan and I have a lot to talk about, but for now, I'm going to enjoy studying his features which have matured after all this time. He never liked keeping a full beard because of how much work it was, but he was always one for keeping that five o'clock shadow on his face. His brown hair is ruffled, a goddamn mess, and my cheeks heat because that's definitely my fault.

Oops?

An idea pops into my mind, and I slip out of bed as quietly as I can without waking him. I go to grab my clothes and instead opt to keep Tristan's shirt on. *When did this get on me?* I bet he threw it over me after I fell asleep. I throw my underwear and socks on since my feet are cold before I trudge out to his living room. I pick up the clothes scattered around his living room and fix anything else that's out of place before I head into his kitchen.

I grab some eggs from his fridge, bread from his pantry and begin to make a simple breakfast. I put some coffee on, hopefully, the right way because his machine is *way* fancier than mine, as I start to make the eggs. Suddenly feeling like it's too quiet in here, I go over to his speaker and turn on some music—softly, so I don't wake him up. I don't know how long it's been since he's gotten a good night's sleep, and I don't want to take that from him.

I mindlessly start to make breakfast, scrambling the eggs and putting the toast in his toaster, before I feel a pair of arms wrap around my center as his chin rests on the back of my head. "I could get used to this every morning."

"What? Actually, eating breakfast and not skipping a meal like you normally do?"

"Seeing you in my kitchen, dressed in one of my shirts." He presses a kiss to the top of my head before pulling away.

I hate how much I already miss the contact. "Can you take the toast out? I'm afraid I'm going to burn it."

"Sure, Liv," he says, placing them onto a plate that I left out. "How'd you sleep?"

I smile, memories bubbling up again. "It's the best I've slept in years," I say, not turning around to face him.

"Me too," I hear him whisper as I scrape the eggs onto another plate. As I turn around, our eyes meet, and goosebumps trickle over my skin. Even after all the time we've spent apart, my body still reacts to him the exact same way it did before. It's like I subconsciously remember how we felt when we were together all that time ago. *And last night.*

I've missed this. I've missed feeling things—emotions, my body coming alive under his stare. "I'm sorry if I woke you. I tried to put the music lower, but it's at the lowest setting."

He's still staring at me. "You didn't wake me."

"Okay." *Is this awkward?* I set the eggs on the kitchen island, before I turn around and grab the other plate, a mug with coffee in it, and set it on the counter. "I just—"

Tristan comes over to where I am, grabbing my hand and lacing our fingers together before he pulls me into him and starts swaying. My hand mindlessly goes to his back, and I follow his lead as we dance in the middle of his kitchen. "The food—"

"Don't worry about it, Liv. We can reheat it," his gravelly morning voice whispers in my ear.

"Okay." He squeezes my hand a few times before we continue swaying to the music that's playing softly in the background. I lean my head against his shoulder as he pulls our joined hands closer to our bodies. He spins me out, and I get pulled back into him before he presses a kiss to my cheek. We stop dancing when my stomach growls.

"We can eat now."

"That was fun. I've never done that before."

"Danced in a kitchen?"

"Yeah, I guess." I softly laugh before meeting his gaze again. "I don't know how to slow dance. It's been years since I even thought about it."

He smiles at me as he sits on his stool, patting the one next to him, and I sit down, too. "I promise we'll have time for more slow dancing in our kitchen in the years to come, but first, come here and eat. I can't have my girl starving."

"Wait, let me get the coffee I made. Still two sugars?" I say as I get up, his arm stopping me.

"I can get it, Liv. Just enjoy breakfast, okay? You didn't have to do this, you know."

"I wanted to. Plus, it was nice to focus on something else for a few minutes." My head drops, remembering all the things my parents said to me last night. "It was them, Tristan. They broke us up."

I see his back tense up before he turns around and comes back over to his stool. "I figured. You were over there for a while. It didn't take much to put the pieces together. Did they say why?"

"They thought they were doing what was best for me. At least, that's what story they're sticking to. They *really* didn't like you, but I assumed they would forget about you like they always did to me. I guess I was wrong." Tears start to flood my eyes, too many emotions overwhelming me at once. "I told them I never wanted to see them again, Tristan."

"Oh, Liv," he says as his arms wrap around me. *Safe.* That's the one thing I've always felt with Tristan—safe in his arms and presence. "It's okay to feel whatever you are."

"Is it bad that I feel relieved?" I ask, hating that I'm over here, relieved that I don't have to deal with my parents anymore when he's missing someone that won't ever come back.

"No, it's not. They were never good to you or your sister. It's for the best right now. In the future, you can decide if you want to give them a second chance. Or you don't. Just because they're your parents doesn't give them the right to tear your life apart when they choose to."

I pull back from his hold, looking into his eyes when I say this. "I'm sorry, Tristan. I'm sorry they did this, and I'm sorry—"

He shuts me up with a kiss, and I'm melting into him before he pulls back. "Liv, stop apologizing for something that you had no control over. I'm glad we figured it out. Now we can move forward without this hanging over us."

"Is that something you want? To move forward...with me?" I ask, doubt creeping into my mind.

"It's all I've wanted for years, Liv. And now that we have this chance, I'm not letting you go. It's always been you and me, Liv. It's always been us." He grabs my hand, pressing a kiss to my knuckles.

"Okay," I whisper. "But maybe we go slow so we can get to know each other again. I'm a mess right now—have been for four years."

"Liv, I'm a goddamn mess too, but unless you forgot—which I'm hoping you didn't—we had sex last night. I think slow is out the window."

I laugh, hitting him in the arm as I do. "I remember, Tristan. I remember it all, and I'm sorry I practically jumped you before we had the chance to talk. I know I said I would call you when I was done, but I was on auto-pilot after I left their house."

"It's okay, Liv. I don't regret a minute of last night. I missed you, and we're talking now, so it's okay." He smiles at me, a real one, and I find myself tearing up at seeing that cross over his face.

"I missed you, too."

"And I have four years of wooing to make up for. Consider this your only warning. I'm coming for that heart of yours, Liv."

I smile as I take a bite of toast, now cold, but I don't care. "It's been yours, Tristan. It's always been yours."

Three Days Later

Tristan: I slipped something underneath your door.

Livvy: I'm not home. What is it?

Tristan: An invitation. I want to take you out on a proper date.

Livvy: Okay...Why didn't you just text me and ask?

Tristan: Slipping a note under your door felt more like us. I look forward to hearing your answer.

Tristan: Have a good shift at work.

Livvy: Thank you. Everyone here keeps asking why I'm so happy...

Tristan: I'm glad that smile is back on your face. I missed it.

Livvy: Likewise, Tristan. I like your real smiles better than the fake ones.

Tristan: I'll see you, Liv.

Livvy: Bye, Tristan.

Chapter Forty-Two

— TO THE MOUNTAINS BY LIZZY MCALPINE

OVER THE PAST FEW days, Liv and I have been slowly reconnecting and spending more time together. It's been unreal. When I first saw her when I came back, I never imagined we would end up where we are. It's been a whirlwind these past few months, and I'm fucking glad it's started to calm down again.

Things on our front are good, but my head is still feeling weighted. I haven't been back home because I can't handle it. I know I can't. I can't deal with walking into my childhood home and one of my siblings not being there.

I haven't even been back to his grave. My sister has been inviting me to go with her the past few times she's gone, but I've come up with excuses anytime she asks. It's too much. It's too hard, and I don't like who I am when I think about Tobias.

I like who I am when I'm with Livvy. She makes me feel happy. I can laugh at the jokes she makes because everything feels lighter when I'm with her. I'm thankful as fuck that she wanted to be with me again. I was a fucking asshole to her these past few months. I said things I didn't mean out of sadness and grief, but that's never an excuse. I should never have hurt her, and I should never have pushed her away. Thankfully, she's forgiven me, but I haven't forgiven myself for how I acted toward her. I'll spend the rest of my fucking life making it up to her.

But when I'm by myself, everything comes crashing down again, and I'm reminded of the fact that my brother isn't here anymore. The responsibility of his death weighs over me like a two-ton brick that I can't put down, and I don't know how to let go of it. It's like I'm tied at the ankles, constantly being dragged down by the guilt.

If I had reached out more, called more, went to see him and noticed that something was wrong, then maybe I could've saved him from himself. Maybe he wouldn't have chosen to do what he did, leaving the rest of us behind to grapple with the aftermath.

My little brother was silently struggling, and I never saw it—none of us did. But that doesn't excuse the fact that I should've seen all the signs. I'm his older brother. For fucks sake, it's my job to see when my siblings are struggling, and I didn't.

I fucking failed.

Tobias was like a warm breeze in the spring, always making the people around him feel a bit lighter, a bit happier. Now it's like I'm stuck in the cold, waiting for his light to shine again and knowing it won't.

I shake off the thoughts as best I can, wanting to focus on why I left my house in the first place. It's around six PM, and my girl is at work. She closes tonight, and I'm on my way to pick up a few things. Did I come to this grocery store so that I could see her? Of course, I fucking did. Is it farther than a different grocery store by our place? Also, yes, but I don't care. Ever since we decided to move forward, I can't get enough of her. If I thought my obsession with Liv during college was too much, it's nothing compared to what it is now.

Olivia Hart has and always will be, my fucking undoing.

I park and step out of my Audi, a pep in my step that wasn't there before, as I head into the store. I round the corner as I pick up a basket, headed straight for where I know my girl is.

When I see her laughing and smacking Cal in the arm, I feel peaceful. Content. *Happy.* I head to the counter when Cal sees me. "Liv, he's here."

"Who?" She turns to look at me, a smile gracing her face. "Tristan! What are you doing here?" I hear her playing music from the same pink speaker she's always had.

"Grocery shopping," I say, lifting the basket into view. "It's a plus that I get to see your beautiful face."

"You're too sweet. What are you getting?"

"Dinner, but it's a surprise. I'll see you in a few, okay?" I tell her, quickly heading away from the counter so I can gather all the things I need.

What Liv doesn't know is that I'm taking her out after her shift for a picnic in the park. I've been wanting to do something special for her, and I think she'll love this. Even though it's freezing cold outside, I'm improvising with the next best thing—a car picnic. I grab some fancy bread, some salami and cheese, and some of Liv's favorite crackers. I have to go pick up the other part of our dinner—the main course—after I'm done here. I pass by the floral department, grabbing a few different bouquets, unsure of which one I like the best before I head to the checkout. I pay for my things, but before I leave, I stop by Liv's department again. "Miss Hart?"

She turns around from where she was cleaning the back counter. "Tristan? I thought you left already."

I say nothing as I hand her the flowers, a smile gracing her face. "For you, pretty girl."

"Thank you." She takes a big sniff of the flowers. "They smell wonderful. I can't wait to see how they look in my apartment."

Maybe I should get her some more for my apartment... "I'll be back to pick you up when your shift ends. Sound good?"

"Sounds great!" Her smile punches me in the chest. God, I've missed those smiles. I'll forever try to coax those out of her as many times as I can.

"I'll leave you two be. Don't work too hard."

I hear Livvy laugh as Cal answers me, "We won't!"

As I wait by my car, gloves on my hands because of how fucking cold it is, I shake off the nerves I'm feeling. Livvy and I have gone on dates before. We've hung out one-on-one lots of fucking times, but I'm still scared for some reason. The two of us have been here before, and I think part of me is still worried that it's too good to be true. That it might end up like it did last time, but I know that Liv is just as in this as I am.

But that didn't stop what happened. Even though I know it wasn't actually us, part of me thinks that one day, Liv will see how broken I am and not want to deal with me anymore.

My mind is not kind to me lately, but that's why I wanted to surprise Liv with a date. I have all of her favorite snacks, her favorite music loaded onto my phone, and blankets in case she gets cold.

December is around the corner. Which means the snow has officially started to dust the streets, making it fucking freezing out. Part of me misses the warm weather in California, but nothing will ever beat seeing Liv all bundled up as she heads out of the entrance, a familiar hat sitting on her head. *So that's where that went...*

"You know I've been looking for that hat for about four years now."

Her head shoots over to where I stand, leaning against my car, more flowers in hand. "Tristan, what are you doing here? Have you been waiting for me all night?"

"Of course, I have, pretty girl. I'm taking you out, after all."

She shuffles over to me, her winter boots scraping against the pavement. "I thought we were going later. I was going to get all dressed up and not be in my gross work clothes."

I lean into her, pressing a kiss to her cheek. "Liv, you should know already that I don't give a fuck what you're wearing. You'll always look like the most beautiful girl in the room. Now, your chariot awaits," I say, motioning her over to my car while grabbing her work bag from her. I open the door for her, and she slides in, her mouth dropping open before I shut the door again, a huge smile crossing my face.

After I place all of her things in my trunk, I slide into my seat, looking over at Liv's beautiful face as she sees what else is in my car.

Bouquets. Not enough to fully fill my car up, but enough to get that look on her face—confusion mixed with surprise and happiness. At least, that's what I see on her face. "What is this, Tristan?"

"I missed a few years of being able to get you flowers, so I thought I'd make up for it."

Her hand goes to her mouth, surprise still flooding her features, before she speaks again. "This looks like you bought out the entire floral department."

"And if I say that's exactly what I did..." I trail off, turning on my car as I smirk.

"Tristan! They're going to hate you tomorrow!"

"I know, but it was worth it to see that smile on your face," I say, putting my car into drive. "Are you ready for our date?"

"Of course I am." And as I drive away from the place where Liv and I first connected, a sudden pang of nostalgia hits me.

But these days, I'm only trying to look forward.

Emphasis on the word *trying*.

Chapter Forty-Three

December 11th

— FOREVER WINTER BY TAYLOR SWIFT

Staring at my phone at yet another unread text to Tristan, my heart slowly starts to sink. We were supposed to go out for breakfast this morning, and I've sent at least ten messages about it since last night—all of them have gone unanswered.

Part of me feels like I should be angry, but something doesn't feel right. We've been having the best time reconnecting over the past few weeks, and it's unlike him not to text me back after this long. *I wonder if he's home...*

My feet move before I'm aware, and soon enough, I'm knocking on his door. "Tristan! Are you okay?" It's around eleven a.m., and he normally wakes up early to go for a short run. Tristan was always the morning person in our relationship, and I was the night owl. When he sleeps, he goes to bed early. There have been a few times recently when I stayed over at his place where he left me to write at his desk while he went to sleep. I end up crawling into bed with him a few hours later, his body wrapping itself over me like it was always meant to.

A few more knocks and no answer later, I turn his handle, only to find his door unlocked. "He needs to stop leaving this unlocked so much."

I enter his place, shouting his name a few more times, but already knowing it's empty. My body knows when Tristan is around; the air often feels different, and I don't sense any other energy in here. *Where could he have gone?* I take the opportunity to look around and see if anything could clue me into where he is, but everything looks to be in order. No bookshelves are overturned, and no tables and chairs are knocked over.

Everything looks perfect—as if he wasn't even here last night.

We were going to hang out last night, but Parker and I had girl time with Cassie over FaceTime. We all watched *Mean Girls* together and ate ice cream. It was rather fun, and even though we were miles apart, it still felt like old times.

But Tristan told me he was going to bed last night while I was with the girls. So, where could he have gone? And why isn't he texting me back?

My mind flashes to the worst-case scenario—car accident, and he's dead in a ditch somewhere—and I shake that out immediately. I'm sure I'm overreacting, but I have that sinking feeling in my stomach, and it won't go away.

I pull my phone out and swipe to Teagen's number, pressing the call button before I press my phone to the ear. "Hello?"

"Hi, Teags. It's Liv."

"Hey, Liv! How's everything?"

"Um, fine. Have you seen or talked to Tristan in the past twenty-four hours?" My hand starts shaking, nervous for her answer. I don't know what I'm supposed to do if she says no.

"I haven't. Why? Is something wrong?"

"I don't know. We were supposed to get breakfast this morning, but he hasn't answered me since yesterday, and he's not at home."

"Oh. Well, we haven't seen him since he left. He hasn't been back here, and we don't want to press him about anything. We figured he'd come back when he was ready. He probably hasn't even opened the letters that Tobias left us."

In all the chaos of the past few weeks, I had forgotten about that. Tristan mentioned it briefly before, but all his grief has taken a backseat the past few weeks—or at least that's what I thought. Was he still shoving his feelings down, or was I distracting him from it? "Do you think that could've caused him to disappear? Do you think he finally read it and needed some space?" Too many questions race through my head.

Did he run back to California?

Is he lost and can't find his way back home?

Is he gone forever this time?

God, I feel sick.

"Fuck." Teagen's curse brings me out of my spiral. "I forgot what day it was."

"What does that have to do with anything?"

"It's Tobias' birthday today. He would've been twenty-six today. Fuck, how did I forget that was today?" I hear her voice start to strain.

"Teags, you've got a lot going on. It's okay. Do you or your family need anything? Can I get you guys anything?" I feel like I can't breathe, but this isn't about me now.

"If you could find Tristan, that would be a help. I don't want my mom worrying about anything else, especially today." Teagen sighs heavily across the line, and I can tell that she's now shouldering all of what Tristan used to. Teags has stepped in to take care of her mom and Theo, and she's as exhausted as Tristan used to be.

"I'll keep you updated as best I can. Try not to worry too much, okay? And don't forget to feed yourself today. Maybe even nap, if you can."

"I'll try, Liv. You—" she starts to speak, but the phone cuts out.

"Teags? What did you say?"

"You don't think he would go to the cabin, do you? Like Tobias did…"

"I—I don't know. But I think that's the first place I'm going to check," I tell her, the sinking feeling in my gut now full-on nausea at this point. If he's at the cabin where Tobias died, then what does he plan on doing? And why didn't he tell me about going? And when did I forget when Tobias' birthday was?

"Be careful, Liv. It's supposed to snow. Maybe I should go with you."

"Tristan would kill us both if he found out we trekked the four-hour round trip to the cabin if he wasn't there. I'm going to ask Harry if he's free. If not, I'll go myself. Just take a day, Teags. Take a day for yourself, or call my sister and hang out with her. That way, I'll know you're okay."

"Okay, Liv. Keep me updated, okay?"

"I will. I love you, T."

"I love you too. I'm glad you and my brother figured your shit out. I've missed having you around."

That punches me right in the chest. I've missed it too. "Me too."

"Good luck, Liv," she says before I hang up, immediately pulling up Harry's contact.

Liv: Are you busy right now?

Harry: Not at all. What's up?

Liv: Are you up for a road trip?

"Can you drive faster?" I ask, my leg nervously bouncing in Harry's passenger seat.

"No. It's snowing Liv. I'm not getting us into an accident. Just trust me, okay? Tristan is fine. He's probably not even up here." Harry's trying to soothe my nerves, but it's not helping. I can tell he's worried too, because his eyebrows have been furrowed since he picked me up. We've been driving for two hours, and according to the directions that Teagen gave me, we should be there by now. The snow is slowing us down, and images of what I could find when I get there are scaring me.

"But what if he is? Harry, I've ignored all of his grief that past few weeks. I'm doing a pretty shit job as a girlfriend."

"Is that what you guys are?"

Shit. "I don't really know." We haven't labeled it quite yet. I think we've just been enjoying each other in the same proximity lately.

"Even so, you've only been doing your best, Liv. Tristan is the one who likes to run, remember? You've been good for him, though. He smiles more when you're around. It's like you make the clouds go away when you're around him."

"Yes, but I shouldn't be distracting him from his grief. I should be helping him through it." Harry turns onto a driveway, the snow piling up, but I see another car in the distance. It looks like Tristan's Audi. "I can't go farther than this, or we'll be stuck. Do you want me to go with you?"

He starts to unbuckle his seatbelt, but I stop him. "No. No, it's okay. At least we know he's here." I check my phone, going to text Teags, when I notice that I have no service up here. "Dammit."

"No service?"

"No. Can you call Teagen when you get back to reception and let her know we're okay?"

"Of course. Good luck, Liv. Give him my best, okay?"

I lean over and hug Harry. "I will. Thank you, Harry. For everything."

"Anything for you two, Liv. You know that." I practically dash out of the car, the wind whipping against my hair, snow falling in front of my eyes as I try my best not to slip and fall.

When I get up to the cabin, I can barely see what it looks like. It seems like it's been snowing up here longer than it was back home, and the thick white snow is making it hard to see. *I hope Harry makes it back okay.* The sun is still out, technically, but the snow clouds make it a bit darker than usual for the mid-afternoon.

I take the steps slowly, and by the time I reach the covered porch, I hear the faint sound of music playing in the house. Not wanting to wait any longer, I push the door open and am met with a cozy entryway, a few hooks in front of my face where jackets should be. "Tristan?"

"Liv?" I hear him faintly say, unsure of where he is in the cabin. It's quite a large space, but the only way is forward. I step through and am met with a large open family room, the logs of the house on full display. I hear the fireplace crackling and am grateful for the warmth because of how cold it is outside. To the left looks to be the dining area and kitchen, I'd assume.

When I look to the right, I see what looks like an office, a candle flickering on the desk. I head over and when I see the room in full view, I see Tristan on the floor, leaning against the big, wooden desk, an envelope in his hand, and a glass of whiskey on the floor beside him.

"Baby, are you okay?" I don't rush him yet, even though every part of me wants to. I need to gauge how he's feeling. I can't tell from the blank expression on his face.

And then he breaks.

His face crumbles as I watch his knees come to his chest and his head fall. I rush over, sitting in front of him, trying to help in any way I can. A painful sound comes from him as tears pour out of his eyes. "It's okay, Tristan. It's okay. I'm here. You're okay."

— SOMEONE TO STAY BY VANCOUVER SLEEP CLINIC

LIV FRANTICALLY REPEATS A bunch of phrases, but I can barely hear her over the ringing in my ears. I didn't expect to see her here, and I think I might be dreaming or something, but I feel her touch, so she must be real.

How did she get up here?

Tears continue to leak out of my eyes as all the emotions I've held in for the past few months come out of me at once. It all feels like too much. Hell, it felt like too much last night when I drove up here.

I was going crazy in my apartment. His letter was burning a hole in my kitchen drawer, and when I looked at my phone to text Liv back, a calendar notification came up instead.

Tobias' 26th birthday.

Not only had I forgotten my dead brother's birthday, but I forgot to turn off the alarm I set to alert me the day before. I never wanted to forget anyone's birthday, so I set those reminders up a few years ago.

Just seeing that banner on my phone sent my mind into a tailspin. I couldn't breathe in my apartment. I needed to get out. I needed to go somewhere far so I could hear myself think, and before I knew it, I was driving and ended up here. I had no clothes, nothing except my phone, his letter, and a bottle of my favorite whiskey that Tobias and I used to share.

I think I came here because I wanted to see if his presence might still be felt where he was last. This place, this cabin, this *room*, is where my brother's story ended. This is where he stopped being Tobias. His last breaths were taken as he sat at this desk and wrote letters to our family, knowing that we would read them after he was gone.

I feel like I'm gonna be sick.

I've been pushing all of these thoughts aside for months. I know that. I'm fully fucking aware of that. But I don't know what the hell to do anymore. I failed. I failed to see him struggling. I failed to help him when he needed it.

I failed at being his big brother and the one person he could always count on.

I. Fucking. Failed.

And because of that, all I have left of him is this letter. The last things I'll ever hear him read to me in my head are whatever words are on this paper. What if I forget what his voice sounds like in the future? What if I start to forget all the memories we made together? What if one day I speak about him for the last time, and I don't realize it?

"Tristan, baby, you have to breathe with me, okay? You're going to pass out if you don't. Focus on me, please. Please, just please." Liv presses her forehead against mine, and through the blur, I see those beautiful blue eyes lock on mine.

I try to do what she says, but I can't. It's all coming up—the sadness I feel, the disappointment, the anger.

It's too much. I can't fucking do this. But at the same time, I have to read this letter soon, or I'll go crazy not knowing what the last thing my brother wanted to say to me was. "Letter."

"What, baby?" Liv asks, her face frantically searching mine. I suddenly feel horrible for dragging her into this. She shouldn't have to deal with all my shit, with the mess that has become of my life these past few months, but I also know that I need her.

She's the only one I want to see me like this—the only one I trust to watch my body crumble in front of. This is the second time I've broken in front of her, yet she still came for me. She still found me and wanted to help me through it.

I'm never alone when I have her, of that I've always known. "The letter." My voice comes out unrecognizable even to me as I hand her the now crumpled envelope. "C-Can you open it for me?"

"Of course I can."

What she doesn't know is that I'm giving her the hardest part. The part that I haven't been able to do for months. Opening it has always seemed like a mountain I didn't want to climb. Because opening it was me admitting that my brother was never coming back, and the thought of that being real didn't make sense. I could never wrap my mind around that—the finality of his death.

That's the thing about when someone dies; they're the ones that are gone forever, leaving the survivors to grapple with the loss. How I'm supposed to continue on with my life, knowing he's not here to live it with me feels insurmountable. I know that in time, it's supposed to get easier, but I don't see that ever happening. Every single second since I got that call, I've missed him. Every song I play reminds me of him and a time of our lives that we shared, and I hate it.

What's left if my brother is gone? This letter? No. No piece of paper could ever compare to him and who he was. He was the best of us. I'd give any amount of money, any amount of time, to see him for even one more minute.

Life is just time with the ones you love and the ones that love you. It's all the moments that you wish you could relive, the memories that you reach out to grasp, only to realize it already happened. You can't get them back when someone is gone. You can't climb into a memory and sit there until the pain stops, no matter how much I wish I could.

He was my brother, for fucks sake. He grew up with me. The two of us were kids together before Theo and Teags came along.

I wish he stayed a little longer. I wish I could go back to the last time we had dinner together. In hindsight, I would've stayed longer with him, too. I would've had a dessert or another drink. I would've laughed more at his jokes that he told to see me smile. I would've told him that I would love him even when he felt like his world was crashing down, even when his mind told him that he wasn't worthy of feeling all the love he gave to everyone else.

I would've told him that I love him even when he's not around to see it.

But now he's gone, and he'll never know any of that.

Liv appears back in front of me, or maybe she's been here the whole time, the letter in her hand but not stretched out to me. She knows I'll take it when I'm ready, but how can anyone be ready for something like this? How do I prepare myself for the last words my brother wrote to me? "I miss him, Liv. I fucking miss him."

She's crying now, too, her voice tight with pain. Little does she know that she's my life vest in the ocean of my grief that's trying to tear me down. She's the light at the end of this long and dark tunnel. "I bet, wherever he is, that he misses you, too."

That kills me because I think he'd be disappointed in me for how I've been acting the past few months. I practically abandoned my family to sort through my shit while we're all going through the same thing. If he could see me now, I don't think he'd be proud. I shake my head, no words able to get out.

"You don't have to do this now, Tristan. There's no time limit on this." Her hands are caressing my arms, comfort seeping from her touch like it always does.

"I can't keep living like this, Liv. You deserve better than someone who's stuck in their grief. I promised you that we'd move forward, and I meant it. I want to at least try."

"I'll be here for you regardless of that, baby. If you sink, then I'll pull you up. That's what you did for me all those years ago. It's my turn to help you this time, so let me. Let me help you through this at whatever pace you want." Her lips press a kiss on my wet cheek.

"Okay."

Before we say anything else, I reach my hand out, fingers grasping around the envelope and pulling it over to me.

"I'm gonna read this now. And after, I'm going to fall. I'm going to fall to the lowest point that I'll ever be at because I know you'll be here to pull me up after." Tears fall from her eyes as mine meet hers.

"I'll always catch you when you fall, Tristan. I'll always be here to pull you up." Her fingers lace with mine as I open the envelope, finally reading what I've spent months avoiding. It's only a page when I unfold it, the handwriting familiar, his name signed at the bottom.

Tristan.

My big brother. Stop blaming yourself for my actions. I know you're going to. I know you're going to retreat into yourself and run away like you always do, but I'm telling you not to. I need you to understand something—it's not your fault.

It's not your fault that I feel like this. It's not your fault that nothing feels right to me—my job, my life, my body, my brain.

I'm just broken. I feel cracked, with no glue or tape able to patch me back up.

Thank you for making me who I am today. I'll never forget growing up watching you have it all together, and how you took care of us after Dad died. I know we always joke around with you, but I don't think I've ever thanked you properly.

So, thank you, Tristan. Thank you for stepping up. Take care of Mom, Theo, and Teags for me, okay? I doubt I need to tell you that, though. You've always taken such good care of us.

I hope you get your happy ending.

I love you forever, big brother.

Tobias.

By the time I'm done, Livvy catches me. She catches me as I keel over, my body no longer able to be upright. She holds me as I fall, throwing a rope down the hole I'm in for when I need it later.

And before I know it, I either pass out from all the emotions or sleep finally takes me.

Chapter Forty-Four

— 'TIS THE DAMN SEASON BY TAYLOR SWIFT

MY EYES OPEN, BUT not much light comes through. The pounding in my head is pissing me off, and when my surroundings come into view, all the memories of the past two days come rushing into my head.

There goes my one split second of amnesia. Reality always hits you in the face first thing in the morning.

I can barely feel anything from all the tears that I shed yesterday, my sinuses swollen as fuck, and when I reach the side table in my room, a body stops me.

Liv. My girl. I forgot that she was here, but how did we get up to my room yesterday? And how long have I been asleep?

"Since yesterday afternoon. I was afraid that you were in some sort of coma or something." Liv's groggy morning voice comes through like music to my fucking ears. *I must've said that out loud.* "How are you feeling, babe?"

I take a moment to ponder that question. How do I feel? Like shit, honestly. But my shoulders feel a little lighter, the weight not as crushing today. I'd like to think that crying every tear out of my body probably helped that, but I think Liv also has something to do with it. Her presence always makes me feel a bit more like myself.

My Livvy. My tether. My rope. My fucking lifeline. She's saved me more times over the past few months than I care to admit—whether from myself or my emotions. "I feel like shit. But a little better than yesterday. Like one percent better."

"Little progress is still progress, Tristan," she says, her hand running down my naked chest as I notice that my clothes are different. "And don't ever scare me like that again. If you get that low again, you call me. No more running."

"No more running. I didn't mean to scare you. I'm sorry. Did you change my clothes?"

I feel her nod against me. "I found some sweats and stuff in your closet."

I forgot that I left some stuff behind and never came back for it before I moved to California. Good thing I did, or else I'd still be in my jeans, and whoever sleeps in jeans is a fucking psychopath. "Thank you."

"Anything for you, Tristan. You know that."

I grab her face with my chin, wanting to see her eyes while I say what I'm about to. "Not just for the clothes, Liv. Thank you for being here. Thank you for coming back to me, no matter how many times I pushed you away. I'm so fucking sorry for how I acted before. I'm so fucking sorry for all of it."

She presses a light kiss to my lips. "Stop apologizing, Tristan. You were hurt, angry, and grieving. It was all too much for you at once, and I knew that. I've moved past it, and you should, too."

"I know, but—"

"None of that matters now, Tristan. It's just us."

That phrase brings an idea into my head. "Stay here with me."

"What?"

"Stay here with me. Just for a few days, please." I don't know what she'll say, but I feel like this could be good for us. I need a few days to calm down from the emotional high that was last night—and the past few months or years, I guess. It's all been too much. Staying in the cabin for a few days, disconnected from the world and all the shit it keeps throwing my way, is just what I need. "It won't be long, Liv. We both could use a disconnect."

"I have to call work, I can't—"

"They'll understand. If you tell them what's going on, they'll get it."

"I don't have service up here, though."

"Liv, I'll take care of it," I say, wrapping her body up in mine. "I haven't been able to feel you in my arms for four years. I've woken up without your face for four years. Please, just give me the weekend. That's all I'm asking for right now. The weekend."

"I don't even have clothes. I didn't pack a bag since I didn't know if you were here." Her mind is going a thousand miles a second. I can tell because her eyes are shooting all over the place. I force her gaze to mine, wanting to stop her from overthinking.

"Wear my clothes, Liv. We can run to the general store in town for anything else you need. Please, just until Monday. We can drive back then."

"Okay," she whispers against me. "I'll stay."

I can't stop myself from kissing her after those words leave her mouth. She practically melts into me, and we spend the rest of the morning tangled up in the sheets, memorizing each other's bodies again as if it's the only thing that matters.

"TRISTAN, LET ME HELP you!" Liv screams as she runs out of the cabin, mismatched shoes on her feet as her arms stretch out to mine. She takes two bags from me before I follow her inside.

"Baby, it was only a few bags. I didn't get us that much."

"I know, but still. I wanted to help."

I press a kiss on her head as I shut the door with my foot. "Thank you. I'll put all this away if you want to get back to your book."

"Are you sure?"

"Positive." Before I left, Liv was one hundred pages into one of her most anticipated reads this year. I didn't even ask her to go with me because I knew better than to get in the middle of Liv and her books. So instead, she wrote me a list of things to get for her and sent me some money after I got the Wi-Fi working this morning.

I declined her payment and got everything on her list—some clothes, snacks, a charger, and warmer socks. I also grabbed some food for us to make a few meals over the next two days.

As I start to put things away, I reminisce about all the fun times I spent here as a kid. I was wondering if those memories would feel tainted by what happened here a few months ago, but I don't feel that way.

This space feels like him now. It doesn't feel like our family any more, just Tobias. This was the last place he lived, and now it will forever carry his memory—of that, I'll make sure.

After I'm done putting all the groceries and clothes away, I search the house for Liv. She was sitting in front of the fireplace on the couch before, but when I got back down to the first floor, I didn't see her. I check the one place that I know could capture Liv's attention, and when I enter the library, I see the back of her head poking up from the chair that faces the window.

This was always Teags and my mom's favorite room in the house. They used to sit in here for hours and read whatever book they were lost in at the time while me and my brothers played video games or fucked around outside.

I'll always remember the memories we created here, but I wouldn't hate creating some new ones with my family and Liv. In fact, that sounds perfect to me. I think I'll start right now.

I softly pad over to behind the chair Liv is in, taking in the surrounding room. Shelves line every single wall, partially filled with books and dust. Teagen's library is much more impressive at home since she and my mom turned the office into their reading nook.

Liv turned the chair to face the window instead of the glass center table that my mom bought for the room, the rug still as soft as I remember it. I take a quick peek over Liv's shoulder, browsing the page she's reading on her phone, and discover that she's reading some dirty little things—and almost the entire page is highlighted. "You know I could do that to you if you want. All you have to do is ask, pretty girl."

Liv is still wearing one of my old t-shirts, and the image of her in that, reading what she is, has me thinking all sorts of things. "Is that so?" she asks, her voice lower and sultrier than before. *My girl is turned on.*

"Careful, baby...Don't talk to me in that voice unless you want me to do something about it." I snake my hand around the chair, my hand finding that pretty throat of hers, lingering but not squeezing yet.

"I want you to do something about it, Tristan. So do it." I squeeze her neck, my rings looking so fucking good wrapped around her.

"Beg."

"Tristan, please," her voice comes out in a whisper, her eyes blazing into mine. "Touch me."

That's all I need to hear before I grab her arm, her phone falling out of her hand as I do before I pull her against me and lift her off her feet. Liv's legs wrap around my waist before I push her against the bookshelves, her breath catching as I do, but I know it's not from pain. "Is this how you want me to fuck you? Pressed against the things you love so much?

Screaming *my* name so you can remember that there's nothing fictional about me?"

Her pupils are *huge*, and her pulse is going crazy, probably about as crazy as mine is. Liv's hands go to my hair as I find that spot on her neck that she loves so much, my already hard dick pressing right where it wants to be. God, this girl is my fucking weakness. I can feel how fucking wet she already is through her leggings. "Tristan, I need you. Don't make me wait."

"Whatever you want, Liv." I drop her down, peel all of her fucking clothes off, along with mine, but before I lift her back up, I sink to my knees. "Fuck, just one taste, though."

My tongue meets her needy pussy, already wet and dripping for me, as I taste my favorite thing in the fucking world. My tongue laps at her clit, sucking on it before I give some attention to her entrance. God, I could do this all day. "You taste like my fucking undoing, Liv."

"Tristan, shit," she breathes, her hands gripping my hair as if she'll fall without it. "I need you to fuck me. Please."

"Come here, baby," I say, getting off my knees and lifting her into my arms again. My dick lining up perfectly with her pussy, and in one thrust, I'm buried.

"Fuck." Livvy moans. I give her a second to get used to me before I start moving. "Faster, Tristan. I want to be fucked."

Fucking hell, I love how vocal she is about sex now. "You feel so fucking good," I say, moving in and out of her. The only sounds filling the room are the sounds of us. I *love* it. I love hearing what I do to her, and I love that I'm the only one who will hear her screaming my name as she comes in a few seconds. "I'm gonna go harder, Liv."

"Okay, I can handle it."

I tuck a loose strand of her hair behind her ear. "I know you can, pretty girl." And then I'm fucking her so hard that I hear some of the books fall off of the shelves, our movement too much for them. I'm hitting her favorite fucking spot, and then I feel her pussy clench hard around my dick. "Are you gonna come all over my cock, baby?"

"Yes, please, just don't stop," she moans as I pump into her, my thrusts fast and hard, how she likes it before I feel her legs start to shake, her pussy clenching around my dick like a fucking vice. Liv starts to unravel, her moans indecipherable. "Tristan."

"Fuck, Liv, just hearing that out of your mouth is making me close."

"Then come, Tristan. Please." Her hand yanks part of my hair back before I feel my spine tingle, my own orgasm coming in a flash. All I see are stars as I fill Liv's pussy, her pants, and moans on replay in my head.

As we both come down, I find Liv staring at me intently. "Something on your mind?"

"I think I love you."

I press a soft kiss to her lips. "Glad we're on the same page again, Liv. I've loved you for four fucking years, and I don't plan on stopping anytime soon." I set her down, grabbing some tissues to clean us both up. The two of us get our clothes back on, and I wrap my arms around her, her head leaning back against my chest as we look out the window. It's snowing again.

It's snowing again, and I remember what it feels like to love and be loved by Livvy. I owe most of the good days of my life to her, and I know all the future ones are hers, too. "Thank you for sticking around, Liv." *At the cabin and in life.*

"It's been a difficult few months, but I'm glad we ended up here." She leans her head back, smiling at me, and it's like I'm witnessing all the lights in my head turn on after a string of endless darkness.

"Me too. I love you, Oliva Hart. This impromptu break from reality has been wonderful, but you're not just mine for the weekend. I want all your days, all your highs and lows from here forward."

"I love you too, Tristan West. I'll be yours for however long you'll have me, you know that." I smile, wrapping my arms tighter around her before I hear her stomach grumble. "Any chance we can make lunch?"

Anything you want, pretty girl. I'll give you all that I have. "Of course we can."

Chapter Forty-Five

— HOME BY PHILLIP PHILLIPS

THE DRIVE BACK HOME has been quiet so far, only the music that I'm playing heard softly in the background as my thoughts race.

I love Tristan. He loves me. But what are we going to do? This weekend has been great; being able to separate from the real world and disconnect has helped clear my head, but now more things are crowding it.

Tristan still technically lives in California. He was only back indefinitely, at first. Have I splintered his plans? Am I forcing him to stay in Pennsylvania because of me? Would I move to California if he asked? *I think I would.* But how do I know what's right for me? I feel like I just got back on my feet from whatever funk I've been in, and it's mostly thanks to him. What am I supposed to do now? Which path ahead do I take? Do I let it all work itself out and hope for the best?

What if the bubble we've been in pops, and I lose him again?

Ugh. I hate my brain sometimes.

"Something on your mind, Liv? You have your 'thinking too hard' face on."

It's adorable that he still knows all my facial expressions. I thought I had forgotten all of his, but those seemed to linger too. "I was just thinking about us."

That causes a smirk to appear. "What about us?"

"Everything, I guess. Where we go from here. What we're going to do about..." I trail off, not having the right word for whatever situation we're in.

"What we're going to do about the fact that I still live across the country and where that leaves us?"

God, of course, he knows. Tristan always was a mind reader of sorts. I never really had to say anything for him to be able to tell what I was thinking. My face usually gives everything away. "Well, yeah."

Tristan laughs as he pulls the car over, putting it in park on the side of the road. "Tristan, I wasn't trying to make this a whole thing, and we don't have to talk about it right now."

"I know there's nowhere for you to pace your thoughts out, but slow down for a second, Liv. If it's itching at your mind, let me try to ease it." He pulls my face in, pressing a kiss to my forehead. For a moment, my thoughts calm, and I silently thank him for always being able to do that—get me out of my head when it's too much.

"I don't want to pressure you into deciding. We have time. I'm just scared."

"What are you scared about, pretty girl?"

"I'm scared that this is all going to end badly again, and I don't want that. I want you and only you, but I don't want either of us to be unhappy in whatever we decide."

He takes a deep breath before he speaks again. "Liv, I've been unhappy for four years. Ever since we got broken apart, I've been unhappy. Now that I have you again, it's all I need. *You* bring me happiness just by being in my presence. I'm going to keep my job, but ask if I can work remotely from here. A few of the other guys I know do that, and they love it."

"I can't ask you to upend your whole life in California to stay here with me."

"Liv, I didn't have a life in California. There was no living without you. I practically floated my way through the days out there. I thought leaving was the only thing I ever wanted, but somewhere along the way, all I started to want was you."

Tears start to flood my eyes. "Would you really come back here for me? You would leave California just to make it work for us?"

"I left once, and everything fell apart. There's no way I'm making that same mistake when we're back together. I'm not leaving you again, Liv. That's a fucking promise. Where you are is where I want to be. So, if you're here working at the grocery store, then I'll be here too."

"Tristan, I don't know what to say." I'm overwhelmed, but not with confusion. With love. With admiration and happiness for the man in front of me. "I love you."

"I love you too, Liv. It's us against the world, right?"

"Always." I lean into him, pressing a quick but deep kiss to his lips. He groans when I move back into my seat.

"God, I'm fucking hard as a rock just from you kissing me."

I chuckle. "Good. You're mine, Tristan. You said so yourself."

"Damn fucking right." He smiles at me before turning his blinker on and starts to drive back home. He switches the song a few times before landing on one that he likes, softly humming the words. "This was Tobias' favorite song."

"I can take it off of the playlist if it's too much." I go to switch the song on his screen, but his hand stops me.

"Don't." He smiles, a touch of something hidden under it. "It's okay. He used to whistle to this song while I drove. I never thought I knew the words, but I guess I do."

It's funny the things you remember after somebody passes away. The song you never thought you memorized has a place in your head. The scents that linger and remind you of them. The receipts left from that trip to the grocery store were still scattered in their car or room. There are all of these little remnants that they were once on earth, except for them, and isn't that the one thing everyone would rather have? Nobody wants the things they leave behind, just the person they lost, but that's not how it works.

That's really all we become after we leave, pieces scattered on the lives of the ones who loved us like small flecks of dust in the air.

I turn to Tristan, watching his grief flash on his face before it turns into a small smile, a tear running down his cheek. I wipe it away with my thumb before I turn the song up and start humming it along with Tristan, letting him know that I'm here with him as he drives us home.

АN HOUR LATER, TRISTAN parks the car at our apartment complex, but neither of us gets out right away. I feel like we both know that as soon as we do, everything changes. It's simultaneously exciting and terrifying. But before our next chapter starts, I need to get something else off my chest. It hasn't been there long, but I've been thinking about it a lot recently, and I think I'm finally ready to admit it. As soon as I say it out loud, it will become a real thing, and maybe that means it will seem less scary. "Tristan, can I tell you something?"

"Livvy, you can always tell me anything. You know that."

"I know, but this is a big thing." I turn in my seat to face him. Tristan grabs my hands, holding them in his, silently giving me strength to speak. "I think I want to quit my day job at the store."

His eyebrows shoot up, obviously not expecting what I said. "Oh, really? How long have you been thinking about this?"

"A few weeks. Ever since my mom made the comment she did when I last saw her."

"Liv, your mom said that to hurt you. Don't take what she said to heart if it's not truly what you want."

I shake my head at him. "I know, but that's the thing though. I *do* want to quit that job. I feel stagnant there, and I've saved a lot of what I made from the book royalties and paychecks that I think I'll be okay."

He smiles at me, caressing his thumbs over my hands. "Liv, no matter what you want to do, I'll support you every step of the way."

"I'm gonna do it. I'm going to quit so I can focus on writing. Even if I only last a year and have to get another job to support myself, at least I can say I tried."

"Liv, you won't need to get another job. I believe in you and your writing, and we'll be fine, anyway."

"How can you be so sure?"

"Liv, I work in tech in Silicon Valley." he throws a smirk my way. "I'm good at saving too, and I'll support you or both of us if I have to."

"No, babe. I can't let you do that." I feel weird when anybody buys me something as simple as a coffee. I also never borrow money from anyone because I hate the feeling of owing someone back. "We'll figure it out when or if it comes to that but—"

Tristan grabs my chin, bringing me in for a quick kiss. "Livvy, baby, you let me chase my dream four years ago. Please let me help you chase yours."

"A—Are you sure?"

"Yes, I'm absolutely sure. Based on how well your first book did, I'm sure there are thousands of readers out there who will love your next book. You're fucking talented, Liv. I can see that, your readers see that, and it's high time that *you* see that."

"Okay. I'll put my two weeks in," I decide. "I can do this."

"You already did this, Liv. Your first book was a fucking hit. You need to realize that you made your dreams happen, not me or anyone else. *You* did it, pretty girl. Your talent, your genius, your words made it happen." Tristan almost sounds choked up as he speaks, his head leaning forward onto mine. "And I'm so fucking proud of you."

Just hearing him say that is making my eyes burn. "Thank you. My only regret is that you weren't beside me to celebrate."

He presses a quick kiss to my forehead. "Oh, but Liv, we'll have so much more to celebrate in the future, and I'll be standing right next to you, cheering you on the entire time."

"I love you, Tristan."

"I love you too, pretty girl. Are you ready to go inside now?"

I take a deep breath before I open my door. "I'm ready."

Chapter Forty-Six

December 23rd

— MARJORIE BY TAYLOR SWIFT

Teags: Are you coming home for Christmas? Mom was asking about you…

Tristan: I'm not sure, Teags.

Teags: Bring Livvy. It'll be like that one Thanksgiving when we met her.

Teags: Well, it won't be exactly the same, but you know…

Tristan: I'll think about it.

Teags: That's all I ask.

Teags: I miss you, big brother.

December 25th

I SET MY PHONE on my coffee table, panic racing through me before I hear the door swing open, Liv's eyes glancing around my place before they land on me. Her face worried as she sits next to me. "I'm here, babe. What's wrong?"

God, I love this girl. "Will you come to dinner with me tonight at my house? Teags asked me a few days ago, and I told her I'd be there."

"I'd love to. I didn't have any plans tonight anyway since Bree is at some event with Connie." Her smile lights up my world, reminding me why I'm still standing. The world may be a huge place, but I'm thankful that I ended up living at the same time as Olivia Hart.

"I don't know why I'm so nervous about this. It's just going home. It shouldn't be that big of a deal."

Her hand reaches up, cupping my face. "You haven't been home in a while. You've always been the one to take care of everyone else, to take the brunt of the weight when it comes to your family. For the first time in your life, you put yourself first, and I think you feel guilty for doing that. You think your family feels you were selfish for what you did, but I can almost guarantee that they don't think that."

"But I was selfish, Liv. I feel guilty for not seeing them since the funeral, I—I let them down, didn't I?"

"No, baby. No, you didn't. Us older siblings always feel like that—like we're letting people down by putting ourselves first. You feel like you always have to set a good example. You have to show your younger siblings what not to do in life. Your mistakes feel heavier because they always seem to be watching you, and if you fail, that means you've failed them somehow. They're older now, Tristan. They're figuring their own path out just like you are. I think sometimes we forget that it's everyone else's first time growing up, too. Teags and Theo understand why you haven't been around, but I think they miss their older brother."

God, she's right. Of course, she's right. I grew up practically becoming another parent after my dad died. I helped get my siblings ready for school, helped them with their math homework, and read books to Teags so she could go to sleep. I did all of that when I was still a kid. I'm not blaming my mom, absolutely not, but I've had the weight of all of it on my body for years. In all this time, I think the first selfish thing I've done is not go home after the funeral. Even when I was in California, I was always checking in with my family so I could make sure that the world wasn't falling apart without me there. It didn't, of course, but I spent most of my days worrying about them rather than enjoying the life I was supposed to be building. "You're right, Livs."

"Of course I am. I'm an older sister, after all. I practically invented worrying and feeling like I was never doing enough." Her smile breaks through my mess. "Are you ready to go home?"

"I'm ready. But home to me will always be when I'm next to you, Liv." I wrap my arms around her, breathing in the feeling of utter contentment that she always seems to bring me. "No matter what universe we're in, I'll always want to be here with you."

"I love you. Now, let's get ready for dinner since we're already running late." I look at my phone, the clock reading three PM. *When did it get so late?*

I laugh as Liv pulls me off of the couch and into my room, the two of us getting ready to go to dinner with my family.

It feels just like old times, and I wouldn't have it any other way.

❧

Walking into my house for the first time in months, my heart is practically pounding out of my chest. I shouldn't be this nervous to come home, but I am. Everything Liv said earlier is true. I feel guilty, selfish, and like the worst son and brother ever for what I did. I'm a goddamn coward, and I know I have to talk to my mom about all this, but I'm scared to.

"You're doing great, baby." Liv squeezes my hand as I go to help her out of her coat. The house is decorated in typical Christmas fashion. Even our tree is up, shining in the window when we drive up to the house.

"Tristan!" Teags says, giving me no warning before she barrels me with a hug.

"Hi to my favorite sister," I say, squeezing her with my arms. God, she looks so different. It's only been a couple of months, but I swear she looks older. I've always heard that death and grief make one feel older, but I guess I never understood that until now. Theo comes over to us as Teags pulls away from me, and even he hugs me.

"Welcome home, Tris." He claps his hand on my back before he pulls away.

"Hey, bud." I see Teags and Liv hugging, a huge smile on both of their faces, making my heart warm at the sight. "Where's Mom?"

"Kitchen," Theo says, heading back toward the living room. Teags, Liv, and I follow, and as I breathe in the familiar scent of Christmas dinner, sentimentality washes through my body.

I spot my mom making dinner, and she looks better than I thought she would, all things considered. She's got her usual red outfit that she wears every Christmas. Liv shoots a smile my way, giving me confidence as I leave her to talk to my siblings and get reconnected. "Hey, Mom. Do you want me to set the table?"

"Tristan, my dear." She pulls me in for a hug, and I let her. "I'm glad you're here."

Tears flood my eyes before I blink them away, not wanting all my feelings to muddle my thoughts yet. "I've missed you guys. Look, about what I did—"

She pulls away from me, transitioning back to making dinner. "Darling, you have nothing to apologize for. I'm your mother, after all. I know you all better than you know yourselves."

"Just let me say this, please. I'm sorry for leaving you guys back then, and I'm sorry for leaving you after the funeral."

"No apologies necessary. Your dreams always were bigger than this small town. I knew you'd achieve great things, Tristan. I'd never regret letting you leave, no matter how much we missed you. Sometimes, to grow, you have to leave the place where your roots are, and I'm so proud of what you've accomplished."

"Thanks. It was good to get some distance, but somehow, I knew that I'd be back. I just wish it wasn't for what happened."

"Me too, darling. I miss him every second, but I know he's watching over us. I know he's still around, even if not physically."

I look over at Liv and my siblings, all sitting around and chatting by the fireplace. Liv is talking animatedly about something while Teags watches her. Theo is even smiling, grabbing his water bottle off the floor before taking a sip. "You're right. Now, I'm going to set the table so you can get back to cooking, okay?"

"Okay, honey. Also, I'm glad Liv is here. I need her to sign my copies of her book. They're on the bookshelf in the office."

I smile, knowing Liv is going to get all flustered about her book. "I'll let her know." I grab all the things I need before I head into the dining room to set the table. I set out six places, making sure to leave a spot for Tobias. It's a new tradition I'm hoping to start with the family.

No matter where he is, he'll always have a spot at the table. Tobias' memory will never be forgotten as long as my siblings and I have any say about it. He might be gone, but he won't disappear from our hearts, our heads, and our lives.

He'll always be my little brother, and this will always be the place we grew up surrounded by love, light, laughter, and happiness. *That* is what I choose to remember about him. Not how I failed or disappointed him but how we lived and grew up together as brothers.

Tomorrow, I might feel completely different, but being back here just amplifies the memories I have with him. This house is like a time capsule for me, shining the brightest memories I have with Tobias on the walls all around.

I thought coming back here would bring it all up, and I'd want to punch something. But as I take a deep breath, hearing laughter come from the next room where my family is, I feel a bit clearer.

As we all sit down for dinner a few minutes later, I'm the first to speak. "I'm thankful to be back here with you all. Even though we're one short, I know he's here with us. I know he'll always be around no matter what we're going through. I wish he knew that we were always around for him, too. To Tobias. We miss you, and we'll love you forever."

"To Tobias." Everyone says, and as dinner continues, I can feel all the love spread across the room.

I think somewhere out there that Tobias can see us, and he'd be happy that we're all here. There will never be moving on from what happened, but we can always move forward, the grief and sadness fading more every day, but never disappearing.

Chapter Forty-Seven

January

— SWEET NOTHING BY TAYLOR SWIFT

As I finish typing out the final edits of my second draft, I silently take in everything I'm feeling. My eyes close as I sigh heavily to myself, hearing the door of my office click open.

"Hi, pretty girl. How's writing going?"

I open my eyes, meeting his, as I see a plate of brownies in front of me. "What's this?"

"Brownies to celebrate a hopefully finished second draft?" He questions, waiting for confirmation that I did, in fact finish my draft today like I said I would. "I used your recipe and followed it to the letter, so they should taste good."

"I just finished. I thought I had more to say, but this ending feels perfect to me. I'm excited to do my last read-through before I send it to early readers and my editor."

"Look at you go, Liv." he leans across my desk, pressing a kiss to my forehead. "I'm so proud of you, Author Olivia Hart."

Any time I hear that word, I get all flustered. I never really considered myself an author after all these years. I figured one book didn't suddenly make me one, but Tristan is constantly calling me that, letting my imposter syndrome know that it's a big fat liar. "Thank you, my love."

He sits in the chair across from me, smiling big and wide as he takes a bite of a brownie. "I think this is my favorite room in our new place."

"Mine too." I smile, looking around at my beautiful home office.

Tristan and I finally got our own place together after living apart all these years. It's a beautiful three-bedroom home that we've only begun to start decorating. My office was the first thing to be fully furnished. Tristan built me bookshelves that line the walls of the room, and on the one behind me, he's placed all my copies of my book that I have now. I used to only have a few lying around and not on display, but I'm proud of my debut book, and now I have an entire shelf dedicated to it.

Parker was upset that I moved out, but she's still only a few minutes away from us, often coming over for movie nights with her boyfriend. Tristan and I approve of him—he's almost too perfect for Parker—and it's been nice having him around. He and Tristan often talk baseball while Parker and I watch our favorite shows. We even have a game night a few times a week, with our siblings joining when they can.

Cassie and Bryce are still miles away but going strong together. I think they're going to settle down soon, but not without traveling to a few more countries first. Parker and I have calls with her all the time, still staying in touch after all these years.

Harry still hangs out with us all the time, and all the boys are going on a trip soon. A guys' weekend so they can de-stress. Harry is bringing his girlfriend over next week for dinner so she can meet us, and I've been more excited than Tristan has been. I love watching the people we love find happiness.

My parents and I haven't talked since that day I walked out of their house, and I'm okay with that. I finally feel free of their hold after all these years, and I wish I had the guts to do what I did sooner. But it's all fine now, and that's all that matters.

Bree's been out of the country, but she swore to me that she would be back by the time my next book releases, to which Tristan is throwing a huge party for. I can't wait to celebrate this one with all the people I love the most in the world. "I love our home together, Tristan. It's everything I could've imagined."

"I've never loved a space more knowing you're in it." He rises out of his chair, coming over to my desk as he sits on it. "Now, can we celebrate you finishing your draft properly?"

I smirk, knowing what's coming. "Of course we can. I *did* make you read the smut I wrote just to make sure it made sense. I'm—" Before I can finish my sentence, Tristan lifts me up bridal style, carrying me to our bedroom.

Only he doesn't go to our bedroom. He swings our front door open, bringing a rush of cold air onto my skin. Goosebumps travel up and down my arms as he sets me down on the snow. "Tristan! It's cold!"

"I'll warm you up after, but we have to celebrate with snow angels. It's tradition."

It's tradition. Those two words do more for me than anything else. Tristan knows how I feel about them. Now, here we are, starting our own ones in the first home we have together. My smile beams from my face as I see him start to move his arms and legs, snow splashing on my face from how fast he's moving. I start to move, too, smiling and laughing as I remember the first time we did this.

Life with him these past few weeks has been nothing short of a dream. Waking up next to him every single day is all I've ever wanted since my parents broke us apart all those years ago, and now I have that.

I always thought my dream was to figure out who I was in life, who I was meant to be on this weird floating rock that we call a planet. But now my dream is him. Happiness with Tristan is all I want going forward. Life will never be always good or always bad, but with him, it's worth living. Tristan still has days where his grief overwhelms him, and I carry him through that. Just like he carries me through the days when I feel like I'm not good enough.

After so many years of hurting, after so many conversations where we hurt one another, the two of us have carried each other through it all. Every obstacle we face now or in the future, we face together, and I will forever be thankful that we finally made it here.

It took us four years to get here. With all the possible roads we could've taken, I'm glad we took the hardest one, the one that nobody else would want to take. Because now there's nothing we can't face together. We clawed at our happiness until it let go of us, marks ripped into it, showing that we were there.

Now our happiness sits on our chests, warming us from the inside out and casting a light onto everything around us.

I see him sit up, snowflakes stuck to his hair and clothes as I turn my head to face his, feeling the cold snow freeze my cheek. "How do you feel?"

"Happy," he tells me.

I smile at him. "Me too."

"Good. It's my job, after all—making you feel that way." He stands up, holding his hand out for me as I take it.

"Can we make some hot chocolate to go with our brownies?"

"Absolutely we can," Tristan says, pressing a kiss to my lips before he lifts me up again, carrying me back into our home.

Our home that's filled with everything the two of us could ever want—pure happiness and warmth.

Chapter Forty-Eight

March

— FINE LINE BY HARRY STYLES

"GOD, I'M SO NERVOUS," I say to myself, sweeping some highlighter onto my cheekbones. My sophomore novel comes out tomorrow. Tomorrow. As in—my eyes swing to the clock in the bathroom—six hours from now. In six hours, my book will be available at a bunch of stores and in e-book form.

I wasn't this nervous for my first one to come out because I had zero expectations for it. I wrote it to get through a really bad period of my life. This book release feels different. It's an entirely new story and characters, and I'm not sure if people will like this one as much.

Putting a book out into the world is terrifying, but it's also the best thing ever. I love it, and I hate it. I'm sweating, and I'm freezing. I don't know what I am right now except nervous.

"People are on the way, Livvy. Are you almost ready?" Tristan asks me while he steps into the bathroom, already dressed. He looks stunningly handsome in his black slacks, dress shoes, and black button-up. His rings on his fingers look like the centerpiece to his outfit with how much they standout. "You look absolutely beautiful."

"You're quite handsome yourself. Are you sure this party is for me?" I smile at him in the mirror, putting the final touches on my makeup.

"This party is for my beautiful and talented author girlfriend. She's releasing her second novel that's going to top the charts tomorrow." Tristan comes up behind me, placing his hands around my shoulders. "She also happens to be *my* favorite author."

My cheeks heat, and all these compliments make me want to shrink into myself. "Thank you, baby. I'm excited."

"You also look terrified, Liv. It's a launch party with all of our friends. We're going to drink wine, you're going to sign books for them and take a bunch of pictures, and then later, we'll celebrate just the two of us."

"Oh, really? Just the two of us, huh? And what does that entail?" I smile, already knowing what it means.

Tristan's hand finds my neck, squeezing lightly before he kisses my cheek. "It means recreating chapter twenty-five of your book."

Oh my. "That sounds perfect."

"Oh, it will be, Liv. Now, let's go enjoy your launch so we can enjoy each other later. Are you ready?"

"I'm ready, Tristan."

"You're amazing, Liv. I'm so fucking proud of you."

"I love you. Thank you for always believing in my stories as much as I do."

"I'll never stop shouting about your books until I'm dead. Even that might not be able to stop me." Tristan steals a kiss from my red lips, before he drags his eyes up and down my body. I decided to match my book cover with a deep maroon dress that goes to above my knee, black sheer tights, and some cute maroon heeled boots that I found.

"Let's go get ready for our friends," I say, pulling him out of the haze he was in. When we get to our living room, Tristan turns on the music, the playlist being the one from my book before he lays out snacks and such. "Do you think they're going to like the dedication?"

"I think they're all going to love it, Livs. Now, stop worrying, and let's go have fun."

We've invited his family over, my sister, the boys, along with Parker to celebrate my release day. I'm glad I'm doing this the second time around.

Tristan's by my side cheering me on, and all of our friends have made the trip back to Pennsylvania just for this—sans Cassie and Bryce due to some family trouble. I couldn't feel more loved if I tried, and after all the years, I felt lost and confused. Finally, finding the path I was meant to be on feels extraordinary.

I never thought I'd make it here. I thought I was doomed to wander down the same old beaten path that I'd been on since high school. But somewhere along the way, I found the direction I was supposed to go in. I saw the path that I wanted, so I forged it myself. *I* did that. Me. For the first time in a long time, I'm proud of myself. I'm proud of figuring out what I wanted and how I didn't let anyone tell me that I couldn't do it.

I'm fucking doing it. I fucking did it, and now I'm happy as ever. Now, I'm spending time with people who choose to be around me because they love me, not because they feel obligated to.

I was always the one to plan parties for everyone else while all my accomplishments were left behind. Maybe someone would text me, or maybe not. It used to hurt always being the person to remember and plan things for other people's big moments, only for them not to reciprocate. Tristan planned this entire night and invited all of our favorite people. It feels good to have someone plan something *for* me for once.

I'm feeling the sun from both sides—the rise and the set—with all the love that will be around me tonight.

For now, I'm going to enjoy this night. Because if there's one thing I've learned over the past year, it's that life is short, and I want to spend it surrounded by my favorite people while I still can.

A few hours and many signed books later, and the night is slowly coming to an end. Before everyone can sneak out of the party, I tap on my wine glass and ask for their attention. "Hello, everyone. I wanted to thank you all for coming to celebrate my second novel coming out tomorrow."

"Woo!" My sister screams.

"Damn right!" Dom yells after, making everyone laugh.

"Dude," I see Tristan elbow him, which makes me laugh even more.

"Thanks, guys. This one is very different from the first one, but it still feels so close to my heart. I wanted to shift from a typical romance novel and focus on how platonic love can be just as beautiful as romantic love. This book is like a love letter to you all. To the ones who've supported me on this journey unconditionally. This couple gets their happily ever after, but not without the help of the people who love them both the most. I wanted to write about life and how it can knock you down sometimes, but also how you can get back up again."

I hear a few sniffles in the crowd as I see Tristan's mom, my sister, and Teags wipe their eyes with tissues. "I love each and every one of you so much. And now, I'm going to read you the dedication from my book. I'm sorry for keeping it a secret the past few weeks, but I wanted to do it like this because it means a lot to me."

Tristan hands me a copy of my book, and I flip it to the front. I take a deep breath before I say it, not wanting all the emotions I'm feeling to stop the words from coming out. "To anyone who has ever struggled silently while feeling the weight of the world on their chest." I take another steadying breath before I say the rest. "And for Tobias, whose smiles now paint the sunsets we see every night. You'll forever be missed."

Tears leak out of my eyes as I notice that everyone else around me is crying, too, including Tristan and the boys. Teags and Bree are hugging, Bree's head on her shoulder, offering comfort to her. Tristan is rubbing his mom's back, tears coming down both of their faces. It hasn't even been a year yet, but when I wrote this book, I knew I wanted Tobias to be a part of it. The main male character is one who struggles silently until he finally asks for help from the ones he loves, kind of like Tobias.

He'll forever be immortalized in my book, and that was a gift I wanted to give Tristan and his family. "I'm sorry for the tears, but I hope you all enjoy reading the story as much as I did writing it. Thank you for coming."

After I'm done, everyone comes over to hug me, saying their congratulations and goodbyes since it's so late. Tristan's mom pulls me aside before she leaves and hugs me until I can't breathe. "Thank you, Olivia. I know this story is going to be as beautiful as the first. I'm so proud of you, darling."

"Thank you. I'm honored to have his name in my book. It's the least I could do."

"He would've loved it, Liv. I'll see you and Tristan for dinner on Sunday, right?"

"We'll be there." I smile as she pulls back from me, squeezing my arm before Theo offers her his arm. "Bye, Theo!"

"Bye, Livvy. Love you to pieces."

"Love you too." I smile. The West family never fails to make me feel like one of their own, Bree included. They've taken us in and given us a family when our parents didn't step up.

I hug my sister and Teags goodbye. She's preparing to go to Los Angeles tomorrow. A brand is flying her out for a shoot so I won't see her for a few weeks. "I'm so fucking proud of you, Livvy."

"Thanks, Bree. I'm proud of you pretty much every single day of my life." I smile, knowing that a few pieces of how I see Bree ended up as part of the main female character in my novel. "Is that my jacket, by the way?"

She looks down at her outfit, mindlessly shaking her head at me. I know she's lying because I've been looking for that since I moved out of my apartment. I assumed Parker had it, but now I know that my sister stole it from my closet. Even though her wardrobe is filled to the brim with designer outfits, she still steals my clothes, makeup, and shoes. "I have absolutely no idea what you're talking about, but I must be going. I have an early flight. I love you! I'll scream about your book forever, I promise!"

I laugh as she skips out of the house, the pep back in her step that I thought she had lost a few years ago. I love seeing her happy, and I'll do anything I can to keep it that way.

"Teags, I love you girl."

I feel her cheeks lift up as I hug her. "I love you too, sis."

"Dive home safe, and tell that boyfriend of yours I say hi." Much to Tristan's dismay, Teags has a boyfriend. They've been dating since January, so it's still new, but he's not very happy with him. He's a sweet kid, and Tristan only dislikes him because of who he's dating. No guy in the world will ever be good enough for Teags, according to Tristan.

The boys all hug me at the same time, just like they used to, and I feel squeezed with love before they let go. "I love you, idiots. Thank you for coming."

"We wouldn't have missed this for anything, Liv." Harry smiles at me.

"Liv, you know we'll always be here for you. We do like you more than that one." Ethan says, pointing to my handsome boyfriend who's leaning against the wall, letting me have my moments with our guests.

"And if he ever starts to bore you to death, you know who to call." Dom winks at me, still flirting with me after all these years just to get a rise out of Tristan.

"Wait, I have to tell you guys something." They all eye me curiously, waiting for what I have to say. "Thank you for sticking by him when I couldn't be there."

All their faces fall at the same time, obviously not expecting that I was going to say that. Harry comes in for a hug first before they all do again. "No problem, Livs. I'm glad you guys figured it out after all these years." Dom whispers to me, not wanting everyone else to hear him not be an asshole for once. He's got a secret soft side to him, and I know when he's ready to settle down, he'll make someone very happy.

"Okay, party's over. Get the fuck out." Tristan deadpans, opening the front door to usher them out. "I'll see you guys."

As he closes the door, I slump onto our couch, happiness swirling around me after the festivities tonight. "I'm exhausted, but that was so freaking fun."

"I'm glad you had a good night, Liv." Tristan leans over me, kissing me until I'm breathless. "I'm gonna start cleaning."

"I'll help! I need to keep moving, or I'll fall asleep." I grab a few glasses and head to the sink. While I wash them out, Tristan cleans the snacks up. I remember dreaming of the day when he and I cleaned our own place together after a party, and now that we're doing it, I feel emotional. All the roads that led us here were tough, and now we can finally be happy and exist together in the same atmosphere.

Half an hour later, my phone ringing breaks me from my thoughts, and as I head to the coffee table where I left it, I notice that it's my sister. *She probably forgot something here.* That's one thing about Bree—she can never keep track of anything unless it's glued to her. "What did you forget this time? I can try to drop it off before—"

"Liv, he's getting out. They're letting him out."

Him. Her stalker. My blood runs cold, and my face must be white because Tristan is looking at me with concern etched on his face. "That's not possible."

"Connie just called me. It's real, and it's happening. What the fuck do I do, Liv?"

Only one answer comes to mind as I think about how fucked up this is. How are they letting him out after what he did to Bree? How is that fair at all? "We'll figure this out, Bree. I won't rest until you feel safe. I'm calling Vince tomorrow to see if he'll come back."

"Thanks, Liv. I'll try texting him later since I still have his number, but I have to go. I hung up on Connie as soon as she told me, and she's calling me back."

"It's fine, sis. I love you," I say before she hangs up. I could hear the fear in her voice, and after not hearing it for so long, my heart sank. She *just* started feeling like herself again, and now the asshole is getting out of prison. It's not fucking fair. None of it is.

"Liv, what's going on?"

"Bree's stalker is getting out, and she's terrified," I say before he wraps his arms around me. This is my safe place. Tristan knows that. His arms make me feel like nothing can hit me when they're around me. "I don't know what to do."

"Whatever we do, we do together, Liv." Tristan's hand meets my chin, his eyes blazing into mine. "Your sister is family, and family protects each other. We'll get through this."

"I know we will," I say as he wraps his arms around me and begins to sway.

For the next hour, Tristan and I dance in the living room together, feeling more whole and content than ever before. Later that night, we fall asleep next to each other, limbs intertwined as if we can't get close enough. The next morning, we wake up, and he presses a kiss to my forehead before he asks me how I slept.

Life is as we wanted it to be, and all the roads we didn't take look bleak compared to the one we were on.

Epilogue

— LONG STORY SHORT BY TAYLOR SWIFT

WHEN I WAS LITTLE, I never could've imagined that I'd end up here—browsing the aisles of the grocery store with the love of my life. We're trying to figure out what to make for dinner over the next week.

Tristan and I always grocery shop together. In the months we've been back together, we've argued, we've made mistakes, but we always get through it as a team.

Nothing in life will ever be one hundred percent perfect. There will be times when we fail, times when we feel like our mistakes have come back to haunt us. I admit that sometimes I feel like I knew more back then—back when I didn't have as many experiences under my belt. I always had that same steady pattern of life—school, work, getting into college. I knew what was coming next.

Now, I know nothing. I don't know where the future is going to go. I don't have that same steady schedule to keep me tethered to what's next. It all feels like chaos. The unknown of what comes next, the life that is yet to be lived by you in the coming years—it's terrifying. I was always scared of choosing the wrong path that would lead to my life feeling flat, doing the same thing over and over every day until I die.

But it's not *always* like that. Sure, there are some days when I wake up, write, eat, and then sleep, often waking up the next day to do it all over again. But that's the thing I love about life—I also have days where I feel like I made all the right decisions.

I don't think I'd want all my days to be exciting and full of adventure because the quiet days with Tristan are also some of my favorites. I like going to the grocery store and running errands with him. I like knowing what will happen when I wake up those mornings.

Now, as I browse the produce section of the store, checking out the oranges, I feel lucky. Never in my life did I think I'd feel as content as I do now. Tristan peels my oranges for me when I'm too busy writing, and I love him a little more every single day than I did the last. I thought it would stop and slow down, but each time we watch the sunset from our porch, I fall a little bit deeper. Every sunset I see is better, knowing that he's looking at the same one. Every night, we make it a tradition to sit on our porch, drinks in hand, as the sun lowers and paints the sky with colors. Sometimes it's beautiful, and other times the sky is dark, and the rain comes, but no matter what, we always end up in the same place.

Happy as we tangle up in our sheets, whispering to each other how much we love one another. No matter how many things change, that will always stay the same.

After you graduate and are thrust into the real world, you think that independence will come quickly and life will sort itself out. Everything always feels so uncertain, and I still live in that uncertainty every day. I never know if a book I put out will find its audience of people who can relate to it, but I do it anyway. Because my words have impact and meaning, and if I feel a certain way, that means someone else probably does too.

At the end of the day, we're all just people. People who are living on this giant floating rock in the middle of space, who have no idea what any of it means. I don't know what the point is as much as anyone else does. We all keep that in the back of our minds, subconsciously or not. It lingers there, that question of what all this is meant for.

I don't know if there is an answer, but I do know that Tristan makes every day worth living while we're on this earth.

Life always sorts itself out. And the one thing that I wish I could tell my younger self is to take a few deep breaths because life is a rollercoaster, and we're only just getting on it.

I'd tell her to savor the goodness that comes now and then. Savor those moments when you feel like nothing could get better because, at some point, it will, and you'll want to capture that, too.

You'll fall from the stool you're on, and you'll get back up, dusting yourself off like you always have. The only change from then to now is that you have someone by your side to pick you back up, especially those days when you feel like you can't do it alone.

"Are you ready to go home?" Tristan asks me as we get to the front of the store.

Home. He feels like home. Our house feels like home, and I'm thankful because we built that home together. "Yes."

I used to think that I would live with the feeling of being stuck in my past.

Now, I'm embracing the future and the chaos that comes with it because that's where the opportunities come from—to learn, grow, and change. And for once, I'm not scared. I'm only excited to meet all the future versions of me that I've not yet met.

I know I'll make them proud.

Acknowledgements

I would not be able to do any of what I do without the incredible people that support me through this process.

Lexi—Your dedication to my stories is something I'll truly never forget. You were one of the first people who ever believed in me and my words, and I'm grateful for your friendship every single day. I truly could not do any of this without you. Thank you for always being by my side and loving my stories as much as I do!

Han—The covers you design are the most beautiful representations of my stories. I can't believe how far we've come, and I can't wait to see what you create in the future because I know it's all going to be beautiful.

Josh—Thank you for making me believe in the love that I write about. No fictional man could ever compare to you.

Sarah Bailey—I'm thanking the universe for bringing us together. I'm so happy you got to read this story early and help me make it better, and your reactions to it will forever be some of my favorites. I'm convinced you, Lexi, and I were stars together.

Cassidy Hudspeth—Thank you for proofreading this book for me! You made the process so easy, and I am so glad to know you!

Ellie at Love Notes PR—Thank you for making my release so easy and smooth. Your help with ARCs and the cover reveal made my job so much easier, and you're just the sweetest human ever.

Emma Jane at EJL Editing—Thank you for being the best editor I could ask for. I love working with you and you truly make my stories shine.

My beta readers—Drew, Maine, Jan, Meaghen, and Amy. I'm so grateful for you all and how you make my stories better. I trust you all with my words and delusions and I don't even want to imagine a life without you all in it. I'm so grateful that on this giant floating rock that I get to know you all.

Mom—Thank you for believing in me and my stories, and for reading every single one. It's easy to write about a strong single parent when I had you as a role model my entire life.

Taylor Swift—Thank you for folklore and evermore. Your love for storytelling and writing about your own life situations has inspired me since I could remember.

To the readers—Thank you for giving my story a chance. I never thought anyone would care about all the weird thoughts I had, and apparently some of you do. Thank you for giving my stories a little tiny piece of your heart. It means more than you know.

To myself in April 2023—Who would have thought an idea you had in your last semester of college would turn into this? I'm proud of you for making it through, and even more proud that you turned such a hard part of life into something beautiful.

Also By Emily Tudor

About the Author

Emily Tudor creates characters and stories about platonic and romantic love for anyone and everyone. She lives in the state of New York and loves listening to music and creating stories. She loves Marvel movies, the song *mirrorball* by Taylor Swift and buying too many books when she already has many to be read at home.

You can find her on Instagram at:
@authoremilytudor
@emil.yslibrary